I0572738

Unearthed

The Liminal Veil Series: Book One

Breanna Perez

The Third Raven Publishing

Copyright © 2025 by Breanna Perez

All rights reserved. No part of this book may be reproduced or transmitted in any form or by any means, electronic or mechanical, including photocopying, recording, or by any information storage and retrieval system, without written permission from the publisher, except in the case of brief quotations embodied in critical articles and reviews.

This is a work of fiction. Names, characters, places, and incidents are either the product of the author's imagination or are used fictitiously. Any resemblance to actual persons, living or dead, events, or locales is entirely coincidental.

First Edition, 2025

Published by **The Third Raven Publishing**

For Addy, Ezra, and Atlas —
My little loves, I want you to know that you can accomplish anything
you put your minds to. It is never too late to follow your heart and chase
your dreams.

For Anthony —
My rock and my greatest supporter. You gave me the space and confidence to complete this dream. My unofficial editor, graphic designer, and
love of my existence — this book would not exist without you.

For Mom —
Who has told me, and everyone else, for my entire life, that I was meant
to be an author. Thank you for planting that seed in me and watering it
continually.

For Jana —
My cosmic twin, my steadfast cheerleader, my forever friend. This book
exists in part because of your faith, your encouragement, and your unwavering friendship. Thank you for being one of my very first and fiercest
supporters.

For my In-laws —
Who have believed in me and encouraged me with love and kindness
throughout this entire journey.

Author Message

I don't write stories that shock you on page five.
I don't throw pain, spice, or trauma at you just to keep you turning pages.
I write stories that ruin you slowly.
Layer by layer.
Until you don't even realize how deep you've fallen—
until it aches in your chest long after the last page.
The Liminal Veil is about found family, soul ties, ghosts, curses, and the quiet kind of love that saves you when you didn't know you needed it. It's about darkness that creeps, not crashes. Beauty that lingers, not blinds.
Pain that is earned, not exploited.
These books are meant to haunt. To break you softly. To stay with you when the lights go out.
So if you're here for the slow ache, for the ruin that feels inevitable and unforgettable—welcome. Step into the Veil.

Content Warnings
This story contains sensitive themes, including:
Childhood trauma and abuse (non-graphic references)
Alcohol use and underage substance/tobacco use
Grief, death, and depictions of spirits/ghosts
Implied sexual assault (not shown on page)
Please take care of yourself as you read. **Your wellbeing comes first—skim, skip, or pause whenever you need.**

"Some spirits seek rest. Others want retribution."
Ash Hollow miner's journal, 1893

Prologue

The bus carried me farther than I'd ever been, but the ride itself felt unreal—half-dream, half-nightmare. Sleep tugged at me in jagged waves I couldn't quite give in to. Heat and noise pressed from all sides: bodies crammed shoulder to shoulder, the sour bite of beer on someone's breath, music leaking tinny and relentless through headphones. The girl next to me had her face pressed to the glass, neon hair catching in the sunlight, mascara smudged like shadows under her eyes. Everything around me seemed worn thin, waiting to split.

Then the bus jerked to a halt, slamming me into the seat in front of me.

I stepped off into another world.

The festival sprawled out in the clearing ahead, a neon fever dream of movement and sound. Strings of mismatched lights dangled from the trees, casting crooked halos over clusters of tents and makeshift stalls. The scent of earth, sweat, and something sickly sweet clung to the humid air. Music pulsed in the distance—thick, bass-heavy beats, the kind you feel more than hear, like they were pressing into your ribs from the inside out.

I should've felt excited—anything, really. Instead, there was only the ache of exhaustion, the gnawing emptiness inside me that no amount of noise could fill. I swallowed against the lump in my throat and adjusted the strap of my bag, trying to shake the unease crawling up my spine.

I didn't belong here.

A cluster of people nearby burst into laughter, passing around a joint. A guy in a tattered denim vest slung an arm around a girl's waist, spinning her into the chaos of the crowd. Everything was too bright, too loud. My skin buzzed like it wasn't fully mine. I needed silence. Air.

The woods waited, dark and patient.

I slipped past the crowd, reaching into my bag and pulling out my pack of cigarettes. A few were bent from being shoved at the bottom, but I managed to fish out one that wasn't broken. I sparked my lighter, shielding the flame from the breeze, and drew in a lungful of menthol. The bite of it steadied me, though the forest ahead swallowed the light as I stepped toward the trees.

The deeper I went, the more the music dissolved into the hush of the forest. Cool air brushed my skin, carrying the damp tang of earth. The trees stretched taller here, branches arching like skeletal fingers. Somewhere ahead, water stirred—a faint lapping, the crisp scent of it cutting through the humidity. Each step pressed me into a stillness that felt weighted, as if something unseen was watching, waiting.

And then, I felt it.

A sharp bite in the air.

I stopped in my tracks, the warmth of early summer suddenly and inexplicably gone. Just moments ago, sweat had gathered at the nape of my neck, my shirt clinging to my skin from the humidity. But now, as I stepped out of the treeline, a chill wrapped around me, sharp and unnatural. My breath curled in front of me in thin, silver wisps.

The leaves around the shoreline, once green, were now brittle and brown, some even rimmed with frost. The sun still burned in the sky above, but its warmth no longer touched me. The ground beneath my feet was hard, the mud near the water's edge frozen in thin, glassy sheets. The smell of crisp, cold water filled my nose—clean, metallic, like ice cracking over a deep river.

The lake stretched out before me, impossibly dark and still, its surface smooth as glass except for the faintest ripples that spread outward from the center.

And then I saw him.

A boy stood at the water's edge, bare feet pressed into the half-frozen mud. He wasn't monstrous—just wrong, in a way that made my stomach twist. Too still. Too silent. His head tilted, listening for a sound I couldn't hear. His blonde hair, damp and clinging to his forehead, dripped water onto his pale skin. His clothes were soaked through, the leather of his jacket gleaming wet in the strange, cold light. But the thing that made my breath catch—my pulse stutter—were his eyes.

He was looking through me.

Cold bled into my fingertips, spreading up my arms and through my chest. I wanted to move, but I couldn't.

"You see me."

His voice was a whisper that curled around my bones, soft but undeniable.

I swallowed. "Yes."

The cold deepened.

"No one ever does."

The words felt heavy, laced with an unspoken meaning I couldn't grasp. The boy took a step forward, the water barely rippling around his ankles. My instincts screamed at me to back away, but I stayed rooted to the spot, heart hammering.

He raised a hand, fingers trembling slightly. I didn't realize I had mirrored the gesture until I felt it—cold, wet, and electric the moment our fingers touched, and the world around me shattered.

Water.

It was everywhere—rushing over me, filling my lungs, crushing my chest. My vision blurred, the lake swallowing everything, dragging me down, down, down—

I was him.

Thrashing. Desperate. My limbs were weak and my body too heavy. The surface above me warped, the light a distant blur through the water. My throat burned and my thoughts frayed. There was no air. No way out. No—

I tore free with a gasp.

The world snapped back into focus, the trees swaying gently around me, the lake lapping at the shore. I was back. But the boy—

He was still there.

Only now, he wasn't standing. He was crouched in front of me, close enough that I could see the way his lashes clumped together, still damp. His jacket was suddenly on my shoulders, heavy with damp leather, scented faintly of sandalwood. I hadn't seen him move. I hadn't felt him place it there. His lips parted like he wanted to speak—

Then the wind rose, brittle leaves scraping the ground.

When I blinked, he was gone.

Only a whisper remained, answering my unspoken question.

"Kai."

A name. Just a voice in the wind, but it sent a shiver down my spine.

I turned back to the water, but it held nothing. Still, deep in my bones, I knew—he hadn't left. And out there, beyond the treeline where shadows thickened, something else was watching.

Chapter One

inn staggered through the trees, her breath tearing from her in shallow, uneven bursts. The world around her felt too sharp—branches tore at her sleeves, the damp earth beneath her shifting with every unsteady step.

Somewhere beyond the thinning treeline, the festival still carried on, neon lights flickering like a pulse, bleeding through the darkness.

But she barely noticed.

Because all she could see was him—the boy in the lake, with hollow, icy blue eyes. His presence pressing into her chest like unseen hands, suffocating and cloying. The cold that still clung to her, not just on her skin but beneath it, burrowed into her marrow, as if it had been stitched into her bones.

She could have believed she'd dreamed the whole thing—that she'd imagined the cold, the lake, the drowning.

But something kept her from being convinced.

A warm leather jacket.

It enveloped her, too solid to be a figment of her imagination. It clung to her like a second skin, its scent curling around her like smoke—leather and rain.

But there was more than just the jacket.

Something knocked against her side with every frantic step.

Thump. Thump.

Finn slowed, just enough to shove her trembling hand inside the pocket.

Her fingers brushed against something small and cool. It pooled against her skin like liquid silver.

She pulled it out, her breath catching.

A crescent moon pendant, delicate and smooth. The metal glinted dully in the fractured light filtering through the canopy. A chain dangled from her fingers, but the clasp was rusted and broken.

Her stomach lurched.

Had this been his?

None of this made sense.

She sucked in a breath, gritted her teeth, and forced herself forward.

One step. Then another.

She broke through the trees too fast—

And nearly collided with someone.

"Whoa."

A firm hand caught her wrist, steadying her.

Finn gasped, snapping her head up.

The guy in front of her had loose curls of auburn hair, catching the festival lights behind him. But it was his eyes that stopped her—piercing amber, sharp and knowing, like they could see straight through her.

He didn't let go right away and she realized, belatedly, that she was shaking.

Then he smirked, tilting his head.

"You look like you've seen a ghost."

Finn jerked her arm back. Then—her gaze searched upward, and she froze.

She had just realized that the sky was black.

That wasn't right.

It had been midday when she wandered into the woods. The sun had been high, burning against the back of her neck. She had only been gone... what? An hour? Two?

Her skin prickled, a cold wave washing over her.

She must have looked as dazed as she felt because the guy didn't move.

His gaze stayed fixed on her, assessing.

Finn shuddered hard, betraying the words she spoke next. "I'm fine," she muttered, dragging a hand through her short dark hair, trying to shake off the chill clinging to her skin.

He just studied her.

At some point, he'd crossed his arms, the shift in movement pulling back the sleeves of his hoodie.

Dark, intricate tattoos crawled up his forearms, coiling over his skin before disappearing beneath the fabric. The details blurred in the dim light, but the bold lines seemed steady and grounded—everything she wasn't.

He was calm and unshaken.

And Finn? She felt like she might unravel right here and now.

"If you say so."

His voice was calm and easy.

Like they were just two strangers making small talk.

Finn forced herself to breathe.

He shifted, stuffing his hands casually into his pockets. But there was something deliberate about it—like he wanted her to know he wasn't a threat.

"Not really my business, but you probably shouldn't be wandering out here alone. Some people at these things can be... sketchy."

Finn let out a dry, humorless laugh. "Yeah? Thanks for the warning."

His smirk returned, but this time, it wasn't sharp or amused. There was something about it that felt... understanding.

"Well, in case you change your mind about needing a little self-preservation..."

He tipped his head toward a rusted old Bronco, parked just beyond the clearing. The moonlight caught the dented metal, a relic of another time.

He was offering a way out without saying it outright.

She wasn't sure what to do with that.

So she just nodded, turned, and walked away.

"Name's Eli, by the way."

His voice carried after her, unhurried.

Finn didn't look back, or answer, but could still feel his eyes following after her.

The night pressed in, thick and breathless, the air humming with voices and laughter, the thrum of the bass vibrating through the trees.

The bonfire crackled, sending up a spray of embers, little dying stars swallowed by the dark. The scent of charred wood mingled with sweat, beer, and something acrid that stung at the back of Finn's throat, enough to make her eyes water.

She sat on a half-rotted log, the damp wood pliant beneath her fingers, crumbling under her grip. Someone pressed a warm bottle into her hands.

Whiskey.

The first sip burned, seeping through her insides like a slow-flowing magma. She grimaced but gulped it down, chasing the way it dulled the sharper edges of her thoughts, smoothing out the jagged places.

Around the fire, punks sprawled—patches and spikes, tattered denim and scuffed boots, a world apart from the spectacle of the festival.

Finn didn't belong here.

But she didn't belong anywhere.

"Hey, new girl."

The voice slurred, thick with alcohol and bad intentions.

A guy with a buzzed head and a stretched-out tank top leaned in, his breath hot and sour. "You got a name, or do I just call you 'quiet and mysterious' all night?"

Finn rolled the bottle between her palms.

Her mother used to say that names carried power, that they could shape a person, bind them to something bigger than themselves.

But the name Seraphina had never felt like hers.

"Finn," she mumbled.

The guy leered. "Cool. You party, Finn?"

Before she could answer, he shoved a small white pill into her palm.

She stared at it, her fingers closing around the tiny thing, as if trapping it there might keep her from making a decision.

Maybe it would make everything easier. Maybe it would make her forget.

Forget the way her stepfather's voice could slither under her skin like oil, thick and suffocating. Forget the way her mother had stopped looking her in the eyes. Forget the boy in the lake, with his drowning stare.

Her fist clenched tighter.

"You don't have to take that."

Finn turned.

Eli stood just beyond the firelight, leaning against a tree, hands tucked into the pockets of his jeans. Shadows flickered over his face, carving sharp edges into his features. His curls fell loose over his eyes, obscuring whatever expression she might've tried to read.

He was watching her.

Not judging or pushing.

Just there.

She didn't answer him.

Instead, she knocked back another swig of whiskey, and let the burn hollow out the hesitation, scorching it into nothing.

She turned back to the guy and held out her hand, fingers unfurling slowly.

He just blinked at her.

Then, with a shrug, he plucked the pill from her palm and tucked it back into his pocket. No argument.

Eli didn't leave.

Finn could still feel him there, just at the edges. A steady presence.

Something about the way he stood—loose, casual, but there—unnerved her.

The night blurred.

More drinks. More laughter—thin and weightless, slipping through the cracks of reality.

The fire stretched and swayed, its glow licking up into the dark like reaching fingers. Sparks snapped and curled into the night, vanishing before they could touch the sky. The world tilted, sound and light folding in on themselves until everything felt too loud and bright—too wrong.

A hand slid over her knee.

The buzzed guy was even closer now. Far too close.

"You good?" His voice was thick with liquor, his fingers creeping higher up her thigh.

She flinched.

The fire warped, doubled, flames stretching in her vision like liquid light. Shapes bled together at the edges, indistinct—movement distorting like a dream she couldn't wake from.

"No," she tried to say, but the word caught in her throat. Her tongue was too bulky in her mouth, her limbs burdensome, and her vision spiraling.

The heat of his breath brushed against her ear, damp and cloying.

She couldn't move.

Couldn't breathe.

Then—

He was gone.

The moment snapped like a rubber band pulled too tight.

Air rushed back in, sharp and electric, setting her nerves alight.

Finn blinked hard, her vision struggling to focus, to make sense of what just happened.

Eli stood over him.

The guy was sprawled in the dirt, dazed, his body half-lit by the fire's glow. His face bore a stunned expression, the confusion in his eyes slow to catch up with reality.

"The hell, man?" he slurred.

Eli didn't even look at him.

His gaze flashed to Finn—unreadable, but burning through the distance between them.

Then, without a word, he offered his hand.

She stared at it.

She could stay and drown herself in whiskey and firelight, let the heat and the noise pull her under, pretending none of this was real.

Or she could leave.

Her fingers trembled as she reached for his hand.

Eli pulled her up, his grip steady as she swayed.

"Come on," he murmured.

She didn't argue.

The fire danced behind them, its heat dissolving into the cold hush of the trees as Eli led her away. The festival lights pulsed somewhere behind them, but they felt worlds away now—distant and unreal.

Finn barely registered the shape of his car as Eli pulled open the passenger door, guiding her inside.

She slumped against the seat, exhaustion sinking into her, heavy and inescapable.

"Come on," Eli said again, gentler this time.

He helped her into the back. A sleeping bag—old but warm, carrying the scent of fabric softener and the faintest trace of cigarette smoke—was spread beneath her. She collapsed onto it, and something unfamiliar settled into her bones. Safety.

Eli crouched in the doorway, backlit by the dim dome light—until, for a moment, he wasn't Eli at all. The light blurred, softened at the edges. A memory swam into view...

The glow of a nightlight. The scent of lavender and something sweeter—vanilla, maybe, or honey. My mother's hands, warm and careful, tucking the blankets around me. Tucking me in like I was fragile, something worth protecting. Her fingers brushed over my forehead, smoothing back my unruly waves of hair.

"You're safe now, my angel. My little seraphim. Sleep."

I believed her.

Back then, I always believed her.

The memory fractured, dissolving as quickly as it had come.

Finn's throat tightened.

She nestled into the sleeping bag, pulling it around her, chasing the waning warmth before it could slip away.

Eli quietly shut the door.

And for the first time in a long time, Finn let herself close her eyes.

This time, when she let sleep take her—she wasn't afraid.

Chapter Two

unlight pierced Finn's groggy eyes as she stumbled out of the Bronco. The kaleidoscope fever dream of last night—swirling lights, tangled sounds, firelight flickering against strangers' faces—felt like something distant and untouchable, an illusion dissolving in the hush of morning.

But the stench of charred wood and booze still clung to her clothes, securing her in the aftermath.

She felt hollowed out.

The leftover whiskey in her stomach churned, acidic and unsettled. She braced herself against the vehicle, squeezing her eyes shut, willing the world to stop tilting.

Then—

"I was wondering when you were going to come back to the land of the living."

Her eyes snapped open.

Eli leaned against the hood, arms crossed, watching her with quiet amusement.

The morning sun caught in his curls, turning auburn to gold, softening the hardened look in his eyes.

She blinked, her mind sluggish, still dragging itself through the fog of last night.

"I told myself I wouldn't babysit," he said, his tone level but edged with dry humor. "But I also figured I'd stick close. Just in case."

Just in case.

The words settled between them, lingering like the last traces of smoke from the fire.

Finn swallowed dryly, her throat tight.

"I guess it's a good thing you did."

The words came out sheepishly, her voice tattered at the edges. Guilt sat heavy in her chest, thick as oil, clinging to the spaces between her ribs.

"But I'm okay now. Really. Thanks again."

She stared down at her boots—scuffed, dirt-caked, a reminder of where she'd been. Already planning to walk away.

Already wondering where the hell she would go.

Eli didn't call her a liar, but he didn't look convinced either.

He just studied her–really looked at her.

Like he could see the ghosts clinging to her skin.

"You don't have to be okay."

His voice was quieter now. Measured.

She folded her arms tightly across her ribs, pressing until the ache gave her something else to focus on.

She didn't know what to say. So she said nothing.

Eli exhaled, pushing off the hood.

"Come on."

A nod toward the passenger door.

"You need a ride."

Finn bristled at the knowing tone in his voice.

She could disappear back into the woods, and try to find her own way.

Could find another group. Another fire. Another bottle.

Another way to forget.

But she was so damn tired.

And Eli?

He was still standing there, holding the door open.

Waiting.

After a long moment, she stepped forward.

She climbed into the Bronco, sinking into the tattered seat where fraying fabric barely held the stuffing inside.

Eli shut the door behind her.

The sound of it echoed through her, final and certain.

The vehicle rumbled beneath them, the low growl of the engine filling the silence.

The festival faded behind them, the memory of its lights and noise dimming into the hush of the forest, swallowed by distance and dawn.

Finn watched it vanish, her breath fogging against the window.

She felt the insistent pull of exhaustion.

But underneath it—something else.

Something unsettled, coiled tight inside her chest.

Eli didn't ask where she was coming from, or why she'd been alone in the woods.

Didn't ask what she was running from.

Instead—

"So... Do you have a destination in mind, or are we just burning gas?"

Finn turned her head, her reflection ghosting across the glass.

She hadn't thought that far ahead.

"I..." Her voice came slow, hesitant, like it had to fight its way through the fog in her mind. She sighed.

"I don't know."

Eli made a low, thoughtful sound.

"Well, that's not ideal."

She huffed a dry laugh, the sound barely there. "Tell me about it."

His fingers tapped an unhurried rhythm against the steering wheel.

"No friends to crash with? Family?"

Her stomach twisted.

She shook her head. "No one I can go to."

That was the truth. Maybe not the full truth—but enough of it.

Eli just nodded, his eyes still fixed on the road.

"Alright."

The silence stretched between them again, not awkward or tense, just... there.

Finn pulled her knees up, curling into herself.

"What about you?" The question slipped out before she could second-guess it, surprising even herself. "Where are you from?"

Eli smirked, his gaze flashing to her briefly before returning to the road.

"Here."

She raised an eyebrow. "You mean the festival?"

"Nah." A lazy shake of his head. "The town outside it. Been here my whole life."

Finn frowned.

"I didn't think people actually lived out here."

"Most don't." He shot her a sideways glance, the corner of his mouth quirking. "I'm one of the unlucky few."

There was something teasing in his tone—light. No trace of bitterness.

And Finn felt something stir—a shadow of a smile, hesitant and unfamiliar.

"You don't sound like you hate it."

He shrugged, one hand loose on the wheel. "I don't. Not really. It's quiet. You just gotta know where to look for something interesting."

"Like a music festival in the woods?"

"Exactly." He grinned. "Or a girl who looks like she's seen a ghost."

Her chest tightened.

She turned back to the window, watching the road unfurl ahead of them—dark and endless, blurring past like something slipping out of reach.

Eli didn't take it back. Didn't pretend he hadn't seen something in her last night.

He just let it be.

After a while, Finn sighed, dragging a hand through her tangled hair, fingers catching on knots she was too tired to care about.

"So what's the plan, then?"

Eli cast her a sidelong look, his fingers still tapping a more restless beat against the steering wheel.

"For you?" He shrugged, voice casual. "Dunno. You comfortable crashing at my place?"

Finn blinked, not sure she'd heard him right.

"What?"

His grip adjusted on the wheel like he'd said something completely normal, like they weren't still steeped in the aftermath of a night neither of them fully understood.

"My place," he repeated, the words effortless. "That's where we're headed." The drumming of his fingers picked up speed, something un-thinking in the movement. "I mean, unless you had a better idea."

She turned to study him, searching for something beneath the easy cadence of his words.

"You don't even know me."

Eli smirked, a lazy curve of his lips, eyes still on the road.

"You don't know me either, and yet you got in my truck."

Finn started to argue, but the words never made it out. She shut her mouth, pressing her back into the tattered seat, gaze drifting toward the blur of trees outside the window.

He wasn't wrong.

The Bronco groaned as it rolled into town, tires kicking up loose gravel as they passed a warped wooden sign:

Welcome to Ash Hollow, Wyoming

The letters were faded, paint peeling at the edges like they were trying to let go.

The road narrowed, pulling them into a single stretch of forgotten America—buildings standing shoulder to shoulder, their wooden bones worn from a century of wind and time.

Finn shifted in her seat, the town settling around her as she watched it unfold through the window.

The first thing she saw was an old diner, its red-and-white sign so weathered the letters barely clung to the surface.

The Lantern Diner.

A handful of cars sat in the lot, dust settling over their windshields like they hadn't moved in hours. Through the wide front window, a lone waitress wiped down the counter, her movements slow and practiced—the kind of repetition that seeped into your being.

Next came a gas station, or what was left of one. It looked like it had been through at least three different owners, none of them caring enough to replace the flashing OPEN sign hanging in the window, stubbornly clinging to life.

Two pumps stood out front, rust creeping along their edges. One of them was wrapped in a plastic bag—out of service, probably for good.

A man leaned against the doorway, his thick flannel tugged tight against the morning chill. A cigarette burned low between his fingers, smoke curling lazily past the brim of his ball cap, which was pulled down so far Finn couldn't see his face.

Still, she knew he was watching them.

Further down, a squat wooden building with graying white paint bore the fading words:

Ash Grocery.

Finn had seen places like it before—where everything was overpriced, the milk was always a few days from sour, and the produce sat bruised beneath dim fluorescent lights.

The kind of place that only stayed open because there was nowhere else to go.

The whole town felt... paused.

Like time had loosened its grip, leaving the buildings to sink, inch by inch, into the earth.

Finn rubbed her arms, trying to shake the feeling.

"No hotel?" she asked.

Eli's smirk was barely there, his eyes steady on the road. "There's one."

Finn frowned. "I haven't seen it yet."

"That's because it's the kind of place you don't want to see."

He said lightly, but something in the way he said it made her stomach flip.

She turned toward him. "What do you mean?"

He sighed, fingers tapping against the wheel again—a habit Finn was starting to recognize. "I mean, it's the kind of place I wouldn't leave you alone in. Ever."

That was enough.

She sank deeper into the seat. Even if the hotel had been decent, it wasn't like she could afford even a single night.

Then, almost offhandedly, Eli nodded toward the road ahead.

"So, my place it is?"

Finn's mind raced.

Her instinct was to refuse. To say she didn't want to impose, and that she'd figure something else out, but she had nowhere to go.

Her throat felt tight as she forced herself to speak. "Just for a little while," she said carefully, as if saying it out loud made it more true. "Until I can figure something out."

Eli smirked but didn't argue. "Right. Just until then."

She didn't like the way he said it—like he knew something she didn't.

But she was too tired to push back, or pretend she had anywhere else to be.

The road stretched ahead, pulling them out of town, where somewhere beyond the trees, a house waited.

The deeper they drove, the thicker the forest grew—ancient trees pressing in from both sides, their gnarled branches laced together overhead. Even though the morning still lingered, the sunlight barely touched the ground, stolen by the dense canopy.

It felt like another world. A place untouched.

Finn sat rigid in the passenger seat, her gaze passing between Eli's profile and the endless stretch of trees. The road had gone too long without a house, without any sign of life other than the shifting shadows that moved with them.

Then, suddenly, the woods parted.

The trees thinned like a held breath releasing, and golden light spilled into an open clearing. The house appeared all at once—like it had always been waiting at the end of this road.

It wasn't grand, but it wasn't small either. A two-story cabin, rustic but strong, the kind of place that had settled into the land instead of standing against it. The covered porch was wide, its wooden beams untouched by time. It was easy to picture someone standing there with a steaming mug of coffee, watching the mist rise off the treetops.

It was a place that felt rooted.

Eli swung the truck into park and hopped out, moving toward the house with easy familiarity.

Finn stayed in her seat, her grip tightening around the hem of her hoodie.

It wasn't fear, exactly.

But uncertainty pressed against her sternum, locking her in place.

Eli made it halfway up the porch steps before realizing she wasn't following. He turned, his brows knitting together before something softer took over.

He came back, opened her door, and leaned down to meet her gaze.

His hand extended toward her, palm up.

"It's okay," he said, "You don't have to be nervous."

Finn's throat tightened.

"I'm not nervous."

That was the lie she wanted to tell.

Instead, she let out a breath, and slipped her hand into his. His skin was warm, his grip firm but brief—the second she was on her feet, he let go, giving her space.

She followed him up the porch steps, through the front door, stepping into the kind of entryway that only ever existed in houses that had been lived in for generations. The wooden floors had been worn down by footsteps, scuffed but polished with care.

Eli tossed his keys onto an old entry table, the surface scratched and faded with age.

"Pops?" he called.

A voice answered from deeper inside—a low, gravel-rough drawl that sent a shiver up Finn's spine. Not from fear, but from something else. Something unfamiliar.

Eli led her through a wide doorway, and Finn trailed after him into the kitchen.

The first thing she noticed wasn't the scent of coffee, or the well-loved wooden table at the focal point of the room.

It was the motorcycle.

A whole dirt bike was parked in the middle of the kitchen, cardboard shoved beneath the tires to keep the oil from staining the stone floor. And bent over it, turning a tool in his calloused hands, was a man Finn could only assume was Eli's father.

He was lean but strong, built from work rather than vanity. His curly gray hair was cut short, streaked with remnants of black, the silver at his temples catching the light. Wire-rimmed glasses sat low on his sharp nose, stubble shadowing his jaw. His jeans were stained with oil, his Harley Davidson t-shirt threadbare from years of wear.

He didn't look up when they entered.

Eli leaned casually against the counter, nodding toward the bike.

"Really, Frank? In the kitchen?"

The man twisted the wrench one last time before exhaling, finally looking up. His eyes—steel gray and sharp—landed on Finn.

He studied her for a long moment, then nodded once. Like her being here had already been decided.

Finn wasn't sure what to make of that.

"Had to fix the throttle," Frank said simply, wiping his hands on a rag. His voice was deep, even-tempered, the kind that made people listen. "Figured it'd be warmer here than the garage."

Eli huffed, shaking his head.

Frank's gaze turned back to Finn, unreadable but not unkind. He didn't press her with questions or demand explanations.

Somehow, that made Finn even more uncertain.

She wasn't sure if that was a good thing or not.

Finn stood stiffly, feeling awkward in the quiet that followed. She could still feel Frank's gaze—not piercing or judgmental, just assessing. Like he was taking her measure without needing to ask.

Eli, as if mentioning the weather, nodded toward her.

"Finn's gonna stay in the extra room."

Frank didn't flinch. He just nodded, like it was already settled.

Eli glanced over at her again, eyes landing on the small purse slung across her chest.

"She doesn't have much with her." He said it casually, though the tone in his voice felt heavier than the words themselves. Then, with a shrug, "I figured some of Mom's old things might fit her."

Finn's stomach clenched.

She could tell, just from the way he said 'Mom's old things', that his mother was gone.

And yet...

Even with the tools, the motorcycle in the kitchen, the no-nonsense practicality of the space, there was a warmth here. Something untouched by loss. A feminine presence that lingered, even in absence.

Eli eyed her up and down. "She's about Mom's size. If a fair bit shorter." His voice held a spark of amusement.

Finn's cheeks burned. She was only 5'2" in her chunky-heeled combat boots.

Before she could respond, something suddenly clicked in her mind.

She gasped.

Eli's brows lifted, while Frank's narrowed.

"My jacket," she whispered—Kai's jacket.

Her hands clutched at empty air where the fabric should have been. Panic surged through her like a wave.

She'd had it at the bonfire... the necklace was in the pocket...

Eli exhaled, relief settling across his face. "Oh—yeah, I got it," he said, like he'd thought something was actually wrong. "I went back for it after I got you in the truck last night. I'll grab it."

Without another word, he pushed off the counter and strode out of the kitchen, leaving Finn standing under Frank's silent gaze.

She tried to focus on anything but him—her eyes drifting over the butcher block countertops, the little plate of half-eaten toast streaked with dark berry jam, the leaning tower of cookbooks stacked on a shelf against the wall. The kitchen, much like what little of the house she'd seen so far, was rugged but well-loved, marked by time and use.

Then Frank finally spoke.

"So." His voice was low and even. "My boy brought home another stray?"

Finn's head snapped up.

From someone else, those words might have been biting. But from Frank, they weren't unkind. If anything, there was something knowing in his tone, carrying an edge of familiarity. Like this wasn't the first time.

A faint involuntary smile tugged at the corner of her lips. A small rush of warmth pressed against her ribs. "Yeah... I guess that's an accurate take."

His expression softened. The same, almost imperceptible, smile she'd seen on Eli curved his lips. He leaned back, resting his forearms on his knees, his steel-gray eyes still studying her.

"You don't have to be uncomfortable here," he said simply. "Eli's brought in his fair share of wayward souls. Plenty of wanderers. But..." He tilted his head, gaze narrowing.

"Never a girl."

The words landed heavier than she expected. Finn's chest tightened, but before she could find a response Eli reappeared, striding back into the room with the leather jacket slung over one arm.

"What're you two talking about?" he asked, tossing it onto the back of a chair.

Finn barely heard him.

Her fingers were already reaching for the jacket, clutching the creased leather as she pulled it toward her. It was heavier than she remembered.

Frank didn't look away from her as he answered Eli. "Just letting her know you can show her where to find some of your mom's old clothes." His voice was casual, but there was something unreadable in his expression. "And she can take whatever she needs."

Eli nodded, glancing at Finn. "That cool?"

Her fingers curled into the jacket, gripping the worn edges between her thumbs and forefingers. The leather was supple from years of wear, carrying a warmth that wasn't hers. It felt like a history she wasn't sure she had the right to hold.

She hesitated. The kindness was unexpected, unfamiliar in a way that made her chest ache.

She should say something. Anything.

Instead, she just nodded.

Eli's smile was small but certain. "Alright then. C'mon, I'll show you."

And just like that, she followed him.

Chapter Three

inn trailed behind Eli as they moved through the house, her eyes tracing the space around her. The layout was... uneven. It felt like a house that had grown over time rather than been planned—rooms added as needed, walls adjusted, spaces shifting and reshaping to fit the lives inside.

The kitchen gave way to a cozy, unpretentious living room with the same worn-in, well-loved feeling.

The first thing Finn noticed was the fireplace. It took up nearly an entire wall, its stonework rough and uneven, cut from the same rugged material as the kitchen floor. It looked like it had been built not for beauty, but to endure. The wood floor around it bore a soft sheen, footsteps having pressed familiar paths into the grain.

Everything in the room spoke of comfort over design. The deep couch, its cushions settled into familiar shapes. The coffee table, scarred by time, its wood marked with hundreds of moments. A couple of old blankets, folded neatly over the arm of a chair—the kind of detail that belonged to a home, not just a house.

Against one wall, a wooden writing desk caught Finn's eye. At first glance, it looked like chaos. Spools of wire, stray feathers, and tiny glass beads scattered across the surface. But beneath the mess was a rhythm—a purposeful, practiced disorder.

Fishing lures, she realized.

Frank's, she suspected.

Finn hung onto the details, on the small fragments of someone's life present in the space.

She felt like she was standing in a house that had a heartbeat.

She might have dawdled longer, but Eli was already moving, guiding her past the living room and into a short hallway.

The walls were lined with framed photographs—snapshots of time, frozen in their glass prisons. Some were crisp and clear, others yellowed at the edges. Finn's fingers twitched at her sides, resisting the pull to reach out, to trace the ridges of the frames as if that might somehow press her fingertips against the past.

Most of them were of Frank and Eli.

Eli as a boy, perched on the edge of a dock, his feet dangling above dark water, grinning like he knew a secret the world hadn't figured out yet. Frank, younger, standing beside an old Harley, his arm slung over the shoulder of someone just out of frame. A few grainy black-and-white photos of Frank in his youth, his face less lined but still carrying that same unreadable weight.

Finn's stomach twisted.

Nothing was missing. Not visibly, anyway. There were no empty hooks, no sun-bleached outlines of frames that had been taken down. And yet... she felt it.

An absence.

Like the ghosts of missing pictures still clung to the walls. Like there were places where something—or someone—should have been.

She didn't know how she knew that.

But the feeling sat in the back of her mind, unshakable.

At the end of the hall, a screen door stood half-open, leading to what looked like a sunroom. A slant of honeyed light cut across the floorboards, dust softly swirling in its path. Finn barely had time to take in the glimpse of wide windows and morning light before Eli veered right, leading her up a narrow staircase.

The stairs were steep, the kind that demanded attention—one misstep, and you'd be sent tumbling. Eli climbed them without hesitation, his movements sure and practiced. Finn followed, her boots making gentle thuds against the wood, the steps groaning under the shift in weight, as if waking from a long rest.

At the top, she expected a hallway, a landing, something that led somewhere. Instead, she was met with a wall—plain, unmoving. A short corridor stretched left and right, but Eli didn't turn either way.

Instead, he reached up, fingers catching a pull-string. With one firm tug, the attic stairs unfolded like an invitation, creaking as they stretched downward.

Eli climbed first, disappearing into the dim space above. His footfalls barely made a sound, as if the attic already knew him.

Finn took a breath and followed.

The ladder wobbled beneath her, but she moved carefully, her fingers gripping the edges of the wooden rungs. The air grew cooler as she ascended, carrying the scent of dust and time.

When she reached the top, she pulled herself into the attic, taking in the space around her. It was quiet. Not just in sound, but in presence, like a place waiting to be remembered.

Eli flicked on the light, the dim glow spilling into the corners.

And as Finn took it all in, something settled over her—something delicate and uneasy, like walking through the remnants of a life that had once been whole.

The floorboards beneath her steps groaned in protest, wood whispering its years into the air. The space was thick with the scent of time itself—dust and cedar, laced with something softer. Lavender, maybe. Or dried roses. A scent that didn't belong to the bones of the house, but to the memory of someone who once lived here.

As Eli moved toward a stack of boxes, Finn let her gaze wander.

This wasn't just storage.

This was Nancy's space.

The name surfaced unbidden, like a breath against her mind.

Racks of simple dresses lined one side of the attic, their colors faded but carefully preserved. A pair of heavy wooden wardrobes stood nearby, their doors slightly ajar, as if someone had reached for them again and again over the years, until they no longer fit snug in their frames. Along the farthest wall, boxes were stacked carefully, each one bearing the same name in neat, looping script—Nancy.

Finn stilled.

She had already known, somehow, before she saw the name. As if the space itself had spoken it to her.

Eli had mentioned his mother's things, but standing here—surrounded by them—she realized just how much of Nancy still remained in this house. Not in dust, or forgotten things, but in presence.

But none of it held Finn's attention quite like the vanity.

It stood at the farthest end of the attic, nestled beneath the eaves as if it had always belonged there. Large, ornately carved—a thing of beauty, even now, wrapped in the hush of time. The dark wood was etched with floral patterns and curling vines, their intricate details still visible despite the dust that had settled into the grooves. The mirror, though dulled by years of stillness, caught the dim light in a way that made its reflection feel almost alive, shifting with every breath.

The surface was littered with forgotten relics, each one wrapped in a delicate film of dust.

Perfume bottles, their glass bodies ambered with time. Tubes of lipstick, some uncapped, revealing deep reds and soft pinks. Little pots of blush, their lids painted with flowers that had long since faded.

And makeup brushes, their carved wooden handles smooth from years of use. Finn reached for one, her fingers barely grazing the bristles.

Soft. So impossibly soft.

A breath caught in her throat, though she wasn't sure why.

She had never been the kind of girl to linger in front of mirrors. Never cared much for powders or perfumes.

But now, standing here, the past pressing in around her, she couldn't look away.

Not from the mirror.

Not from her own reflection.

And certainly not from the dull ache growing in her chest, as if she had stepped into a space where she was not meant to exist—yet somehow, inexplicably, she did.

Her turquoise-green eyes reflected back at her, vivid against the attic light. The contrast of pale skin and inky hair had always felt sharp, almost unnatural. But now, caught in the mirror's reflective glow, there was something else—something she had never let herself acknowledge. A gentle, understated beauty.

She exhaled, a breath barely there, her fingers hovering above the vanity's surface, dust rising in whorls beneath her touch.

And then—she wasn't alone.

Eli stood behind her, a cardboard box frozen mid-lift in his arms.

His eyes were wide, lips parted, as if something in him had stalled the moment he saw her there. He wasn't just looking at her. He was seeing her.

The air between them stretched, taut and humming.

Then their gazes met in the mirror.

And the spell broke.

Finn turned away too fast, stomach lurching, shame rushing in like a river.

She had touched his mother's things.

Her hands curled into fists at her sides, the press of her nails sharp against her palms. She took a hesitant step forward, the attic walls seeming to inch closer.

"I—" she started, but the words tangled in her throat.

She didn't even know what she meant to say. I'm sorry? I shouldn't have?

But Eli still hadn't spoken.

And the look in his eyes—was it shock? Grief? Something else entirely?

Finn hesitated, the softness of bristles already fading from her fingertips.

And then, without thinking, she blurted, "Your dad is quite the jack-of-all-trades."

The words landed between them like a pebble in still water, breaking the silence but not quite shattering it.

Eli blinked, pulled from whatever had gripped him just moments before. He shifted, like shaking off the remnants of a half-formed thought, then let out a low, amused breath.

"Yeah," he said, tilting his head. "He is. But how do you know that?"

Finn latched onto the change of subject, grateful for something solid to focus on. "The motorcycle in the kitchen," she started, her voice steadying. "The fishing lures on the desk. And all the hand-carved woodwork around the house." She gestured vaguely, as if to encompass the whole place. "Just... little things."

Eli's expression wavered—something quivering just beneath the surface—before the corner of his mouth quirked up. "You're pretty damn observant."

She gave a small shrug, brushing it off with a quiet satisfaction.

But then Eli narrowed his eyes, something thoughtful creeping into his gaze. "Alright," he mused, "but how'd you know he did all the carvings?"

Finn paused, considering.

Because the house itself spoke of his presence, his craftsmanship woven into every detail, every careful cut of wood. She couldn't explain how she knew—it wasn't logical. It was just... something she felt.

Her lips parted, then closed again.

She shrugged once more, lighter this time, as if the answer didn't matter. "I just did."

Eli studied her for a long moment, before he huffed a laugh, shaking his head. "People wouldn't think it, just looking at him." His gaze shifted toward the attic stairs, as if he could see straight through the floorboards to where Frank was likely still working in the kitchen. "Or me, for that matter."

Finn arched a brow, wordlessly prompting him to elaborate.

Eli smirked, but there was something self-aware in it. "Most people take one look at either of us and figure the motorcycle thing." He shifted the cardboard box in his hands, getting a better grip on the edges. Then he tipped his chin toward the vanity. "But not... this."

Finn followed his gaze.

The intricate woodwork, the delicate carving—it was beautiful. It was precise. Made by hands that understood both patience and tenderness.

Made with care.

She exhaled softly, dragging her gaze back to Eli just as he let out a breath and sank onto the attic floor. The old planks groaned beneath him, sending up a wisp of dust. He didn't seem to notice, but Finn coughed lightly, waving a hand in front of her face before lowering herself beside him.

She sat carefully, tucking her legs beneath her, her knee nearly brushing against his.

For a moment, neither of them spoke.

That was when it hit her.

She wasn't uncomfortable.

She wasn't waiting for the slow creep of unease to settle in, for the instinct to pull away before she even realized she was doing it. Her skin didn't prickle and her hands didn't go clammy.

For as long as she could remember, Finn had avoided closeness. Even with those who had once felt like home. She had spent years perfecting the art of distance, of making herself small, of ensuring no one got close enough to notice the way she flinched when they did.

But now—here, in this dust-laden attic—she felt none of that.

Eli sat just inches away, his presence unintrusive. His warmth was subtle, resting just beneath the stillness.

And she felt... fine.

No, more than fine.

Safe.

The realization should have bothered her, should have sent her pulse skittering in warning, made her shrink back into herself before she had the chance to question it.

But somehow—it didn't.

And that might have been the strangest part of all.

Eli shifted the box onto his lap, peeling back the flaps with the ease of someone who had done this before—someone who had sat in this attic, alone, sifting through remnants of a life left behind.

Inside, the contents were folded neatly. Blouses in deep jewel tones, soft sweaters with stretched cuffs, the fabric worn but lovingly preserved. The faint traces of faded perfume rose up as he lifted the first piece, his thumbs brushing over the fabric as if reacquainting himself with something long absent.

There was reverence in the way he handled them.

Without a word, he passed the blouse to her.

She took it, her fingers slipping over the delicate weave, the memory of warmth still soaked in its fibers. She wasn't sure what she had expected, but the feel of it in her hands was... strange. Like she was holding a piece of someone else's story, unsure of the role she was meant to play in it.

They fell into an easy rhythm after that.

Eli would pull out an article of clothing, pass it to her, and she would inspect it, placing it into one of two piles—the ones she would keep, and the ones she wouldn't.

They did this for a long time, the attic stretching around them in patient silence. Dust drifted in the dim glow of the overhead light, settling over the moment like a quiet benediction.

When the first box was empty, Eli took the discard pile without question, placing it back inside before reaching for another.

That's when Finn noticed: he never asked which pile was which. Never clarified.

And yet—without fail—he knew.

There was never a pause or misstep. He simply gathered the ones she had rejected and moved on, as if he could read her choices without needing to be told.

Finn found herself stealing glances at him, watching the unspoken understanding in the set of his shoulders, the certainty in his movements.

"How do you know?" she wanted to ask.

But she didn't.

Instead, she let the moment be.

By the time they had gone through the last box, Finn had a small but sufficient collection—more than she had anticipated, and certainly more than she had dared to hope for.

Eli seemed to sense they were finished. He consolidated the remaining clothes, making space in one of the empty boxes for Finn's chosen items.

They both stood, Eli scooping up the box as if it weighed nothing, then turning off the light.

Finn followed him back out of the attic, her boots careful on the wooden steps.

But just as she was about to cross the threshold, she hesitated.

She found her gaze back on the vanity, now draped in shadow. The mirror, once fogged with dust, had turned into something darker—a well of ink.

For a brief moment, it looked bottomless.

And then—

Movement.

A glimmer of something just beyond the glass.

Finn's breath caught, her pulse stuttering.

The reflection of long, swooping hair, there and gone in an instant.

By the time she blinked, by the time she dared to look again, the attic was just as it had been before—silent, still and empty.

She hurried after Eli, descending into the warmth of the house below.

Chapter Four

he attic stairs folded up with a *thunk*, disappearing into the ceiling as Frank's voice carried up from below.

"Heading to Danny's!"

Finn glanced at Eli, one brow lifting.

"Hardware store," he mouthed in explanation before calling back down, "Got it! We'll meet you at the shop around one."

A low grunt was Frank's only response, followed by the creak of the front door swinging open and the muted thud as it latched shut. The house fell into silence, the kind that settled deep and unhurried.

Eli nodded toward the hallway, motioning for Finn to follow.

They moved down the left corridor, past the open bathroom door. Finn caught a glimpse of an old clawfoot tub, its porcelain surface worn with time but still gleaming. There was something lonely about it. As if it had seen decades of long, contemplative soaks but had gone unappreciated for some time.

She let the thought slip away as Eli stopped at the next door, pushing it open with his shoulder.

"This is all you," he said, stepping inside and setting the box down on a short dresser tucked between the doorway and a small bed.

Finn followed him in, her gaze sweeping over the space with curiosity.

It was small, but not suffocating. No tinier than what she'd had before—but somehow, this felt different. Lighter. The kind of space that invited breath instead of pressing in on it.

The bed, simple but welcoming, was covered in a pale blue duvet, the fabric soft-looking, in the way of things that had been used and loved rather than simply placed for show. Plush decorative pillows were messily arranged at the head.

For the first time since entering the home, Finn didn't feel like she was intruding.

There wasn't much else in the room—a modest wardrobe stood against the opposite wall—but what drew Finn in was the window nook directly across from the bed.

She drifted toward it, her fingers skimming the edge of the deep blue curtains. Silver thread stitched tiny constellations into the fabric, catching the bedroom light. The stars shimmered faintly, like the hush of the night sky just before dawn.

A breath slipped from her lips as she traced the embroidery, something unguarded stirring in her chest. She turned back to Eli, a beaming smile lighting up her face.

"Thank you."

Eli's smile was instant, and just as sincere. "Don't even mention it."

He lingered in the doorway for a second longer before nodding toward the hall. "Get settled in. I'm gonna take a quick shower."

Then, with a wink, he added, "I'll try to save you some hot water."

Finn let out a laugh as he turned, opening the door directly across from hers. He hesitated in the frame, half-turning back toward her.

"If you need anything," he said, nodding toward the room he was about to step into, "this is me."

And with that, he disappeared inside, the door shutting behind him.

Finn shut her own door then turned to the box on the dresser, lifting out the folded garments one by one. With careful hands, she smoothed each piece before tucking it into the empty drawers, giving them a place. Making them hers.

The fabrics smelled faintly of dust and time, holding the imprint of years untouched. She made a mental note to ask Eli about the laundry situation later—she wanted to wash them, to breathe new life into them, to make them feel like more than borrowed memories.

Her fingers found a pair of wide-legged jeans, the denim softened by wear. She held them up against herself, testing the length—a little too long, but nothing she couldn't work with. She set them aside, pairing them with a crushed velvet blouse in a shade of deep ruby. The fabric pooled like liquid between her fingers, smooth, rich. The sleeves stretched long, past her thumbs—something to hold onto.

It was perfect for the day.

And then—

A cold realization swept through her, sharp as a blade.

She had no change of underwear.

The thought struck like a slap.

The warmth in her limbs evaporated.

The air in the room felt thinner.

And suddenly, she wasn't in Eli's house anymore.

She was there. A memory crashed over her, dragging her under before she could fight it.

— — —

I'm back in my old room.

My hands won't stop trembling. My pulse is frantic, hammering against my ribs, my limbs weak from the fading rush of adrenaline. Every breath is shallow, uneven, rattling in my chest like a bird trapped in a cage.

My body aches.

The searing pain across my arms, back and thighs pulses in time with my heartbeat—raw, burning. But it barely registers. The trembling drowns out everything else.

His voice still clings to the air, thick with venom, poisoning the space around me.

The words slither under my skin, sinking deep, just like the leather of his belt—

"Harlot."

"Disgrace."

"Meant to stay pure and blameless, like an untouched lamb."

The things he implies. The sickness in his tone.

The way his eyes move over me.

The reek of whiskey on his breath.

My stomach turns, but there's nothing in me to throw up.

Then, after it's over—after the rage drains from him, leaving him red-faced and panting—he bends down.

Caressing my face.

His fingers feel wrong.

Wrong in a way that makes my skin crawl, and bile surge up my throat.

"You're supposed to stay Daddy's sweet girl," he murmurs, his voice thick and syrupy, curdled with something worse than anger.

His tongue flicks out, wetting his lips.

His gaze sweeps over me in a way a father's never, ever should.

Then, as if nothing happened, he stands. Re-loops his belt. And walks out.

Click.

The lock turning on the outside of my door sends ice through my veins.

— — —

Finn jolted back into the present, the world around her snapping into focus too fast, too sharp.

Her hands clutched the edge of the dresser, her knuckles bone-white against the dark wood. She forced herself to loosen her grip, but the phantom pain still lingered, pulsing hot along the bruises on her back—old wounds reigniting, her body remembering before her mind could catch up.

Her stomach churned. The air felt suffocating, as if the past had wrapped itself around her throat, squeezing tight. Her skin was damp with sweat, and her heart a frantic, stuttering thing. She hated how easily her past could sink its claws into her and pull.

You're not there.

The words barely formed in her mind before she forced herself to stand straighter, to inhale deeply. To remind herself.

You're not with him. You're here. In Eli's house. In your own room.

She tried to steady herself. Her arms wrapped around her torso, gripping her own elbows as if she could physically hold herself together.

She had survived that night.

She had survived every night after.

And she would survive this, too.

Her breath came slower now, though not steady. But it was enough. Enough to push back the darkness, enough to remind herself she was free.

Carefully, as if testing the strength of her own limbs, Finn took a step back from the dresser.

She was still trembling. But she was standing.

That had to count for something.

The knock came again—firmer this time. She'd just realized it wasn't the first one.

"Finn?"

Eli's voice, edged with concern.

She blinked, the shadows of memory receding just enough for her to remember where she was. The scent of dust and flowers. The home that wasn't hers but had offered her something close. The press of her own arms wrapped tight around her.

She sucked in a breath, tried to steady the uneven rise and fall of her chest.

"Yeah..." Her voice was barely more than a whisper. "Come in."

The door creaked open, and Eli stepped inside.

And in an instant, Finn knew—he saw her.

Saw all of it.

The tear tracks carving pale rivers down her cheeks. The way her skin, already fair, had drained to something near translucent. The deep hollows beneath her eyes, darker now, sharp with exhaustion and ghosts she couldn't shake.

Eli didn't speak right away. Didn't ask.

He just... looked at her.

And she hated it.

Hated the way his eyes traced the remnants of something she didn't know how to hide. Hated that he had caught her like this—stripped bare by a past that still had its grip on her.

Her fingers dug into her arms, nails pressing hard against the fabric of her sleeves.

She needed to say something. Needed to shake off his gaze, the quiet kindness in it.

But she couldn't.

Because the way he was looking at her wasn't pity, or discomfort.

It was careful and genuine.

Eli stood in the doorway, damp ringlets of hair falling against his forehead, the shoulders of his black t-shirt darkened with moisture. She hadn't even heard the shower run.

His eyes took her in—her tear-streaked face, the rigid way she held herself.

And then stepped forward.

Warm hands found her shoulders, impossibly gentle. His grip wasn't forceful, wasn't demanding—just there, steady against the tremor in her limbs. His thumbs brushed over the fabric of her sleeves, grounding her in a way she hadn't realized she needed.

His gaze searched hers patiently, looking for answers she didn't know how to give.

"What's wrong?" His voice was soft. "What happened?"

Finn blinked at him, vision still blurred with tears she hadn't realized were still falling.

A wobbling hiccup slipped from her throat.

She sucked in a breath, tried to find her footing, tried to gather the frayed edges of herself back together. But when she finally spoke, her voice wavered, fragile and thin.

"I just realized I don't have a change of underwear."

Eli stilled.

He simply blinked at her, as if trying to piece together a puzzle that didn't quite fit.

A pause stretched between them—long enough that her own words settled, ridiculous in the wake of whatever storm had just overtaken her.

Then Eli exhaled, his brows drawing together, mouth tugging downward in confusion.

"Okay..." he said, carefully. "I'll take you to get some after we're done at the shop. Is that okay?"

Finn's head bobbed as she nodded, her voice slipping out more child-like than she meant for it to. "Yes... please."

Eli gave her shoulders the smallest, reassuring squeeze before nudging her gently toward the bed.

She let him.

Because at that moment, it felt easier to let Eli keep her steady than to try and do it herself.

Eli lifted a finger—a silent gesture—before turning and slipping from the room with swift steps.

Finn sat motionless, staring at the empty doorway, her breath still uneven, listening as his footsteps faded across the hall.

Barely a minute passed before he returned.

He carried a small bundle in his arms. Without a word, he set it beside her.

Seven neatly folded pairs of socks. A pair of pristine white boxer briefs. And a towel—plush and thick.

Eli stooped down so their eyes were level, his presence unshakable.

"I left more than enough hot water for you," he murmured.

"If you need anything—anything—just call for me."

A promise.

Finn swallowed hard, nodding numbly. Her fingers brushed over the towel, over its impossible softness, as if testing the reality of it.

Then he stepped back, granting her space.

Slowly, she rose to her feet, her limbs lighter but no less fragile, as though she were balancing on something just shy of solid ground.

She slipped out of the room and into the bathroom next door. Steam still hung in the air, hovering along the edges of the mirror, clinging to the porcelain tub.

Her movements were slow as she undressed and her pulse still unsteady as she stepped inside the scalding stream of water. It stung where it hit her skin, biting and soothing all at once.

Eli remained where he was, standing in the space she had just left. He didn't move, didn't exhale, not until he heard the latching of the bathroom door shutting behind her.

Only then did he let out a breath.

And Finn—standing beneath the rushing heat, beneath something she hadn't dared let herself feel before—finally let herself believe, if only for a moment, that maybe, just maybe...

She didn't have to run anymore.

The warmth of the shower still clung to Finn's skin as she stepped into her room, steam trailing behind her like a last fleeting breath.

Across the hall, Eli's door stood ajar. Not wide enough to be an invitation, but not fully closed either. An offering. A silent "I'm here".

She didn't acknowledge him. But she felt it—his presence and awareness, the sureness of someone who was watching over her without asking for anything in return.

Instead, she moved to the bed, where the leather jacket lay draped over the edge, waiting.

She hesitated only a moment before reaching for it, fingers clutching the material. Then she grabbed the small canvas purse she'd abandoned earlier, the strap twisted, forgotten in a heap on the floor.

Sitting down, she slid a hand inside, fingertips brushing over the scattered remnants of her life. A compact powder foundation. She clicked it open, tilting the mirror toward her face.

Steam had left her skin flushed, the heat painting her cheeks with the kind of color she had long since learned to erase.

Too alive. Too exposed.

She ran the applicator over her skin, dulling the warmth, evening her tone until she looked more like herself. Or at least, the version of herself she was used to seeing.

A quick swipe of mascara, darkening her lashes, pulling familiarity back into her reflection.

Then her fingers slipped into the deep jacket pocket. Searching.

There it was.

The crescent moon pendant.

She pulled it out, turning it over in her palm, running a tender fingertip along its surface. The metal was smooth, worn down by time or touch.

By him.

The unknowable significance of it pressing into her like a poised wail.

A tether to something unfinished.

A question waiting to be answered.

She slipped her fingers beneath the rusted silver chain, carefully seperating it from the pendant. The brittle metal links crumbled under her touch, aged beyond repair. The broken clasp dangled, useless, before she turned to the small dresser beside the bed.

She halted.

Should it be thrown away? It didn't have any purpose now, right?

But still, she didn't. Instead, she tucked it into the top drawer, shutting it gently. As if discarding it entirely would be too final.

Reaching back into her purse, she pulled out a black leather choker. A small, broken heart pendant dangled from it, a relic from another time. Another version of herself.

She unclasped it, letting the heart slip from her fingers into the depths of her bag. Forgotten.

The crescent moon belonged there now.

Sliding it onto the choker, she fastened it securely around her neck.

The moment the metal touched her skin—

A soft clearing of a throat came from just outside her door.

"You ready to go?"

Eli's voice was calm and even. No knock or intrusion. Just waiting for her.

Finn cast one last look at her reflection. She traced her fingers over the pendant.

Then, without a word, she rose and opened the door.

The drive through town had been quiet, but as Eli pulled up in front of the shop, Finn's gaze snagged on the sign above the door.

The Lost Boys Tattoo Shop.

The lettering was bold and beautiful—standing out like a fresh scar against the weathered bones of the town. Unlike the sagging storefronts and sun-bleached awnings surrounding it, the shop looked cared for. Maintained. As if someone had refused to let it wither.

Finn tilted her head, studying it. "Your dad runs the shop?"

Eli smirked as he cut the engine. "You sound surprised."

She shrugged, still taking in the sign, its edges catching in the afternoon light. "I guess I just didn't think about what you guys did."

Eli stretched, his fingers resting against the cracked steering wheel before he finally moved to step out. "Well, he'd usually already be inside, but knowing my dad, he's still over at Danny's, talking his ear off."

Finn raised a questioning brow as she followed him onto the sidewalk.

Eli shot her a knowing grin as he fished a set of keys from his pocket. "You'd think they were old sewing club ladies with the way they go on."

As the door swung inward, a tiny set of bells jingled, the chime lingering in the air longer than it should have.

Like the shop was waking up.

Like it had been waiting for them.

As Eli stepped inside, flipping on the lights, the shop blinked to life in a hum of fluorescence, casting soft hues over wooden floors and walls that seemed to breathe with a life and history all its own...

She took it in, absorbing the details like ink sinking into skin.

The waiting area was small, intimate in a way that felt intentional. Four wooden chairs, each uniquely hand-carved, sat neatly arranged, their cushions indented from years of patrons coming and going. The carvings weren't as elaborate as the ones back at Eli's house, but they carried the same craftsmanship, the same patient touch of hands that had shaped them with care.

Between the chairs, a sturdy wooden table bore a scattering of tattoo magazines—edges curled, pages softened with time and use. Finn recognized some of the covers, old editions she had flipped through at the grocery store back home, never daring to purchase one.

Against the far wall, a massive grandfather clock loomed, its presence somehow both stately and unnerving. It looked like it belonged in some gothic manor rather than a backwoods tattoo shop, its face a filigree of gold and deep-set numerals. The hands ticked forward with a measured beat, the sound filling the space like a heartbeat, metronomic and unrelenting.

Directly across from the waiting area, a pass-through framed a simple desk, its surface aged but tidy. A blocky desktop computer dominated the space, its monitor tilted a bit askew. A landline phone rested beside a thick, leather-bound appointment book, its pages dog-eared and filled with scrawled names and dates, some scratched out, others squeezed tightly into the margins as if time itself had to be forced into place.

Eli moved through a swinging door beside the pass-through window, disappearing into the heart of the shop.

Finn stalled for only a moment longer before following, drawn deeper into a space that already felt like it knew her better than she knew herself.

Two workstations spread out before her, each marked by the imprint of the artist who used it.

One side of the room was grungy, alive with organized chaos. The walls were a collage of old rock band posters, framed records with cracked glass, and striking paintings of the woods—each a different season caught in stunning detail. Autumn leaves burned in hues of gold and rust, winter scenes dripped in stark whites and icy blues, and deep midnight forests pulsed with an eerie, dreamlike glow. The brushstrokes highlighting every gnarled, twisting tree.

The opposite side was its contrast—structured and industrial. Dark-stained wooden panels lined the wall, each carved with an artist's precision. Interwoven among them were tattoo flash designs and airbrushed artwork depicting old gears and mechanical parts, tangled together like a machine with no clear beginning or end.

She took one look at the space and knew—without a doubt—which side belonged to whom.

Crossing her arms, she turned to Eli with a raised brow. "So when you and your dad said 'the shop,' you meant a tattoo shop."

He let out a sharp, amused huff. "Oh. Yeah. Guess I forgot to mention that part before."

Finn shook her head, impressed. "I mean, I guess that sort of makes sense."

Her gaze wandered toward his arm—the inked sleeve stretching from his wrist to his elbow. Without thinking, she reached out, the tip of her finger breezing over the design.

The tattoo was a contradiction—dark and chaotic, yet intricate and strangely elegant. The longer she looked, the more layers revealed themselves. Shadows spiraling. Shapes shifting in and out of each other, never quite settling. It felt almost like a dream unraveling, surreal and just shy of ominous.

Eli went unnaturally still beneath her touch.

Finn caught the shift and remembered herself, quickly pulling back. She tugged at the collar of the leather jacket draped over her shoulders, for something idle to do with her hands.

"I guess the motorcycle sort of threw me off," she murmured, "I was picturing, like... a chop shop."

His lips twitched, the tension melting just enough to let a grin creep in. "Well," he drawled, "we do a fair amount of fixing things. Just not the kind you're thinking of."

Finn huffed softly, but didn't argue.

She had a feeling this place was full of things she hadn't expected.

And Eli, more than anything, was one of them.

She took a step back, suddenly aware of how close she and Eli had been standing. A thin breath slipped past her lips as she turned, retreating toward the front desk. She sank into the office chair behind it, the old thing creaking grumpily beneath her. Its metal base wobbled, but didn't give—one of those relics that felt like it should've collapsed years ago, yet somehow still held firm.

She barely had time to settle before the distinct scrape of a key turning in the back door echoed through the shop.

Frank stepped through, balancing a tray of coffees in one hand and a box of pastries in the other. He barely spared Eli a glance before setting everything down on the desk—right next to Finn.

"You already found your workstation, huh?" His voice carried that same dry amusement, the kind that made it hard to tell if he was joking or not.

Finn blinked, caught off guard.

He reached for his coffee but hesitated, his brows furrowing as his gaze slid to her, then to Eli, then back again.

"Wait..." His voice shifted, curiosity laced with something sharper. "How old are you?"

The question hit like a gust of cold air.

She stiffened, lips parting, but no words came out.

Frank just watched her, expression firm but not unkind—just calculating, like he was fitting together the pieces of a puzzle he hadn't realized was missing one.

Eli, on the other hand, had suddenly become very invested in opening the box of pastries.

When she finally spoke, her voice was steady, but there was an edge to it—something fragile. "I turn eighteen next week."

A hush filled the space, deep and unwavering.

Then Frank exhaled through his nose, shaking his head like he should've known all along.

"Well," he said, voice slipping into something lighter, as if the moment had never carried much importance at all. He reached for a napkin, tearing it in half before grabbing a pastry. "That's easy enough. We'll just pay you under the table and keep you off the payroll 'til then."

Then, with a wink—the kind Finn had seen Eli throw around more than once—he popped a bite of pastry into his mouth.

Beside her, Eli, mid-bite of a croissant, let out a muffled snort of laughter.

The tension that had coiled tight in Finn's chest began to un-spool. It had been a joke—mostly. But the ease with which Frank said it, like the decision had been made the second she answered, settled the gnawing inside her.

Like she belonged here.

Like they'd already decided she did.

She reached for one of the coffees, wrapping her hands around the cup's warmth, drawing peace from it.

Frank took a seat in one of the rolling tattoo chairs, sipping his own coffee with a thoughtful hum. "You ever worked a front desk before?"

Finn shook her head.

"Well," he shrugged, unbothered. "Lucky for you, I'm a real easy boss."

Eli scoffed around another bite. "You're easy. I'm a nightmare."

Frank didn't even look up. "That's why she's not working for you."

Finn bit back a smile, her fingers tightening around the cup as she lifted it to her lips.

The shop felt comfortable.

It shouldn't have—not yet, anyway.

But somehow, it already did.

Finn leaned against the brick wall behind the shop, its rough surface pressed into her back. The alley was still—just the occasional rustle of wind and the distant purr of a vehicle somewhere down the street.

She pulled a cigarette from her pack, rolling it idly between her fingers before sparking her lighter. The flame wavered in the late afternoon air before catching, the tip of the cigarette flaring as she inhaled. The first drag hit her lungs with a familiar burn, centering her.

It had been a whirlwind of a day.

Not busy, exactly. Just constant.

Only two clients had come through, but even in the slow stretches, there was always something to do or learn.

Frank made it easy. He never barked orders, never made her feel like some kid fumbling her way through a job she wasn't cut out for. Instead, he turned every task into a learning moment, something she could carry forward.

He showed her how to sanitize the workstations properly, where the ink bottles were kept, and how to restock the disposable needles from the supply drawers. Everything explained in an even, methodical way—like second nature to him, like he'd done it countless times before and would never grow tired of passing it down.

And Eli—Eli had his own way of teaching.

While Frank had been hunched over a large piece for a buff, bald guy named Brett, Eli had pulled her aside at the desk. His voice was low, conspiratorial, as he tapped a finger against the appointment book.

"Alright, rule number one—if a guy named Randy calls, schedule him, but only when my dad's available. Otherwise, I'll mysteriously be sick that day."

Finn smirked. "Bad client?"

He sighed, a long-suffering sound, rubbing his arm absently. "He just tells the same five stories every time, and they're all about fishing. I hear enough about fishing at home."

She was about to tease him, but before she could, Brett pulled her into the conversation with Frank—folding her into the melody of the shop like she had been there for years.

Brett didn't seem like a particularly sharp man, but he had a presence that made up for it. He was the kind of guy who could light up a room without even trying, all booming laughter and exaggerated hand gestures, his enthusiasm infectious. He told wild, meandering stories while Frank worked, cracking jokes that made Finn roll her eyes but giggle all the same.

And now—

Now, she was here.

She exhaled slowly, watching a ribbon of smoke curl into the dusky evening air.

Behind her—the low buzz of a tattoo gun, the occasional murmur of voices filtering through the crack under the back door.

She had needed a second to breathe.

At some point, while Frank had been finishing up Brett's dragon tattoo, she had caught Eli's attention, pulling her cigarette pack from her purse and tilting in the direction of the back door—a silent question.

He had met her gaze, and with an understanding smile, gave a single nod.

Now, standing alone in the alley, she finally had a moment to process.

This place—this shop and these people—felt different.

She should have been overwhelmed, thrown into a world she didn't know, a job she hadn't expected. But somehow, she wasn't.

It had been... easy.

That thought settled warm and unfamiliar, just as the hairs on the back of her neck rose.

Her breath hitched mid-inhale, fingers tensing around the cigarette.

The air had shifted.

It was subtle, the kind of change that couldn't be seen—only felt. A pressure, like the charged air before a lightning strike, sending a ripple down her back.

Finn stilled, turning her head just enough to glance toward the shadowed end of the alleyway.

It looked empty.

But something about it was off.

Her pulse drummed a little louder in her ears. A slow, deliberate exhale left her nose as she forced herself to steady.

For a brief second, she considered crushing out the cigarette and heading inside.

But she didn't.

Instead, she lingered.

Just long enough to see if anything lingered back.

Chapter Five

 sensation slithered up the back of Finn's neck, an invisible touch that lifted the fine hairs along her skin. A ghost of pressure. A presence without substance.

She took another drag, menthol smoke sitting sharp and cool on her tongue, willing it to steady her.

She waited.

Inside the shop, the world carried on, punctuated only by the muffled cadence of distant conversations.

Everything in there was normal.

But out here—

Something was watching her.

Finn knew that feeling too well.

Then—

A shadow shifted.

Finn's pulse hastened as a man emerged from the darkness, moving with uneven steps.

At first, he barely seemed human. His shoulders hunched forward, his head dipped low, long matted hair spilling over his face in greasy clumps. His clothes were a patchwork of salvaged fabric, stitched together in places like they had been collected rather than chosen.

But his boots—scuffed hiking boots—still had life in them. Used, but sturdy.

He stopped a few yards away, peering into the dumpster behind the neighboring building.

Finn watched him in silence.

Closer now, she could see the way his hair clung to itself, tangled and unkempt. The way his movements were short and lurching. He rummaged through the trash with the kind of patience that only came with routine.

Then, without a sound, he moved again.

Finn tensed as he shuffled past her.

He didn't stop at the shop's dumpster. Didn't acknowledge her either.

But as he passed—

She caught it.

A fluid shifting. A sliver of movement beneath the wild tangle of hair.

An eye.

Just a glimpse—there and gone. But it was enough.

He saw her.

Not the way strangers saw each other on the street.

No, it was deeper than that.

It was the kind of gaze that latched on, that pressed against her skin like a brand.

And then—

Her vision adjusted.

Her breath turned to ice in her throat.

The shadows in the alley—what she had dismissed as a trick of dim light—weren't shadows at all. A mass of darkness hovered just behind the man's shoulders, shifting at the edges, barely distinguishable from the early evening itself. At first, it undulated—like smoke trapped inside a jar, restless and shapeless.

Then, it solidified.

And it took the shape of a man. Tall and looming.

Suspended just above the ground.

The man shuffled past, seemingly oblivious to the shadow moving with him.

For a split second, she almost—almost—felt relief.

Then—

The shadow turned its head.

Its body remained still, motionless as death, but its head snapped toward her in a movement too sharp, too sudden.

It had no mouth. No nose. No skin.

Only eyes.

They burned through the darkness—glowing and shifting like a lantern's flame caught in the wind.

A sudden, bone-deep cold slammed into her, sinking through her skin like talons, wrapping around her lungs.

Her knees gave way, and everything blurred.

A hand on her shoulder. Warm. Solid.

A voice—far away.

"Finn."

The warmth pressed firmer, pulling her back. A gentle shake.

"Hey. Finn."

Her eyes fluttered open. The alley was now empty again. The man, and the shadow, gone.

Only the distant sounds of the town remained, with the glimmer of a streetlamp casting pale light against the pavement.

Eli was crouched in front of her, his hands still on her shoulders. His brows were furrowed, concern creasing his face as he studied her.

Finn blinked. Her lips parted, but no words came.

He scanned her expression before his gaze shifted downward.

Reaching out and plucking her cigarette from the pavement, still half-lit and smouldering.

As if she had only been out for a minute.

A muscle in his jaw twitched. He flicked the cigarette away before offering his hand.

"Come on," he said, voice steady. "Let's get you inside."

Finn followed Eli back into the shop, forcing her shoulders to stay loose, her movements even.

Like Eli hadn't found her in a strange state—again.

Like he didn't have some uncanny instinct for when she was unraveling.

She kept pace behind him, but the moment they were fully inside, she veered hard to the right.

The small industrial-looking restroom sat near the back, its metal door open just an inch. She slipped inside, shutting it behind her with a resonant *thunk*.

She turned on the faucet. Cool water rushed over her hands. Scrubbing at her fingers, washing away the scent of cigarettes, and the feeling of something colder that had no business clinging to her skin.

She braced her palms against the sink, head bowing forward, watching as droplets slipped off her fingertips.

"Just breathe."

She lifted her head.

Her reflection stared back.

Pupils too wide, swallowed the green, and eyes ringed in shadows smudged like bruises. Her face was the same—but wrong. Not in a way anyone else would notice, but in the way it felt.

Like she wasn't entirely here.

Like some part of her was still out there, in that alley.

She adjusted her expression.

Relaxed her jaw, softened her gaze, and unfurrowed her brow.

She took a breath. Then another.

Normal.

She looked normal.

Or at least—as normal as she was going to get.

With one last steadying inhale, Finn grabbed a rough brown paper towel, dried her hands, and stepped back into the shop.

The bells over the front door jingled, their chime crisp and bright as Brett waved over his shoulder.

"See ya later, Finn!"

Finn forced a smile, lifting a hand in a small wave. "See ya, Brett."

The door swung shut behind him, cutting off the last echoes of his voice.

She felt Eli's gaze before she could even turn.

So she didn't.

Instead, she focused on Frank.

If he noticed the shift in her, he didn't show it.

"Alright," Frank said, pulling her into motion, stepping toward one of the stations. "Let's work on breaking everything down properly."

Finn latched onto the moment like a lifeline.

She nodded, locking onto Frank's movements, his steady voice guiding her through the steps—how to dispose, sanitize, and reset. What got tossed, what needed to be wiped down, and what got put back exactly where it belonged.

She paid attention, taking in every detail.

Letting the clean, logical process fill the space in her mind that threatened to turn back toward the alley.

Eli was still watching.

She could feel it—the pull of his attention, even as he wiped down his own station with slow, methodical sweeps.

But Finn just kept working.

Like nothing had happened, and everything was fine.

Finn wiped down the counter one final time. The sound of routine settling over the shop like a closing note in a song.

Frank exhaled a satisfied sigh as he stretched, rolling his shoulders before reaching for a couple of tied-up trash bags.

"Alright, kid," he said, turning toward Finn. "Before we head out, mind running these out back to the dumpster?"

The air seemed to shift—tighten.

For a second, she didn't move or even breathe.

The alley surfaced behind her eyes. That impossible darkness. The sense of something watching. The burn of those lantern-flame eyes.

Some of the color drained from her face.

But before she could react, Eli's voice cut through the moment.

"I got it, Pops."

Casual. But Finn caught the edge beneath it—no hesitation, no room for argument. Just a seamless intervention.

He grabbed the trash bags without waiting for a response, brushing past them toward the back door.

Frank didn't question it, but he watched. The way Eli had stepped in so fast and the way Finn's shoulders had gone taut. The way she was still gripping the rag in her hand like it might keep her tethered to the moment.

"Alright then," Frank said, his tone easy. "Come on."

He walked to the front door and stepped outside.

Finn followed, exhaling softly as the night wrapped around her, cool and soothing, a stark contrast to the warmth of the shop.

They stood there in silence, the town settling into the hush of evening.

Frank crossed his arms, staring absently through the shop window as Eli moved through the dim interior, shutting off lights one by one.

A moment passed. Then another.

And then—without looking at her—Frank spoke.

"You did good today," he said. "Real good."

Finn blinked.

Something in her chest shifted, caught off guard by the certainty in his voice.

"I mean it." His eyes stayed on the shop, his expression even. "You picked things up fast. You were focused. You impressed me today." A small nod. "And I don't say that lightly."

Finn swallowed around the unexpected lump in her throat.

She hadn't realized how badly she needed to hear that.

She tugged at the leather sleeves still draped over her shoulders, shifting her weight awkwardly.

"Thanks."

Frank hummed in response, the low sound punctuating the moment.

They stood side by side on the sidewalk, their reflections darkened by the shop window—two figures suspended in the dim glow of the streetlamp, the world around them hushed and waiting.

Then—his voice, lower now.

"There's something more going on with you."

Finn's breath snagged in her throat.

Frank didn't turn his head or try to meet her eyes. Just kept his gaze on the window, as if he could see the truth there without looking at her directly.

"I won't try to drag it out of you," he said simply. "Not my style."

Finn stayed perfectly still.

He was giving her an out. A way to slip past this moment, to pretend it hadn't happened. But he was also giving her something else—an opening. A door left cracked, should she ever decide to step through it.

"If you ever need to talk..." He tilted his head, his reflection shifting with the movement. "I'm here."

A bridge, if she chose to cross it.

Before she could decide what to do with the moment, the front door swung open, the chime of the bells breaking the stillness.

Eli stepped out, locking the door behind him.

Frank clapped him on the shoulder as he stepped past toward his truck. "Alright, let's go."

"Actually, I need to take Finn over to The Hollow Stitch first."

Finn frowned inquisitively, shifting her weight. "The what?"

He didn't answer. Instead, he turned toward Frank. "There's a couple things Mom didn't have in her stuff that Finn needs."

Heat crept up Finn's neck. She averted her gaze, suddenly wishing she could disappear into the pavement.

Frank just nodded, unfazed. "Alright, no problem." He pulled open the door of his old pickup, tossing his keys in his palm before climbing in. "I'll meet you two back at home."

Eli turned to her, hands stuffed into his jacket pockets. "The Hollow Stitch isn't far. Thought we could walk."

Finn's brows lifted slightly. "Walk?"

He shrugged. "Yeah. A little walk in the fresh air. It sounds nice."

A huff of amusement left her. A smirk ghosted the corner of her lips. "Alright, fine."

They started walking, their footsteps soft against the pavement.

The town felt different—quieter, heavier. The warm glow of the streetlights stretched long, moths dancing frantically against the bulbs.

Eli moved at an easy pace, his hands still tucked in his pockets, his gaze meandering toward her. "So, what'd you think?"

Finn glanced at him. "About?"

He gestured vaguely behind them. "The shop. Your first day. Working with me and the old man."

She didn't have to think about it.

"I had a really good time."

Eli's grin was slow, lazy. "Yeah?"

She nodded, "Yeah. It was... fun. More fun than I thought working would be."

The words slipped out before she could stop them, drifting into the cool evening air like a leaf caught in the wind—fleeting and unguarded.

Eli turned his head, his brows lifting just enough to signal curiosity but not enough to pry. "You've never had a job before?"

She considered lying, offering up something easy and forgettable. But her hesitation, however brief, had already given her away.

"I wasn't... allowed to."

The admission sat between them, dissolving into the darkening evening like mist. The second it left her lips, she wished she could take it back and fold it into herself, before he had a chance to pick it apart. But there was no taking it back. It was out there, raw and unprotected.

She waited, bracing for the inevitable shift—for pity. Or the carefully measured words that often followed moments like these. But Eli just kept walking, his expression unchanged, his pace steady, as if she hadn't said anything at all.

No murmured apologies. No questions that would force her to reach into places she wasn't ready to go.

And somehow, that was almost worse.

She forced herself to keep moving, restless with the effort of holding herself together. He knew there was significance behind what she had said. And still, he let it be.

The tension that had knotted in her stomach loosened as they reached The Hollow Stitch.

Tucked between two aging brick buildings, the boutique exuded a kind of charm. Its dark wooden sign swaying gently from an iron bracket, gold lettering catching the glow of the nearest streetlight. The street around them had softened in the hush of nightfall. The air carried the faint scent of moisture, like an impending rain. A bell rang out softly as a customer slipped out, the sound like wind stirring chimes on an old front porch.

Through the glass, the display was warm and inviting—earth-toned sweaters draped over mannequins, their fabrics lush-looking, like they begged to be lived in. Shelves were neatly stacked with folded denim, a small rack of scarves in muted autumn hues swaying near the door, the golden glow of the interior spilling onto the sidewalk like a sliver of warmth against the cool dusk.

Eli reached for the handle, pulled it open, and stepped aside just enough to let her pass. "After you."

She obliged, and the warmth wrapped around her instantly—not just the heat, but the feeling of it, the sense of familiarity woven into the air itself. The scent of soft cotton, aged wood, and something faintly floral, like lavender tucked into linen drawers, settled over her, soothing in a way she hadn't anticipated.

For now, she let it calm the restless, untethered part of her.

And for the moment, she let everything else fade into the background.

Chapter Six

entle music hummed through the space—something indie, and calming, the kind of melody that wrapped itself around the space like a slow-sung lullaby.

Finn inhaled deeply, letting the warmth of it settle over her.

She wasn't used to places like this.

The boutique was small but curated. The way the clothing racks were arranged, fabrics draped in a way that made everything feel luxurious—untouchable, but begging to be touched. The wooden floors creaked beneath her boots as she stepped forward, the sound a reminder of her presence in a space that didn't quite feel like she belonged.

Her fingers trailed over a knit sweater, the material plush beneath her touch, the kind of softness that made her think of warmth and comfort—a life where things like this were easy. For a moment, she let herself imagine what it might be like to own something like this, something just because it made her feel good.

Then she turned the price tag over.

$58.

A familiar tightness swelled in her chest. She skimmed past it, reaching for something else.

$72.

Her fingers barely grazed the edge of the hanger before she let go, retreating as if the fabric itself had burned her.

She should have known.

Her eyes wandered toward a rack of plain T-shirts—something simple, something small.

$32.

Her stomach tensed.

She rubbed the sleeve of her jacket between her fingers—not to ground herself, not for comfort, but because it was something to hold on to. The leather was stiff, unfamiliar, making her feel like an imposter in her own skin. She hadn't broken it in yet, hadn't worn it long enough to forget it was never really hers to begin with.

She should just tell Eli she'd make do.

Before she could convince herself to step back, to walk out before the boulder on her chest grew too heavy, his voice came from behind her.

"The shop closes in thirty."

Finn turned at the sound of Eli's voice, her brows drawing together at the unfamiliar edge in his tone.

Uncomfortable.

Eli wasn't the kind of person who got uneasy, at least not in any way she had seen. But now, his hands were shoved deep into his pockets, his shoulders a little too tense, and his gaze fixed on nothing in particular. He looked almost... bashful.

She wasn't sure what to make of it.

"Oh," she murmured, not quite sure what else to say. Then, realizing she had just been standing there, she added quickly, "Sorry."

She turned before she could overthink it, making her way toward the far wall, where an entire display of women's undergarments was arranged in neat, folded sections.

As she moved, she stole a glance back at Eli.

He was still standing where she'd left him, staring at a rack of scarves with a level of interest that was entirely too intense to be real.

Finn couldn't help but appreciate that, for this part, he gave her space. She turned back to the display.

It bothered her that she hadn't even thought about such a basic need.

Frank had kept his late wife's things but there were obvious gaps, items that weren't there for her to borrow.

And now, standing in front of an entire wall of options, a strange discomfort settled in, creeping beneath her skin.

Everything looked so... delicate.

Soft lace, embroidered details, sheer panels that felt entirely too revealing. Even the simple silk sets looked elegant, but in a way that felt too intentional, too sensual—like wearing them would be some kind of unspoken admission.

These were the kind of things her stepfather thought she wanted to wear.

The thought struck like a slap, sharp and sudden, knocking the breath from her chest.

"Harlot."

The word slithered into her mind, dripping with the same sickening sneer of judgment he had always used against her—for existing, for breathing, for daring to be.

Her fingers dug into the hem of her jacket sleeve.

Out.

She forced the thought away, shoving it back into the darkness where it belonged.

Out.

She didn't have to live under that voice anymore.

OUT.

She quickly gathered a few pairs of the least lacy, least frilly, options she could find. Soft cotton. Simple cuts. Nothing sheer, or delicate, nothing that would make her feel like she was wearing someone else's skin.

She didn't check the prices. Didn't stop to second-guess. She just needed to be done.

Turning, she held the fabric a little too tightly in her hands and made her way toward the checkout.

Eli was still planted exactly where she'd left him, his entire focus locked onto that rack of scarves, his expression one of deep, unwavering concentration, as if deciphering their patterns was a matter of life or death.

Something close to a smile tugged at her lips.

She reached the counter and placed the items down with more care than necessary, handling them as though they might break apart in her hands.

There was no one there. The register sat untouched, the space behind it empty. The store, once so warm and welcoming, now felt eerily still, the soft music in the background suddenly more noticeable.

She glanced around, fingers brushing the edge of the counter. Waiting and listening. But no one appeared.

She wasn't the type to demand attention, to call for help when it wasn't freely given. Most of her life had been spent that way—in the background, unnoticed, blending into spaces rather than claiming them.

But the shop would be closing soon, and Eli had already been scrutinizing the scarves for long enough.

Her gaze landed on a small, golden bell perched near the register.

For a second, she stalled, her fingers hovering just above it, like pressing it might break the stillness in a way she wasn't ready for.

Then, with a breath, she gave it a gentle ring.

The chime barely had time to settle before a voice called from the back.

"Coming!"

A moment later, a young woman slipped through the beaded curtain from the back, smiling warmly, as if she had been expecting them all along.

Finn took her in quickly.

She looked to be around the same age, but taller by at least three or four inches, with a curvy, feminine build that filled out her fitted top in a way that made her seem effortlessly confident—at ease in her own skin.

Her short hair was styled in a tousled pixie cut, the same warm brown as her doe-like eyes. Bold eyeliner wings swept up at the outer corners, sharp, accentuating her round features in a way that made the contrast work. There was something cool about her, like she knew exactly who she was and never had to second-guess it.

"Hey there! Sorry about that—I didn't realize there was anyone up here."

Her voice was bright as she slipped behind the counter. She picked up the panties and scanned them swiftly, her hands moving in quick, fluid motions.

"Alrighty," she chirped. "Your total comes to $56.78. Cash or card?"

Finn's stomach went tight.

Fifty-six dollars.

Her grip on her purse strap stiffened, the rough canvas pressing into her palm.

She should have checked. Should have looked at the price tags, or picked less.

But she needed them.

And she couldn't exactly ask to put them back now.

Forcibly she made her voice steady. "Um... cash."

She unzipped her purse, reaching inside. She had enough—just over, actually—but her hands wouldn't cooperate. The bills were right where she had tucked them, but her fingers felt slow and uncoordinated, like they didn't belong to her.

The cashier, at least, didn't seem to notice.

She tapped idly at the register, waiting, patient, as if she had all the time in the world.

And then—

"Hey, Finn!"

She flinched, her fingers fumbling in her purse as Eli appeared at her side, all casual ease, like he hadn't just startled the hell out of her.

She looked up, mid-search, as he grinned down at her.

"I almost forgot to give you this."

He held out a folded hundred-dollar bill, pinched between his fingers like it was nothing. Like it wasn't the exact solution to her problem at this moment.

"Pops said to give you this for today."

The words fell slowly, like she had to absorb them piece by piece.

Eli stood there, arm extended and waiting.

Finn, meanwhile, felt like she was moving in slow motion, her fingers still buried in the tangled mess of her purse, her pulse unsteady from trying to scrape together the total.

Her hands were still shaking.

Once her mind caught up, and her hands remembered how to work, she took the money quickly, not wanting the moment to stretch any longer than necessary. "Thanks," she murmured, slipping the hundred into her purse, blending it with the rest of her crumpled bills.

She didn't want to look like she had nothing before Eli handed it to her, and she didn't need it for this—she'd rather save it. Groceries. A buffer. Something that was hers.

To make it seem natural, she pulled out a few smaller bills, holding them toward the cashier.

But the girl wasn't looking at her anymore.

Her wide, doe eyes had gone even rounder with recognition, caught somewhere between disbelief and excitement.

But she wasn't looking at Finn anymore.

She was looking at Eli.

"Oh my God," she breathed, almost laughing. "Eli?"

Eli, to his credit, didn't seem remotely fazed by the reaction. He just gave her an easy smile, hands still stuffed back into his pockets like this happened all the time.

"Hey, Sarah."

Finn's gaze flashed toward Eli.

So, they knew each other. But then again, of course they would, in a town this small.

Sarah's expression brightened even more, the kind of excitement that felt reserved for rare sightings—not just a friendly reunion, but something closer to recognizing a celebrity.

"Wow, I haven't seen you around in forever! Where the hell have you been?"

Eli gave a shrug. "Out of town. I did a guest spot at a shop a few states over."

Sarah's brows shot up. "That's huge!"

"Yeah, I've been doing a lot more traveling lately. Which is why me and my dad hired my friend Finn here to help manage things at The Lost Boys."

His friend.

Not untrue, she supposed, but the way he said it felt pointed. Like something he wanted to be clear.

Sarah looked at Finn, her smile tightening, a subtle shift—so small, it might have gone unnoticed.

But Finn caught it.

Something behind her eyes, brief and fleeting, gone in a blink before it could fully settle.

And then she recognized it.

Jealousy.

It wasn't blatant. Just a quick, instinctive glimmer before Sarah smoothed it over with a neutral expression.

It was only then that she seemed to remember Finn was still standing there, hand outstretched, and money waiting.

"Right," she muttered, grabbing the cash and turning toward the register.

Finn adjusted the bag in her grip as they turned to leave, fingers tightening around the crinkling plastic. The receipt was tucked neatly inside, the transaction complete.

As she turned to follow Eli back out, he spoke over his shoulder.

"See you around."

Sarah's face lit up instantly, that same starry-eyed glow returning in full force, as if Eli's presence alone had a gravity that pulled her back in.

"Bye, Eli," she breathed airily, like she had to remind herself to actually speak.

Finn pressed her lips together, saying nothing.

They had taken just a few steps when Sarah's voice rang out again.

"Fran, was it?"

Finn turned back, unhurried and unreadable, recognizing this for exactly what it was.

A test.

Sarah's smile was pleasant but just a little too measured, waiting to see how Finn would react.

She didn't hesitate as she met Sarah's eyes, expression calm, unfazed, and delivered the correction.

"It's Finn."

Sarah's brows lifted, absorbing it with a hollow sort of grace, as if the mistake had been entirely unintentional. "Oh, right. Well—"

She extended her hand.

Finn paused—not long enough to be obvious, but just enough to feel it. She didn't want to touch her.

But refusing would feel too much like conceding.

So, she stepped forward, closing the short distance between them, and reached across the counter, clasping Sarah's hand in her own. Her grip was firm, her skin warmer and her palm broader than Finn's.

It was quick, nothing more than a polite exchange.

But in that brief moment, the light of the candle next to the register caught the crescent moon pendant at Finn's throat, hitting it just right, making it gleam gold for a split second.

And in that instant, Sarah's expression changed.

Her smile faltered—not dramatically, but just enough for Finn to catch the brief glint of recognition in her widening eyes.

A crack in the mask.

The shift lasted no more than a heartbeat before she smoothed it over, slipping back into composure, but there was something missing now. The warmth from before had thinned, her once-bright expression dimming.

"I guess I'll be seeing you around," she said, releasing Finn's hand.

Finn didn't reply. She only took a step back, feeling Eli waiting for her near the door, his presence palpable.

She met Sarah's gaze for just a moment longer, then nodded once and turned, stepping out into the cool night air.

Chapter Seven

The Hollow Stitch faded behind them, its warmth already distant—the door chime a thin echo.

Finn's fingers curled lightly around the plastic shopping bag handle, the crinkling sound barely audible over the fall of their steps. But her thoughts weren't on the bag, or the cold creeping in through her sleeves.

She kept mulling over the way Sarah's expression had shifted—the widening of her eyes, the way she had tried too quickly to smooth it over.

Finally, she broke the silence.

"She didn't like me."

Eli snorted softly. "Nope."

She glanced up, arching a brow. "Not even surprised I clocked that, huh?"

He huffed out something between a chuckle and a sigh, shaking his head. "Not even a little."

His expression shifted—less amused, a little annoyed.

Finn narrowed her eyes. "Alright, what's the deal?"

He stuffed his hands deeper into his jacket pockets. His lips pressed together in a brief, thoughtful line before he finally spoke.

"It's stupid."

Finn shot him a look.

"Oh, now I have to know."

Rolling his shoulders, he sighed like he was reluctantly settling in for a story.

"Back when we were younger, Sarah was getting picked on by some older guys. It was getting kind of bad, so I stepped in."

Finn breathed a quick laugh. "Of course you did."

He shot her a sideways glance. "What's that supposed to mean?"

"Nothing. Just—White Knight complex much?"

Eli laughed under his breath, shaking his head. "Shut up."

But he didn't deny it.

She could picture it so easily. A younger Eli, hot-headed but kind, throwing himself into the middle of someone else's problem just because it was the right thing to do.

He rubbed the back of his neck, the other hand still firmly tucked in his pocket. "Anyway. Ever since then, Sarah has had this... thing for me."

Finn nodded slowly. "And you don't reciprocate."

Eli let out a flat, unamused laugh. "Not even remotely."

"So, you avoid her."

He nodded in agreement. "Whenever possible."

She hummed, turning that over in her mind. It wasn't exactly surprising—the way Sarah had lit up the second she saw him, the way her eyes had flashed to Finn, assessing and measuring.

But something about it still felt... off.

As if reading her thoughts, Eli added, "You wanna know the real awkward part?"

Finn glanced at him. "There's more?"

He rubbed his temple briefly before muttering, "She came into the shop last summer to get a tattoo from me."

Her curiosity sharpened; she gave him a *look*.

"Please tell me she got your name."

Eli groaned. "Worse."

"Worse than your name?!"

He hesitated, exhaling like he was already regretting this conversation. "Okay, not worse than asking me to tattoo my own name on her. But still—really uncomfortable."

Instead of explaining right away, he reached out, his index finger brushing against the pendant at her throat.

Finn stilled.

The touch was brief, but not as brief as it should have been. His fingertip slipped, grazing just below the pendant, skimming the hollow of her throat before he pulled away.

Heat crept up her neck, but Eli didn't seem to notice. He just let out a dry chuckle, shaking his head.

"That," he said, nodding toward the pendant. "Right there. She got a crescent moon, same as yours."

Her brows pulled together. "Why would that be uncomfortable?"

Eli looked like he was still debating whether to elaborate.

"She came in saying she wanted something small and meaningful. I figured, sure—until she told me where she wanted it."

He ran a hand down his face, shaking his head. "Right between her breasts."

Finn let out a loud snort, but he wasn't finished.

"And if that wasn't bad enough, she kept—" he gestured vaguely, "pushing them together, shifting and leaning in every two minutes; I must've told her five times to sit still or I'd lose my lines."

Finn pressed her lips together, trying—and failing—not to smirk.

"That bad, huh?"

Eli shot her a look, unimpressed. "Finn, I was so close to telling her to find another shop."

They arrived at the Bronco, and he exhaled as he reached the driver's side door.

"So, yeah. She definitely didn't like you."

He'd just pulled the truck door open when a sound broke the stillness of the night.

A shuffling noise. Subtle—the uneven movement of someone trying not to be heard.

Both Finn and Eli turned at the same time.

And then—

A figure peered around the side of the building.

Finn's stomach plummeted.

It was the man from the alley.

A small gasp slipped out before she could stop it.

Eli noticed immediately. His head shifted, his focus snapping from the man to her.

"What?" His voice was low, cautious. He angled in front of her without thinking, like instinct told him to close the space between them—hands out of his pockets now, shoulders squared.

Finn didn't answer right away.

Her heart was pounding too fast, her mind racing.

The man wasn't moving toward them or making any obvious threat. He was just... watching. Hunched, like he was still deciding whether he'd been seen.

But Finn had seen him.

And she knew what was following him.

Eli's attention stayed locked on her, his expression tightening. "Finn. What's up?"

Her mouth felt dry, but she forced the words out.

"I saw him earlier, behind the shop."

She didn't elaborate.

But she saw the shift immediately—the way Eli moved even closer to her, his focus sharpening, giving her his full attention. His usual easygoing stance gone, something guarded settling into his posture.

"Did he—" His voice was edged. Now serious and protective. "Did he say or do anything to you?"

No, he hadn't.

Not in the way Eli meant.

But the memory of that thing behind him—the shadow with lantern eyes—sent a cold ripple through her.

"No. But..."

She let the words hang, unfinished.

Eli exhaled before glancing back toward the man. The tension in his shoulders eased slightly, but not completely.

"That's just Josiah." His voice softened a fraction, like that was supposed to explain something.

Finn frowned. "Who?"

Eli nodded toward him. "Josiah. He's kind of a... local."

She kept watching the man, trying to reconcile the name with the figure standing in the dark. Josiah wasn't looking at them anymore. Instead, he had turned his head, as if listening to something only he could hear.

Eli kept talking, his tone even and casual.

"He's... not really homeless, exactly. More like off-grid. He lives out in the woods, mostly off the land. Only comes into town when things get rough for him out there."

Finn's hand reached up unconsciously, fingers wrapping around the pendant at her throat.

Eli's tone remained relaxed, as if this was nothing unusual.

Like he was trying to convince her it wasn't worth worrying about.

"He doesn't talk much. Mostly just scavenges. Goes through trash, looks for stuff he can use. But he's never bothered anyone."

She nodded, more out of habit than certainty, and forced herself to look away. "Yeah. Okay."

Eli studied her for a moment, like he was deciding whether to say more, then exhaled and pulled open her door.

"C'mon." He nodded toward the cab. "Let's go home."

Finn hesitated, stealing one last glance over her shoulder.

Josiah hadn't moved.

But behind him, in the darkness—

Something shifted. The same needle-prick cold gathered at the base of her skull.

A shape, tall and unnatural, just beyond his shoulder. Its edges unstable, shifting in and out of focus, like it wasn't fully there.

Or like it was trying not to be seen.

She tore her gaze away and climbed into the truck.

Eli rolled the Bronco to a stop in the driveway, the engine idling before he cut the ignition. The night was still and cold, the air rushing in as Finn pushed open the door and stepped out.

As they entered the house, warmth met her immediately—drifting in from the living room—a steady, ambient heat that suggested Frank had gotten a fire going.

She hadn't realized how cold she was until now.

The scent of burning wood hung in the air as she followed Eli into the kitchen.

Frank wasn't there.

But two plates sat on the table.

Simple turkey sandwiches, steam still lifting from the toast where the turkey met the bread. No chips or sides—just easy, filling and warm.

Eli huffed a small laugh, stepping past her and pulling out a chair. "The old man's version of a hot meal," he mused, gesturing to the sandwiches.

It wasn't just food.

Frank had made two plates, knowing they'd be home late, and they'd probably be hungry.

Knowing she would be here.

A heaviness pressed against her chest—unexpected and unfamiliar. She let out a slow breath, steadying herself before moving toward the table.

Eli was already digging into his sandwich, leaning back in his chair with a relaxed posture. "You hungry?"

Finn nodded, sliding into the seat across from him and setting her shopping bag on the floor beside her.

The house was quiet, wrapped in the kind of stillness that only late nights could bring. The only sounds were the occasional shift of Eli's chair as he ate and the distant crackle of the fire in the next room.

Finn chewed slowly, her thoughts unwinding, stretching thin beneath the silence.

The day had been a blur. A strange and twisting current she hadn't quite found her footing in.

Her first shift at the shop. Sarah's odd reaction. Josiah. And the thing that hovered over him.

Seeing spirits was nothing new, but this had felt different—wrong in a way she couldn't explain. There had been something deliberate in the way the shadow had moved, the way it had turned toward her.

A shiver prickled at the base of her neck.

Across from her, Eli tore through his sandwich like he hadn't eaten in days, each bite quick and automatic, his focus solely on the food in front of him.

Finn smirked faintly, taking another slow bite, the contrast amusing.

She had just swallowed when the sound of footsteps broke the hush.

She looked up as Frank stepped into the kitchen, an old, dog-eared book tucked beneath one arm. He didn't say anything at first, just moved to the fridge and pulled it open with the ease of routine.

"You two want a pop?" he asked, already reaching inside.

"Hell yeah," Eli answered emphatically.

Finn nodded, grateful for the offer.

He tossed them each a can before cracking his own open, the soft hiss of carbonation breaking the stillness.

She popped the tab on her own soda and took a deep sip, the sharp fizz cutting through the last remnants of unease clinging to her ribs.

Frank glanced toward their empty plates, his mouth twitching. "Figured you'd both be starving."

He gave a small shrug, something almost apologetic in his tone. "Sorry it wasn't much of a meal. Didn't have a chance to go grocery shopping before this one—" he nodded toward Eli "—came back into town."

Eli laughed, taking a long gulp of his drink before setting it down with a soft thunk against the table.

"Yeah, well, let's be honest," he said, leaning back in his chair. "You're not exactly the shopper of the house."

Frank let out a deep, hearty laugh—louder than Finn had heard from him before.

It was a warm and genuine sound.

"That's the damn truth."

Eli shot Finn a look, tilting his head. "We'll go first thing in the morning. That cool with you?"

"Yeah, of course." She smiled, nodding.

Frank sighed, still chuckling under his breath as he shook his head and took another swig of his soda.

"Appreciate it."

He exhaled, stretching, rolling his shoulders like a man who had carried a lifetime of work in his muscles.

"I'm heading to bed," he said, already moving toward the hallway. "You two don't stay up too late."

Eli smirked, glancing at Finn as Frank disappeared down the hall. "Early to bed, early to rise. That's him."

Finn hummed in agreement, taking another sip of her soda.

She was still getting used to this—simple normalcy, the shape of belonging.

In the fireplace, a log shifted and hissed.

For a breath-long moment, the room's warmth thinned—like a door had opened somewhere she couldn't see.

Chapter Eight

he house felt different at night—not eerie, just the kind of stillness that made everything feel softer, like the walls themselves had exhaled.

Finn padded down the hallway toward the room that had become hers. Frank had already disappeared into his own, and Eli had hung back in the kitchen, finishing his drink and stretching his legs. She didn't mind one bit. She appreciated the silence.

Even so, something felt denser now, the events of the day had finally caught up with her.

Setting her shopping bag on the small dresser beside the bed, she let out a breath and unzipped her canvas purse. There were a couple crumpled bills still there, along with the smooth hundred Eli had given her. She pulled it out, unfolding the crisp paper and staring at it for a long moment.

It was nothing to him. Like handing her money wasn't a big deal at all. As if it didn't mean survival.

She pressed her tongue against the inside of her cheek as she folded the bill and tucked it away. Then, unconsciously, she reached for the pendant resting against her collarbone.

Her gaze drifted to the darkened window across the room. Her reflection stared back, but her thoughts weren't here.

They were still in The Hollow Stitch.

Still caught in the glint of recognition in Sarah's eyes. The way her pleasant mask had slipped, just for a second.

Finn's grip tightened around the pendant as she exhaled, pushing the thought away.

She'd think about it tomorrow.

For now, she just wanted to sleep.

Finn tugged off her jeans, the tension easing from her body. The relief was immediate, her muscles uncoiling and stretching as she let herself relax.

She turned toward the window—catching her reflection again.

And laughed.

She was still wearing Eli's boxers.

The memory surfaced all at once—this morning's chaos, the borrowed clothes, and the way Eli had taken it in stride. He had rolled with it, but not without that brief, hesitant look before ultimately deciding not to pry.

Still grinning, she pulled open a drawer and grabbed something fresh. Slouchy black pants and an oversized gray T-shirt with baggy sleeves. Clothes that didn't cling, that gave her breathing room.

She tugged the shirt over her head, her fingers instinctively brushing over her arms as the fabric settled.

The sleeves didn't quite reach her wrists.

Her hands moved without thinking, turning her arms this way and that, scanning the skin beneath the low light.

She didn't think her stepfather's belt had landed there.

But that last "punishment" had been a blur of blows and pain, of breath forced from her lungs faster than she could pull it back in.

Her eyes traced over her pale skin, searching for shadows beneath the surface.

Nothing... Good.

She let out a big breath, only now realizing she had been holding it.

Moving toward the jacket where she'd discarded it on the bed, she reached for the choker where she had looped the crescent moon pendant earlier. Her fingers slipped behind it, unclasping it carefully before tucking it back into the pocket. The supple feel of the leather settled beneath her palm as she smoothed it down.

She wasn't sure why, only that it felt right leaving it there.

With that last thought, she turned for the door.

A glass of water. That was all she wanted—something to wash away the lingering sweetness of soda before bed.

But the moment she pulled the door open—

She nearly collided with Eli.

He stood just outside, fist raised mid-motion, caught in the exact moment before knocking.

For a second, neither of them moved.

Eli blinked, his expression shifting from surprise to amusement before he let out a chuckle.

"Well, damn. Great timing."

His fist lowered, and with his other hand, he held out a bottle of water.

Finn stood still, momentarily thrown.

How did he always seem to know?

Like there was some invisible thread between them, pulling his thoughts in sync with hers before she'd even formed them.

Eli caught her pause and gave the bottle a small shake, wordlessly nudging her to react, to move.

"Hydration." His voice was teasing, but there was a warmth behind it. "Gotta balance out the sugar after all that pop."

A breath of amusement left her lips as she reached for it, fingers brushing against his for half a second before she stepped back.

"Thanks."

She started to turn, her trip to the kitchen now unnecessary, but before she could take a step—

"Hey."

Eli's voice stopped her.

She glanced back, bottle still in hand, watching as something almost sheepish flashed across his face.

"Wanna play some video games?"

Finn wasn't sure what she had expected when Eli led her into his room, but whatever it was, this wasn't it.

It was as if his tattoo station had expanded and spilled over every surface, every wall—a collision of ink, art, and sound, all contained within a space just big enough to hold it.

The room wasn't much larger than hers, but it felt full. Not cluttered, just lived-in.

One wall was lined with wooden shelves, built with the same craftsmanship as the shop's furniture. She could tell, immediately, that Eli had made them himself.

They were packed—rows of vinyl records pressed tight together, a record player nestled on the nearest shelf, stacks of art books worn soft at the edges, novels piled in loose clusters. Some were books on technique, others fiction—a mix of classic literature and modern fantasy, their spines creased and handled. Read, time and again.

Then there were the history books.

Thick, aged tomes with gilded lettering and faded covers—books about Ash Hollow.

Ghost stories, forgotten myths, unexplained disappearances. Some focused on the town's general history, others on the strange happenings buried beneath its past.

Finn resisted the urge to pull one from the shelf.

And then—

The milk crates.

Stacked along the bottom shelf, each a different color, filled to the brim with old Nintendo game cartridges.

She couldn't help the slight tug at her lips.

Eli moved toward the shelves, flipping through one of the crates before pulling out a cartridge. His eyes gleamed with excitement, like he had been waiting for this moment.

"This one."

He crouched in front of the TV—a screen just a little too big for the space, but somehow fitting perfectly in the landscape of his room.

As he set up the game, Finn hesitated before finally easing onto the end of his bed.

It was small, like hers, with a simple wooden frame and a forest-green bedspread, smoothed neatly over the mattress.

Her gaze drifted across the room, tracing over the details, taking in everything she hadn't noticed at first.

Band posters lined the walls, much like the ones decorating his tattoo station—bold and chaotic, a testament to Eli's restless energy.

But they didn't hold her attention.

The paintings did. Dozens of hand-painted canvases stretched across the walls, each one saturated with color, and thick with texture. The rich gleam of oil paint caught the light in a way that made the images feel alive.

Like they were breathing.

Finn's eyes moved from one to the next, drawn into deep forest scapes. Close-up views of mushrooms blooming from fallen logs, a herd of deer grazing in a patch of sunlight. The brushstrokes were careful yet bold, each piece carrying a subtle confidence.

Admiration rose in her chest before she could stop it.

She wasn't sure why it felt so visceral.

Then—

She froze.

Her fingers tightened against the fabric beneath her.

One painting stood out from the rest.

A lake with dark water stretching beneath a sky too vast and open. The trees surrounding it were painted in deep, earthy hues, the edges softened by the same masterful blending as the rest of his work.

But there was something about it—something off.

The longer she stared, the stronger the feeling became.

It looked like the lake where she had met Kai.

And the longer she looked, the more she felt that unnerving pull.

That sensation like she was being watched.

Before she could stop herself, the words slipped out.

"Eli... when did you paint this?"

His head snapped up, his attention breaking from the game. His eyes glinted with a sudden edge, studying her for a second before following her gaze.

He stood and moved to stand beside her, his posture shifting as he took it in.

"Oh, that one."

His voice slowed, thoughtful. A pause—not hesitation exactly, but careful, as if he was measuring his words before deciding how much truth to give her.

"It's actually a lake over by where the festival was," he said finally.

Her stomach tightened.

Eli ran a hand along the back of his neck, his brows drawing together like he was trying to find the right way to explain.

"I was out there last year." His voice was more careful now, like he was deliberately placing each word. "Looking for... something."

The phrasing fell between them, incomplete.

Finn didn't miss the quick dash of his gaze toward her, the way he seemed to be gauging her reaction before continuing.

"Didn't find... it."

The air shifted.

Something about the way he said that, the careful way he left it open-ended, made Finn uncomfortable.

He wasn't lying, but he wasn't telling the whole truth either.

That wasn't like the boy she was coming to know.

Eli always seemed casual and relaxed, always at ease. He didn't tiptoe around words, or edit himself.

But now—

Now, he was mindfully choosing his words.

Finn kept her expression neutral, forcing herself to stay steady.

Eli gently shook his head, as if shaking off whatever had passed between them, moving back into something familiar.

"Anyway," he said, his voice lighter now, "the look of this lake really caught me."

His gaze on the painting, but distant, like he was being pulled back into the memory.

Finn stayed still, waiting.

"It was cold," he said, his tone more introspective. "Not quite winter. That weird in-between where the air cuts through your clothes, but the trees haven't fully given in yet."

She could picture it as he spoke—the skeletal branches, the breeze carving ripples across the surface, shifting like something moving beneath.

"Something about the water," he murmured, tilting his head. "It was dark. Almost... inky."

His fingers twitched at his sides.

"Made my hands itch to paint."

The words stayed with her—not just the meaning, but the way he said them. The pull of something he hadn't fully understood but had needed to capture anyway.

"So I snapped a picture with my phone to use as a reference and started painting it that night when I got home."

Finn forced herself to keep the steady expression she'd set on her face.

She had to play this off.

So she exhaled and let her gaze move across the canvas again, taking in the careful strokes, the richness of color, and the way the water looked like it moved.

"It's stunning," she said finally, keeping her tone light.

She hoped all he heard was admiration, and not the way her heart was pounding beneath it.

Hours stretched into the night as Eli and Finn let the day slip away, their focus narrowing to the game in front of them.

Finn was terrible. Absolutely, spectacularly terrible.

She had never been allowed to play video games growing up. Before her stepfather had come into the picture, it had been just her and her mom, and her biological father had never been in the picture.

Anytime she'd ask about him, the answer had always been the same.

"It's not important. It's you and me against the world, always."

That hadn't ended up being true.

Money had been tight back then, so consoles and games weren't an option. Instead, their nights had been spent at the library checkout desk, stacking up old VHS tapes and as many books as her little arms could carry.

So, safe to say—

Eli absolutely wrecked her.

"Damn, Finn, are you even trying?" he teased after his third consecutive win, his thumbs moving effortlessly over the controller.

Finn groaned, letting her head fall back against the wall. "I'm trying! This game is just dumb."

"No, you just suck at it."

She jabbed an elbow into his ribs, making him lurch to the side.

"Whoa—cheap shot!"

She grinned. "Gotta use whatever I've got."

They kept playing, laughter slipping easily between them, making their movements looser and their reactions slower. The space between them shrank as their shoulders bumped, their knees knocked together—neither of them acknowledging it, neither of them pulling away.

Eli kept winning, but Finn didn't care.

She loved every second of it.

By the time she finally peeled herself away, exhaustion settled deep in her limbs, leaving her body light and relaxed. Stretching her arms overhead, she pushed off the bed with a sigh.

"Alright, I concede. You're better than me."

Eli grinned broadly. "Obviously."

She rolled her eyes. "Goodnight, loser."

"Goodnight, sore loser."

Still smiling, she shook her head and made her way toward her room, the last traces of laughter still lingering in her chest.

The night had washed everything else away—the unease, the questions, and the fear she hadn't wanted to name.

By the time she collapsed onto her bed, sleep pulled her under within minutes.

And at first, it was peaceful.

But it didn't last.

– – –

I wake up in darkness.

Thick. Suffocating.

The air is stagnant, pressing down against my skin like something alive.

I don't know where I am.

I don't know how I got here.

I inhale, but it's like breathing through soaked cloth—the scent of earth and smoke thick in the air, coating my throat, my lungs.

I reach out, hands brushing cold, damp stone.

Walls.

Tunnels.

I turn blindly, searching for something—anything—but there's only twisting darkness.

And then I hear it.

A sound behind me.

Not an echo. Not my own footsteps.

Something else.

Something coming.

A sudden, sharp clatter of loose stones, the shift of something moving fast.

I bolt forward.

I don't know where I'm going—I just run.

Faster.

My feet scrape against the uneven stone, the skin splitting raw.

The thing behind me doesn't stop.

It's closer.

I swear I can feel its breath at my back, the cold coil of something unnatural reaching for me.

I push harder.

I'm gasping, lungs burning, but then—

Light.

A faint glow ahead, cutting through the dark, just beyond the twisting corridors.

I run toward it.

The walls narrow, the ceiling lowering, pressing in closer, closer—like the tunnel itself is trying to swallow me whole.

I reach the mouth of the tunnel and hurl myself forward.

The wooden boards at the exit splinter and snap as I crash through—

And suddenly, I am free.

Cold air slams into me.

I hit the ground hard, coughing, my palms skidding against frozen dirt.

I push myself up, struggling to find my breath—

And then I see it.

The lake.

It stretches out before me, the water as black as ink, still and waiting.

The sky above is a dull, pallid gray, thick clouds stretching across the horizon, smothering any sign of stars or moonlight.

The wind moves through the trees, but the water does not ripple.

Until, in the shallows—a figure moves.

Kai.

His back is to me, his fair hair slicked against his pale skin, wading forward, deeper and deeper, the water climbing up his spine.

A pulse of dread strikes through me.

What are you doing?

I take a step forward—

And I see him.

Eli.

He stands just feet away, facing the haunting scene taking place, still and focused.

An easel is before him, a canvas stretched wide, and in his hand—a paintbrush.

Slow. Methodical.

The bristles drag over the canvas, stroke after stroke, capturing the scene before us.

Not reacting.

Not stopping it.

Just painting.

"Eli?"

My voice comes out hoarse, but he doesn't turn.

I take another step forward, my pulse pounding in my ears.

"Eli, what are you doing?"

Nothing.

He keeps painting, as if he can't hear me.

As if I'm not even here.

The wind shifts, the air carrying the scent of wet earth and something burning.

My chest tightens.

"Eli, stop him!"

Finally, he stops.

His brush stills against the canvas.

Slowly—so slowly—he turns to face me.

And my breath is stolen from my lungs.

His amber eyes are gone.

In their place—

Flickering flames.

The fire dances, alive inside him, licking at his skin but never consuming it.

I stumble back.

He watches me, silent.

Unblinking.

The wind howls over the lake.

I can't move.

Then—

The flames swell.

The fire inside him burns hotter, brighter, spreading—his skin cracking, hellish light spilling through the fractures.

And just as the heat lashes out—

– – –

Chapter Nine

er body jolted upright, breath shuddering as panic crashed through her.

For a moment, she wasn't in her room, where the soft hush of morning light was filtering through the curtains, the faint creak of the house settling—none of it felt real. Her mind was still somewhere else, wrapped in the suffocating darkness. The flames of something watching.

Rap-rap-rap.

Knuckles against wood.

Then—Eli's voice.

"Rise and shine, loser! Daylight's a-burnin'!"

Burning.

The word struck like a live wire, sizzling through her chest.

She squeezed her eyes shut but the dream clung to her, tangled in her limbs, thick as smoke in her lungs.

She could still see Eli, standing at the edge of the lake.

His face was familiar—strong lines softened by unruly curls, the boy she had already come to feel like she knew. But his eyes—

Flames.

Flickering with their own life, like they had always been that way.

A tremor rolled through her as she forced herself to move, her fingers untangling the twisted duvet, letting the real world press back in.

Another knock, gentler this time.

"C'mon, Finn. Don't make me come in there."

His voice was light. Completely normal.

She exhaled slowly, feeling her pulse thrum against her skin.

No fire. No lake.

Just Eli. Just this morning.

She forced herself to answer, voice rough with sleep.

"Yeah, yeah. I'm up."

A pause, then the sound of footsteps retreating down the hall.

She sat motionless, staring at the empty space ahead of her, the echoes of the dream still licking at the edges of her mind.

Finn headed straight for the bathroom, first gathering some of the clothes she'd pulled from the attic—a long-sleeved black tee that looked like it would hug her waist more than anything she was used to wearing, and a nearly new pair of acid-washed jeans.

They were still a little dusty. She had meant to ask Eli about the laundry situation but she'd forgotten. Another thing to deal with eventually.

Tucked under her arm were the clothes she'd chosen, a fresh pair of panties and—because she had no shame—Eli's socks. Thick and warm, objectively better than anything from the boutique.

A quick, no-fuss shower ensued, followed by a finger-brushing—mental note: buy a toothbrush.

She moved easily through the house, heading downstairs, feeling more settled than she probably should have.

The living room was empty, though a coffee mug sat abandoned on the table, the liquid inside long since gone cold.

The scent of fried potatoes and eggs drifted through the air, an invitation pulling her toward the kitchen.

As she stepped inside, Eli was already at the stove, scooping scrambled eggs and hashbrowns onto a plate.

Without turning, he grinned.

"Well, there's our very own Sleeping Beauty." He shot her a glance over his shoulder, eyes alight in that mischievous way of his. "Thought I was gonna have to send the seven dwarves up there to get ya."

Finn scoffed, sliding into a chair with a playful scowl.

"That's two different stories, dumbass."

Eli set the plate in front of her with a smirk.

"Eh, potato, pat-ah-to."

He gestured to the food with an expectant nod.

"Speaking of potatoes—this grocery trip is way more dire than I thought, 'cause this," Eli motioned toward the plate, "is just about all the food left in the house."

Finn twirled her fork between her fingers before taking a bite. "So what I'm hearing is, if I had slept in a little longer, I might've missed out on breakfast entirely?"

Eli snapped his fingers. "Exactly."

She huffed, rolling her eyes, but the food was warm and filling, settling comfortably in her stomach.

It wasn't much, but it was tasty. Solid and simple, something to start the day.

They sat across from each other, the easy quiet between them becoming familiar despite how little time they'd known each other.

Eli hunched over a notebook, scrawling out a grocery list, his handwriting a little messy, his concentration deep enough that his tongue pressed against the inside of his cheek. Every so often, he'd tap his pen against the page before glancing up.

"You like this?"

and

"What about that?"

Sometimes, he'd toss in his own preferences, a running commentary of things he loved, and things that just weren't worth the hassle.

Finn realized—he wasn't just making a list. He was including her.

Asking what she liked and making space for her, in ways that no one had in so long.

It was such a menial thing, but it felt unbelievably nice.

To be considered and have someone think about what she might want to eat.

To have someone cook for her, without expecting anything in return.

She let the moment settle around her as Eli kept writing.

And then—her eyes caught on his hand, the way his pen moved smoothly over the page.

Laundry soap.

Her body reacted before her brain did.

"Oh! Laundry!"

She lunged forward, her chair screeching horribly against the stone floor as her hand smacked down onto Eli's notebook with enough force to send his pen flying into the air.

They both froze, watching as it arced dramatically before clattering to the floor.

Eli turned back to her, eyes wide, caught somewhere between amusement and deep betrayal.

"What the hell was that?"

Finn, completely unfazed, smoothed her sleeve between her fingers.

"I've been meaning to ask what the laundry protocol is around here," she admitted. "Your mom's clothes were packed away really well, but they were still kinda dusty."

She plucked at her sleeve, as if expecting a theatrical puff of dust to rise off of it for effect.

Eli snorted, shaking his head as he leaned down, swiping his pen off the floor.

"Laundry's in the garage. The machines are old as hell, but you can use them whenever."

Finn nodded, satisfied—then hesitated.

"Oh, and I also need a toothbrush," she added as an afterthought. "Forgot to grab one yesterday."

Eli froze mid-motion, his pen hovering just above the page.

"Wait."

His tone shifted, like something had just hit him.

"A toothbrush? What have you been doing?"

Finn stilled.

Then, slowly, she lifted her index finger and shrugged.

Eli recoiled so hard it was a full-body reaction.

"Oh, girrrrrl." He dragged the word out, shaking his head in mock horror. "We better get out of here and get that taken care of."

Still shaking his head, he turned back to the notebook.

With deliberate, exaggerated flair, he boldly scrawled across the page: *TOOTHBRUSH FOR FINN.*

Finn rolled her eyes, but her lips twitched into a smile.

She was already starting to like mornings here.

As they finished up at the kitchen table, Finn pushed her chair back, stretching.

"I'm just gonna run upstairs and grab my jacket."

Eli nodded, tapping his pen lightly against the notebook before tearing off the sheet and folding the grocery list.

"No worries. I'm gonna check in with my dad real quick, see if he needs anything added before we head out."

He pushed back from the table and headed toward the garage.

Finn took the stairs quickly now; the hesitation she'd felt yesterday was gone. She barely even thought about it—until the last step.

Her boot slipped. Just a quick misstep. It was nothing that would've sent her sprawling, but enough to jolt her back into awareness. She caught herself fast, her pulse jumping before she even had time to process it.

Instinctively, her eyes flitted around, scanning the space as if someone might have seen her.

But she was the only one inside the house.

A breath left her, half amusement, half exasperation. Shaking her head at herself, she continued down the hall toward her room.

And then—she stopped.

It took a second for her mind to catch up, her feet already still before she fully understood why.

She'd walked past the open bathroom door and at first, it hadn't registered. Just a passing blur, a moment of motion that shouldn't have been there. But something in her brain caught onto it, something instinctive and uneasy.

Her pulse ticked up.

For the briefest moment, she could have sworn she had seen someone, standing in the center of the bathroom, and looking out.

The thought sent a ripple of dread through her, bouncing inside her ribcage. She knew it was probably nothing. Just a trick of the eye or a shadow in the wrong place.

But still, she faltered.

Then, feeling ridiculous, she stepped back and into the doorway. Easing into the room, her breath was tight as she reached for the shower curtain. Her fingers curled around the fabric, then yanked it aside.

Only stillness, save for the slow drip from the faucet. A single drop breaking the silence as it hit the porcelain.

Finn let her breath out sharply, the tension unwinding from her shoulders.

She flexed her fingers against the sleeves of her shirt, losing herself in the feel of fabric beneath her hands as she turned for her room.

Shrugging into her leather jacket, she grabbed her choker and fastened it around her neck, the cool metal settling against her collarbone like an anchor.

Without another glance toward the bathroom, she headed for the stairs and took them two at a time.

When she reached the bottom of the stairs, she let her steps slow, but the restless energy still lingered in her limbs. She made her way through the house swiftly. Pushing through the front door, she stepped onto the porch, drawing in a deep breath of morning air.

The coolness of it filled her lungs, crisp and clean, chasing the last traces of unease from her mind.

And then—something else.

A pleasant smell threaded through the cold, a blend of scents drifting on the breeze, soft and inviting.

Finn's eyes wandered, searching for the source.

Quickly finding it.

A lone coffee mug, resting on the wooden porch rail.

She stepped closer, inhaling deeply.

Coffee.

Cinnamon.

Lavender.

The fragrance curled around her, rich and lingering.

The mug wasn't steaming, but the scent still hung in the air, woven into the fabric of the morning.

Her brows pulled together as she studied it, something about the scene feeling both ordinary and significant all at once.

Just then, Eli appeared from the garage, holding up his folded grocery list.

"Good to go?"

He didn't wait for an answer, already heading toward the Bronco.

Finn hesitated before following, her voice slipping out before she could think better of it.

"Do you guys just not finish your coffee?"

Eli slowed, turning back with a look of mild confusion.

Finn gestured toward the mug on the railing.

Then, as if realizing how random the question must have sounded, she quickly added, "There was another one inside. In the living room. It looked like it had been sitting there a while."

Eli followed her gaze to the mug, his expression unreadable.

Then—

"Oh. That."

A pause.

Then, quieter—

"Yeah..."

His eyes lingered on it for a second longer before he turned away, climbing into the driver's seat.

Finn slid into the passenger side, settling her hands in her lap, watching him carefully.

There was something more. She could feel it.

"Yeah, that's something Dad always did for Mom."

His voice had shifted, distant but not heavy.

"He'd make sure we both let her sleep in every Sunday morning, and he'd make her coffee just the way she liked it."

His hands flexed briefly on the steering wheel, lost in memory.

"He'd set it out on the front porch, where she liked to drink it. I swear she could smell it all the way upstairs, 'cause she'd always come down right after to drink it while it was still steaming."

His lips twitched up, like he could still see it.

Finn didn't say anything at all.

She just let the moment settle between them, like the scent of cinnamon and lavender still hovering in the air.

Chapter Ten

he old steed roared to life, a deep, steady vibration beneath them as Eli backed out of the driveway and turned onto the road.

The morning air carried the scent of pine and damp earth, the kind of clean sharpness that awoke the senses. Sunlight filtered through the canopy of trees lining the road, pine needles lush, and leaves full and vibrant, shifting with the breeze. Dappled patterns of gold and green danced across the pavement, flickering against the hood as they passed beneath the branches.

The only sounds were the low hum of the engine and the gentle whir of the tires rolling against the road.

It was an easy silence that didn't need to be filled.

Then, as they passed the first stretch of businesses along Main Street, Eli finally spoke.

"So, that's Danny's Hardware," he said, nodding toward a brick store-front with a hand-painted wooden sign above the door.

Finn recognized the name immediately—Frank had mentioned Danny the day before.

A man stood just outside the shop, leaning against the railing, a styrofoam cup in hand.

Even from here, Finn could tell—Danny had a presence.

He was older, tall and broad, his dark skin touched with deep lines of laughter and experience. His hair was ashy grey, cropped close to his scalp, and his beard neatly trimmed in the same salt-and-pepper shade.

His eyes, though—they were sharp. Quietly attentive, taking in everything around him with a pointed kind of awareness.

He wore a plain denim work shirt, the sleeves rolled up to reveal strong muscled forearms. The fabric was soft with years of use, but clean and well-kept. Paired with sturdy boots that looked to have walked through years of hard work.

Even now, standing in the golden light of morning, he looked unshakable—like a man who had seen everything, weathered every storm, and had come out stronger for it.

As they rolled past, Eli lifted a hand in an acknowledging wave.

Danny responded with a slow, deliberate nod, his large hand lifting in return.

There was something in his expression—not just acknowledgment, but something warmer.

A fondness.

But then—his eyes flashed toward her.

And just like that, the warmth cooled.

Not entirely—just a degree.

Like he was taking stock of her. Trying to place her.

Eli didn't seem to notice. If he did, he didn't think much of it. His attention had already shifted as they passed another business.

"That's The Drug Shoppe."

Finn raised a brow. "The what?"

He smirked. "Yeah, yeah. Weird name. But it's the oldest business still standing in town. Been here since the late 1800s."

Finn's gaze drifted toward the display window where vintage medicine bottles, glass apothecary jars, and hand-rolled cigars sat carefully arranged, like artifacts in a museum.

"They still have one of those old-school soda fountains inside," Eli added. "Like straight out of a 1950s movie."

Finn smiled at the thought.

The whole town felt like it had been paused in time.

Every storefront and sign, every pressed brick held the mark of history, as if each belonged to a different era entirely.

Then, up ahead, the road curved—

And the atmosphere shifted.

To their right, beyond a low stone wall, the land stretched wide and uneven.

A vast cemetery.

The ground sloped gently toward the tree line, where the forest pressed at the edge of the graves.

Headstones stood in varying states of decay—some polished and new, others worn by time, their engravings softened, fading into nothing.

Scattered among them, small American flags fluttered in the breeze, their colors muted by morning light.

A low, silvery mist drifted through the grass, weaving between the stones, delicate and wispy above the dew.

"This place looks ancient," Finn murmured.

Eli nodded, one hand resting on the steering wheel, the other drumming absentmindedly against the gear shift.

"It is. This town used to be a coal-mining hub—before it all went to hell."

Finn turned toward him, intrigued. "Coal?"

He nodded. "Yeah. That's what really put this place on the map. Men came from all over, hoping to strike richer materials—silver, maybe even gold." He glanced in her direction, taking stock of her reaction before continuing. "There was a big mining accident in the 1940s. It killed a bunch of workers. People say that's when things started going downhill."

A chill worked its way down Finn's spine, quiet but insistent. There was something about that, something that sat wrong in her bones, though she couldn't say why.

Eli's voice remained casual and unaffected. "By the time my dad was a kid, the mines were long shut down. Some people stuck around, but most left."

The town's past settled between them, heavy in the silence that followed.

And then—

A church rolled into view.

At the far end of the block, it loomed over the smaller buildings, its towering presence steadfast and impossible to ignore. Dark stone walls, blackened with age, made it feel less like a place of worship and more like a sentinel pulled from another time, meant to keep watch rather than welcome. The steeple's peak speared the pale morning sky like a blade.

But it wasn't just the size that made Finn's skin prickle.

Something about this place felt wrong. Cold.

Like it didn't belong.

Beside her, Eli's grip on the steering wheel tightened, a subtle motion, barely there, but she caught it. "That's St. Sebastian's."

His voice was still light, still casual—but too casual. Like he was making an effort not to put importance behind the words.

Finn just stared, the unease pressing deeper into her core.

The massive wooden doors were shut tight, but the stained-glass windows took shape above, twisting light into strange, unnatural colors as the early morning sun skittered across them. Blues too deep, reds too sharp, casting warped shades against the stone.

Finn's pulse quickened.

The sight unsettled her, an inexplicable unease biting at the edges of her awareness.

Beside her, Eli let out a slow breath through his nose. "Creepy as hell, right?"

Finn swallowed. "Yeah."

Eli shot her a glance but didn't linger. Instead, he tapped his fingers against the steering wheel, nodding toward the church.

"Well, half the town's gonna be in there soon. It's Sunday morning."

Finn shifted her gaze to the empty lot beside it.

She could already picture the scene—cars pulling in and the doors swinging open, people stepping out in pressed clothes and stiff smiles. Filing inside and taking their places.

Eli turned down another street, and just like that—the moment passed.

The church faded into the rearview mirror.

A few minutes later, the grocery store came into view.

Eli pulled into the lot, parking near the entrance. "Alright, let's get this over with before we end up living off canned beans for the rest of the week."

Finn snorted, unbuckling her seatbelt. "Not a fan of canned beans?"

"Not exclusively."

She rolled her eyes, stepping out onto the pavement, but her mind was still back at the church.

Finn glanced around, taking in the handful of cars scattered through-out the lot. It was quiet, the slow lull of morning settling over everything. Eli veered toward one of the cart corrals, grabbing a cart—or buggy, or whatever they called them out here.

With a smirk, he gave it a lazy push in her direction. "Alright, let's do this."

Finn nodded, falling into step beside him as they made their way toward the entrance.

The moment they stepped inside, a wave of warmth enveloped her, cozy and inviting.

The store was clean and tidy—much neater than she was used to. No cluttered aisles or buzzing fluorescent lights casting everything in a harsh glow. No overpowering scent of detergent like in the bigger grocery chains.

Instead, a softer atmosphere filled the space, made richer by the blend of smells drifting through the air.

Freshly baked bread.

Sweet, buttery pastries.

Rich, brewed coffee.

Her stomach growled, reminding her that she hadn't eaten much that morning—just the eggs and potatoes, a meager portion of each, enough to curb her hunger but not satisfy it.

Her gaze fell on a quaint coffee kiosk near the front of the store.

A few customers were gathered around, stirring cream and sugar into their drinks, chatting as the world outside remained slow and still.

Behind the counter, a woman moved swiftly, pouring steaming cups of coffee with practiced ease.

She was older yet striking, her features elegant, but softened by time.

Something about her felt familiar.

The way she carried herself, the soft focus in her eyes, the way she had her gray-streaked hair pinned back—it reminded Finn of someone.

The thought surfaced before she could stop it.

"She reminds me of my hometown librarian."

Eli shot her a glance, curiosity flashing in his honeyed eyes. "Yeah? Where's home?"

It was a simple question—one people ask all the time. But for some reason, it felt like more than it should.

Maybe because home didn't feel like the right word anymore.

She swallowed down the pang of nausea and gave a small shrug. "Colorado."

Eli pressed lightly. "Where in Colorado?"

Another pause, just long enough for her to consider dodging the question. But finally, she muttered, "A little nowhere town called Estes Park."

Eli's lips twitched, like he was filing that away. "So, you're a mountain girl, huh?"

Finn huffed a small laugh. "Something like that."

He pushed the cart forward. "Alright, mountain girl—let's get some groceries before we end up living off my dad's expired ramen stash."

Finn arched a brow, giving him a look of mock incredulity. "So there's canned beans and ramen now? Sounds like there's more sustenance in the house than you were letting on."

Eli grinned, shrugging one shoulder. "I prefer to call it strategic rationing."

Finn let out a dramatic gasp. "Ah, I see. A survivalist."

"Exactly."

She rolled her eyes but followed, trailing just a step behind. As they passed the coffee kiosk, her gaze strayed toward it once more.

The woman wasn't looking at them, but for a brief second, Finn swore the subtle crease between her brows had deepened.

Eli moved through the aisles with determination. Finn watched as he pulled the grocery list from his pocket, scanning it briefly before reaching for each item with purpose, barely pausing before marking it off with a stroke of his pen.

It wasn't just efficient—it was calculated.

After a few more aisles, she started to notice the pattern. His list wasn't random. Everything was written in the exact order they'd need to grab it in the store.

She watched as he reached for a bag of flour without hesitation, tossing it into the cart and checking it off in one smooth motion. He wasn't just quick; he was deliberate, moving through the store with a kind of certainty that felt second nature.

It was impressive.

And maybe just a little intimidating.

Finn exhaled a laugh, tucking her hands into the pockets of her jacket. "I don't feel like I'm being much help."

Eli glanced at her, completely unbothered. "That's 'cause you're not."

She shot him a mock-offended look, but he just shrugged.

"I've been doing this forever. I know this place like the back of my hand. You'll learn it before long. Then you'll be of more assistance to me."

Then, almost as an afterthought, he added, "Not that I mind. I'm just grateful for the company."

Finn blinked.

Her mind shifted to Eli and Frank—the way they coexisted in quiet familiarity. They didn't talk much, but there was a steadiness to their silence, an understanding woven into their routine.

She hadn't thought about it before, but now the thought stuck.

Did Eli get lonely?

She thought back to last night and the way his face had lit up when she'd agreed to play video games with him, the energy in his movements as he set everything up.

Like it wasn't just about the game, it was about having someone there to play it with.

She didn't know what to say, so she just smiled softly instead.

Eli didn't seem to notice. He was already rounding the end of the aisle, turning into the next.

The cereal aisle.

Finn followed, about to step in beside him when—

"Uh-oh."

Eli's voice was low, but there was something pointed about it.

Her gaze snapped ahead.

And then—she saw.

Sarah.

A few yards down the aisle, she stood near the shelves, examining a box of granola like she had all the time in the world. Her light brown hair, just long enough to tuck behind her ear, was swept neatly away from her face, framing her soft features.

Then, as if sensing them, her eyes darted in their direction.

The moment she spotted Eli, her face lit up.

"Eli!"

Her wave was exaggerated, too enthusiastic—like she wanted to make sure everyone saw her greeting him.

Eli's smile was tight but polite, as he lifted a small, barely-there wave.

Then, before Finn could react, he pivoted smoothly, steering the cart into the next aisle instead.

"We can circle back to that one," he said, nonchalantly.

But just before they turned the corner, Finn caught it—

Sarah's gaze dashed toward her, sharp and unguarded, narrowing just slightly.

A clean, cutting look.

Finn's stomach twisted, but she kept moving, matching Eli's pace.

They just let the moment slide away, disappearing into the next aisle.

Eli steered the cart, calm and methodical, completely in his element.

Finn, however, was plotting.

She had barely glanced at his list earlier, but now that she understood just how precisely he had mapped everything out, she was determined.

As he rolled the cart forward, she peeked over at the page in his hand, scanning for the next item before he could reach for it.

Stewed tomatoes.

Her lips twitched and before Eli could make his move, she grabbed the first thing her fingers landed on—a completely random can—and tossed it into the cart.

Then she turned to him, triumphant, mischief sparking in her eyes.

Eli glanced down into the cart, then back at her.

His eyes widened, his mouth dropping open in mock horror.

"You monster!"

Finn burst into laughter, and Eli barely lasted a second before joining in, his full-bodied laugh filling the aisle.

"What even is this?" he asked between chuckles, reaching into the cart and holding up—

A can of creamed corn.

Finn blinked in surprise.

"Oh."

Now it was her turn to be horrified.

"That's worse than I intended."

Eli laughed even harder, shaking his head. "You replaced stewed tomatoes with creamed corn?"

Finn cringed. "Listen, I panicked."

He tossed the can back into the cart, scoffing, like it had personally offended him.

"Oh no, it's staying now. You did this."

She practically shouted out, "That was a mistake."

Eli smirked, raising a brow. "That's what they all say."

Finn rolled her eyes, but she could feel it—the warmth settling in her chest, their laughter lingering somewhere deep and safe.

Eli shook his head, still chuckling as he pushed the cart forward.

"Okay, Missy." He shot her a pointed look. "If you want to be so helpful, why don't you head over to the produce section and grab these?"

He held the list in front of her, tapping a few items further down the page.

She gasped dramatically, pressing a hand over her chest like she'd just been knighted.

"What an honor," she declared. "To be entrusted with such a vital mission."

Eli nodded solemnly. "Only the most capable of grocery operatives can be trusted with produce selection."

Finn lifted her chin, feigning great pride. "I won't let you down."

With exaggerated purpose, she turned on her heel, striding off with confidence.

...For about five steps.

Then she slowed to a stop.

She turned back around, face drawn as her act completely unraveled.

"Where... is the produce section?"

Eli's grin widened as he fought back laughter. "Wow. That was fast."

Finn sighed dramatically, trudging back toward him, shoulders slumping in defeat. "I regret to inform you, sir, that I have failed my mission."

He finally snorted, jerking his thumb over his shoulder toward the front of the store. "It's by the entrance. Big displays of fruits and vegetables. Can't miss it. Though... I guess you already did."

Finn nodded firmly, straightening like she was snapping back into character. "Right. Of course. This is fine. All part of the plan."

"Uh-huh." Eli winked, already turning back to his cart. "Good luck, Agent Finn."

She rolled her eyes but couldn't stop the small grin creeping onto her lips as she turned back toward the entrance—this time, actually knowing where she was going.

With Eli's direction fresh in her mind, Finn found the produce section with ease.

The moment she stepped into it, she pulled up short.

She had assumed—wrongly—that a grocery store in a town this small would have produce past its prime. Overpriced and half-wilted.

But that wasn't the case at all.

The section was overflowing with some of the freshest, most vibrant produce she had ever seen.

Crisp greens, golden pears, and plump berries bursting with color. Everything looked rich and impossibly fresh, like it had been harvested that morning. Each display had a small, handwritten sign boasting organic and locally grown, listing the exact farm, garden, or orchard it had come from.

Finn ran her fingers over the leaves of a head of lettuce, impressed at how alive it felt beneath her touch.

This was the kind of selection she'd expect from a high-end market—not a small-town grocery store.

She took her time, carefully mulling over the freshest bundles, the juiciest apples, and the most crisp greens.

For a moment, it was peaceful.

And then—

Something shifted in the corner of her vision.

A movement. Someone was striding toward her—fast, with intent.

It caught her attention immediately.

Finn turned just in time to realize who it was.

But by then—it was too late.

Sarah was already on her.

The carefully constructed pleasantness she had worn at the boutique? Gone.

Sarah's face was set, her expression twisted in pure, unfiltered anger.

And before Finn could react, Sarah grabbed a fistful of her jacket.

The sudden force yanked Finn forward, her boots scuffing against the linoleum.

"What the hell is this?!"

Sarah's voice rang out, shrill and seething—loud enough that a few nearby shoppers turned their heads.

Finn gasped, her pulse spiking, but Sarah wasn't even looking at her face.

Her eyes were locked on the jacket, burning with fury.

Like it offended her just by existing.

"Where did you get it?!"

Finn opened her mouth, but Sarah didn't give her the chance.

Her gaze lifted incrementally higher—

Latching onto the choker.

And then—her other hand shot out and the clasp at the back of the choker snapped.

The crescent moon pendant slid off, hitting the floor with a sharp, metallic clatter.

The sound rang through the aisle—unnaturally loud.

Finn stumbled back, breaking Sarah's grasp, her breath caught in her throat and the sting of broken skin burning where the chain at the back of the choker had been torn away.

Her mind raced to catch up, but everything was happening too fast.

Sarah didn't move. She stood rigid, fists clenched and chest rising and falling with unsteady breaths.

And her eyes—

They weren't just filled with jealousy. Or pettiness.

This was something deeper, and colder.

Something dangerous.

Chapter Eleven

inn couldn't move.

Her body froze; her mind struggled to process what had just happened.

The sting at her neck sharpened into a steady pulse, radiating outward from where the chain had snapped free.

Slowly, she pressed her palm against the tender spot, fingertips brushing over the irritated skin—but her eyes never left Sarah.

The girl stood, chest heaving and face flushed with rage. Her eyes burned with venom.

Something too intense for a simple rivalry.

Then—

"What the unholy hell is going on here?!"

Eli's voice sliced through the thick tension, sharp and demanding.

His cart sat abandoned at the edge of the produce section as he strode toward them, his sharp eyes darting between them, taking in everything—their rigid stances, Finn's stunned expression, and Sarah's barely restrained fury.

And then—he saw it.

His expression shifted, confusion giving way to something colder, sharper.

Finn caught the way his brows knit together, his gaze darting from her wide eyes to Sarah's scarlet anger—

And finally, to the pendant lying on the floor between them.

The shift in energy was immediate.

With Eli's sudden presence, some of Sarah's heat drained—not entirely, but enough.

Finn's pulse pounded, her throat tightening as she fought against the heat prickling behind her eyes.

She wouldn't cry.

Not in front of Sarah.

Eli's gaze resumed its bouncing between them, frustration mounting with the silence.

"Well? Someone wanna clue me in?"

Finn didn't answer. She couldn't.

Instead, she kept her focus locked on Sarah, waiting.

Sarah's jaw tensed.

Then, through clenched teeth, she spat out—

"They aren't hers."

Eli's frown deepened. "What?"

Sarah's glare snapped to him, sharp and burning. "They aren't fucking hers."

Without another word, she turned on her heel and strode out of the store.

She didn't look back. Didn't acknowledge either of them even a moment longer.

Finn remained still, her body refusing to move.

The choker lay between her and Eli now. The crescent pendant gleaming faintly under the lights.

Sarah was gone.

But her words lingered, thick as smoke, refusing to clear.

Eli bent down slowly, his movements purposeful as he reached for the pendant lying on the linoleum floor.

He turned it over in his fingers, then inspected the broken clasp on the choker, his brows knitting.

"Well, the clasp is definitely broken," he murmured. "But I think I can fix it back at home."

His voice remained calm and steady. Normal.

Finn didn't feel normal.

Not even close.

Eli held the pendant out to her, palm open, waiting. The leather choker dangling, limp, looking as dejected as she felt.

Then, carefully, she reached for it.

She took it, the metal a familiar shape—only heavier now, like it had kept a piece of the moment. Heat, too. Or maybe that was her skin. She thumbed the crescent's edge and slipped it into her jacket pocket.

Even the jacket felt different now.

Bigger.

She kept her gaze on the floor, willing herself to breathe, to steady the unease clawing at her insides.

She could feel Eli's eyes on her, the way he was watching and waiting, sensing the shift in her posture, the way tension had locked her shoulders in place.

His voice was soft when he finally spoke.

"Hey."

Finn swallowed down the lump that formed at his patient tone.

"What happened?"

She wanted to answer, or to somehow explain.

But when she finally found her voice, it was softer than she intended.

"I'm... I'm not really sure."

She glanced around, tilting her head and searching, as if the air might hold an explanation—something that made sense.

But there was nothing.

No logic or reasoning.

Slowly, she forced herself to meet Eli's gaze.

His eyes were steady and warm, full of quiet concern.

"She just came at me... grabbing me."

Her fingers grazed the front of her jacket, pressing against the spot where Sarah's grip had been moments ago, like she could still feel the phantom pressure.

"And she just..."

Her jaw tightened, the words slipping from her lips.

"...ripped my necklace off."

The sentence felt hollow, too simple to encompass what had actually taken place.

A slow, creeping cold wrapped around her, winding through her limbs.

Without thinking, she crossed her arms over herself, pulling them in tight.

Just like she had yesterday, when Eli had found her in her room.

When she had slipped back in time.

But this wasn't her stepfather, and this wasn't the past.

So why did it feel just as suffocating?

Eli started unloading the cart on the belt, and Finn automatically stepped in to help.

It didn't take long to notice—even in this, he was meticulous.

Each item had its place. The heaviest things went first, followed by the mid-weight items, and finally, the delicate ones—bread, eggs—were stacked carefully at the end.

Finn watched him for a moment before muttering, "Do you have OCD or something?"

Her voice carried a teasing edge, but it wasn't as sharp as before. The usual lightness wasn't there.

Eli noticed.

He didn't look at her when he responded, choosing instead to keep his focus on the task at hand.

"Nah, I just like being efficient."

Finn let out a hum, shifting her attention to the cashier as the total climbed higher than she expected.

A familiar tightness gripped her entrails.

She reached into her purse, fingers searching for the hundred-dollar bill Eli had given her the night before. It wouldn't cover much, but she needed to contribute.

Eli caught the movement immediately. "What are you doing?"

Finn glanced up, holding the bill between her fingers. "I've gotta pitch in something. I'm going to be eating this food too."

She extended the money toward him, but Eli didn't take it. Instead, he waved her off, shaking his head.

"That's not something you need to worry about right now."

His voice was firm, as if the matter had already been settled.

Finn hesitated, gripping the bill for a second longer before tucking it back into her purse.

Without another word, she focused on loading the grocery bags into the cart, moving quickly, keeping her hands busy.

Eli exchanged a few pleasantries with the cashier, offering a polite nod and a quiet thank you before helping Finn finish loading.

Neither of them spoke.

But something about the silence felt heavier than what was becoming normal for them.

She wasn't sure if it was Sarah's words still lingering in the back of her mind or the way Eli had dismissed her attempt to help.

Either way, it settled deep in her chest, pressing down and refusing to fade.

As they wheeled the cart away from the register, Finn expected Eli to head straight for the exit, but instead, he veered toward the coffee kiosk.

She glanced up at him, brow furrowing. "What are you doing?"

Eli smirked. "I noticed you eyeing the coffee stand when we got here. And I swear I heard your stomach growling"

Finn opened her mouth to argue, but before she could, the warm scent of cinnamon and coffee curled around her again, rich and inviting. Okay, maybe she had been enticed by it.

Eli pulled the cart up beside the counter, where the woman working moved easily, pouring fresh coffee, her hands sturdy and expression calm.

"Morning, Clarabell," Eli greeted, his tone teasing.

The woman chortled, shaking her head as she wiped her hands on a cloth. "You know you can just call me Clara."

Eli grinned. "Yeah, but where's the fun in that?"

Clara turned her attention to Finn, studying her with curiosity before nodding lightly. "So, you're the mountain girl."

Finn blinked. "How did you—"

Clara lifted a shoulder in a shrug. "It's a small store. I heard you two talking when you came in."

Finn exhaled a small laugh, shaking her head. "Right. That makes sense."

Clara smiled knowingly, then gestured toward the menu behind her. "So, what'll it be?"

Finn glanced at the neatly written chalkboard, scanning the options before deciding. "Caramel macchiato, please. Oh! And a chocolate croissant"

Clara immediately got to work, her hands going through the motions like second nature. As she steamed the milk, she spoke offhandedly, voice light but certain.

"Funny thing, actually—I'm from your hometown."

Finn froze, her fingers tightening on the edge of the counter.

"What?"

Clara glanced up briefly, offering a small smile. "Yeah. That little 'nowhere town'? That's where I grew up."

Finn stared at her, caught between surprise and something else she couldn't quite place.

"That's... weird."

Clara let out a soft chuckle as she wrapped Finn's pastry in wax paper. "It is, isn't it? Two mountain girls, ending up in the same little mining town."

Finn nodded absently, still processing as Clara turned toward Eli. "And what about you? Anything today?"

Eli leaned casually against the counter. "Just a black coffee."

Clara smirked. "Simple man."

"Something like that."

She poured the coffee without hesitation, setting both drinks, and the neatly wrapped croissant, on the counter before ringing them up. Eli pulled out his wallet before Finn could even think about trying, handing over the cash without a second thought.

Clara gave him the change, offering Finn another thoughtful glance as she did.

Finn forced a small smile, murmuring a little "Thanks" as she picked up her items.

She took a sip, the warmth settling in her chest, but the conversation lingered.

Of all places...
What were the odds?

Chapter Twelve

The cart jostled over the uneven pavement, but Finn barely noticed. Her thoughts were too tangled, caught between Sarah's violent outburst and Clara's offhanded revelation, trying to make sense of two things that had nothing remotely to do with one another—but somehow left her with similar feelings of unease.

She bit into the croissant; the chocolate went silky, but her stomach stayed tight.

Sarah's anger. Clara's ease.

One had grabbed her like she was stealing something that wasn't hers.

The other had smiled like it was nothing at all.

Beside her, Eli kept sneaking glances in her direction, measuring her silence, waiting to see if she'd break it. He didn't push. Not yet.

When they reached the Bronco, he popped open the back, the hinges creaking in protest. They worked in sync—Finn passing over the bags and Eli stacking them neatly inside.

And then, finally—

"What are the chances?"

His voice was light, but there was an edge to it, like he'd been turning the thought over in his mind since they left the store.

Finn handed him another bag, keeping her eyes down, pretending to focus on the task.

Eli took it, set it in place, then threw her another glance.

"You and Clara. From the same town, both ending up here. That's wild, right?"

She nodded slowly. "Yeah. Wild."

Eli studied her, waiting, but she didn't offer anything more.

He exhaled, shaking his head as he secured the last of the bags.

"I mean, really—what are the odds?" His lips twitched, something like amusement flickering at the edges. "She said it like it was no big deal."

Finn took a sip of her drink, the sweet caramel mingling with the dark chocolate.

It should have been comforting, but it wasn't.

And Eli kept talking.

That's when Finn realized—that was the point.

He wasn't just fixating on Clara because he was curious. He was redirecting her, steering her attention somewhere else, away from Sarah and the way her hands had latched onto Finn's jacket like she had the right to rip it away.

And—it worked.

The tension that had wrapped around her moments ago loosened, her mind shifting, untangling itself from the scene in the store.

She let out a small huff, shaking her head. "Guess I'll have to start calling her my long-lost hometown cousin or something."

Eli's grin was immediate, satisfied that she was playing along. "Oh yeah, I'm sure she'd love that."

They finished loading the last of the groceries, and Eli swung the back shut, dusting his hands off before turning back toward her.

"Alright, let's get home before my dad decides to try cooking something up with the rations and burns the house down."

Finn laughed, lighter now, the sound pushing away some of the tension that still clung to her.

Maybe Eli had the right idea, and it wasn't worth overthinking.

Maybe Clara's connection to her was just a weird coincidence.

Maybe Sarah's reaction wasn't as deep as it had felt.

As Eli pulled out of the grocery store parking lot, Finn realized he was taking the same route home as yesterday. No detours. No winding back past the church or slow roll past the cemetery.

She was grateful.

The last thing she needed was to see that dark, imposing structure again—or the endless rows of gravestones stretching toward the treeline, whispering stories she wasn't ready to hear.

They drove in silence, the Bronco humming beneath them, the morning sun creeping higher. But before they actually headed home, Eli made another stop.

Finn glanced up as he pulled into the old gas station, easing the truck toward the only available pump.

"Want anything from inside?" he asked, already hopping out, stretching his arms before heading toward the store.

Finn hesitated, then shrugged. "A Dr. Pepper?"

She wasn't sure why she asked, like it was a question.

Eli smirked, shaking his head as he pulled open the door. "Alright. But I think you'd like the homemade version from the soda fountain at the drugstore better. We'll get one next time."

Finn huffed a small laugh, tucking her hands into the sleeves of her jacket.

She didn't doubt he was right.

Eli disappeared inside, and she leaned back against her seat, exhaling slowly.

Then—she remembered. There *was* something else she needed.

She pushed open the passenger door and hurried after him.

Inside, the gas station smelled exactly how she imagined it would—faintly musty, tinged with burnt coffee and oil-soaked concrete. The air was thick with it, clinging to the walls and the floors, even the shelves stocked with dusty snack foods.

The attendant behind the counter barely moved as she rushed past, though his tired eyes narrowed in recognition. She ignored it, too focused on weaving through the narrow aisles, searching for Eli.

She spotted him near the back, standing in front of the refrigerated sodas, just as he grabbed hers from the cooler. His gaze lifted up as she approached, brows lifting.

"Everything good?"

Finn felt her face heat slightly.

This was stupid.

But still—

"Can you do me a favor?" she asked, shifting a little uncomfortably.

Eli's expression softened immediately. "Yeah, of course. Name it."

She glanced toward the counter before lowering her voice.

"Can you buy me a pack of smokes?"

For a second, Eli just blinked at her. Then—

He laughed.

Not mocking. Just genuinely amused.

"Yeah, sure." He smirked. "You could probably just get 'em yourself. Todd asks for ID out of formality, but I've never actually seen him look at the birth date."

Finn huffed out a breath. Good to know.

Still, she followed him to the counter, standing just off to the side as he paid for the gas, her soda, and a pack of menthols.

And sure enough—

Todd barely glanced up.

"ID."

Eli handed it over lazily, one-handed, like it was just another step in a routine.

Todd grunted, barely even pretending to look at the card before sliding it back across the counter.

Finn hadn't thought twice about it—until Eli tucked it back into his wallet, and she caught a glimpse of his name.

Eli Ashford.

The sight of it tugged at the edges of her mind, like a loose thread she couldn't quite pull free.

It should have been insignificant, but somehow, it wasn't.

And maybe the strangest part of all—

She hadn't known his last name until now.

By the time they stepped outside and made their way back to the Bronco, Eli moved toward the pump, grabbing the nozzle and setting it into the tank.

Finn climbed into the passenger seat, absently spinning the name over in her mind, trying to pin down why it felt familiar.

Ashford.

It nagged at something, just out of reach. But no matter how many times she turned it over, nothing came.

A minute later, Eli slid into the driver's seat, tossing the pack of cigarettes into her lap.

"Nasty habit," he said, his voice dipping into something mockingly parental.

Finn rolled her eyes, picking up the pack and stuffing it into her jacket pocket. "I know, I know."

Eli chuckled, turning the key in the ignition. "Every smoker knows that."

Then—without a word—he held out his hand. Expectant.

She narrowed her eyes but didn't question it. She pulled the pack back out, ripping off the plastic and flipping it open before sliding one between her lips. Then, she tapped another loose and handed it over.

He took it with an impish smirk, reaching into the center console for a beat-up old lighter. He flicked it once. Twice. Then, on the third try, the flame caught.

The soft glow danced briefly between them as he leaned in to light hers first, then his own.

They both inhaled slow and deep, the burn easing into Finn's lungs as Eli shifted the truck into drive.

Smoke floated around them, trailing lazily out the open windows as the town slipped past.

For a while, the only sound in the cab was the occasional pop of burning tobacco.

Then—

"Ashford."

Eli shifted his gaze off the road, toward her, for just a brief moment. "Huh?"

Finn tapped the ash from her cigarette out the window. "Your last name. Ashford."

He gave a nod, exhaling a stream of smoke. "That's me."

She was quiet for a moment before asking, "You think it's weird?"

He glanced at her again. "Think what's weird?"

Finn shifted, eyes fixed on the road ahead. "That we didn't know each other's last names until now."

Eli let the thought sit for a beat, like he was actually considering it. Then, finally, he shrugged. "Hadn't really thought about it, to be honest."

Finn hummed, taking another slow pull from her cigarette.

He watched her for a second longer before nodding toward her. "So? What's yours?"

She hesitated. Not because she didn't want to tell him, but because for the first time, she realized she wasn't sure if it even felt like hers anymore.

Still, she answered. "Rowan."

Eli flicked ash out the window, raising a brow. "Finn Rowan." He tested the name, rolling it over his tongue like he was seeing how it fit.

Finn huffed a small, almost amused breath. "Seraphina."

He blinked. "Huh?"

She smirked, tilting her head. "Seraphina Rowan."

Eli studied her for a second, his expression thoughtful. "Seraphina." He let the name settle, before giving a slow nod.

Then, his lips twitched.

"Huh." He mused thoughtfully.

Finn narrowed her eyes. "What?"

He shot her a small smirk. "We're both named after trees."

She snorted, shaking her head. "I don't think Seraphina is a tree."

Eli just tapped his temple knowingly. "No, but Rowan is."

Finn paused, the realization clicking into place. She hadn't really thought about that before.

"Oh."

He smirked again, taking another drag from his cigarette. "So I guess that makes us a couple of forest kids, huh?"

She exhaled a laugh, turning her gaze back out the window as the scenery of Ash Hollow rolled by.

Finn hooked her fingers into the thin plastic loops of the grocery bags, hoisting them up as she followed Eli toward the house. Each bag was loaded, the weight pulling against her arms, so she could only manage two at a time.

Eli, on the other hand, seemed determined to turn it into a personal challenge.

He stacked as many bags as humanly possible, his arms loaded past the elbows, the plastic digging into his skin as he staggered forward. His face reddened from the effort, but his grin never wavered.

By the time they reached the porch, he still refused to set anything down, instead shifting awkwardly to hold the front door open for her.

She shook her head, equal parts amused and exasperated. "You know you could just—"

"Absolutely not." Eli's voice was tight with strain as he heaved his ridiculous load inside.

With an unceremonious thud, he dropped the first armful onto the counter, then let the rest collapse onto the floor.

Finn rolled her eyes fondly as he slumped against the counter, flexing his fingers like he had just fought for his life.

"You act like you just climbed a mountain."

Eli exhaled dramatically. "Don't underestimate the struggle." He shook out his hands like he could still feel the plastic cutting into his skin.

Finn was already heading back outside, head nodding along with '80s rock music pouring from the open garage door. The sound mixed with the scent of pine and gasoline, the morning air still cool despite the creeping summer heat.

She grabbed four more bags—lighter ones this time—and turned back toward the house.

Eli met her there just as she did, snagging the last few. They walked side by side up the porch steps, the plastic crinkling between them.

"Why does it always seem like so much more food when you actually have to put it away?" Eli mused, shifting the bags against his chest.

The side of Finn's mouth quirked. "Well, the prospect of living off canned beans and stale ramen makes anything more than two bags of groceries feel excessive."

He scoffed, nudging the door open with his foot. "I'll have you know, I can get very creative with my canned goods."

She laughed openly as she followed him inside, setting her bags down on the counter. "Oh yeah? Like what—canned bean soufflé?"

Eli grinned, unbagging a frozen pizza and tossing it into the freezer. "Please. My usual diet is a delicate balance of artistry and class."

Finn plucked a box of frozen waffles from one of the bags, holding it up between them. "Yeah? Real sophisticated."

He gasped in mock offense, snatching the box from her hands and shoving it into the freezer before she could say anything else. "Waffles are a delicacy."

They worked through the bags at an easy pace, not yet automatic, but comfortable. Eli pointed out where things went as they unpacked—where to store dry goods, where to stack the cans, and which cabinet held the plates and glasses.

Finn followed his lead, making a mental map of the kitchen as she tucked items away, their movements occasionally overlapping—a brief hesitation here, a near bump there—but nothing awkward. Just learning.

She had just pulled the last thing from her bag—her new toothbrush, still sealed in its plastic packaging—when Eli grabbed a hefty grocery bag full of frozen foods and hooked his other hand around the handle of a bulky jug of laundry detergent.

"I'm gonna take this stuff to the deep freezer," he said, jerking the bag of frozen goods in the direction of the garage—he lifted the detergent—'and drop this by the washer while I'm at it.'"

Finn nodded. "Yeah, I'm just going to put this away."

Eli didn't ask what "this" was. He just gave a lazy salute, hefting the jug to his forehead, and headed toward the front door.

The bathroom light buzzed softly as she flipped it on. The air carried the faint scent of Eli's soap—fresh and lightly citrusy. It wasn't overpowering, just a delicate part of the space.

Her eyes landed on the sink.

Two toothbrushes sat in the holder—one deep green, the other a dulled yellow, its color faded from use.

She stalled.

It was such a small thing. Just a toothbrush and an empty slot. But something about it felt more monumental than that.

She peeled open the packaging and slid her new, bright blue, toothbrush into the holder beside the others, and stepped back, studying them.

Three in a row.

The sight of them—lined up together like they had always been that way—made something in her stomach twist. Not with fear, or unease, but with something softer.

Finn pulled her gaze away before she could dwell on it too long.

She made her way back to her room, heading straight for the neatly packed drawers where she had stored the clothes from the attic. The ones that had once belonged to Nancy.

One by one, she unfolded them, tucking each piece back into the box they had brought them down in.

Then, with much less precision, she grabbed the heap of dirty laundry she had left piled on the window nook and tossed it on top.

She figured now was as good a time as any to finally wash her clothes.

Eli and Frank were already out in the garage, and from the way Eli had described the machines, they were ancient compared to what she was used to. She didn't want to risk breaking anything—or worse, flooding the garage—so she'd have him show her how to work them.

And maybe, just maybe, she could pretend the lingering twist in her stomach was about that.

As she made her way down the stairs and out the front door, a thought surfaced—uninvited, unwelcome, but persistent.

Back home, laundry had been her job.

So had the dishes, scrubbing the floors, vacuuming—every chore in that house had fallen to her. Not because of fairness, or because her mother had asked. But because *he* had made sure of it.

There had been a time, before the marriage, when housework had felt different. She and her mother had made it fun, turning chores into games, racing to see who could fold laundry the fastest, singing together as they worked. It had never been a burden. It had been theirs.

But after the wedding, everything changed.

It hadn't taken long for him to put them in their places.

At first, he had been the perfect gentleman—charming and affectionate, full of grand gestures and sweet words, just as he had been when he convinced her mother to marry him. But once they moved into his house, the illusion cracked.

The love bombing stopped, and the control began.

Her mother wasn't allowed to work anymore. Most days, she read religious books in the sitting room, or more often, shut herself away in the bedroom, growing quieter and smaller. A shadow of the woman she'd once been.

And Finn?

She was left to pick up the slack.

On weekends, when he was home from his high-paying sales job—the one that kept them in that pristine house, the one he never let them forget—he watched her.

She would feel his eyes on her as she scrubbed the kitchen floor, on her hands and knees, as early as eleven years old. She would sense his overbearing presence in the doorway of the laundry room, whiskey glass ever present in hand, as she handled his clothes.

His stained, stale, sweat-reeking clothes.

Finn's breath caught, a sickening churn of bile rising in her throat. For a split second, the present blurred, slipping into the past.

But—

This wasn't then, and this wasn't his house.

The thought moored her to the present, pulling her back before the past could take hold.

She exhaled, slow and steady. Then, adjusting her grip on the box, she hoisted it higher on her hip and stepped outside.

The early afternoon sun had burned away most of the morning chill, but a whisper of last night's coolness still clung to the shade, lingering like a ghost in the untouched corners. As Finn followed the worn footpath around the house, her steps crunched softly over gravel and fallen pine needles, the earthy scent rising with each step.

The garage door stood wide open, spilling its world into the afternoon air—the tang of motor oil and sawdust, the sharper bite of metal, and Eli's ever-present playlist weaving through it all.

Finn hesitated at the threshold, just for a second, just watching.

Frank stood at a workbench, head bent over something small, hands moving with the agile grace of someone who had spent years perfecting his craft. Across the garage, Eli was half-hidden behind his dad's truck, wiping grease from his hands with a streaked rag, his movements unhurried.

For a brief moment, she let herself take it in.

This space, this life—it was nothing like the one she had come from.

There were no eyes tracking her every move, no expectation for her to make herself more miniscule.

She wasn't being watched or controlled.

She wasn't small here.

The thought settled something deep inside her.

Shifting the makeshift laundry basket higher on her hip, she finally stepped inside, her voice light as she called over the music—

"Hey, can I get a crash course in antique laundry machines?"

Frank looked up from his work, his focus momentarily breaking as he registered Finn's presence. A strange, conical magnifying lens sat over his left eye, making his usually keen gray gaze look unnervingly large beneath the glass.

Finn tilted her head, caught off guard by how it distorted his face, giving him the wild-eyed look of a mad scientist.

Frank smirked, clearly catching her reaction. "You never seen a loupe before?" He tapped the glass.

Finn shook her head, her attention drifting downward.

In his palm sat a vintage gold pocket watch, its delicate inner workings exposed like the insides of something alive. Tiny gears and springs gleamed under the workshop light, their thin layer of oil catching the glow. In his other hand, Frank held an impossibly small tool, working with the steady exactness of someone well versed in such mechanisms.

Finn stepped closer, drawn in. "It's beautiful."

Frank gave a hum of agreement, his focus redirected. "Used to belong to my great grandfather. It's been through some things."

His tone was casual, but something in it made Finn pause—like the history was pressed into the watch's casing, more than just time woven into its gears.

Eli, still wiping grease from his hands, leaned lazily against the workbench. "Don't let him fool you. He's been messing with that thing since I was a kid. Pretty sure it's just an excuse to tinker."

Frank huffed, eyes still trained on the intricate mechanics. "While some things should be forgotten, others deserve to be looked after."

The words were simple, but the way he said them made Finn's skin prickle.

Her grip on the box was slipping, the corner digging into her arm as it shifted. She adjusted her hold, clearing her throat. "Uh—so, crash course in antique laundry machines?"

Frank set the watch down carefully on a clean cloth before straightening. "Alright, let's see if you can handle 'em."

Eli scoffed. "They're not that bad. Just don't make the mistake of starting a load and thinking you've got time to do something else. If you're not here to stop the spin cycle manually, you might as well say goodbye to whatever's inside."

Finn groaned dramatically. "Great. A haunted washing machine. That's exactly what I need in my life."

Frank chuckled, shaking his head as he gestured for her to follow. "C'mon, mountain girl. Let's see if we can't keep your clothes in one piece."

Finn blinked.

Mountain girl.

Her gaze flashed toward Eli. He wasn't looking at her—suddenly very focused on scrubbing grease from his already wiped clean hands.

They must have talked about the grocery trip.

A spark of curiosity flashed in her mind. Had Eli mentioned anything else? Had he told Frank about Sarah? About the way she had grabbed Finn's jacket—Kai's jacket—like it physically hurt her to see it? Had he repeated the sharp, venomous edge in Sarah's voice when she spat, "They aren't hers"?

If he had, Frank didn't show it. His expression remained light, and his tone too casual to be anything but deliberate.

Finn exhaled, pushing the thought aside. Instead, she focused on the phrase still lingering in her head, rolling over like a stone in a stream.

Mountain girl.

She followed Frank toward the laundry machines, the words settling into her mind, lingering like the last trace of an echo.

Chapter Fourteen

The laundry lesson had gone better than Finn expected.

The machines were, in fact, primitive—clunky, and temperamental in ways that made her grateful she had asked for help instead of blindly diving in. She could easily imagine the disaster that would have unfolded if she'd started a load and walked away, only to return and find the entire garage submerged and clothes chewed to tattered bits.

But Frank had been as patient and straightforward as he had been when teaching her the shop duties. No wasted words, no condescension—just a clear, simple breakdown of how things worked and what not to do unless she wanted to destroy everything.

By some miracle, she had managed to get her clothes clean without catastrophe.

Well.

Almost.

Eli plucked the freshly laundered pair of his white boxers from the box, holding them up between two fingers. The fabric had taken on a faint, but unmistakable, purple hue.

His socks had suffered the same fate.

He stared at them for a long moment before exhaling through his nose, resigned, like a man shouldering an impossible burden.

Finn pressed her lips together, fighting a laugh. "Listen, in my defense, I did not see that happening."

He shot her a slow, skeptical look. "You washed my stuff with your purple hoodie."

"Yeah, but—" Yeah, but what? That she hadn't been thinking? That it was an accident? Both were true, but neither would save her from the inevitable teasing she was about to endure.

Frank saved her, making a sound suspiciously close to a chuckle before clapping Eli on the back. "Guess you're wearing lilac now, kid."

Eli groaned, shaking his head as he tossed the stained boxers back into the box. "You're lucky I like you, mountain girl."

Finn flashed him a smile. "Oh, I know."

They moved to leave the garage, Finn carrying an armful of freshly laundered shirts while Eli balanced the heavier box of folded clothes against his side.

As they stepped into the sunlight, Finn's gaze drifted back toward the open garage—toward the farthest corner, where something caught her eye.

Against the far wall, half-tucked behind an old shelving unit, stood two bikes.

One was sleek and black, silver spokes glinting in the daylight. The other—the one that made Finn pause—was painted the same soft, powdery blue as the duvet in her room. The exact same shade.

A basket was fastened to the front, its edges frayed with time.

She shifted the warm bundle of clothes, fingers pressing into the fabric as she nodded toward the blue bike.

"That one yours?"

Eli followed her gaze, his expression unchanging as he answered. "Nah," he said easily. "It was my mom's."

Frank stepped closer, rubbing his hands together as he took in the bikes. A fondness settled into his face, softening the edges of his usual stoicism.

"Me and Nance used to take these out on days like this," he mused, his voice dipping into memory. "We'd ride for miles, just to see where we'd end up."

Finn let her eyes trace the lines of the bike—the seat worn from use, the subtle scuffs along the frame. It was clear it had once been cared for, but time had left its marks.

Frank's gaze drifted back to them, something knowing in his smirk as he clapped his hands together. "You two should take 'em out for a spin."

Finn looked up, meeting his eyes, then glanced over at Eli.

For half a second, Eli's expression was unreadable. He shifted slightly. Then, just barely, the corners of his mouth lifted. His eyes scoured the bikes, something playing behind them—excitement, maybe even anticipation.

He was waiting for her answer.

She glanced at the blue bike one more time before looking back at him.

Laundry had been the one thing she needed to get done today, and that was already completed.

Maybe this could be next.

"Alright," Finn said, shifting the shirts to the other arm. "Let's do it."

Eli's grin widened instantly, something flashing in his amber eyes—something almost eager.

Frank nodded in approval, already stepping forward to roll out the black bike first. "Go on, get that stuff back upstairs. I'll give 'em both a once-over, make sure they're good to go."

Eli didn't need to be told twice. He adjusted his grip on the box, jerking his chin toward the house. "C'mon, mountain girl. Let's move."

She followed him inside, but the feeling stayed with her.

Something about this moment felt like more than just a bike ride.

Finn shoved the last of her clothes into the drawers, not bothering with neatness this time. Her mind was already elsewhere—on the bike ride, the way things felt different between her and Eli, and how easy it was to fall into this rhythm with him.

Then her eyes landed on the faintly purple boxers sitting on top of the pile.

She smiled impishly, plucking them up before heading across the hall.

Eli was bent over, lacing up his sneakers, completely unaware as she tossed the boxers at him.

They landed squarely on his head.

Finn bit the inside of her cheek, barely holding back a laugh as she dropped onto his bed beside him.

With exaggerated slowness, Eli reached up, pinching the fabric between two fingers and peeling it off. He turned them over in his hands, inspecting the new color like it was some kind of personal betrayal. Then, with a long, suffering sigh—

"Unbelievable."

Finn grinned. "I think the color suits you."

Eli shot her a look, balled them up, and chucked them back at her. She dodged easily, laughing as they bounced harmlessly onto the bed beside her.

"You're lucky I have a forgiving heart, Rowan," he said, shaking his head as he stood.

"Oh?" she pondered. "And what exactly am I being forgiven for?"

He huffed, stretching his arms overhead before reaching for his jacket. "For my future suffering when I inevitably run out of clean underwear and I'm forced to wear those."

Finn leaned back on her hands, legs swinging. "Just wear them. Who's gonna notice?"

Eli grabbed the boxers again, shaking his head. "Please, Rowan. You really think I can just wear purple boxers and no one will notice?"

She crossed her arms, smirking. "Who's gonna be looking?"

He pressed a hand to his chest. "Please. You underestimate my stud status."

She arched a brow. "You do not give off casual-hookup energy."

He gasped. "How dare—"

"Enigma, then," she said, moving for the door.

"Casanova," he corrected, snatching his jacket. "Put some respect on it."

As Finn and Eli stepped outside, the sharp hiss and rumble of an air compressor filled the air, cutting through the stillness of the afternoon.

By the time they entered the garage, the compressor let out a final burst of air before clicking off, leaving a faint metallic hum in its wake.

Frank was crouched beside the black bike, giving one of the tires a firm squeeze. "They were a little flat from sitting so long," he said, standing up and dusting off his hands. "Didn't find any holes, though, so they should hold up just fine."

Eli stepped forward, running a hand over the handlebars. "Feels good as new."

Frank huffed. "Yeah, well, don't go wrecking 'em on your first ride."

Eli shot him an incredulous look. "Wow. The faith you have in us is inspiring."

Frank turned his attention to Finn. "You ever ridden trails like these before, mountain girl?"

Finn let out a short laugh, shaking her head. "The irony of everyone calling me that is, despite growing up tucked into the mountains, I never really spent time in them."

Eli's expression shifted to mock outrage. "No biking? No hiking?"

She shrugged. "I didn't have anyone to go with."

For a moment, the words hung heavier than she'd meant them to. But before either of them could respond, she tilted her chin toward the bike in front of her, shifting the conversation. "But I'm comfortable on a bike. I never got my license, so I biked everywhere I needed to go back in Colorado."

Frank nodded in approval. "Good. Means you won't go flying into the trees five minutes in."

"I don't know, Pops," Eli grinned maniacally. "She might surprise us."

Finn rolled her eyes. "Just for that, I hope I leave you in my dust."

"Oh, it's like that?" his smirk deepened.

Frank chuckled, stepping back toward the workbench. "You two go on before it gets too late. And try not to break anything—bikes included."

Eli swung his leg over his bike effortlessly, kicking up the stand with the heel of his shoe. "No promises."

Finn watched him for half a second, then gripped the handlebars of Nancy's bike and hopped on.

The seat fit beneath her like it was made for her.

But that didn't make sense—Nancy had been taller.

She shifted, testing the fit, her fingers gripping tighter as realization settled in. Frank must have adjusted it.

A heat flared in her chest.

She exhaled, steadying herself just as Eli leaned toward her, amusement lighting up his eyes.

"You ready, mountain girl?"

Finn lifted her chin. "Born ready."

With that, they pushed off, rolling out of the garage and onto the road. The breeze kissed her skin, and for the first time in a long time—she felt weightless.

The wind whipped through her hair, sending loose strands flying into her mouth as she let out a sharp *whoop* toward Eli.

She had no idea where they were going, but she didn't care.

Eli was ahead of her, his long, reddish curls trailing behind him like the fiery tail of a rocket. At her exclamation, he glanced back. His eyes were alive with the same wild, reckless, joy thrumming through her veins.

Then he whooped right back—louder and unrestrained.

Finn laughed, the sound carried away by the wind. She pedaled harder, heart hammering, the bike beneath her feeling like an extension of herself. The late afternoon air was thick with the scent of sunbaked earth, balmy against her skin.

For the first time in as long as she could remember—there was no past pulling her back.

Just the road, the speed, and the wind.

And the boy ahead of her—burning like a comet.

Still grinning wide, Eli eased off the pedals, letting his speed drop. Finn followed his lead, coasting before gently braking.

He veered onto an old dirt road she hadn't even noticed—a narrow, overgrown path just wide enough for a single vehicle, though any car trying would have to fight through the branches reaching from both sides.

Now that their pace had slowed, they rode closer together, side by side, their breaths still a little ragged from the rush of their ride.

They let the crunch of their tires against the dirt fill the space between them.

Then Eli, still catching his breath, glanced over. "You know... the bikes were one of the things my parents really loved doing together."

Finn looked at him, silently encouraging him to go on.

"They didn't have a lot of hobbies in common," he continued. "They were both happy doing their own thing most of the time, but... this? They made time for it."

His voice softened, thoughtful.

"It wasn't even about where they were going. Half the time, they just rode for the sake of it. A reason to be together, away from everything else."

Finn realized that's exactly what this was.

She watched him as he spoke, the warmth in his expression, and the way his golden-brown eyes glimmered with memory.

Finally, she spoke up, asking, "Did you ever go with them?"

Eli let out a short laugh, shaking his head. "Nah. They usually had Clara watch me while they went. Or I'd hang out at the hardware store with Danny until they got back."

Finn frowned. "You think they didn't want you to slow them down?"

"That's what I thought at the time," Eli admitted. "I was, like, five or six, and I wasn't exactly a pro at riding a bike back then. So yeah, I figured they just didn't want to deal with me struggling to keep up."

He exhaled, his gaze drifting over the sun-dappled path ahead.

"But the older I got, the more I think it was really about them having that time as a couple, instead of as parents."

Finn let that thought settle between them, picturing Eli's parents riding side by side, just as the two of them were now.

Then, softly, she asked, "What about you and Frank? Did you guys ever go on bike rides... after?"

She didn't have to say after what.

Eli shook his head, fingers tapping absently against the handlebars. "No."

His voice was quiet but certain.

"He put the bikes away after," he added, patting the grip like one would the neck of a horse. "I haven't seen him take this out since."

Finn didn't press, and Eli didn't say anything more.

The road had taken on a slight incline, subtle but insistent. Not enough to make the ride difficult, but enough that Finn could feel it in her legs, a slow burn that built with each push of the pedals.

It stretched on like that for a while, until the ground evened out again.

Her mind wandered.

She thought about Frank and Nancy riding this same path, their laughter carried through the trees.

Had it looked the same back then? Had the forest pressed in this closely, or had the trees been more contained in their time?

Had Frank glanced over to find Nancy smiling, breathless from the ride? Had she challenged him to a race, her voice teasing as she took the lead?

Eli was still silent beside her, eyes on the road ahead.

And for the first time, she wondered—if Frank had never taken his bike out again, why had he been so quick to suggest that she and Eli take them out today?

Eli's posture shifted—just barely. His head tilted, his gaze sharpening as it locked onto something up ahead.

Then, without warning, he stopped.

Finn barely had time to react before she was skidding to a halt beside him, tires kicking up a thin cloud of dust. She braced herself against the handlebars, blinking at him.

"A little warning next time?"

Eli didn't answer right away.

He sat motionless, one foot balanced on a pedal, the other planted firmly on the ground. His gaze was fixed on the treeline just ahead—a mysterious expression clouding his face.

Finn followed his line of sight, but all she saw was more of the dense forest. Just trees and shadows, just—

"I wanna show you something."

His voice cut through, but he still didn't look at her. Instead, he swung off his bike in one swift motion, leaning it against the trunk of a nearby tree.

Finn hesitated for only a second before doing the same.

Eli was already moving, stepping toward the trees with a sort of purpose. She watched as he reached for a section of overgrown foliage—thick, tangled branches curling together like fingers trying to keep something hidden.

Then, like drawing back a curtain, he swept them aside.

A path.

Narrow and dark, barely visible beyond the knot of branches. The dirt trail twisted into the trees, gobbled up quickly by the vast forest.

Finn's pulse picked up.

Her fingers flexed at her sides, brushing against the fabric of her jeans, grounding herself in the feel of something solid.

She shot Eli a look. "Do I even wanna know how you found this?"

Finally, he glanced at her. A smirk teasing at the corner of his lips.

"Only one way to find out."

Finn followed Eli deeper into the trees, the narrow path winding ahead of them like a snake slithering through the underbrush.

It wasn't treacherous—no sheer drops or tangled roots waiting to take her down—but it wasn't a casual stroll, either. The uneven ground forced her to watch her step, and low-hanging branches clawed at her sleeves, reaching out like grasping fingers.

The further in they went, the heavier the air became.

It wasn't just the humidity—though that was part of it, the way the warmth of the day felt trapped beneath the thick canopy, suffocating the breeze.

It was something else.

Something darker.

The trees pressed closer together still, their limbs tangling overhead, stealing more and more of the afternoon light. Shadows stretched long, pooling into one another, but she could still make out Eli's shape ahead of her. He moved through the overgrown path with familiarity, barely needing to slow his pace.

Every now and then, he glanced back over his shoulder, amusement dancing across his face when he caught her carefully navigating the uneven ground.

"Not backing out yet, are you?" he teased.

Finn huffed, brushing a clinging spiderweb from her shoulder. "Not a chance."

He chuckled, turning his gaze forward. "Good. You'll wanna see this."

She glanced around, taking in the eerie hush that had settled over the forest. The further they got from the road, the quieter it became—like the trees themselves were swallowing sound.

The silence pressed in, stretching too long and too thick.

Finally, she broke it. "So... where are you actually taking me?"

Eli didn't answer right away. He stepped over a fallen branch, then turned, offering his hand to help her across. She gratefully gripped his forearm for balance as she hopped over.

Only once they were moving again did he finally say, "The main mineshaft."

"The mines!?"

Eli nodded, his voice easy, but something weightier sat just beneath the surface. "Yeah. It's been closed up forever, but... no one's really supposed to go there."

Finn's steps faltered before she caught herself. "Wait—so we're not supposed to be going there?"

A grin grew, but he didn't deny it. "Not technically."

"Fantastic. I love a good trespassing adventure." She groaned.

Eli laughed, the sound low and throaty. "Relax. It's not like we're doing anything wrong, exactly. It's just—" He hesitated, choosing his words carefully.

"They say it's cursed."

Slow goosebumps sprouted down Finn's arms.

The air felt heavier now, thick with something she couldn't quite place. But she tried to shake it off, keeping her tone light. "Oh, great. So not only are we trespassing, we're also waltzing onto haunted land. I love that for us."

Eli smirked, his voice dipping back into a teasing tone. "I mean, that's what they say. You know how small towns are."

"Superstitious?"

"Paranoid."

Finn's brows pulled together. "Paranoid about what?"

Eli exhaled through his nose, pushing a low-hanging branch out of the way. "When we were kids, the adults told us stories about the miners' spirits. Said if you got too close, they'd drag you underground to suffer with them."

Her stomach twisted.

He caught the look on her face and chuckled. "It was just their way of keeping kids from messing around near the mines. They're old—no one knows when a tunnel could collapse. They just didn't want us getting crushed."

Finn nodded solemnly, but something about it didn't sit right.

The silence here was different.

The kind that settled deep into the trees, into the ground itself. Even the wind felt hesitant, slipping between the branches like it didn't want to linger too long.

She kept her voice casual. "So... you don't actually believe in all that ghost story stuff?"

Eli smirked. "What, you do?"

Finn's fingers flexed at her side, but she didn't answer.

They just kept moving, the forest thickening around them, pressing in closer, leading them toward something Finn wasn't sure she wanted to see.

That creeping sensation had been tugging at Finn's spine for minutes, subtle at first, but now impossible to ignore.

The feeling of being watched.

Not just a fleeting paranoia—something purposeful. Something unseen, tracking her every move from just beyond her line of sight.

She forced herself to keep her gaze ahead as the trees thinned, shifting from the dense, suffocating press of the path into something more open. The thick canopy fractured, slashes of golden afternoon light finally cutting through, breaking apart the shadows.

The air lightened.

Finn exhaled slowly, releasing some of the tension coiled in her chest.

Then—

"There it is," Eli murmured, his voice carrying something almost reverent.

He had stopped just ahead, his frame blocking whatever lay beyond.

She stepped closer, peering around him—

Everything inside her lurched and the world twisted.

The ground was gone beneath her feet.

Her vision snapped, severing from the present—

– – –

I'm deep underground.

The blackness is thick, pressing in from all sides. The air is wrong, thick with dust, laced with something stale.

Then—

An explosion.

The tunnel shook, a deafening boom cracking through the earth.

Wooden beams splintering. The ceiling collapsing.

Stone is raining down in suffocating sheets.

And the screams—

Raw. Choking. Desperate.

I'm not just seeing it, I am in it.

Trapped.

Buried.

The heaviness of the earth above crushing, final and unyielding.

Somewhere in the chaos—voices pleading.

A flash of pain—

And then—

Something is yanking me backward.

A force hooked behind my ribs, tearing me free.

The cries stretch away, swallowed by the dark as I'm flung backward—past falling rock, past the wreckage of the collapse—

And suddenly—

I am outside.

Watching.

The mine's entrance gaping before me, black and endless.

Then—

Thick wooden beams slam down, sealing the opening.

The tomb is shut.

A final, brutal silence.

And then—

Gone.

– – –

Reality slammed back into her as her knees hit the ground.

The rough grit of dirt and stone pressed through her jeans, dragging her back to the present. Her breath came hard and uneven, chest rising and falling in sharp bursts. Sweat slicked her forehead despite the shade beneath the trees.

A voice—so close, laced with concern.

"Finn?"

Eli was crouched in front of her, hands braced on his knees, his brows knit together. His eyes darted over her face, scanning for something—an answer, an explanation, anything that made sense.

"What the hell just happened?" he asked. "You just—your knees buckled. Are you okay?"

The vision still clung to her, the echoes of the collapse ringing in her ears, the cries of the trapped miners fading like ghostly whispers. But she couldn't—wouldn't—explain it. Not here. Not now.

She exhaled sharply, forcing steadiness into her voice. "I'm okay."

His gaze lingered, unconvinced, like he was peeling at the edges of what she wasn't saying.

"Finn—"

She wiped her hands against her jeans, shaking off the tremor in her fingers. "I just lost my footing. That's all."

Eli wasn't buying it.

His stare held for a beat too long, searching.

Finn forced a small, tight-lipped smile. "Seriously. I'm fine."

Another moment passed before he finally exhaled, the tension in his shoulders easing—just a little, just enough.

"Alright," he said, voice lighter now, though there was still a thread of skepticism beneath it. "Guess that means you're still good to go inside, huh?"

Her stomach dropped.

Inside?

Her muscles locked before she could stop them, feet rooted to the earth.

Eli, oblivious to the way her entire body had tensed, tilted his chin toward the mineshaft entrance. The wooden beams stood just as they had in her vision—an unyielding barrier. A seal.

"C'mon," he said, flashing a smirk. "You didn't think we came all this way just to look at the outside, did you?"

She forced her arms to relax at her sides, though she wasn't sure who she was trying to convince. Slowly, she stepped forward, trailing a fraction behind Eli.

The entrance loomed ahead, half-swallowed by the creeping wild vines and undergrowth wrapping around the beams like nature itself was trying to pry them open.

She kept close to Eli, just a step behind, his solid presence acting as a buffer between her and the dark threshold ahead.

It looked just like it had in her vision.

Only older and decayed. More final.

Like the earth had never truly let go of what was buried beneath.

The wooden beams sealing the mine had been worn down by time, their once-sturdy planks splintered and sagging under the weight of creeping moss.

Finn's stomach tightened.

She didn't know if it was because of what she had just seen, or because she could still feel the foreboding press of unseen eyes.

Eli stepped forward, gripping an aged board, and with little effort—

Crack.

The board came loose in his hands, dust billowing from the break.

Grinning in satisfaction, he set it aside carefully, brushing off the remnants of decay like he was handling something fragile but familiar.

Finn had settled onto a nearby boulder, watching him work, her expression guarded. She wasn't sure what she was waiting for—herself, maybe, to feel differently. But she didn't.

Eli turned toward her, a roguish smirk tugging at his lips. "Just as easy as I remember."

But then—he really looked at her.

The smile faded.

Her face was too pale, her arms still wrapped around herself as if holding something in. The faint shadows that always lingered beneath her eyes looked darker now, like something had settled behind them, deep and unmoving.

Eli exhaled through his nose, then crouched in front of her, waiting.

Finally, Finn forced out the words.

"I can't go in."

He searched her expression.

Finn shook her head, swallowing thickly. "I just... I can't. I don't know why. I just know I—"

She hesitated, fingers gripping the fabric of her sleeves.

She didn't finish the sentence, because she didn't have to.

Eli glanced back at the mine, at the gaping darkness beyond the broken beam, then back at Finn.

At the tension in her shoulders and the way she was still pulling herself inward, like she was bracing for something unseen.

He sighed, nodding. "You're probably right."

She looked wary, not expecting him to give in so easily.

Eli rubbed the back of his neck, his gaze shifting toward the mine again. His voice was more thoughtful now.

"It's been years since I went in," he admitted. "Who knows how much worse the tunnels are now."

With that, he sank down beside her, stretching his legs out in front of him, fingers idly tracing patterns in the dirt.

Then, after a moment, he said, "I used to come here a lot when I was younger."

Finn turned her head, watching him.

He didn't meet her gaze.

"It felt like... I don't know." His voice was lower now, like a confession. "Like I was drawn to it. Like my own little rebellion against the warnings not to."

Finally, he glanced at her, something unreadable behind his gaze—not just curiosity, but something deeper. Something that had been there long before this moment.

"Guess I never really thought about why."

His voice carried a mindful edge, like he was only just realizing something about himself.

"I guess I also didn't think about why I felt the need to bring you here today."

Finn's breath caught, but she stayed silent, watching him.

Pulling his knees to his chest, he fixed his gaze on the mine entrance. His eyes, usually so sharp and full of mischief, had taken on a faraway look, like he was sifting through old memories, trying to piece something together.

"I never told a soul about coming here," he admitted. "Never came with anyone else before."

His admission settled between them. He wasn't just talking about sneaking off as a kid or breaking some silly rule. He was talking about trust. About choice.

Finn studied him carefully, watching the way his jaw tensed and his fingers sifted the dirt.

Why her?

She didn't ask. She wasn't sure she wanted to know the answer.

The silence between them stretched, present but not uncomfortable. She could feel the undefined meaning of his words pressing in, but she refused to let him sit with it alone.

So she let out a slow breath and offered, "It's peaceful here. Quiet."

Her gaze drifted toward the trees, the fading light filtering through their tangled limbs. The hush of the forest wrapped around them, heavy but not suffocating.

"A good place for thinking," she continued. "I always dreamed of having somewhere like this growing up."

The words left her before she could stop them, a little too honest and exposed. She cut herself short, realizing too late that she'd let another piece of herself slip through.

But when she turned to Eli, expecting curiosity or concern, she found neither.

Instead, something in him seemed lighter. Like her words had eased something for him, even if just a bit.

His lips curved into a wistful smile—one she felt mirrored on her own.

For a long moment, they just sat there, letting the silence stretch onward, neither of them in a rush to fill it.

Then, finally, Eli let out a slow breath and pushed himself to his feet.

"C'mon," he said, holding out a hand. "It's getting late. We should head back before it gets too dark."

Finn hesitated only a moment before slipping her hand into his, letting him pull her easily to her feet. His grip was as warm and steady as she'd come to expect.

He added lightly, "Not to mention, I'm starving."

Finn huffed a laugh, grateful for the shift in mood.

Eli lingered just a second longer before turning back toward the path.

And just like that, they left the mine behind.

Chapter Fifteen

he ride back no longer hummed with the same exhilaration that had sent them flying down the road before.

Finn's mind was still tangled in the vision, unwilling to let it go.

The rush of wind against her face should have been enough to clear it, to push it into the background where it belonged. But beneath the cool evening air, she could still hear them—the distant, echoing screams of the men buried beneath the earth.

She tightened her grip on the handlebars, forcing herself to focus on the present, on the steady pedaling, and keeping pace with Eli instead of slipping back into the past.

The road stretched on, their tires kicking up soft plumes of dust. They didn't speak much, but they didn't need to.

Some things weren't meant to be put into words. Not yet.

By the time they rolled back into the driveway, the sun had dipped lower, bleeding gold and orange across the sky, sinking toward the tree line.

Eli veered toward the garage first, and Finn followed, both of them propping their bikes back against the wall where they belonged.

Frank wasn't there.

She had half-expected to find him, still hunched over the workbench, tinkering with that pocket watch. But the space was empty, his tools resting neatly where they'd been hours ago.

Without a word, they headed inside, both grabbing bottles of water from the fridge and downing half the contents in greedy gulps.

Still no Frank.

No sound of movement or scent of dinner filling the air.

Eli pulled the bottle from his lips, brow furrowing.

"It's way too early for him to be in bed," he muttered, more to himself than to her.

Finn watched as he started toward the stairs, likely heading to check his dad's room.

But before he reached the first step, the creak of the screen door echoed through the hall.

Eli turned, and Finn did too, something pulling her forward as she stepped past him toward the sound.

The sunroom was dim, bathed in just the golden light of early evening. The glow filtering softly through the dirty windows, painting everything in amber hues.

It was breathtaking.

The sunroom was alive.

Greenery spilled from every surface, vines clinging lazily along the edges of the glass, trailing down from hanging planters in leafy cascades. The air carried the scent of earth and something faintly floral, warm and rich, like a place that had been lived in—loved—for a long time.

On one side of the room, wicker patio furniture sat nestled beneath the windows, the cushions plump and inviting.

But it was the other side that stopped Finn in her tracks.

Easels lined the far wall, each one holding a painting, vibrant and bathed in color.

A wildflower meadow, glowing beneath the sun. A sunrise spilling light across rolling hills. An apple orchard in full bloom, petals caught mid-drift in the breeze.

She stepped forward, drawn to them.

Eli's voice was quiet when he spoke. "This was my mom's sanctuary."

Finn could feel it in the room, in the warmth of the brushstrokes and the way everything here had been preserved.

She traced the edge of an easel lightly with her fingertips, taking in the way each painting held so much light, so much life.

"Now I know where you get it," she murmured.

He let out a small, self-conscious huff. "I don't know about that. She painted things people actually wanna look at."

Finn turned to him, shaking her head.

"No," she said, clear and certain. "She painted how she saw the world."

Her gaze drifted back to the easels.

"You do too."

Eli didn't answer, but something in his expression shifted—a glimmer of thought behind his eyes.

Then his attention was drawn past her, out the wide sunroom windows.

Finn followed his gaze.

Outside, in the backyard, Frank stood near the firepit, stacking thick logs. The flames were already climbing, their glow flickering against the deepening sky.

Eli exhaled through his nose, a slow smirk tugging at the corner of his mouth.

"Guess we found him."

Eli and Finn stepped out onto the back porch, the evening air filled with the scent of burning wood. The fire crackled steadily in the pit, casting shadows across the yard.

Frank was adjusting the logs, his face illuminated in the golden light. He nudged a stray ember back into place with the toe of his boot before finally looking up.

Eli huffed, crossing his arms. "What are you doing, old man?"

"Well," he said, with a dry look and a gruff, "figured you two had a big day. Stocking up the house and taking the bikes out."

His gaze flashed to Finn. "He work you too hard yet?"

Finn smirked as Eli scoffed. "*Pfft.* She's still standing, isn't she?"

Frank just gave her a small, knowing grin, then motioned toward the cooler beside the three camp chairs he'd arranged around the fire. With a suctioning *pop*, he lifted the lid.

Inside, nestled in a bed of ice, were bottles of water, sodas, hotdog buns, and two packs of hotdogs with all the fixings.

Then he leaned down, grabbing a bundle of sharpened wooden sticks from beside his chair. Handing one to each of them and keeping the last for himself.

"Figured roasting dogs on the fire sounded simple and nice."

Eli clapped Frank on the back, grabbing some logs to really get the fire going, while Finn eased into the middle chair, the warmth of the flames licking at her skin.

Once the fire was properly roaring, they each skewered a hotdog, holding them over the flames until the skins split and sizzled.

Finn's: ketchup and relish.

Frank's: just mustard.

Eli's?: Everything.

Sauerkraut. Relish. Mayo. Mustard. Ketchup.

She stared at it, expression pinching.

Frank took one look and let out a low whistle. "Son... that's a monstrosity."

"That's gonna be all over your face in thirty seconds." Finn snorted.

He just grinned proudly, taking a massive bite, completely unfazed as half the toppings dripped onto his hand.

"You eat like you don't plan on seeing another meal." Frank said, shaking his head.

Eli shrugged, licking the mess off his fingers with a smirk. "Gotta enjoy life, Pops. Even the messy parts."

Finn chuckled, sinking deeper into her chair.

The fire crackled, filling the spaces between them with its steady song.

The night settled around them with the scent of burning wood and the distant chirp of crickets beyond the tree line.

They ate their first hotdogs with the kind of ravenous focus that only came after a long, exhausting day. No talking, just the steady chorus of chewing, swallowing, and the occasional rustle of the fire as the logs shifted.

By the time Finn finished her last bite, she was already reaching for another, adjusting her roasting stick over the flames. Eli, just as eager, did the same—holding his next hotdog expertly over the fire with one hand as Frank leaned over to the cooler.

With a rustling of ice, he pulled out three sodas, setting his own in the cupholder of his chair before tossing one to Finn.

She barely caught it, the condensation slick against her fingers. The tab popped with a satisfying hiss.

Frank tossed the last to Eli, who snatched it one-handed without breaking his focus on the fire.

Settling back into his chair, Frank stretched out his legs with a content sigh, the firelight flickering in his tired eyes.

"Alright," he mused, casting a glance between them. "Anybody got any scary stories?"

Finn and Eli exchanged an amused look, but neither spoke up.

Frank sighed exasperatedly, shaking his head. "Figures," he muttered. "Leaving it up to the old buck."

He leaned forward, staring into the fire. The glow of the flames deepened his expression, thoughtful and distant—like he was sifting through a lifetime of stories, deciding which ones were worth telling.

Finn watched him carefully, with no intention to speak.

She didn't even realize she was going to.

Her tongue moved before her good sense could catch it. "What about a story about the old mine?"

The second it left her lips, a hush seemed to settle over them—the fire suddenly too loud in her ears, the night going a little too still.

Eli's gaze snapped to her, something shadowed behind the curiosity in his eyes.

Frank's fingers drummed lightly against the side of his soda can.

His jaw worked for a moment before he exhaled.

"Well now," he murmured, his voice carrying a different weight than before. "That's a hell of a thing to ask about."

The fire popped, sending a spray of embers into the night.

Frank watched them rise, glowing red against the dark.

Then he leaned back in his chair, the firelight flickering over his face, carving deep shadows into his features. He let the moment settle, gaze dashing between them, gauging their anticipation.

"You know," he began, his voice dipping lower, "any kid who grew up in Ash Hollow has heard some version of this story."

Finn shifted, fingers tightening around the cool metal of her soda can. Eli remained still, but she could tell—he was listening just as intently.

Frank took an unhurried sip of his drink before setting it aside.

"They say the mine was cursed from the start," he continued, his tone slipping into something almost casual—like he was reciting a well-worn tale passed through generations. "Back when the mines were booming, men came from all over the country, chasing the promise of fortune."

He tipped his chin toward Eli. "Silver, coal, lead... hell, some thought they'd even strike gold."

His voice carried that edge of knowing—of something unspoken beneath the words.

"But what most people don't know," he added, his sharp eyes gleaming in the firelight, "is that it wasn't the cave-in that doomed the mine."

Frank let the pause stretch, drawing them in before continuing.

"The collapse? That was just the final nail in the coffin."

The fire spat another ember into the dark, momentarily casting his face in an eerie, molten glow.

"Things had already been going wrong long before that," he murmured, his voice turning thoughtful. "Men vanishing in the tunnels. Tools going missing, only to turn up rusted and broken—like they'd been buried underground for decades."

Finn swallowed hard. "What happened to the men?"

She wasn't sure she wanted to know the answer.

Frank exhaled, shaking his head. "No one knows. They'd clock in for their shift, head down into the tunnels... and never come back."

The fire crackled between them, its steady hiss filling the silence, stretching into the space where answers should have been.

"Some folks said they ran off," Frank went on, his voice quieter now, like he was speaking more to the flames than to them. "That the work was too damn hard, and the conditions too rough. Maybe they just packed up and left."

His gaze flickered, distant, reflecting the orange glow of the fire.

"But the men who worked beside them?" His jaw tensed slightly. "They didn't buy that."

A sharp pop from the fire made Finn jump, the moment fracturing like splintered wood.

Frank let out a breath and leaned back again, stretching his legs, and letting the story settle into the night before continuing.

"Then came the cave-in."

His voice dipped just enough to send a shiver trailing down Finn's spine.

"They say it happened during the night shift," he murmured, tapping his fingers against the armrest of his chair. "An explosion—one meant to blast open new seams of coal. Only... something went wrong."

Finn didn't realize she had wrapped her arms around herself until her fingers pressed painfully through her shirt. She already knew where this was going.

"Instead of simply breaking through rock," Frank continued, rubbing a hand along his jaw, "the tunnels collapsed."

The fire cast shadows across his face as he spoke. "They say you could hear the rumble from miles away."

His voice lowered.

"Like a beast waking up underground."

Finn's stomach knotted.

She had heard it, too.

She had felt it herself.

The vision lurched forward in her mind. The suffocating dark. The screaming. The sound of the earth caving in and sealing the men inside.

Finn forced herself to focus, to keep herself anchored here—by the fire. To the present. But the past, and the echoes of it, still pulled at her psyche.

Frank leaned forward, his voice dipping lower still, nearly lost beneath the crackling fire.

"The worst part?" he murmured, his words barely more than a breath.

"No one went in to dig them out."

Her stomach hollowed out, a creeping, ice-cold dread spilling through her veins.

"Wait... what?" she managed, her voice thin.

Eli spoke next, his tone flat. "They just... left them."

Frank nodded, slow and deliberate.

"The mining company called it a lost cause," he said, his voice heavy. "Said it was too unstable. That there were no survivors, so what was the point?"

The fire snapped sharply, sending a spray of embers skyward. Neither Finn nor Eli flinched this time. Neither moved at all.

Finn swallowed against the dryness in her throat.

She could still hear them. The men from her vision, screaming for help as the walls caved in around them. She could still feel the impact of those wooden boards slamming into place—sealing them in.

"So they just... closed the mine?" Her voice was strained.

Frank exhaled sharply, shaking his head. "They didn't just close it."

Bending down, he picked up a small rock, rolling it between his fingers, the rough edges catching against his calloused skin.

"They boarded it up," he said. "Sealed it shut. And they made damn sure no one ever went in again."

Finn barely breathed.

Because she had seen it happen. Lived it.

The terror of being buried alive. The desperate cries swallowed by the earth.

Frank turned the stone over once more, then tossed it into the fire. It disappeared instantly, consumed by the flames.

"They say those men never left," he murmured.

The night seemed to still.

Finn's heartbeat pounded against her ribs, sharp and insistent.

Frank's face was unreadable, his gaze dashing between them, searching.

"Kids in this town have been warned for generations," he said. "Stay away from the mines."

The look in his eyes intensified.

"Because if you get too close..."

His voice dropped to a whisper, something almost devout.

"They'll pull you down with them."

Finn kept her eyes locked on the flames, her mind tangled in the echoes of her vision—the deafening explosion, the choking dust. The hands clawing at collapsing rock.

For a moment, no one spoke.

Then Eli let out a short laugh, shaking his head. "Damn. Spooky campfire story, Dad."

Frank smirked, stretching back in his chair, clearly pleased with himself. "Well, I can't let the title of local storyteller go to waste."

Eli huffed, grabbing his soda. "I'd say you really got Finn good with that one."

She blinked, realizing too late that she hadn't reacted—hadn't laughed or made some sarcastic comment to brush it off. She'd just sat there, too quiet, still tangled in a truth she couldn't explain.

Frank glanced toward her, amused at first—but then something in his expression shifted, his smirk fading.

She forced a smile, though it felt wrong. Hollow.

He let out a satisfied chuckle anyway, finishing off his soda and tossing the empty can into the cooler with a dull clink.

"This old man still has it," he mused, pushing up from his chair, stretching his arms overhead before clapping Eli on the shoulder as he passed. "I'm calling it a night."

As he stepped onto the porch, he cast a glance back over his shoulder. "Make sure that fire's all the way out before you head in."

Eli waved him off without looking. "Yeah, yeah, we got it."

The porch door creaked shut behind him, and just like that, Finn and Eli were alone under the glow of the dwindling fire.

Eli didn't say anything at first, but Finn could feel his eyes on her, steady and searching.

Then, finally—

"Okay," he murmured. "You're acting weird."

She kept her gaze on her hands, watching the faint tremor in her fingers. She clenched them into fists, willing the shaking to stop, but the tension in her body only deepened.

The vision. The mine. Frank's story.

It wasn't just folklore. It wasn't just some ghost story passed down through generations. She had seen it—felt it. And she couldn't keep holding onto that alone.

Her throat tightened, the words catching before they could rise. She exhaled slowly, trying to ease the grip of something unseen wrapping around her.

Then, finally, she turned to Eli.

The moment their eyes met, his expression shifted.

Gone was the teasing, and the easy smirk. The casual amusement.

Instead, there was something stalwart in the way he looked at her. No impatience, or pressure. Just a silent openness, a willingness to listen.

Finn swallowed, pulse stuttering beneath her skin.

And then, in a voice barely above a whisper, raw but certain—

"I need to tell you something."

The fire crackled softly, but Finn barely heard it. The warmth of the flames, the cool press of night air against her—none of it registered.

Her focus narrowed to her heartbeat hammering in her ears as she forced herself to steady her breathing.

"And please, please don't think I'm crazy."

Her voice wavered, carrying something fragile, something barely held together.

Eli's brows knit—holding no doubt, or skepticism, just concern.

"I won't."

He said it with certainty, no hesitation in his voice. No questions or reassurances, just unwavering trust.

"Look, Finn... we haven't known each other long, but I think we both know this isn't exactly a normal friendship."

His lips curled, not into a smirk, but something understanding.

"I've trusted you with things I've never said out loud before," he continued, his voice strong and sturdy. "I hope you can trust me, too."

Finn swallowed hard, something tight and aching settling in her chest.

She took a breath—shaky, uneven—letting it out all at once.

And then, she told him.

About her gift. The way she had always felt, and seen, things others couldn't. How the world had never felt quite as empty as it should.

She told him about Josiah and about the thing that loomed behind him, its burning eyes flickering like lantern flames.

She told him about the mine. The explosion. The thundering rumble of the collapsing tunnel. The trapped men screaming, clawing for escape, their terror still pulsing in her chest like a heartbeat.

And then—about the boy by the lake.

She left out the word ghost.

Not because she didn't think Eli would believe her.

But because she wasn't sure she was ready to say it out loud.

Her voice faltered near the end, her fingers tightening around each other in her lap, knuckles pale against the firelight.

Eli didn't interrupt.

He just listened, eyes steady and shoulders relaxed, taking in every word.

Letting her speak and be heard.

Before Eli could say anything—before she could second-guess herself—Finn pushed forward, telling him the last part. The part she had been most afraid to share.

Her nightmare.

She told him about the lake, the one from the painting in his room. The same lake where she had met the boy.

She told him about *him*.

How he had been standing there at the end of the dream, his silhouette framed against the water, an easel set up before him. How Eli had been painting, each brushstroke concentrated, his focus unwavering.

And how, when he finally turned to face her—

His amber eyes had been filled with fire.

He didn't flinch, or speak.

Finn's heart pounded.

She had told him everything.

And now, he just sat there. Silent.

The longer the silence stretched, the heavier it became, pressing against her, wrapping around her like a slow-closing fist.

Maybe this had been a mistake. Maybe she shouldn't have said anything.

Maybe—

She willed herself to breathe, but the pressure of his silence was unbearable. Finally, she lifted her gaze, searching his face for something—anything.

Tears burned behind her eyes, threatening to slip free.

And then, he looked at her.

His expression wasn't one of doubt, or disbelief.

It was something deeper. Something she didn't understand.

Her voice was barely above a whisper. "Eli?"

A tear slipped down her cheek.

And finally—finally—he spoke.

Eli's voice was calm, but there was something beneath it, something wound tight and waiting.

"What was the boy's name?"

Of all the things she had just told him, that was what stuck with him?

She hadn't been sure what to expect, but it wasn't this. The way his expression sharpened, his focus narrowing in on that single question like it was the only thing that mattered.

She didn't know why, but relief flooded through her. He wasn't pulling away, or looking at her like she was insane. He wasn't dismissing her.

She let out a slow breath, and let the name slip from her lips.

"Kai."

She swallowed, steadying herself. "He told me his name was Kai."

The change in Eli was instant.

His entire body went rigid, his normally warm features going pale. His hands, once resting idly on his knees, balled into tight fists.

The fire crackled, a log splitting apart with a loud snap. But Eli didn't react. He just stared, unmoving, his jaw clenched so tightly she thought his teeth might break.

Finn's stomach twisted.

He knew that name.

Eli gave a small shake of his head, as if trying to dislodge the thought, his curls bouncing with the movement.

"No..." The word was barely audible, more breath than sound. "No, that can't be right."

His brows furrowed, his whole expression tightening like he was trying to force a puzzle piece into place, but it wasn't fitting.

For the first time since she'd met him, Eli looked completely lost.

Finn watched, heart pounding, as the sure, unshakable boy in front of her started to unravel.

Eli was supposed to be the grounded one, the logical one who had everything figured out.

She was the one who teetered on the edge, always seconds from coming undone.

But now—

Now, it was him.

Finn sat frozen.

She had trusted him with this. With all of it.

And now—now he was shutting down.

Panic furled tight in her chest, rising like acid in her throat. Was he going to reject her now? Pull away and pretend none of this had happened?

Her pulse roared, viciously.

Before she could lose him, before the moment slipped too far, she reached out with an unsteady hand and placed it gently on his arm.

Eli stilled.

The quiet murmurs under his breath stopped cold.

Slowly, cautiously, he lifted his gaze to hers.

Their eyes locked—both of them shaken, both standing at the edge of something neither could take back.

Finn gulped hard, her voice a sliver in the night.

"He put the leather jacket on me."

Confusion flashed through the storm in Eli's eyes, but he didn't move.

"He gave it to me by the lake, before he... disappeared." The last word stuck in her throat.

She searched his face, willing him to believe her.

"I found the crescent moon pendant in the pocket," she continued, her voice gaining strength, solidifying with each word. "The one Sarah ripped from my neck."

Eli's fingers twitched, and his throat bobbed with a hard swallow, the muscle in his jaw ticking as it clenched and unclenched.

His nostrils flared. His gaze darted away, for just a second, like he couldn't look at her. Not yet.

Then, finally, he exhaled.

It was unsteady, just barely there.

And when he spoke, his voice was raw.

"...That was Kai's jacket."

The words settled between them like a stone dropping into deep water—silent, but impossible to ignore.

Finn barely breathed.

"And the pendant..." His voice was rough at the edges now. "The crescent moons... that was their thing. His and Sarah's."

His eyes lifted to hers.

And in them, there was no room for doubt.

Just fear—and recognition.

Just the slow, sinking feel of something that had been waiting in the dark, creeping closer with every second.

Finn watched as Eli's lips parted, as if he wanted to say more, to fill the hollow space between them. But when he finally spoke, his voice barely carried over the fire's dying crackle.

"...Finn, Kai's been missing for over a year."

The words hit like a cold wind, cutting straight through her.

The tears that had been pressing at the edges of her vision finally slipped free, hot against her skin. She barely managed to find her voice, the sound broken and fragile.

"Eli..." Her breath wavered, her body trembling.

She blinked hard, but it didn't stop the fresh wave that followed.

She knew it. Had felt it deep in her bones, but saying it aloud—giving it shape, and truth—

It was like forcing herself to let go of something she had never really held at all.

"Kai's dead."

The fire's last ember flickered weakly.

Then, just like that, it burned out.

The night stretched around them, vast and silent.

Eli didn't move or speak.

But Finn could feel it, pressing in from all sides.

Everything had changed.

Chapter Sixteen

li exhaled a single word into the dark.

"...Shit."

Finn watched as he swiped a hand down his face, dragging it over his mouth before letting it drop heavily to his side. His jaw still tense and his throat bobbing with a silent swallow, like he was wrestling with something he couldn't quite put into words.

Something had shifted.

It wasn't just realization—it was acceptance.

Like a truth he had been avoiding had finally caught up to him.

Then, without a word, Eli stood.

It wasn't abrupt, but there was an urgency in the way he rose to his feet, his gaze never leaving hers. Before Finn could react, his hands found her arms—not gripping, not forcing, just silently reassuring.

And then, in one sure motion, he pulled her against him.

Her breath caught, her body tensing for only a second before she let herself sink into him. His arms wrapped around her, firm and secure, holding her close to the warmth of his chest.

She pressed her cheek against him, feeling the steady, solid rhythm of his heartbeat beneath her palm. Strong. Real. Unwavering.

And then—she broke.

The emotion she had been holding back for too long crashed through her like a tidal wave, breaking past every barrier she had tried to build. A ragged sob tore from her throat, wretched and unrestrained, her shoulders shaking with the force of it.

And Eli didn't let go.

He only held her tighter, as if bracing against the storm, as if trying to shoulder some of the burden pressing down on her.

As if, somehow, holding onto her might keep them both from falling apart.

Finn had no more tears left. The storm inside her had spent itself, leaving behind only exhaustion—deep and resounding, like the still air after a dense rain. Her body felt lighter, yet hollow, like something had been pulled from her and left behind in the ashes of the fire.

She exhaled a slow, unsteady breath and stepped back, just enough to meet Eli's eyes.

The warmth of him still lingered against her skin.

The fire had long since burned down, but in the dim light of the night, his gaze remained unwavering.

Finn swallowed against the tightness in her throat and whispered, "Thank you."

She didn't have to explain.

Eli didn't ask for what.

He just nodded, his silent understanding wrapping around her like an unspoken promise.

For believing her, and not questioning what she'd told him. For accepting it as truth—because it was.

For staying.

Eli let out a slow breath through his nose, then ran a hand through his curls, shaking out the tension in his shoulders before breaking the silence with a dry chuckle.

"Well... that was a lot."

A startled huff of laughter escaped Finn before she could stop it.

"Yeah," she admitted, her voice hoarse. "It really was."

Eli shot her a look—something wry but gentle—before tilting his head toward the house.

"C'mon, mountain girl. Let's go inside."

Finn pressed her lips together, the faintest hint of a smile forming, small but real.

She let her gaze drift back to the firepit one last time. Only blackened wood and faint wisps of smoke remained, twirling in the cool night air.

Something inside her still felt shaken.

But lighter.

And together, they stepped inside.

The house was void of sound. The only noise was the creak of the wooden floors beneath their feet, each step feeling too resonant.

Eli didn't lead Finn straight to his room. Instead, he paused at the top of the stairs, lifting a hand in a wordless motion for her to stop.

Then, with a single finger pressed to his lips, he turned toward the closed door at the end of the right hall.

Frank's room.

Finn held her breath as Eli crept closer, his movements careful—like he was testing the air itself for any shift in sound. He tilted his head toward the door, listening.

Silence.

A long moment passed before he exhaled quietly, nodding to himself in satisfaction.

Then, he pivoted back toward his own room, moving past her with an ease that felt instinctual.

Finn followed.

Eli pulled the door open just enough for them to slip inside.

She hesitated for the briefest second, tension still woven into her muscles. But Eli's gesture toward the bed was silent reassurance.

She perched on the edge, hands knotting in her lap.

Eli didn't sit right away.

Instead, he swiped a hand down his face, dragging exhaustion from his features before finally lowering himself beside her.

"Alright," he said, the words unfaltering. "Let's talk about Kai."

Finn braced herself as Eli leaned forward, his gaze distant.

"When he disappeared, it shook the whole damn town." His voice had an edge now, something simmering beneath the words. "Nothing like that had ever happened here before. I mean—people don't just vanish in a place like this. Not these days."

Finn watched expectantly, letting him unravel the story.

"The FBI got involved. It was that serious." He shook his head, as if even now, it still didn't make sense. "But no matter how much they searched or how many interviews they did, no matter how many times they turned this place inside out—nothing. All that our search parties ever turned up was his bike, dumped off a deer trail by the clearing where the festival was. Besides that, it was like he walked into thin air."

He scoffed, fingers pressing into his temple.

"After a while, they called it. They closed the case, and presumed him dead. Mystery unsolved. Everyone was supposed to move on."

He turned then, his gaze locking onto hers.

"But people don't move on from things like that."

And Finn could see it now—in the set of his shoulders, the dark glimmer in his deep-set eyes.

The implication of it was still there.

Lingering.

Eli shifted, sitting up straighter as he reached toward the bookshelf beside his bed. His movements were casual—but there was a distinctness to them that caught Finn's attention.

She watched as he pulled down a small stack of books, their frayed edges marking years of use. Town history books.

Something about the way he handled them made her pause. His fingers brushed over the spine of one, hesitating for the briefest moment before subtly shifting another in front of it. A movement so minute she might not have noticed if she hadn't been watching him so closely.

But before she could think too much about it, Eli had already cracked open one of the thinner books, flipping through the pages. He didn't skim, or delay—just turned straight to what he was looking for.

And then, from between the pages, he pulled out a folded piece of paper.

Finn barely had time to react before he smoothed it out between them on the bed.

Her breath caught.

It was a missing person's flyer.

Finn's pulse stuttered as she stared down at Kais' face, frozen in time. He looked exactly as he had at the lake—the same sharp jawline, the same blue eyes—but here, he was smiling. A wide, genuine grin that crinkled the corners of his eyes, so different from the solemn, ghostly presence she had met in the woods.

She took in the details.

The silver chain around his neck, barely visible beneath his shirt.

The leather jacket.

She could almost feel it again on her shoulders, the way it had draped over her like a second skin.

When Eli finally spoke, the certainty in his voice left no room for doubt.

"That's him, isn't it?"

Finn forced herself to meet his gaze.

And then, resolutely answered—

"Yes."

She pressed her lips together, exhaling through her nose as her eyes locked back on the flyer.

"I don't really understand it," she admitted. She traced the edges of the paper with her fingertips, feeling its creased surface beneath her touch. She could feel him watching her. Waiting.

She couldn't tell him everything.

Not yet.

Not the fullness of the vision at the lake—the way she had felt the icy water closing over her, filling her lungs. Or the blind panic and desperate struggle against something impossible to fight. How she had drowned with him.

Not the part of the dream—where she had seen him walk into the lake willingly, his body surrendering to the depths like it was the only escape left to him.

Not yet.

"But I know they're connected somehow."

Finally, she lifted her gaze, meeting Eli's eyes, willing him to see how sure she was.

"He's not in the mine," she continued, her voice gaining strength. "At least... not now."

Eli didn't react right away, but kept his eyes trained on hers, searching.

Finn held her breath, waiting for the doubt, for the skepticism—for him to tell her she was wrong.

But it never came.

Instead, Eli just nodded. Slow and thoughtful.

Finn exhaled, the tension in her shoulders easing as he stayed with her. As he simply... listened.

That alone gave her the strength to keep going.

"I can't let this go," she admitted, her voice firmer now. Her gaze dropped back to the flyer, to Kai's frozen smile—so full of life, but so painfully still.

"Kai won't be able to rest until we figure this out. Until we understand what the mines have to do with him." Her throat tightened, but she pushed forward. "I can feel it, Eli. He's slipping. Whatever hope he had of peace... it's fading."

Eli's brows pulled together, his hands pressing firmly against his knees. He didn't speak, but Finn could see the way his mind was working—turning over every piece, fitting it together, feeling the gravity of what she was saying.

"And it's not just him," she continued, "I keep thinking about what your dad said—the way those miners died. Not instantly in the collapse like the company claimed, but trapped. Waiting for a rescue that never came."

Her throat constricted further as she shook her head. "I think they're still waiting. And I think... somehow, that's part of what connects them to Kai."

A hush settled between them, thick and unmoving.

Outside, a soft wind pressed against the windowpane, leaving a faint and hollow whistle to fill the space between them.

Eli exhaled heavily, fingers briefly gripping the back of his neck before he let them drop.

"Okay," he said finally, nodding once. "So, we figure it out."

Finn blinked, caught off guard by how easily he said it.

"You believe me?"

Eli's lips twitched, but there was no amusement in his expression. "I told you, Finn. I trust you. And I know this town has its secrets." His voice lowered a step. "So... yeah. We figure it out."

Something inside her loosened, just a little.

But before she could take even the smallest breath of relief, a new thought surged forward—so sudden it made her stomach drop.

Her pulse jumped, sending her heart thudding unevenly.

Eli caught it immediately. His gaze sharpened, the ease from a second ago vanishing. "What?"

"Josiah," she whispered.

Eli sat up straighter, every fiber of him focused on her. "You think he's connected?"

She nodded, her thoughts spinning, the pieces aligning in ways she didn't fully understand yet. "I don't know how, but... the thing that follows him—it's like it's latched onto him. And what if that's what happens when a spirit like Kai gets... lost?"

Eli didn't move. Didn't blink. The muscle in his jaw ticked, tension rolling through his shoulders as her words settled.

But then he nodded. Not slow or uncertain—just firm.

"Then we better figure this out before Kai ends up like that."

Finn exhaled shakily, wrapping her arms around herself. Her mind still spun with unanswered questions, but for the first time since all of this started, something inside her had shifted.

The fear was still there. The veiled mystery.

But now, they had a direction.

"So, what's our best shot at talking to Josiah?" Finn asked, forcing herself to focus on the next step instead of drowning in the enormity of it all.

Eli ran a hand through his curls, eyes narrowing in thought. "He doesn't come into town much these days," he admitted. "Mostly keeps to himself in the woods. But when it's warmer like this, he shows up more often. We might get lucky."

Finn nodded, turning the idea over in her mind. "And... you've actually talked to him before?"

"Yeah," Eli said, shifting on the bed. "Not often. He doesn't talk to most people. But I've had a few conversations with him."

A beat of hesitation. Then—

"I've helped him out here and there," he added. "Given him some food when I had extra. Even gave him some hiking boots a few months back—his old ones were in rough shape."

That tracked. When she'd seen Josiah outside the shop, she'd noticed his boots—worn but still solid. Now she knew why.

She studied Eli for a moment, warmth growing in her chest.

Of course, he would be the kind of person to look out for Josiah.

"So, we keep our eyes open," she said, mostly to herself. "And if we see him, we try to talk to him."

Eli nodded. "Exactly."

Finn glanced at the history books stacked between them. "Do you mind if I take these to my room? I want to go through them. See if I can pick up on anything."

"Of course. Take whatever you need," he said immediately.

As she stepped toward the door, gripping the handle, Eli's voice stopped her.

"Hey."

She paused, glancing back over her shoulder.

Eli was watching her, his expression softer now, but more certain.

"We can do this," he said, his voice steady. "I know we can. Together."

Finn felt the words settle deep in her chest, solid and sure.

She swallowed past the lump rising in her throat, then gave a small, grateful nod.

Together.

Without another word, she slipped out of the room, the door closing softly behind her.

Finn drifted in and out of sleep, her mind restless, caught between dreams and waking.

There were no nightmares—not really.

But there were images. Flashes and pieces she didn't yet understand.

Kai, standing by the lake.

His gaze wasn't as piercing as before. It was more gentle. Sadder. Like he was waiting for something—waiting for her—but losing hope.

Then—darkness.

The gaping mouth of the mine. Shadows shifting behind the decayed wooden boards, their faces blurred and indistinct.

Except for their eyes.

Burning and flickering like dying embers.

Then—Kai again.

But this time, sitting cross-legged on the dirt floor, folded into the darkness. Candlelight skittered across his face, the glow casting sharp shadows over his features.

He wasn't alone.

But before she could see who was with him—

Light.

A field of wildflowers, golden and endless, swaying gently beneath a mellow sun. The scent of earth and honeysuckle filled the air, soft and sweet.

And just beyond the flowers—

A woman.

She turned to face Finn, her expression muted, but a knowing smile curving her lips.

Her eyes—

Soft, golden brown. Warm as sunlight. Filled with something Finn couldn't name.

A slow breath left her.

And finally—finally—she slept soundly.

Finn moved through her morning with an unfamiliar sense of ease, a luxury she hadn't given herself in days. There was no rush, no pressing urgency gnawing at the back of her mind, just the simple act of going through the motions at her own pace.

She stood in front of the dresser, running her fingers lightly over the fabric of her clothes before finally settling on something basic and comfortable. The decision felt small, insignificant, but it was hers to make. That was enough.

Her shower was longer than usual, the hot water washing away what was left of the exhaustion she hadn't realized was still clinging to her. Steam billowed around the room, wrapping around her, protective and cleansing.

Once she finally stepped out, she wiped a hand over the fogged mirror, revealing her reflection in scattered streaks of clarity. For the first time in as long as she could remember, she didn't look completely drained. The dark circles beneath her eyes had lightened, her skin held a faint flush of color again, and there was something softer about the way she carried herself.

She leaned in, inspecting her face, and on a whim, reached for her mascara. A few extra swipes, a touch of eyeliner, and a quick run of her fingers through her damp hair, smoothing out some of its usual wildness. It wasn't much, but it was something. A small attempt at feeling normal.

By the time she stepped into the hallway, she knew Frank was already awake.

Not because she saw him.

But because she felt it.

A thin layer of mist had still clung stubbornly to the bathroom mirror when she'd gotten there, the last trace of his early morning routine. And then there was the scent—faint but distinct—the deep and woodsy bite of pine tar soap still drifting through the air.

She followed it downstairs, the thick socks Eli had loaned her muffling her footsteps, making her movements nearly silent as she moved through the house. Everything felt calm, the kind of early morning stillness that settled after a long night, when the world was just beginning to wake.

When she reached the kitchen, she hesitated just outside the doorway.

Frank stood at the stove, his back to her, one hand wrapped loosely around the handle of a wooden spoon as he stirred a slow, careful circle in a pot.

She just watched, not stepping forward.

There was something about the way he moved—unhurried, as if he had done this a thousand times before and knew exactly what he was doing. The steam rose up from the pot in soft ribbons, carrying the scent of hot maple and cinnamon through the air, blending seamlessly with the familiar woodsy scent of him.

She had never seen him like this before. Not behind the counter of the tattoo shop, or in the garage, with sleeves pushed up to his elbows and hands stained with grease. This was different. More tender.

It wasn't until she took a slow step forward that something changed.

A scent, faint but unmistakable, wove its way through the air.

Honeysuckle.

Finn's muscles tensed before she could stop them, her mind jolting back to the dream. The wildflowers swaying in the golden light, the air thick with soft, sweet perfume, the warmth that had settled in her chest like something sacred.

And then—

Frank stilled.

His stirring slowed to a stop, his head tilting to the side, as if listening.

A long moment passed.

And then—just as softly as the morning itself—

A small, sweet smile touched his lips.

"Morning, Nance."

Something deep inside of Finn whispered that she wasn't supposed to be here.

That this moment wasn't meant for her.

She took a careful step back, heart thudding in her chest, her breath barely making a sound.

Without a word, she turned—

And quietly retreated, leaving Frank to his reverie.

She moved without thinking, letting her feet carry her somewhere else.

She passed through the living room, her steps silent against the old wooden floor, then slipped down the short hallway that led to the sunroom.

The moment she pushed open the screen door, golden morning light spilled inside, stretching across the floorboards, warming the air with the slow rise of the sun.

She stood there for a second, letting it wash over her, letting it ease the strange tightness still gripping her chest.

Then, she slipped on her boots that sat beside the back door, and she stepped outside.

The backyard was so calm, the kind of early-morning stillness that made everything feel untouched. The air was cool, but the sun was beginning to warm the ground beneath her boots, chasing away the last traces of dawn.

Her fingers found the cigarette pack in her back pocket, the motion automatic.

She tapped one out, set it between her lips, and flicked the lighter. A small flame flared, then disappeared, replaced by the wisp of smoke spiraling into the morning light.

She took a long drag, holding the burn in her lungs before exhaling, watching as the smoke thinned into nothing.

Thinking of honeysuckle. Thinking of Frank. Thinking of Nancy.

The screen door creaked open behind her.

Eli's voice carried toward her, familiar and easy.

"Frank said he hadn't seen you yet, so somehow, I had a feeling I'd find you out here."

Finn didn't turn right away.

She took one last drag, letting the nicotine settle before dropping the cigarette to the ground. Pressing her boot over the smoldering end, she ground it out, the faint crunch of ember and ash filling the silence.

Like closing a door.

Then, finally, she glanced up—expecting his usual smirk, some teasing remark.

But Eli wasn't moving.

He had stopped speaking and was just... looking at her.

Not in confusion. Not in amusement.

But like he didn't quite know what to do with the version of her standing in front of him right now.

An unrecognizable look flashed past his eyes, something like realization threading through his expression.

Finn shifted under his gaze, suddenly feeling more exposed than she had a moment ago. She let out a small, breathy laugh, forcing lightness into her tone.

"What?"

Eli blinked, quick, almost imperceptible. Like he was shaking himself free from a thought.

"Nothing," he said, his head wobbling, but the faintest tinge of pink touched the tips of his ears. Then he cleared his throat, forcing an easy smile. "You just look... bright-eyed and bushy-tailed."

Finn snorted, arching a brow. "Do people still actually say that?"

"I do," Eli breathed a laugh.

But now, as she stepped closer, she saw it—the exhaustion clutching him. His face was a little drawn, his eyes carrying a weariness. Not the kind that came from just missing a few hours of sleep, but the kind that took over when you've tossed and turned all night.

A small knot tightened in her chest.

Was this because of last night?

Had everything she dumped on him—the visions, the mine, Kai—been too much? Had she handed off her burden only for him to take it on himself?

The thought unsettled her, but before it could take root, Eli shifted the moment, pulling her out of it like it was second nature.

"Gimme a smoke?"

She exhaled, pulling the pack from her pocket and shaking out two cigarettes.

She stuck both between her lips, flipped the lighter open, and cupped the flame to shield it from the light morning breeze.

A slow inhale. A steady burn.

She plucked one from her mouth and handed it to him.

Eli took it without question, bringing it to his lips as he inhaled.

The tension between them softened—not gone, but no longer insistent.

They stood there like that, side by side, the morning sun reaching over the treetops, the thin trails of smoke mingling in the crisp air.

And even though neither of them said it, the understanding was there.

Eli wasn't carrying this alone.

And neither was Finn.

They smoked in companionable silence before finally heading back inside.

The scent of maple oatmeal and freshly brewed coffee still hung in the air as they stepped into the kitchen.

This time, Frank was already seated at the table, newspaper in one hand and coffee in the other, his posture relaxed.

Finn greeted him casually, as if she hadn't already seen him earlier.

Frank barely looked up, but a smile tugged at the edges of his mouth—the same one she'd caught earlier before she'd backed out of the kitchen.

"Morning, kid."

Without pausing from scanning the paper, he gestured vaguely toward the stove.

"Made plenty of oatmeal if either of you want some."

Finn had no time to process the offer before movement in her periphery caught her attention—Eli, shaking his head vigorously, his eyes wide in alarm.

His lips formed an exaggerated, desperate plea.

"Don't do it."

Finn had to bite the inside of her cheek to keep from laughing.

She followed Eli's gaze, watching as he side-eyed Frank's bowl of oatmeal like it was to be feared, his expression nothing short of horrified.

It took everything in her not to crack a grin as she turned back to Frank, schooling her face into something neutral.

"I'm actually not really hungry," she said smoothly, the lie rolling skillfully off her tongue.

Before she even finished the sentence, Eli jumped in—way too quickly.

"Yeah, I was already planning on taking Finn over to The Lantern anyway."

Frank let out a small huff of amusement, finally glancing up from his paper. His gaze bounced between the two of them, clearly unimpressed.

Eli didn't flinch, but Finn caught the way his shoulders stiffened.

Frank stared at him for a long moment. Then, with a sharp exhale through his nose, he shook his head.

"Yeah, yeah, go on then. No need to pretend to enjoy this old man's slop."

The words were gruff, but the edges of his face softened. A smirk tugged at the corner of his mouth before he disappeared behind the paper again.

Finn finally let herself laugh.

She followed Eli toward the door, watching as he grabbed his keys from the entry table.

"You wanna grab your jacket?" he asked, absentmindedly.

Finn eyed him with confused curiosity.

"Why?"

Eli flipped his keys in his palm, glancing toward the window.

"It's gonna rain."

She frowned, turning to look outside. The sky was clear and bright, the morning sun spilling through the trees. Not a single cloud in sight.

"Doesn't look like rain to me."

He gave her a knowing look.

"Trust me. I know this place. I'm telling you—it's gonna rain."

Finn tilted her head, considering for a moment before shrugging.

"I don't mind getting caught in the rain."

Eli smirked but didn't argue.

He just pushed the door open, stepping outside as Finn followed close behind.

Chapter Seventeen

The brass bell above the diner door jingled as Eli held it open, shooting Finn a grin over his shoulder.

"You should be thanking me," he said, his voice laced with amusement. "I just saved you from an experience you'd never recover from."

Finn raised an eyebrow as she stepped inside. "Frank's oatmeal?"

"The very one." He nodded solemnly, leading the way. "The smell is a lie, Finn. Deceptive. Downright evil."

She let out a laugh, but any retort she had disappeared the second the scent of sizzling bacon, fresh biscuits, and something sweet and buttery wrapped around her like a hug. Her stomach growled—loudly.

Eli turned to her, eyebrows lifting. "Okay, someone is *hungry*."

Finn huffed, but she couldn't deny it—she was starving.

The diner was pure old-school Americana. Checkerboard tile floors and red vinyl booths with chrome edges. A long counter lined with round stools, each with a crack or two in their pleather seats. A small jukebox sat near the entrance, currently silent. The whole place had likely looked exactly the same for decades, maybe even since before Frank was born.

Behind the counter, a middle-aged waitress with a short brown ponytail and laugh lines around her eyes turned their way, tossing a dish towel over her shoulder.

"Well, hey there, stranger," she called out to Eli, her tone warm and familiar.

"Hey, Sheri," Eli greeted back just the same.

"You kids pick a seat, and I'll be right with you!"

Eli nodded and led Finn past the counter, moving swiftly past a couple of older patrons hunched over their steaming mugs of coffee. They settled into a booth near the back, away from the low murmur of conversation.

Finn leaned back against the seat, glancing around as she took it all in.

The cork bulletin board on the far wall caught Finn's eye—a cluttered patchwork of community announcements, missing pet flyers, and handwritten notes advertising everything from lawnmower repairs to homemade jam. She skimmed over it absently before shifting her focus back to Eli, who was watching her with an amused smirk.

"So," he said, lacing his fingers together and resting his elbows on the table, "are you actually gonna order food, or should I just ask Sheri to bring you a plate of whatever your stomach was just screaming for?"

Finn opened her mouth to fire back, but before she could, a voice cut in.

The waitress had arrived, wiping her hands on her apron as she pulled two menus from under her arm. She handed one to Eli first, then to Finn, her tawny brown eyes twinkling as she took her in.

"So," Sheri said, planting a hand on her hip with a knowing smile, "is this your little mountain girlfriend I heard about, Eli?"

Finn balked. His what!?

Eli groaned, dragging a hand down his face. "Oh my God. I'm never gonna hear the end of this, am I?"

Before Finn could even process a response, her stomach betrayed her—growling again, loud enough that Sheri arched an amused brow.

Eli exhaled, defeated. "Whatever. We need food before she starts scaring the other patrons."

Sheri chuckled, tucking her notepad under her arm. "Alright, alright. What'll it be?"

Finn scanned the menu, but the decision was an easy one. "I'll have the biscuits and gravy, please," she said, setting it down.

"Ooo, solid choice," Sheri nodded approvingly before turning to Eli. "And for you?"

"Cowboy platter," he answered without hesitation, handing his menu back. "Extra bacon."

Sheri smirked like she'd expected nothing less. "Thought so. And to drink?"

"Coffee," Finn said. "Cream and sugar."

"Black," Eli added.

Sheri didn't even bother writing it down. Finn had barely finished speaking before the waitress was already nodding, grabbing Finn's menu from the table. "Coming right up."

She turned to leave, but just as she pivoted, she caught Eli's eye and grinned, tilting her head toward Finn.

"She's cute," Sheri stage-whispered, mischief glinting in her brown eyes.

Heat shot straight up Finn's neck. Her entire body tensed, hands instinctively covering her burning cheeks.

The bell over the front door jingled as another customer entered, but Finn barely registered it, too busy wishing she could disappear into the cracked vinyl seat. Across from her, Eli groaned, shaking his head with a half-laugh, half-sigh—but she didn't miss the way his own ears turned just the slightest shade of pink.

"Yeah," he muttered, reaching for the salt just to give his hands something to do, "gossip travels fast around here."

Finn peeked at him through her fingers, her voice flat. "You don't say."

Eli exhaled a small laugh, swirling the salt in the shaker absently in a circle.

"Welcome to Ash Hollow."

Just as Finn dropped her hands from her face, warmth still flushing her cheeks, her eyes landed on the last person she wanted to see.

The door had barely finished swinging shut behind Sarah, the brass bell above it still jingling softly. Unlike previous encounters, there was no forced sweetness, no thinly veiled malice at the edges of her smile. She didn't glare. Didn't sneer. Just met their eyes with an expression so unreadable it made Finn's stomach tighten.

Cold and distant. Almost... calculated.

Without a word, Sarah crossed the room and slid into the booth directly across from theirs, right in front of the cork bulletin board cluttered with notices and ads.

Finn felt herself shrink, pressing back into the cracked booth. She hated that she reacted at all, hated the fist of unease striking her gut. For once, she was grateful she had left the jacket at home. The pendant, too—tucked safely away.

Beside her, Eli tensed. The easygoing nature from a moment ago drained from his posture, shifting into something more alert, and rigid. His fingers wrapped around the salt shaker, knuckles blanching as he leaned forward just enough to brace himself.

Finn could feel it—the quiet bracing. He was waiting for something. Another outburst or confrontation.

But Sarah just sat there.

She didn't glance at them again. Didn't acknowledge them at all.

The tense atmosphere was palpable between them. Finn forced herself to exhale, stealing a quick glance sideways at Eli. He met her eyes, and in them, she saw it—the same wary discomfort reflected there.

Neither of them liked this.

Seconds passed.

Finn let out a breath and tried to make herself relax. Eli did the same, the strain in his grip easing a bit.

But neither of them spoke.

Sheri returned, breaking the silence with the comforting clink of ceramic against wood as she set their coffee cups down. The sound was a welcome distraction, just enough to pull Finn's focus away.

She gave a small nod of thanks as Sheri placed a tiny tray of cream and sugar beside her mug. The waitress flashed her another warm smile before shifting her attention toward the booth across from them.

"What can I get ya, hon?" she asked, her tone just as light as before.

Sarah didn't glance at the menu.

"Just a coffee."

Her voice was smooth. Even. Almost too casual.

Eli and Finn both heard it. Both registered the careful neutrality in her tone. And though neither reacted outright, Finn felt something unspoken pass between them.

Sarah wasn't here by accident.

Finn stirred sugar into her coffee, keeping her movements controlled, but that nagging feeling didn't fade. Sarah wasn't glaring or making a show of her presence—but that didn't mean she wasn't waiting for something.

She wrapped her hands around the warm ceramic, letting the heat seep into her fingers.

She forced herself to focus on the other surroundings. The murmur of conversations from other tables. The distant sizzle from the griddle. The scent of fresh coffee mingling with butter and syrup.

The place wasn't familiar to her yet, but there was a comforting air about it. A sense of ease held in the worn-out booths and scuffed checkered floors.

Sarah was still there—drinking her black coffee Sheri had quickly delivered, still sitting stiff and unreadable. But she wasn't looking their way. Wasn't doing anything at all.

And maybe that was fine.

Finn tried again to focus on something else. On the cup in her hands. On the stillness between her and Eli—not awkward, not strained, just... there.

On the fact that, somehow—despite everything—she was sitting across from him, having breakfast.

With a friend.

The thought settled in her chest, unfamiliar but not unwelcome.

Finn zeroed in on Eli now. On the way he leaned back against the booth, one arm slung over the top of the seat. He looked relaxed, but she knew better. He was always watching, always keyed into her in a way that made her feel like he could read her temperature just by looking at her.

She took a sip of her coffee, letting the warmth seep inside her before setting the mug down. "So... now that I have a big girl job, I should probably get a cell phone."

Eli's brow lifted, his mouth already curving like he was ready to tease her. "Big girl job, huh?"

She smirked. "That's right. Fully employed and everything. Call me a responsible adult."

He huffed a short laugh, shaking his head. "Okay, responsible adult. Yeah, a phone would probably be a good idea." Then he hesitated, brow furrowing as something clicked in his mind. "Wait. You don't have a phone?"

Finn shook her head. "Nope. Never have."

Eli scoffed, sitting forward like she had just said something completely absurd. "Wait, wait. You mean to tell me you've *never* had a cell phone?"

She just shrugged, stirring her coffee like this was the most normal thing in the world. "Not one my parents knew about."

Just like that, the humor in Eli's face dimmed. Just a fraction. Just enough for her to notice.

"Okaaay..." His voice dipped, slower, more careful. "What does that mean?"

Finn lowered her voice, like she was admitting something mildly scandalous. "I had a tracphone that I kept hidden."

Eli leaned in, intrigued now. "Hidden from who?"

She lifted a brow, giving him a look that said, *'Who do you think?'*

"My stepdad. My mom, too, but mostly him."

Eli let out a short, humorless laugh, his fingers drumming lightly against the tabletop. "Jesus." He took a sip of his coffee, processing that, before tilting his head. "So... what, you just used it for emergencies?"

Finn shook her head. "Not really. I mostly just used it to text Mike."

Eli blinked. "Who the hell is Mike?"

She rolled her eyes, smirking sheepishly. "Relax, Dad, he was just this guy I knew back home."

Eli did not relax. His posture straightened, his expression one she didn't recognize. "Define 'knew.'"

Finn sighed, like this whole conversation was completely unimportant. "He was just a guy who'd buy me smokes when I ran out. We'd meet up in the park, he'd smoke weed, I'd smoke a cigarette, and he'd talk about his garage band or whatever. Then we'd go our separate ways."

Eli's face scrunched disapprovingly. "So, let me get this straight—you had one person to talk to back home, and it was some burnout dude who bought you cigarettes?"

Finn shrugged, picking absently at a sugar packet between her fingers. "I mean, yeah. He wasn't a bad guy or anything. Just... convenient."

Eli didn't respond right away. He watched her, something thoughtful passing over his face like he was turning over a piece of information he didn't quite know what to do with. Then his voice softened, the teasing edge gone.

"Finn... why didn't you have any real friends?"

She froze. Just for a fraction of a second.

The question caught her off guard.

She hadn't really thought about it in those terms before.

For a moment, she considered shrugging again, brushing it off with some dismissive answer. But she didn't.

Instead, she met his eyes.

And with something as honest as she could muster, she admitted—

"I don't know."

Before Eli could respond, Sheri arrived with their plates, sliding them onto the table in a smooth motion. "Alright, biscuits and gravy for the mountain girl, and a heart attack on a plate for our boy Eli."

Eli grinned, rubbing his hands together before grabbing his fork. "You know me so well, Sheri."

"Too well," she shot back, winking before heading off to tend to the other customers.

Finn could have kissed her for the interruption.

She picked up her fork and dug in, her stomach reminding her just how badly she needed this. The first bite was heavenly—dense and buttery, with perfectly peppered gravy soaking into a fluffy biscuit. She practically melted into her seat.

They both fell into the kind of silence that only really good food could justify, Eli devouring his plate like a man starving while Finn took her time, savoring every bite.

Still, even as she ate, something in the corner of her vision tugged at her.

Sarah had stood up, turned fully away from them now, facing the corkboard on the opposite wall.

Finn might have thought nothing of it, except—Sarah wasn't just standing there. It's like she was stalling.

Her hands dug around in her purse, her movements stiff. She shifted her weight from foot to foot, keeping her back to them, her shoulders hunched.

Finn's stomach tightened.

Then—Sarah's arm lifted ever so slightly. Just for a second.

Finn barely caught the motion before Sarah's hand dipped back into her bag, emerging with a few bills. She laid them on the table without looking back, then straightened and briskly strode out of the diner.

Finn released a breath, watching Sarah disappear through the front window.

She turned back to her meal, but suddenly she wasn't hungry anymore.

Eli, on the other hand, was still going.

She sat back, watching as he demolished the last of his food, barely taking time to breathe between bites.

Finally, he swallowed the last bite of hashbrowns, patting his stomach with a satisfied groan.

"That," he declared, "was exactly what I needed."

Finn smirked, setting her fork down. "Clearly."

Sheri returned, scooping up their plates and stacking them in the crook of her arm. She let out a chuckle as she surveyed the damage.

"You kids did a real number on those," she teased before dropping the check slip onto the table—deliberately sliding it in front of Eli.

Then she turned to Finn and began to say, "It was so nice to meet you, mount—"

"Finn," Finn blurted out, cutting her off before she could finish the nickname.

Sheri blinked, then let out a bright laugh, pressing a hand over her heart. "Oh, that's so unique. Just lovely." She beamed at them both before gathering the rest of the dishes and disappearing toward the kitchen.

Eli pulled out his wallet, flipping the check slip over and tucking a couple of bills inside the leather folder. Finn barely registered it. Her gaze had already drifted, idly scanning the room, the hum of the diner settling into something background and distant.

Her stomach was full and still warm from the coffee, the morning routine of a small town rolling on around them.

And then—

Her breath caught.

There, on the corkboard near the exit, was a single sheet of paper that hadn't been there before.

A missing person's flyer.

Kai's face smiled back at her. The same grin. The same clear blue eyes.

Her stomach lurched.

Before she even realized she was moving, Finn's hand shot out, gripping Eli's arm, her fingers tightening against the fabric of his jacket.

Eli followed her gaze, his post-meal contentment evaporating the instant he saw it. His body went still.

"What the f—" he started, but Finn cut him off, her voice low, certain. "Sarah."

Finally, she turned to look at him, and the moment their eyes met, she knew he felt it too.

The world outside of that single sheet of paper, outside of Kai's face, might as well not have existed.

Sarah had put it there.

And she had wanted them to see it.

Eli's face hardened, the warmth of their morning burned away in an instant, replaced by something colder.

Without a word, he slid out of the booth, his movements too con-trolled, too calm. With purposeful strides, he crossed the short distance to the cork board.

Finn held her breath as he reached up and plucked the flyer down. He didn't crumple it. Didn't rip it away in frustration. Instead, with an unnerving ease, he folded it once, twice—hard creases—before sliding it into his pocket.

Only then did he turn back to her.

"You ready to go?" His voice was even. Measured.

Finn swallowed against the tightness in her throat and nodded, sliding out of the booth.

They stepped out of the diner into an overcast morning, the air thick with the promise of rain. The atmosphere had shifted—not just in the sky, but between them.

Sarah had wanted them to see, and whatever the reason, it had changed things.

Without speaking, they climbed into the Bronco just as the first fat raindrops began to fall, dotting the windshield in lazy, uneven splatters. The air was cooler now, carrying the scent of pine and petrichor through the half-cracked windows as Eli turned the ignition and switched on the heat.

Finn didn't ask. She just shook two cigarettes from her pack, lighting them both the way she had earlier. The soft flick of the lighter, the brief flare of flame—then she handed one to Eli.

The ember at the tip glowed bright for a moment before dimming, smoke unfurling into the cab.

They sat there for a long beat, listening to the rain tap gently against the roof, and the occasional distant rumble of a car passing on the roadway beyond the lot. The world outside felt oddly detached—muted by the storm creeping in.

Then, finally, Eli exhaled, breaking the silence.

"What the fuck was that about?"

His voice was low, even, but she could sense the controlled frustration just barely leashed.

Finn didn't answer right away. She watched the smoke pulled toward the cracked window, the soft tendrils dissolving into the moist air. When she finally turned to face him, his expression was already hard, jaw tight.

"All of Kai's missing flyers were taken down after he was pronounced dead," Eli continued when she didn't immediately respond. "People didn't want to be reminded of the missing boy anymore. They just wanted to move on." He scoffed, shaking his head. "And I haven't seen one anywhere in town since."

His hand ran absently over the steering wheel, creaking under his touch. His cigarette dangled between his fingers, forgotten for a moment as he stared through the rain-slicked windshield.

"So why the hell did Sarah put one up now?"

Finn took a slow pull from her cigarette, letting the menthol settle on her tongue before exhaling through her nose. She traced the raindrops on the glass with her eyes, following the way they raced each other down in jagged paths.

"She knew we'd see it," Finn said finally.

Eli didn't argue. His fingers tightened around the wheel.

"She's making a point," Finn continued. "He's wearing the jacket in the photo. And I'm assuming the crescent moon pendant was hanging from that chain under his shirt."

Eli's grip flexed, his knuckles whitening. But he didn't speak.

Finn watched the raindrops gather, merge, and roll away. "Do you think she wanted me to know that she knows for certain they were his?"

He took one last pull from his cigarette, then flicked the smoldering butt out the window. The rain swallowed it instantly.

Running a hand over his face, he shook his head. "I don't know," he muttered. His jaw worked, anxiety tugging at his shoulders. "But whatever this is—whatever game she's playing..."

He exhaled hard, gripping the wheel a little tighter.

"It's not fucking subtle."

Outside, the rain continued its steady descent, streaking across the windshield in silver rivulets. The wipers dragged lazily over the glass, clearing it just enough before the droplets returned, obscuring the road in a hazy blur.

Finn tossed her cigarette out the window, mirroring Eli's movements, then turned fully toward him. Her expression was resolved.

"Look," she started, choosing her words carefully, "I know she's the last person I wanna deal with after what happened at the grocery store, but I don't think we can avoid it. We have to talk to her."

Eli kept his eyes forward, unresponsive.

Finn hesitated for a fraction of a second, then pressed on. "Didn't you say something about her and Kai being friends?"

He gave a single nod. "Best friends. They were always together."

The answer came so matter-of-fact, that Finn found herself studying his face, searching for something deeper—some emotion beneath the certainty. But there was nothing. No hesitation, no glimmer of doubt. Just the truth of it.

She turned back toward the windshield, processing. "Then do you think there's any way Sarah doesn't know something? Anything we could use to piece together the puzzle?"

He watched the wipers sweep another slow arc across the glass before finally answering, his voice certain.

"She knows something." He nodded once, more to himself than to her. "She has to."

That was all Finn needed to hear.

Eli shifted into gear, the tires kicking up a fine mist of rainwater as they eased back onto the main road. The metronomic swish of the wipers filled the space between them, an unspoken agreement settling in the air.

Finn crossed her arms, staring out the rain-speckled window as the town whisked past.

Beside her, Eli rested one hand on the wheel, the other near the gear shift, his fingers flexing as if working through an invisible equation. His focus was locked ahead, his jaw set, but his posture told Finn he was already figuring out their next move.

For now, it would have to wait.

The Lost Boys still needed opening, and Frank was counting on them to keep things running smoothly. Whatever was unfolding between them, the mines, and Kai—whatever secrets Sarah might be holding onto—would have to marinate. At least for a few hours.

Eli let out a deep sigh, as if coming to the same conclusion, then flicked on the turn signal.

"Let's go to work."

Chapter Eighteen

The next few days slipped into a rhythm. The kind of comfortable routine Finn never realized she had craved.

Mornings at the shop were spent learning the ropes, her movements behind the front desk becoming smoother with each passing day. She was getting better at handling scheduling, tracking deposits, and keeping up with the steady hum of shop life.

While most clients didn't return often, Finn was starting to recognize some familiar names and voices over the phone. She knew Danny from the hardware store was coming in for a touch-up on Friday. And Penny, a younger woman working on a sleeve, had popped in a few times—once to pay her deposit, once to confirm the design, and once more just to kill time before her appointment, flipping through flash books while chatting about the work she wanted done next.

Finn liked those small moments of familiarity.

But in little moments, away from Frank's eyes, Finn and Eli were piecing together something else entirely.

They'd wait until Frank was in the garage, tinkering with whatever old relic had captured his attention that day. Or when he went out for errands, running into town to grab supplies.

That's when Finn and Eli would sneak off to his bedroom, shutting the door behind them and spreading books and papers across his bed. The missing flyer still nestled inside one of the books.

Finn took notes while Eli flipped through pages, pointing out passages about the town's mining history, sometimes recalling something Frank had told him long ago.

The Ash Hollow Mining Company.

That's all the books called it. Not the name of the family who ran it, just the company itself.

It had once been the backbone of the town, drawing in workers from all over who were desperate for steady pay, lured by the promise of untouched veins of coal—and maybe even silver or gold if they got lucky. But after the explosion, the company collapsed. No lawsuits. No reparations. Just closed doors and silence.

Everything about it felt off, but nothing concrete had clicked into place.

Not yet.

Some evenings, Finn would cook, partly because she liked it, but mostly because the guys were hopeless in the kitchen. The first night she made chicken and rice with roasted vegetables, Frank patted his stomach afterward and declared it the best meal they'd had in years—which was a clear jab at Eli, who scowled at his dad but kept stuffing his face anyway.

She even spent a few afternoons in the garage with Frank, drawn in by curiosity more than anything. One afternoon, he was fixing up an old radio, fingers working steadily at the inner components. He handed Finn a tiny screwdriver, nodding toward an open panel.

"Hold this still."

She wasn't sure why the simple act made her chest warm, but it did.

She liked watching his rough hands handle fragile things with care. It reminded her that strength and gentleness weren't opposites.

But in the middle of the normalcy, Eli started acting strange.

At first, it was little things—Finn would walk into a room and catch him and Frank talking in low voices, only for them to stop the second she entered.

Or sometimes, Frank would suddenly pull her into the garage to show her something, or give her an extra-long lesson on handling certain tattoo shop supplies, while Eli conveniently disappeared somewhere.

She didn't question it.

Not when Frank was giving her pieces of something she had never had before—a father figure.

If Eli was keeping something from her, or planning something, she let it go.

For now.

Friday morning had arrived. Finn stretched with a groggy sigh, rolling onto her side before pushing herself up. The room was still dim, the morning light barely creeping in through the curtains. She rubbed at her eyes, blinking away the last remnants of sleep.

Then, it hit her.

Her birthday.

She sat there for a second, waiting for the feeling that usually followed that thought. But it didn't come.

With an exhale, she swung her legs over the side of the bed and grabbed a fresh set of clothes from the dresser. Tucking them under her arm, she made her way toward the door, stepping into the hall just as Eli's door swung open.

They locked eyes.

Eli, shirtless and still half-asleep, had his own pile of clothes tucked under his arm. His gaze flashed past her toward the bathroom door.

Finn followed his line of sight.

A single, charged second passed.

Then they both bolted.

Finn lunged forward, but Eli had longer legs. He shoved ahead of her, reaching the door just as she grabbed for the knob. With a triumphant grin, he yanked it open, ducked inside, and—

SLAM.

The door shut in her face.

Finn scowled as she heard him laughing from the other side.

"Seriously?!" she shouted, smacking her palm against the door.

The sound of the shower turning on was his only response.

Huffing in frustration, she turned and stalked back to her room. She tossed her clothes onto the dresser, muttering under her breath about Eli and his unfair height advantage. No point in standing around waiting—she'd just shower later.

The kitchen was silent, the scent of coffee still rolling faintly through the air. Finn rubbed at her arms, glancing around. There was a folded piece of paper sitting on the counter near the coffee pot, Frank's neat handwriting standing out against the notepad paper.

'Had to run into town early. I'll meet you both at the shop later.'

She didn't think much of it. Frank was always up before either of them. Some mornings, she'd wake to find him already sequestered to the garage or gone entirely. The guy was restless.

Setting the note back in place, she moved to the fridge and pulled out eggs and sourdough bread. She wasn't about to sit around waiting for Eli to be done. Might as well make breakfast.

Within minutes, the eggs were scrambled, and the toast was crisp and buttered. She had just finished plating the food when she heard Eli's footsteps coming down the stairs.

He stretched lazily as he entered the kitchen, ruffling a towel through his damp curls before draping it over his shoulders.

Leaning against the counter, he said, "You are getting slow in your old age."

He remembered.

Masking her grin, she grabbed the hot skillet and set it in the sink, running some water into it to soak. She knew full well either Eli or Frank would probably wash it before she got the chance. They always did after she cooked—some sort of silent thank-you.

She set a plate in front of Eli before sliding into the seat across from him.

"You're older than me," she shot back, raising an eyebrow.

"Yeah, but I wear it better." He smirked, taking a bite of his food.

Finn rolled her eyes but didn't argue.

They ate casually, the morning settling between them. As always, Eli finished first. He leaned back in his chair, stretching his arms behind his head.

"Danny's coming in first thing, right?" Finn asked, scooping up the last of the egg with her toast.

"Yeah, and Brett again this afternoon." Eli pushed back from the table, grabbing both their plates. "The guy's practically our most loyal customer at this point."

Finn chuckled, "I mean, he does have a whole sleeve left to go."

"Yeah, well, at this rate, he's gonna end up covered neck to toe." Eli shook his head, rinsing their dishes in the sink like she knew he would.

Finn watched for a second, a small smile tugging at her lips before she stood.

"I'm gonna get ready," she said, pushing away from the table.

Eli nodded without looking back, already scrubbing at the dishes.

Finn headed upstairs, a feeling tugging at her—not weighty or empty. Just... different.

She didn't need anyone to remember.

But still.

It was nice that he had.

Finn stepped into her room, rubbing the ends of her damp hair between her fingers as she nudged the door shut behind her. Steam from her shower still clung to her skin, the warmth fading as the cooler air of her bedroom greeted her. She had already changed into the jeans and hoodie she'd picked out earlier, the fabric still clinging slightly from her skin's dampness.

As she reached for a hair tie, her eyes landed on something small and familiar near the edge of the dresser.

The crescent moon pendant.

Her fingers hesitated before she picked it up, letting the metal rest against her palm.

She had worn it before—because it felt right. The press of it against her skin, the way it sat against her throat. She hadn't thought much about why she wore it. It had simply made sense.

Until Sarah saw it.

Until she tore it from Finns neck.

Her thumb brushed over the broken choker. The leather was frayed where the clasp had snapped, where Sarah had yanked it too hard.

She could fix it.

But something about that didn't feel right anymore either.

Her fingers curled around the pendant. She hadn't realized how much she had grown used to feeling it there—the simple physical presence of it.

Now, without it, her neck felt bare.

Lighter.

She wasn't sure if that was a good thing or not.

Her hand relaxed, and she set the pendant back down on the dresser, leaving it where it was.

She turned away, reaching for the eyeliner she had grabbed from the bathroom, gliding a quick stroke along her lash-line before swiping on some mascara. Running her fingers through her hair, she worked through the strands that had already begun drying into soft waves before pulling it back into a low ponytail.

Her gaze lifted up to the mirror.

Something about her looked different.

Not bad.

Not broken.

Just new.

Finn rolled her shoulders, shaking off the thought.

She grabbed her boots, laced them up, and headed downstairs.

Eli turned the key in the ignition, the old engine grumbling before settling into a steady purr. Finn buckled herself in, adjusting the sleeves of her hoodie as she leaned against the window, watching the town come to life around them.

Ash Hollow was always quiet, but the morning stillness was giving way to movement. Shop owners flipped CLOSED signs to OPEN, sweeping their front steps as they chatted with familiar faces. A woman carrying a woven basket of fresh produce stepped out of Ash Grocery, tucking a graying strand of hair behind her ear as she loaded them into her car. Near the gas station, an older man in a faded trucker's cap stood nursing a Styrofoam cup of coffee, his dog sniffing lazily around the base of a fuel pump.

Small-town life, slow and steady. Finn let herself take it in, her fingers idly tapping against her thigh as the Bronco rolled down the street.

Eli's voice broke the stillness, laced with amusement.

"Alright, birthday girl, pop quiz."

Finn groaned, slumping back in her seat. "You're relentless."

He smiled. "Damn right. Now, what's the most important thing to remember when setting up for a shading session?"

She sighed, but the answer came naturally. "Make sure the artist has the right needles and ink caps ready, plus a rinse cup so they can blend tones without cross-contaminating colors."

Eli nodded. "Good. What needle grouping do I use most for my linework?"

Finn grinned slyly. "Depends on the piece."

He shot her a pointed look and she rolled her eyes dramatically before answering. "For fine-line work, you use a three-round liner. For bold pieces, you go for a nine or eleven."

"Not bad, rookie."

Finn crossed her arms, feigning offense. "You quiz me every damn day. At what point do I stop being a rookie?"

"When you can set up my whole station without asking a single question." He threw her a teasing glance. "And when you stop making that face every time I test you."

"I do not make a face."

"You totally do."

She huffed but couldn't stop the small smile tugging at her lips.

They passed The Lantern Diner, its large windows framing a few early customers sipping their coffee. An older man passing on the sidewalk lifted a hand in greeting, and Eli gave him a nod in return.

By the time they pulled up in front of Lost Boys Tattoo Shop, the morning was in full swing. The shop's sign looked pristine above the door, untouched by time or wear, its bold lettering standing out against the brick façade.

Eli shifted into park, cut the engine, and cracked his knuckles.

"Alright, rookie. Let's see if you remember how to open up."

Finn rolled her eyes again, but grabbed the keys from the console, already unbuckling her seatbelt.

She was still smiling as she stepped out of the truck.

Her boots met the pavement with a familiar crunch, the air crisp and moist from the lingering drizzle. As she approached the front door, her gaze caught the empty parking space beside them.

Frank's truck wasn't there.

That was... odd.

He was usually the first one in, especially when they had an early appointment. She pushed the thought aside, chalking it up to him running late for once, and flipped through the keys on the ring to find the right one. The lock turned with a satisfying *click*.

The scent of disinfectant greeted her instantly, familiar and comforting. Soft overhead light flooded the waiting area as she tapped the switch, casting a warm glow over the four wooden chairs lined up along the wall.

Finn's gaze drifted toward the open pass-through window that connected the sitting area to the tattooing space. Those lights were still off.

Behind her, Eli stepped inside, shaking out his damp curls.

"No Frank yet?" he asked, turning on the open sign.

"Yeah... kind of weird," Finn muttered, sliding the key ring onto her middle finger. "Danny's appointment starts in, like, twenty minutes. I figured Frank would already be setting up by now."

She headed for the door leading into the tattooing area.

The second she pushed it open—

The overhead lights burst to life, flooding the room in a sudden glow.

"HAPPY BIRTHDAY, FINN!"

Finn gasped, nearly jumping out of her skin as Frank and Danny's voices rang out in unison.

The keys slipped from Finn's fingers, clattering against the shop floor.

Frank let out a deep, satisfied laugh, arms crossed over his chest as he leaned against the desk. Beside him, Danny grinned wide, his teeth shining pearly white.

Finn's heart pounded, her pulse still trying to catch up. "What the hell—what's going on?"

Frank smirked, pushing off the desk with a shrug. "Eli and I wanted to put together a little something for your big eighteenth." He nodded toward the desk beside him. "Consider it a proper welcome to adulthood."

Finn followed his gesture, eyes landing on a tray of to-go coffees and, right beside it, a gorgeous apple pie, the golden crust glistening.

And right across the top, carefully piped in whipped cream, were the words:

HAPPY BIRTHDAY FINN

A slow, unstoppable smile stretched across her face, so wide it made her cheeks ache.

Frank stepped closer, resting a firm hand on her shoulder. His sharp, knowing eyes softened just enough to make her chest tighten.

"Happy birthday, kiddo."

Finn swallowed hard, words tangling somewhere in her throat. "I... I don't even know what to say."

Danny snorted, crossing his arms. "You better say something. Me and Frank have been sittin' in the damn dark for twenty minutes."

Laughter filled the shop, easy and unforced. The kind that felt like warmth, and belonging.

Finn beamed at them, heart full to bursting. She glanced around—Frank, Danny, the shop she was beginning to love, and then, finally, Eli.

He stood near the doorway, watching with that familiar smirk—warm and steady, just for her.

Frank pulled open the bottom drawer of the desk and retrieved a small stack of paper plates, a handful of napkins, and a pack of plastic forks. He started plating slices of pie, the spicy, cinnamon-laced aroma filling the shop as he passed them out one by one.

Finn murmured her thanks as she took her plate, settling into the rickety office chair near the desk. It groaned in protest, like it might finally give up, but she was used to its quirks by now.

Danny dropped into the tattoo chair in Frank's section with a satisfied sigh, like he was easing onto his throne. Eli, across from him, spun his own chair lazily from side to side as he dug into his pie. Frank, as always, didn't bother sitting—just leaned back against the desk, fork in hand, already taking his first bite.

For a few minutes, the shop was filled with nothing but the soft scrape of forks against paper plates.

Finn took her first bite, and the second the buttery, flaky crust and spiced apple filling melted on her tongue, she nearly groaned.

Damn, that was good.

They ate in silence until Frank, ever efficient, wiped his mouth with a napkin and broke the moment with a gruff declaration.

"Alright, presents. Then I have to move my truck from the alley, before Sheriff Tundly slaps me with a citation."

Finn paused mid-bite, blinking up at him. "Presents?" she mumbled around a mouthful of pie, barely managing to get the word out before swallowing.

Frank raised an eyebrow, looking almost offended that she'd even question it. "Well, yeah."

Without another word, he reached into his back pocket and pulled out a small manila envelope—folded in half, a little creased—and handed it to her.

Finn wiped her mouth with a napkin before taking it. Across the front, in Frank's familiar scrawled handwriting, was her name. A small smile pulled at her lips as she slid out the piece of paper tucked inside.

"...A W-4 form?" Finn asked, brow furrowing as she held up the sheet of paper.

Frank grinned, that rare, quietly proud smile tugging at the corner of his mouth. "Yep. You're officially an employee of The Lost Boys Tattoo Shop."

Finn just stared at it, the reality of it settling in. Then, her lips curled into a wide grin.

"Thank you, Frank," she said, genuine warmth in her voice before mischief crept into her expression. "Now it'll be even harder for you to get rid of me."

Frank snorted, shaking his head as she set the document on the keyboard to fill out later.

Before she could take another bite of pie, Danny shifted forward in his chair, reaching into the front pocket of his work shirt. With a smooth motion, he pulled out a chocolate bar, its wrapper crinkled from being carried around all morning.

Without a word, he slid out of his seat, stepped over to Finn, and handed it to her with a small nod.

"Never been any good at givin' gifts," he admitted, his voice gruff but honest. "But if I learned anything from my sweet Lorna, it's that, typically, ladies like chocolate."

His nod was short, firm—like that was that—before he turned right back and settled into his chair, already digging back into his pie as if nothing had happened.

Finn blinked down at the chocolate bar, something in her chest tightening in a way she couldn't quite name. It wasn't just the gift itself—it was the thought behind it. The simple, unspoken kindness wrapped in its crinkled foil.

"Thanks, Danny," she said, her voice soft, but a little steadier.

He didn't look up, just grunted in acknowledgement, lifting his fork like a toast before taking another bite.

The tattoo chair in Eli's section creaked as he stood, the sound pulling Finn's attention toward him.

She expected the usual—one of his smirks, a teasing remark, something light and easy. But instead, he looked... nervous.

His cheeks stained a deep, unmistakable red, the flush creeping from his sharp cheekbones down to his collar. And that's when Finn noticed—really noticed—the faintest dusting of freckles scattered across his skin. They were barely visible, so light that you'd only catch them in a moment like this.

Eli walked over, shoulders tight like he was bracing for impact. Then, from his back pocket, he pulled out a small bundle wrapped in paper—a striking shade of turquoise that almost perfectly matched Finn's eyes.

He held it out without a word, his fingers barely brushing hers before retreating to his back pockets the moment she took it.

Finn glanced up at him, curiosity flickering in her chest. He wasn't meeting her eyes. Just watching her hands, the way her fingers traced the smooth wrapping paper.

Carefully, she tugged at the silky black bow binding it together.

The ribbon came undone with a soft whisper, and the paper unfurled, spilling its contents into her lap.

Finn sucked in a sharp breath.

Falling from the wrapping paper was something glistening.

Gingerly, she reached down and carefully lifted a delicate gold chain between her fingers. As she raised it higher, the pendant attached to it caught the light, and for the first time, she saw the details—intricate, precise, every careful cut in the polished wood.

A sun and a waning moon, cradled together.

The moon's gentle curve leaned in, as if drawn into the sun's warmth. The sun's rays curled protectively around it, wrapping it in light.

Not a crescent moon, like the ones Sarah and Kai wore.

Something entirely her own.

Finn turned the pendant between her fingers, a realization settling in.

Eli had made this.

"It's Mountain Ash—Rowan wood," Eli said softly, pulling her gaze back to him.

She blinked at him, still caught in the awe of the pendant now resting in her palm.

"Not easy to come by," he added, "But we don't need to get into that."

His hand left his pocket, rubbing the back of his neck—a rare, almost bashful motion. For once, there was no teasing smirk, no sarcastic remark. Just something unguarded.

Before she could second-guess herself, Finn moved.

She stood, crossing the short space between them in a few quick strides, and threw her arms around him.

The pendant was still clutched tightly in her hand, the chain dangling between her fingers, but all she could focus on was the sturdy feel of Eli beneath her arms.

"It's phenomenal," she breathed.

She felt him tense—just for a second—before he eased into the hug, his arms looping around her with a gentle steadiness.

Then, as quickly as it had happened, the reality of it hit her and she pulled away.

She had just hugged him.

In front of Frank and Danny.

Heat crept up her neck as she pulled back, sneaking a quick glance toward them.

Frank and Danny just... watched.

One looked confused. The other? Amused.

Finn turned back to Eli before she could read too much into it.

"Can you help me put it on?" she asked, holding out the necklace.

Eli blinked, surprised—maybe even pleased—before nodding.

She lifted her ponytail, exposing the back of her neck as he stepped closer.

His fingers brushed against her skin, feather soft, as he secured the clasp. The touch was fleeting—but something about it sent a strange shiver through her.

Then he let go.

The pendant fell into place at the center of her chest, settling against her skin.

A comfortable weight.

The kind she had been missing.

Chapter Nineteen

The day unfolded in warmth and easy laughter—the kind of day Finn knew she'd remember forever.

Danny hung around long after his appointment, trading increasingly outrageous stories with Frank about their younger years. He sprawled comfortably in Frank's tattoo chair, speaking through mouthfuls of flaky crust and cinnamon-laced apples about bar fights, poker games gone south, and the occasional "misunderstood" run-in with the law.

Frank, never one to let a good tale stand unchallenged, scoffed between bites of his own slice. "You got a terrible memory, old man," he grumbled, shaking his head. "Half those stories didn't even happen the way you tell 'em. And the ones that did? A hell of a lot stupider than you make 'em sound."

Finn couldn't stop laughing. The shop hummed with the easy camaraderie. It felt... safe. Light.

She didn't miss the way Eli watched her throughout the day—subtle, like he was cataloging every time she laughed. And every time, a flicker of a smile tugged at the corner of his lips.

By midday, Danny finally stretched with a satisfied sigh, brushing stray crumbs off his lap. "Welp. That was the best damn tattoo session I ever had."

Finn smirked and handed him a paper plate with two extra slices, shaking her head. "For your blood sugar, of course."

Danny took it with a wink. "Damn right. Doctor's orders." He patted his belly, and strolled out whistling—looking far too pleased with himself.

The shop calmed after Danny left. The afternoon stretched ahead, as Finn and Eli cleaned up and prepped for the next appointments.

Around three, Frank started gathering his things, slipping his keys into his pocket. He stretched, rolling out the tension in his shoulders before glancing between the two of them.

"I'm heading out," he announced casually, but there was something else there—an odd little smile lifting the corner of his mouth, one Finn couldn't quite place.

She frowned. "Leaving early?"

Frank shrugged, entirely unbothered. "Danny and I got some fishin' to do."

Finn squinted at him, skeptical. "And you're trusting us to hold the place down?"

Frank leveled her with a knowing nod. "I know the place is in good hands."

There it was again—that same weird little smile as his gaze passed briefly between her and Eli before he strolled toward the door.

Finn frowned, watching him go.

What was that about?

Before she could think too hard on it, the shop door swung open, and in walked Brett—loud, confident, and clearly ready to spend the next few hours in the chair.

Eli had him booked for the afternoon, which meant Finn jumped into action.

She moved through the motions effortlessly, pulling gloves from the box, lining up fresh needles, and filling ink caps. Machine prepped, rinse cup filled, paper towels stacked neatly. Everything exactly where it needed to be.

It wasn't until she finished that she felt Eli's gaze on her—watchful, assessing.

She turned to find him leaning against the counter, arms crossed, that slow realization dawning across his face. He was impressed.

Smugly, she crossed her arms, mirroring his stance. "Well?"

"Touché, Rowan," he murmured, pulling on his gloves. Then, with a wink—"Guess you're not a rookie anymore."

As Eli worked, Finn leaned against the counter near Brett, watching as the needle glided over his skin, leaving crisp lines of ink in its wake.

After a while, Brett tilted his head toward her. "So," he asked, with his usual jovial smile, "how are you liking Ash Hollow?"

"It's growing on me," she replied with a wry smile.

Brett nodded like he'd expected that answer. "Good place, good people." He gestured loosely around the shop. "Hell, this place alone is enough reason to stick around."

Finn cocked an eyebrow. "You sound like the town's official spokesperson."

Brett grinned, leaning back in the chair with the kind of relaxed confidence that made it clear he'd spent a lot of time here. "Gotta talk up the town. It's what we do."

Something about his tone made Finn pause with a ridiculous thought. She narrowed her eyes at him, studying him for a second.

The idea hit her before she could stop it—

Was Brett the mayor?

The second it crossed her mind, she nearly snorted out loud, shaking her head at herself. Yeah, okay, maybe Ash Hollow was small, but not that small.

By the time Eli wrapped up the session, Finn had already slipped into work mode, stepping behind the counter to handle the payment process. It felt natural now, the motions familiar.

Brett counted out the cash and slid it across the counter, but this time, there was a bit extra on top.

Finn raised an eyebrow. "Did you mean to tip so much today?"

Brett smirked, resting an elbow on the counter. "The extras for you this time, birthday girl."

Finn blinked, caught off guard. "But how'd you—"

"Ah," Brett cut in smoothly, tapping his receipt against the counter. "Frank let me know on his way out the door." He gave her a pointed look, his expression sincere. "Just wanted to say—you're doing great. You really add something to this place."

Finn's chest puffed unexpectedly. She hadn't realized how much she needed to hear that.

"Thanks, Brett," she said, genuinely grateful.

Brett gave a lazy wave before heading for the door. The bell jingled softly as it swung shut behind him, leaving the shop suddenly quieter.

Eli swept the ink-stained paper towels into the trash, the soft crinkle of them filling the space. Only once the station was clean did he peel off his gloves, tossing them after. With a sigh, he ran a hand through his curls, shaking them loose.

"Go ahead and lock up the front," he said, rolling his shoulders like he was shaking off the long day. "We'll head out the back when we're done."

Finn nodded, flipping the OPEN sign to CLOSED, twisting the lock into place, and then heading back.

Finn grabbed the disinfectant spray and a fresh cleaning cloth, moving through the space. She wiped down the countertops, carefully organizing supplies, but when she reached Frank's station, she took her time—making sure everything was just the way he liked it.

It felt like a small way to repay him for today.

Even as she moved through the last steps of closing up, Finn couldn't shake the warmth still suspended in her chest. The day had settled in a way that felt different—easier, lighter. She smiled to herself as she bagged up the last of the trash and set it by the back door.

Then she turned—

And paused.

Eli's station was spotless. Everything had been cleaned and reset, put back exactly where it belonged.

Everything except one.

His tattoo machine was still plugged in, the power on, a faint, steady hum filling the space.

Eli leaned back in his chair, one arm slung over the backrest, the other draped across his knee. His lips curled into a smirk as he watched her, his amber eyes alight.

"So," he drawled, tilting his head. "What do you think, mountain girl? Are you ready?"

Then—

BZZ BZZ.

The machine buzzed to life, vibrating softly in his grip.

Finn's eyes widened.

"Wait—get a tattoo? Like, now?"

Eli shrugged, his smirk deepening. "You're eighteen now. What's holding you back? Gotta uphold the reputation of your employers."

Finn huffed a laugh, "Oh, is that a requirement now?"

"Unspoken, but yeah," Eli said, tapping his fingers against the armrest. "No pressure, but you've been here long enough. You're practically family at this point. Gotta start somewhere."

She hesitated, running her fingers over her wrist in thought.

"I mean... I have been thinking about it," she admitted, crossing her arms. "A lot this past week, actually."

Eli's smile faded, replaced by something more curious. "Yeah?"

She nodded, glancing down. "I do want to start getting ink, but... I'm not sure what I want yet. And I want the first one to be meaningful."

Eli held her gaze for a moment, like he was weighing her words.

Then, without hesitation, he nodded. "Fair enough."

With a flick of his wrist, he switched off the machine, the hum fading into silence. He moved smoothly, sanitizing and packing it away without another word. No teasing, no pressure.

Finn let out a slow breath, a small, grateful smile tugging at her lips.

She had a feeling that when she was ready—when she finally knew what she wanted—there wouldn't be anyone else she'd trust more to do it.

As Finn and Eli wrapped up for the night, the last remnants of the day settled into stillness. Eli switched off the shop lights, casting everything into shadow while Finn gathered the final bags of trash, their plastic crinkling against her fingers.

She moved toward the back door, but slowed, something tugging at the edge of her awareness.

Her eyes drifted back to the desk.

The pie box still sat there, a reminder of the morning's warmth, its edges softened from being left out. The last two slices remained untouched beneath the cardboard lid, the whipped cream letters now smudged. It felt wrong to leave it behind, like abandoning something meant to be savored.

Without a second thought, she turned on her heel, crossing the dim shop to scoop up the box, tucking it carefully under her arm.

By the time she reached the back door, Eli was already there, holding it open for her.

The alley stretched out before them, footsteps muted by the patter of rain. The pavement gleamed under the glow of the streetlamp, reflecting rippling halos of light. The scent of damp mixed with the sharp, metallic tang of rain on old iron, the fire escape ladders lining the brick walls rusted at the edges.

Eli stepped forward first, boots scuffing against the wet ground as he strode toward the dumpster. He set his trash bags down with a dull thump, lifting the lid in one smooth motion. The hinges groaned, the sound swallowed quickly by the hush of the rain.

Finn followed, shifting the pie box as she tossed in the bags she carried. Then, balancing the box against her hip, she bent down, grabbing the rest of Eli's bags and swinging them up and over the edge of the dumpster.

As she straightened, a thought struck her out of nowhere.

"Is Brett the mayor?"

Eli, mid-motion, froze for a split second—then let out a sharp, surprised laugh. "What?"

Finn shrugged, brushing a damp palm against her hoodie. "I don't know. He just talks about this place like he's running a campaign or something."

Eli's chuckle deepened, shaking his head as he propped the dumpster lid up with one elbow. "No, he's actually the vice principal of the high school."

Finn blinked. "Huh... cool."

He shot her a glance. "Yeah, that's why he's here so much during summer. He's got the time."

Finn nodded absently, gaze drifting toward the mouth of the alley. The neon lights from the bar down the street bled against the rain-slick pavement, colors rippling with each drop that hit the ground.

Eli shifted beside her, still holding the dumpster lid open. He lifted an eyebrow. "So... you gonna toss the pie box in or what?"

Finn's head snapped toward him, immediate offense flashing across her face.

"There's still perfectly good pie in here," she said, clutching the box closer, as if he had just suggested a crime against humanity.

Eli chuckled, shaking his head. "Alright, keep your sacred pie."

With that, he let the dumpster lid fall shut, the heavy clang echoing off the alley walls before fading away.

Then—

A faint shuffling sound echoed down the alley, just beneath the steady patter of the rain.

Finn and Eli froze.

Their heads turned in unison, eyes narrowing as they peered through the dim haze of streetlamp glow at the far end of the alley.

At first, it was nothing. Just shifting shadows and the endless drizzle, the slick pavement reflecting distorted shapes. The outlines of old crates, a rusted drain pipe, the silhouette of an abandoned shopping cart leaning at an awkward angle.

Then—movement.

A shape huddled beneath the overhang of a back doorway, shoulders curled inward, spine bent like he was trying to fold into himself, to disappear into the rain.

Even before she fully made out his face, she knew. It was Josiah.

Eli didn't hesitate. He stepped forward, moving with that steadiness that made people feel at ease, as if nothing about this moment was out of place. Finn followed a few steps behind—not out of hesitation, but because she was searching.

Is it still here?

Her gaze flitted over the alley, sweeping the edges where the streetlamp glow bled into the shadows, where the rain blurred the lines between what was real and what wasn't.

She didn't just expect it—she knew what she was looking for. The thing that had loomed over Josiah the last time she'd seen him, its presence thick, and dark in a way that went beyond shadow.

But the alley held only the soft hush of rain. No flicker of movement where there shouldn't be, no oppressive force pressing at her senses.

Just Josiah.

His shoulders hunched inward, and his jacket soaked at the edges. He looked less than before—diminished, like something had been siphoning the life from him. His hair hung in wet, uneven strands over his face, masking his expression, but it didn't hide the deep hollows beneath his eyes.

Eli stopped a few feet away, voice careful. "Hey, Josiah."

At the sound of his name, Josiah flinched.

A small movement, barely noticeable, but Finn caught it.

His gaze lifted, sharp and wary, flashing between them. His whole body was wound tight, like a stray animal trying to decide whether the hand reaching toward it was safe—or a trap.

Josiah didn't move.

Didn't speak.

Just watched.

He barely seemed to notice Eli, his attention fixed entirely on Finn. His eyes, sharp and assessing, locked onto hers with an intensity that sent a cold shockwave through her.

Then, in a voice roughened by something deeper than the cold, he said, "You're the one."

Finn felt the words settle inside her, low and certain.

The one?

Her breath faltered. "What?"

Josiah's expression didn't shift. He didn't hesitate, didn't blink. There was no uncertainty in the way he spoke, only fact.

"He told me." His voice was calm. "Told me you can see him."

A steady realization wound through Finn's ribs, clicking into place like something inevitable.

This wasn't a guess.

Josiah wasn't wondering if she could see the shadow that followed him—he knew.

Her pulse quickened, but not from fear. Not from unease.

From recognition.

Like an unspoken truth had finally been given form, turned into something real.

She stepped past Eli, moving toward Josiah with an ease that felt instinctive, as though this moment had already happened before. As though she was simply reaching it now.

Eli didn't stop her. He didn't call after her, didn't ask what she was doing. He just watched.

She handed him the pie box without thinking, barely feeling it leave her hands as she crouched in front of Josiah, rain dripping from the ends of her sleeves.

Behind her, Eli moved just a little closer, standing near the edge of the overhang, where the rain was falling heavier. He didn't quite fit in the narrow doorway, but he stayed near enough to listen, near enough to be present. A steadying force at her back.

But he didn't speak.

He was letting her take the lead.

Finn's voice was even when she finally did. "Who is he?" she asked. "Why was he with you?"

Josiah's gaze flickered, something shifting behind his eyes, a hesitation that hadn't been there before. His fingers curled deeper into the folds of his coat, knuckles pressing against the worn fabric.

For a moment, he looked away, his body tensing, as though testing his words before releasing them.

He finally met her gaze again. Careful. "He comes from the mine."

The mine.

Finn's stomach twisted.

Josiah shifted against the cold metal of the doorway. "They're weak, most of the time. But sometimes... when they're strong enough, they slip away."

Finn didn't move, barely breathed, the words sinking in like stones into deep water.

She understood.

Not in the way someone learns a new fact, but in the way someone remembers something that had been buried just beneath the surface, waiting to be recognized.

Her next words weren't a question.

They were something closer to certainty.

"You lent him your energy, didn't you?" she murmured. "So he could come here."

Finn's voice was gentle, softening at the edges. "They miss the town—the ones from the mine."

His fingers twitched where they were buried in his coat, like some part of him wanted to reach for something that wasn't there.

And for the first time since she had met him—

He looked like he wanted to say more.

Josiah's lips parted, but the words stalled, catching in his throat like something physically resisted being spoken aloud. It was subtle at first—the slight tension in his jaw—but Finn saw it.

Not uncertainty.

Fear.

Not the kind of fear that came from seeing something terrifying, but the kind that came from knowing something he wasn't supposed to. Something that had weighed on him for far too long, pressing down until it was nearly unbearable.

His gaze flickered toward the mouth of the alley, a quick, almost instinctive glance, as if making sure no one else was there, no unseen force listening in. He exhaled slowly, his breath faint in the rain-dampened air.

Then, in a voice barely louder than the rain itself, he said—

"The missing boy."

The words landed hard, and for a moment, it was as if the entire alley held its breath.

Finn's pulse stuttered, her body going still as the realization settled in, solid and undeniable. The truth had been creeping at the edges of her mind, forming just out of reach. But now, hearing it spoken aloud, it finally took shape—became something real.

Beside her, Eli didn't move, his posture rigid, his grip on the pie box tightening.

Finn pushed past the initial wave of shock.

"Kai," she murmured.

Josiah didn't confirm it outright, but he didn't have to. The answer was already there, hanging between them like mist in the rain.

The missing boy.

Kai.

It wasn't just about his disappearance. It wasn't just about his death.

He had been a part of this before he was gone.

Josiah's jaw worked. "When he came, he brought the girl sometimes." He shook his head, a small, certain motion. "But they liked him better. He listened. She... didn't. Or couldn't. They stayed with the boy."

The breath left Finn's lungs in a soundless rush, her stomach dropping, fast, like falling through open air.

Eli didn't move.

Neither of them looked at Josiah.

They looked at each other.

Eyes locked, searching, a silent conversation sparking between them like hot lightning in a summer storm. It didn't need to be spoken aloud. They knew.

Finn controlled her breath, but inside, her pulse thundered. The world beyond this moment felt distant, muffled, like everything had narrowed to the space between them.

Josiah's gaze flickered between them, something unreadable behind his tired eyes—hesitation, regret, or maybe both. Then, softer this time, like he almost wished he could take it back—

"He's not missing... he's lost."

Finn inhaled sharply.

Lost.

Not dead. Not gone.

Lost.

The whirlwind of the word shifting everything she thought she knew.

Josiah exhaled, shaking his head, his expression twisting—not in pain, but in something that didn't quite belong to him. Something borrowed. Something carried.

"It made them sad," he murmured, almost distantly.

Them.

The miners. The ones who had spoken to him. The ones who knew.

Finn's pulse pounded behind her ribs, hard and unrelenting, as the full implication of what he was saying pressed into her chest.

Had she been looking at this all wrong?

Beside her, Eli shifted, his own thoughts no doubt racing.

Josiah's posture tensed, discomfort creeping into the lines of his frame, and Finn could feel it—palpable in the air. He had given them more than enough. He had carried more than enough.

And still, she wanted to ask for more.

But not at his expense.

Not when she could see it so clearly—the exhaustion etched into his face, the burden pulling down his shoulders. He had lived with this, with them, for so long. He had carried the dead just as she had.

A life touched. Tethered. Worn down by spirits.

So instead of pushing, she reached out.

Her fingers brushed gently against his arm, a simple touch, small but deliberate.

Josiah didn't flinch.

He simply looked at her hand, as if the gesture was something foreign to him.

Her voice softened, the words slipping out like an offering.

"I'm so sorry, Josiah."

That got him to look up.

And for the first time, he truly met her eyes.

Something in his gaze softened, the sharp edges dulling, just a little.

Finn offered him a small, genuine smile.

"Thank you for sharing this burden with us." Her voice was steady and warm. "I hope it makes you a little lighter."

Josiah just studied her, as if he wasn't sure how to process those words.

Then, after a long pause, he gave the smallest of nods.

Beside her, Eli finally stooped down, balancing the pie box on his knees, his voice easy but sincere.

"You want a ride?" he asked. "We can take you back toward your neck of the woods. Save you the walk in the rain."

Josiah was silent for a moment, watching the slow drizzle around them.

Then he shook his head. "No. It's peaceful here, watching the rain." His voice was quiet, but certain. "I'd like to stay a bit longer."

Finn and Eli both nodded, accepting his answer without argument.

They stood, turning to leave.

They had only taken a few steps when Finn hesitated.

Without a word, she grabbed the pie box from Eli's hands.

He glanced at her, their eyes meeting.

And without needing to ask, he gave her a small nod.

He already knew her intent.

Finn turned back to Josiah, stepping closer once more.

"Are you hungry?" she asked.

Josiah stiffened, but nodded once.

Finn held out the box.

"I've already had more than enough," she told him honestly. "I'd like you to enjoy the rest."

Josiah looked at the box, then back at her.

For a second, he looked caught off guard—like no one had offered him anything in a long time.

Then, finally, he smiled.

It was small, lopsided, unpracticed, but it was real.

Finn smiled back.

And without another word, she and Eli walked away down the alley, their steps patting against the rain-slicked pavement.

The Bronco doors shut with a solid thunk, sealing them inside.

The world outside had transformed into a blur of rain, the streetlights casting a hazy, distorted glow through the downpour. The rain wasn't just falling anymore—it was pouring, drumming against the roof, cascading in rivers down the windshield, almost as if the town itself was releasing something.

Unburdening.

Finn shivered, her clothes soaked through, the cold clinging to her skin.

Eli was the same—drenched, chilled to the bone.

But still, neither of them moved.

Not to start the truck.

Not to flip on the heat.

They just sat in the stillness, breaths fogging faintly in the cold air, staring blankly out the windows at the empty street.

The tattoo shop was dark now, locked up tight for the night. No warm glow cutting through the storm.

No movement.

Just the two of them, sitting in the murmur of the rain.

Finally, Eli let out a hard breath, the exhale visible in the chilled air.

Then, his voice cut through the silence.

"What... the hell is going on with this town?"

He turned his head toward her now, searching, like maybe Finn had an answer he didn't.

His hands, still damp from the rain, rubbed slowly over his jaw—as if trying to wipe away the heaviness of everything they'd just heard.

"I feel like I stepped into a ghost story."

Finn finally looked back at him, exhaustion sinking deep into her bones.

She let her head tip back against the seat, eyes trained on the roof, listening to the steady drum of rain above them.

Then, softly—

"I think a lot more people are contacted by spirits than anyone realizes."

Eli's brows furrowed, but he didn't interrupt.

"Most just learn not to talk about it." Finn's voice was quiet. "They learn to hold it in."

Her fingers played absently with the wet edge of her hoodie sleeve, gaze distant.

"Like I did. Most of my life."

The words hung between them, meaningful but unafraid.

Like a truth she hadn't spoken aloud before.

A truth she wasn't hiding anymore.

Eli rubbed a hand over his chest, just over his sternum, as if something about her words struck there.

Then, without a word, he reached into his jacket pocket.

Pulled out his keys.

And started the ignition.

Chapter Twenty

y the time Finn and Eli pulled up to the house, the rain had slowed to a steady drizzle, mist curling around the porch lights.

The tires crunched against the wet gravel as Eli parked, the headlights cutting through the damp night.

Neither of them spoke as they climbed out, still cold, damp, and exhausted from everything that had happened.

But the second Finn stepped inside, the scent of buttery, pan-fried fish and crispy potatoes hit her.

The house was warm, a stark contrast to the cold rain still clinging to her skin.

Frank stood at the stove, spatula in hand, flipping a fillet in a cast-iron skillet. A plate of golden, crispy fish already rested on the counter, next to a bowl of roasted potatoes speckled with salt and fresh herbs.

His sharp eyes lifted toward them the second they walked in.

"Took you two long enough."

It wasn't accusing, just... curious.

Finn's mind grasped for an excuse, her thoughts fumbling for an explanation that made sense.

Before she could come up with one, Eli—still shaking water from his curls—jumped in smoothly.

"Finn was picking my brain about her first tattoo," he said, leaning against the counter like it was no big deal.

Frank raised a brow, clearly not fully buying it, but not questioning it either.

Instead, he just flipped the last fillet, letting it sizzle before glancing over his shoulder.

"Yeah? You land on anything yet, kid?"

Finn exhaled through her nose—not quite relief, but close.

She peeled off her damp hoodie, hanging it over the back of a chair to dry before shrugging.

"Still thinking on it," she answered truthfully, finally moving forward to grab a plate.

Frank made a noncommittal noise and turned off the burner, dishing up the last fillet.

"Well, don't overthink it too much. First one's gotta mean something, but doesn't mean it has to be complicated."

He set the pan aside and grabbed a beer from the fridge, twisting off the cap.

Then, in typical Frank fashion, he seemed to let the conversation drop as quickly as it started.

Eli shot Finn a glance as if to say, *"We're in the clear."*

She gave him a small nod back, understanding settling between them.

And just like that, they sat down for dinner—both of them acting normal, despite the very real mystery they were now tangled up in.

The kitchen filled with the clinking of silverware against plates, the warmth of the house reinvigorating her, chasing away the lingering chill of the rain.

The meal was simple—freshly fried fish, crisp roasted potatoes, a cold beer for Frank, and ice water for Finn and Eli—but it was good. Comforting.

Finn and Eli did their best to keep up with the conversation, playing along, trying to keep their minds from drifting back to the alley, to Josiah's words, to the shadow of something lost.

Frank, oblivious to the undercurrent of thoughts flowing between them, told them about his fishing trip with Danny, describing in detail how the old man nearly tipped their boat over trying to haul in a black bullhead catfish "the size of a damn toddler."

Finn managed a laugh.

Eli shook his head. "I bet he'll be telling that story for weeks."

Frank snorted. "Oh, guaranteed. Might even add another foot to the size of the fish by next time you hear it."

It was easy banter, but Finn still caught the way Eli's knee bounced lightly under the table, the way he occasionally pushed his food around his plate—which was not like him at all.

Eli wasn't the type to play with his food.

If he had a plate in front of him, he ate. Plain and simple.

But now? His fork scraped lazy patterns through a stray bit of roasted potato, his mind clearly somewhere else.

And she wasn't any better—her mind still swirling, replaying Josiah's words, the way he had looked at her, the certainty in his voice.

But they both kept up the charade, filling in the conversation where needed, nodding along when appropriate.

Eventually, plates were scraped clean, and Finn and Eli moved to help clear the table without needing to be asked.

Frank leaned against the counter, sipping the last of his beer as Eli rolled up his sleeves and started on the dishes.

Finn took her place beside him, grabbing a clean towel.

Eli scrubbed, then passed the plate to Finn to rinse and dry.

It was a practiced system, easy despite the exhaustion hanging between them.

The kitchen wasn't silent, but the conversation had mostly faded into quiet companionship—the only sounds were the steady rush of water, the clink of dishes, and the distant thrum of rain still falling outside.

And though neither of them spoke about it, Finn knew—

They were still entrenched in the events of the night.

Frank took the last long sip of his beer, his heavy-lidded eyes and the slight slump of his posture making it clear—the afternoon of fishing had taken it out of him.

Whether it was the fresh air, the excitement of nearly tipping the boat, or simply the long hours spent out on the water with Danny, he was too worn out to poke at Eli and Finn's odd behavior.

Setting the empty bottle on the counter with a thunk, he stretched his arms over his head with a low grunt.

"I'm calling it. You two don't stay up too late."

His voice held no suspicion, no prying edge—just the familiar, easy tone of someone who had gotten what he needed out of the day and was ready to shut down.

Finn nodded, finishing the last swipe of her towel over a clean fork before setting it aside.

"'Night, Frank."

Eli barely looked up from where he was drying his hands on a dish towel. "'Night."

Frank gave a small wave as he walked through the living room, his hefty boots thudding across the wooden floors.

They heard him head for the stairs, his steps slowing as he climbed, then fading as he disappeared to the upper floor.

With that, the house fell into stillness.

Just the distant drip of rain off the eaves outside.

Just Finn and Eli, standing in the kitchen, side by side.

They waited a few moments, listening to the house settle.

The distant sound of Frank moving around upstairs eventually faded, leaving only the hum of the fridge, the occasional creak of the house settling.

Finn took a slow breath, her lips parting like she was about to say something.

But before she could get a single word out—

Eli held up a finger.

A silent request for patience.

Finn's brow furrowed, but she obliged, watching as he turned and walked over to the fridge.

He opened it, rummaging for a second before pulling out two beers, setting them with a *clink* on the counter beside her.

Finn looked at them.

Then back to Eli, her expression vaguely reproachful—a silent *"seriously?"* forming behind her eyes.

She went to speak again.

Eli, still unreadable, held up a finger once more.

Wait.

Finn's eyes narrowed further, but she held her tongue as she watched him turn away again, this time crossing the kitchen to a far cupboard.

Without hesitation, he reached inside, pulled out a bottle of whiskey, and held it up for Finn's approval.

The second her eyes landed on it, her stomach tightened.

No.

Her mind flickered—flashes of her stepfather, whiskey glass ever-present in his hand.

Flashes of that first night with Eli, that buzz-cut punk egging her on to take deep pulls from his bottle.

Finn's reaction was instant, forceful.

She shook her head, sharp and final.

Eli caught it immediately. He didn't argue. Just put the whiskey back.

For a moment, he stood there, staring at the open cupboard, fingers drumming absently against the shelf, assessing his other options.

Then, after a beat, he grabbed another bottle.

Tequila.

This time, when he held it out, Finn paused.

Then, with a small shrug, she relented.

Eli, satisfied, closed the cupboard with his elbow.

And just like that, the silent negotiation was over.

Eli tucked the tequila bottle under one arm, grabbed both beers with the other hand, and headed for the stairs without a word.

Finn followed silently in tow, knowing—without needing to ask—that he intended to drink with her.

That much had been clear the second he made her choose a bottle instead of just grabbing one himself.

She didn't expect him to part ways at his door.

Didn't expect him to go to his own room at all.

And sure enough, when they reached the upstairs hallway, Eli moved with purpose, never hesitating as he turned assuredly into her room instead.

Finn stepped in behind him, watching as he crossed the small space, reflecting on the day—her birthday morning now felt like a lifetime ago.

He set the tequila bottle down on her small dresser with a solid *thud*.

Then he popped the caps off both beers, the metal lids clinking against the wood before rolling to a stop near the tequila bottle.

He handed her one.

Finn took it, glancing at the bottle almost reluctantly, fingers curling around the cool glass.

Eli didn't wait for her to say anything.

He simply planted himself in the window nook, back against the frame, knee bent, one boot propped up against the ledge.

And then—without breaking eye contact—he took a long, slow drink of his beer.

Finn hesitated for only a second before she followed suit.

She sat at the edge of her bed, directly facing him, eyes still locked with his.

And then—with equal purpose—she took a deep sip from her bottle as well.

Never breaking eye contact.

Eli's gaze flickered, something knowing, something unreadable in the dim light.

But he just exhaled, swirling the bottle absently in his hand, the liquid inside sloshing against the glass in slow, rhythmic waves.

Both Finn and Eli took another sip from their beers.

It was Eli who finally spoke.

"So you've seen these kinds of things your whole life."

He didn't look at her when he said it.

Just stared into the frothing golden liquid in his bottle, watching the bubbles rise and pop.

Finn let her bottle drop into her lap, resting in the crook of her crisscrossed legs.

"Yeah," she said softly.

She waited for his eyes to meet hers again before continuing.

"Not necessarily like this."

She emphasized the word, making sure he understood.

Eli just watched her, silent.

Waiting.

"But I've always seen... things."

She lifted her bottle again, took a quick sip before pressing on.

"Like people I knew who'd died—yelling into the ears of their loved ones who were still living, like they were desperate to make them hear."

Her voice was even and detached.

Finn set her beer down on the dresser, reaching for the tequila bottle instead.

She uncapped it, took a swig, then wordlessly handed it off to Eli before continuing.

"It wasn't until my teens that those people—the ones who were dead—started realizing I could see them."

She let that hang in the air.

Eli took the bottle, but he didn't drink from it just yet.

He just watched her, processing.

Waiting to see if she had more to say.

And in the dim glow of the room, she did.

Eli finally lifted the bottle, tilting it back for a swig of tequila.

Finn watched him beneath eyelids already growing heavier, the warmth of the liquor buzzing through her.

Eli lowered the bottle with a small exhale, the familiar burn chasing down his throat, and then—without looking at her this time—he asked,

"Did you ever try to tell anyone else?"

Finn's fingers clenched around the bottle as he handed it back.

Instead of answering right away, she took another little swig, letting the sting of it buy her an extra few seconds.

Then, finally—

"I tried to tell my mom."

She set the bottle down on the floor beside her, elbows resting against her thighs, fingers idly toying with the hem of her jeans.

"I told her that her parents—my grandparents—were there. That they were trying to talk to her."

Her voice was steady. Too steady.

"They were pleading with her."

Eli's expression didn't change, but something in his gaze sharpened.

Finn huffed a humorless breath, shaking her head.

"She didn't listen to me anymore. Not like when I was little."

Her fingers picked at a loose thread. "Instead, she took it to her husband."

Eli didn't move, didn't react, but Finn could feel his attention.

Still, she kept her voice even, detached, like it wasn't really her own story she was telling.

"A deacon at the church."

She lifted her head now, meeting Eli's gaze.

"He said I was being plagued by demons."

The words sat thick in the air, the memory clinging to the edges of the dimly lit room.

"That they were trying to trick me."

Finn's fingers went still against her jeans.

The tequila bottle resting between them caught the light, the amber liquid shifting as the silence stretched.

Eli's jaw tightened.

But he didn't say anything.

Not yet.

She stood up suddenly, the motion a little too quick, sending a slow, dizzy wave through her head.

She caught herself, feet planting unsteadily beneath her, then exhaled sharply.

"Can we go out for a smoke?"

Eli didn't hesitate. He stood too—more solid, more grounded than Finn felt right now.

"Yes, please."

Finn didn't waste another second.

She strode straight for her bedroom door, sock-softened steps light but quick, pushing out into the hallway.

Eli followed behind, but not before bending down to grab the tequila bottle from where it rested on the floor.

He didn't say anything about it—just took it with them like it was always part of the plan.

They moved through the house, keeping their steps as silent as possible, their movements instinctively careful despite the haze of liquor.

The cool night air hit Finn the second she stepped onto the porch, sending a ripple of clarity through her as she crossed to the Bronco. Her socked feet instantly soaked by the rain wet earth.

Eli didn't follow.

Instead, he posted up on the front steps, planting himself there, bottle resting against his knee, waiting for her.

Finn rummaged with little grace, pulling out her pack of smokes and a lighter.

She closed the door carefully, casting a quick glance back at the house, making sure they hadn't woken Frank.

Then she turned back to Eli, cigarettes in one hand, lighter in the other, and headed for the porch.

Instead of plucking out a couple of cigarettes, Finn wordlessly handed the pack and lighter to Eli, as if forgetting entirely that having a smoke was her idea in the first place.

Eli didn't comment on it, didn't give her that sideways smirk he usually did when she was being absentminded.

He just shook two loose, taking one for himself.

But instead of lighting it right away, he placed it between his parted lips, letting it rest there as he held the second one out to her.

Finn took it between her lips without question, without thinking, just trusting.

Eli clicked the lighter to life, the small flicker of flame cupped against the breeze, a fine mist of rain still carried on the night air.

As the tip of Finn's cigarette glowed red, Eli muttered,

"Pretty girls don't light their own cigarettes."

Then, with the same sure motion, he cupped his own, sparked it to life, and inhaled deep.

And just like that, the world around them settled again, the buzz of tequila humming steady in their veins, the night stretching on.

The first drag of the cigarette went straight to Finn's head, the nicotine threading through the tequila haze, settling into her limbs.

She exhaled, watching the smoke twist and vanish into the misty air, then picked up right where she had left off.

"My stepfather made sure to drive it home that... what I was seeing wasn't real."

Her voice was quiet, but there was something sharp beneath it, something not yet dulled by time.

As if on instinct, her fingers absently rubbed at her shoulder, where the sting of his belt had once landed, where his lessons had been beaten into her skin, into her silence.

Eli watched her, his cigarette burning idly between his fingers, the way his gaze followed the movement of her hand making it clear that he noticed.

But he still didn't interrupt.

So Finn kept going.

"It never stopped."

She took another drag, her lips parting to let the smoke curl free before she continued.

"But I learned to keep it all to myself."

Her voice was matter-of-fact, but something else was there now, too.

Understanding.

Realization.

"The more I ignored them, the less it happened."

She glanced at Eli now, something distant in her eyes, as if the thought was just setting into place as she spoke it aloud.

And then—

"Until... I left."

There was a finality in the words, the pieces of something slotting together in her mind.

She had been on the road a couple of days by then.

Drifting.

Moving from bus to bus, mile after mile.

And then—the lake.

That was when she saw Kai.

Not as a whisper.

Not as a distant, glimmering vision.

But as something vivid. Something impossible to ignore.

The truth of it settled deep in her chest, humming beneath the warmth of the liquor.

Maybe it wasn't just the place she had left behind that changed things.

Maybe it was her.

Then, finally—

"And met Kai?"

He wasn't pressing. Wasn't doubting.

Just continuing where she left off.

Finn nodded, firmly, without hesitation.

"Yeah."

She took another slow drag, exhaling as she spoke.

"It's like leaving... opened a floodgate."

The misting rain still carried on the breeze, fine droplets catching in the glow of the porch light.

Eli didn't respond.

Didn't push for more.

Instead, he shifted absentmindedly, his body angling closer to hers as a small shiver rolled over her shoulders.

Finn didn't acknowledge it.

Didn't say anything about the cold or the way he moved in just enough to buffer her from the night air.

Eli was quiet for a long moment, his body now just close enough to share his warmth.

Then, finally—

"It's Kai and Sarah, right?"

Finn's cigarette paused midway to her lips as she looked at him.

Something shifted behind her eyes, something knowing, covered, but there all the same.

She didn't have to ask what he meant. She knew.

Eli flicked the ash from his cigarette, his voice lower now, more certain.

"The young man and woman Josiah was talking about."

"Yes."

No elaboration.

She didn't have to.

Eli knew.

They both knew.

The miners.

The restless ones.

Eli took another quick swig of the tequila before passing it back.

"They opened some kind of connection to Kai."

It wasn't a question.

It was a confirmation.

Finn nodded once, pressing the mouth of the bottle to her lips and took a deep swig.

The liquor burned, but she welcomed it.

Eli exhaled his next drag, the smoke disappearing into the damp air before he muttered,

"So that settles it, officially."

Finn glanced over at him, cigarette dangling between her fingers, waiting.

"We have to talk to Sarah."

A solemn nod from Finn. No hesitation. No doubt.

"Yeah."

They finished their cigarettes, stamping them out on the porch and flicking them lazily toward the Bronco.

Eli stretched as he muttered, "I'll remember to pick those up tomorrow so Frank doesn't get irritated."

Finn just hummed in response.

They both knew, somewhere deep in themselves, that neither of them would actually remember.

Finally, they turned back toward the house.

Tried to walk carefully, move lightly, just as they had on the way out.

But it was far less successful this time.

Eli still had the half-empty tequila bottle in his hand, holding it loosely as they stepped through the kitchen.

As he reached the cupboard, he swung the door open, a little too fast, and slid the bottle inside without much precision.

At that exact moment, Finn misjudged the edge of the kitchen table, her hip catching it hard.

A dull thud echoed through the house.

She hissed under her breath, biting back a curse, one hand bracing against the tabletop as she exhaled through her nose.

Eli paused, eyes flicking toward her, but didn't say anything.

Just stifled a laugh, shaking his head as he closed the cupboard and kept moving toward the stairs.

Finn followed, rubbing at her side, their steps careful again—but the damage was already done.

When they got to Finn's room, they didn't talk about it—they just wordlessly crashed onto her bed.

Eli flopped at the foot of it as Finn rolled onto her back at the head.

She tossed a decorative pillow toward him, which he caught and shoved beneath his head.

They lay there—feet to head, head to feet, staring at the ceiling, voices low and slurred as they mumbled about their next step.

Finding a chance to talk to Sarah.

Somewhere between words, somewhere between murmured thoughts and unfinished sentences, they both slipped into a drunken stupor of sleep.

The beer bottles stashed underneath the bed, more promises to remember to clean them up tomorrow.

Neither of them would.
And the night stretched on, silent and waiting.

Chapter Twenty-One

he first thing Finn registered was how bright it was.

Too bright.

The kind of blinding daylight that made her brain stumble through a haze, piecing together why everything felt wrong.

She groaned, pressing her face into her pillow, but the movement made her head throb.

The second thing she registered—

Eli's presence.

A shifting at the foot of her bed, followed by a muffled, groggy "Shit."

Finn peeked one eye open, squinting against the harsh slant of sunlight cutting through the curtains.

Eli was just barely awake, rubbing a hand over his face, his hair an absolute mess, eyes still half-lidded with sleep.

Then—his gaze flashed to the window.

To the golden light pouring in through the glass.

Both of them froze.

There was no mistaking it.

The sun was way too high.

"Oh, no." Finn's voice cracked.

Eli groaned, already swinging his legs over the side of the bed, moving with the stiffness of someone who hadn't meant to fall asleep like that.

Finn pushed herself upright, instantly regretting it as her stomach lurched in protest.

They'd overslept.

Badly.

The night before flooded back in pieces—the porch, the cigarettes, the tequila, the unraveling of memories and realizations—

And now?

They were late.

Finn and Eli stumbled over each other trying to pull themselves together, muttering curses under their breath as they shoved out of her room.

By the time they clattered downstairs, barefoot, hair still a mess, definitely looking like two people who had been up far too late drinking—

Frank was already waiting for them.

Seated at the kitchen table.

Not saying a word.

Just reading the newspaper.

Coffee steaming in front of him, completely unbothered.

Finn and Eli both stalled at the threshold.

Frank didn't even look up.

Just turned a page calmly and took a sip of coffee.

Finally—in that slow, knowing tone—he muttered,

"Mooornin'."

Then, without lifting his eyes—

"You two enjoy your little celebration last night?"

Finn swallowed. Eli scratched the back of his neck.

Shit.

They didn't even try to talk their way out of it.

They just stood there in palpable guilt, neither sure what to say.

Finn hesitated for only a moment before she pulled out a chair and sat down across from Frank, her head hanging in shame.

Eli, instead of speaking, just walked over to the coffee pot, grabbing two mugs from the cupboard.

He brought both cups back to the table, setting one in front of Finn before sitting in the other empty chair.

Finn usually hated black coffee—the bitterness always made her scrunch her nose, always had her reaching for sugar and cream.

But today?

She accepted it without a word.

Just wrapped her fingers around the warm mug and took a slow sip.

Eli did the same.

And together, they sat sipping their coffee, waiting for Frank to tear into them.

But he didn't.

For a few long moments, he just kept reading the paper, turning another page with slow patience.

Then—finally—he folded it closed, setting it aside with a rustle of newsprint.

He leaned forward, eyeing them each in turn.

"Look," he started, voice steady, unreadable.

"I know you're both adults now."

He eyed them each in turn.

"And you're gonna do the kinds of things that all young adults do."

Finn lowered her gaze further, gripping her mug a little tighter.

Eli just sat there, listening.

Frank sighed heavily, shaking his head as he glanced between them again.

"Danny and I spent half the day yesterday talkin' about all the bad decisions we made at your age."

He exhaled through his nose, rubbing a hand over his jaw.

"I guess I just hoped you two were better than us."

The words weren't cruel, weren't harsh—but they landed all the same.

Finn swallowed.

Eli glanced down at his mug.

Neither of them knew what to say to that.

Both Finn and Eli absorbed Frank's disappointment.

Then, at the same time—

"Sorry, Frank."

"Sorry, Pops."

Their voices overlapped, pulling their eyes toward each other for a brief second before Eli—without thinking—jumped in to take the fall.

"It was my idea."

Frank barely blinked.

"Well, yeah." His voice was flat and unimpressed.

Then, without missing a beat, he motioned toward Finn with his chin.

"I didn't think it was this sweet angel's idea."

Eli flushed.

Finn stifled a smile, biting the inside of her cheek to keep it from showing.

A sweet angel.

She'd never been called that before. At least not since her mom used to when she was little.

So this is what it feels like to be a daddy's girl.

Frank leaned back in his chair, bracing his hands against the table.

"Alright." He nodded to himself. "Here's the deal."

Finn and Eli both tensed, preparing for whatever was coming next.

"I'm calling work off today."

Both of their heads snapped up in surprise.

Eli's brows shot up so fast it was almost comical.

"Wait, what?"

Frank didn't acknowledge their shock. Just kept talking.

"For all three of us."

Eli blinked, sitting back like he needed to physically process what he was hearing.

Frank Ashford had never closed the shop on a Saturday.

Not for as long as Eli could remember.

Finn threw her gaze toward him, seeing the same disbelief written all over his face.

Frank, ignoring them, grabbed his coffee and took a sip before finally looking up again.

"We're just gonna treat this one like other businesses treat the day after a holiday."

His eyes slid toward Finn, sly and knowing, the corners of his mouth twitching with restraint.

Finn felt her face warm, realizing what he was implying.

He was calling her birthday a holiday.

Eli huffed out something between a laugh and a scoff, shaking his head.

Frank leveled them both with a firm look.

"You guys recover and enjoy your long weekend. Back at it on Monday. Got it?"

The sternness in his voice was still there, but—

So was the twinkle in his eye.

Finn and Eli didn't push their luck.

They both muttered their thank-yous, grabbing their coffees as they stood.

And then, without a second of hesitation, they booked it out of the kitchen.

No way in hell were they giving Frank a chance to reconsider.

The rain never let up.

It had been nothing more than a fine mist the night before, clinging to their skin as they stood on the porch, cigarettes glowing in the dark, words slipping between them like something sacred—Finn finally unraveling the things she had spent years keeping to herself.

Now, it was steady, pattering against the windows in a rhythmic cadence, a hushed soundtrack to the kind of afternoon that felt like it existed outside of time.

Frank's declaration of their long weekend had been both pointed and merciful. Neither she nor Eli had argued. Instead, they'd taken their coffee upstairs, unhurried, wordless in the kind of way that only came from mutual exhaustion.

They showered. Tried to scrub off last night, the haze of tequila and the dull ache lingering behind their eyes.

By the time Finn tugged a sweatshirt over her damp hair and stepped into the hallway, she caught the sound of music drifting from Eli's room—not the usual rough-edged rock he played downstairs when the garage was open, but something softer.

Low and slow. A deep, bluesy hum that curled through the house like smoke.

She followed it, bare feet whispering against wooden floors, pausing briefly outside his door before pushing it open without knocking.

Eli was sprawled out on his bed, one arm tucked behind his head, an old vinyl sleeve resting on his stomach. He barely glanced at her before nodding toward the stack of records on the floor.

"Pick something."

Finn moved toward the pile, fingers ghosting over the cardboard covers, the scent of aged vinyl mingling with the damp air and faint trace of his shampoo. She flipped through them slowly, the crackle of the record playing beneath the sound of her fingertips as she searched.

Then, the unmistakable opening riff filled the air.

"Baby, please don't go..."

The words slipped out before she even thought about them, her voice barely above a murmur.

Eli's eyes flashed to her, sharp at first, then shifting—something quick and fleeting, there and gone, but not before she caught it.

Recognition.

Like someone had just seen a part of him he hadn't meant to show.

A smirk tugged at her lips. "What? You think I don't know my blues?"

Eli exhaled, shaking his head. "Didn't say that."

But his voice had lost its usual edge. Maybe even a bit impressed.

Finn pulled a record free, holding it up.

His brow quirked. "John Legend?"

"Not just John Legend."

She lifted Lightnin' Hopkins off the platter, slid the John Legend vinyl from its sleeve, and lowered it onto the turntable.

A quiet crackle. Then—*Who Did That To You* spilled into the space, deep and raw.

Eli let out a short laugh, turning onto his side to face her.

"Interesting choice."

Finn leaned back against the wall, drawing her knees to her chest, letting the music sink into her bones.

"Felt right."

The song thrummed between them, deep and low, the kind of melody that filled the spaces between thought and memory.

Eli's fingers tapped absently against his stomach, unconsciously keeping time, his body moving with the music even as his mind drifted somewhere else. Finn sat with her knees pulled up to her chest, her arms draped loosely over them, letting the lyrics flood her senses.

"Who did that to you... you better tell me before I go..."

She exhaled, stretching her legs out, toes flexing against the floor. Last night still clung to her, not heavy, but present—an ache just beneath the surface, lingering at the edges of her thoughts.

"Alright."

His fingers stilled where they had been moving against the fabric of his hoodie, his focus shifting back to her.

"How are we gonna do this?"

Finn blinked, forcing herself back into the moment. "Sarah?"

Eli nodded, watching her closely. "Sarah."

She sighed, running a hand through her damp hair before rubbing her face. "I don't know yet."

But they both knew—they had to figure it out. And soon.

The record spun on, the final chords fading into the soft crackle of static, but neither of them moved to change it. The music still hummed in the air, like something unfinished.

They should have been talking about Sarah, about what to say and how to say it, but Eli's eyes were still on her, searching.

He wasn't waiting for a plan.

He was waiting for her.

"That song."

Finn glanced up, thrown by the shift. "What?"

"Who did that to you."

Eli's fingers toyed idly with the hem of his hoodie, tapping a slow, deliberate rhythm.

"You said it felt right." His voice wasn't questioning, just careful, like he already knew there was more beneath the words.

Finn swallowed, running her thumb along the jagged edge of a hangnail, the other tracing patterns against the fabric of her jeans. She could brush past it, pivot, shift the focus back to Sarah. She could say it was nothing.

But Eli was watching her like he already knew the truth. Like he was just waiting for her to say it.

She could lie.

She'd done it before—dodging, deflecting, tucking things away where no one could reach them. But it remained, coiled and restless, and for some reason, she didn't want to shove it down this time.

So instead, she exhaled, fingers pressing lightly into her knee before balling into a loose fist.

"It just... reminds me of something."

Eli just nodded, waiting.

Finn's throat felt tight, her pulse drumming beneath her skin, too fast, too uneven. And then, before she could stop herself—before she could decide whether she even wanted to—she let it slip.

"Someone."

The word was almost hesitant, like an old scar traced beneath the fingertips, still holding the faintest echo of pain.

Eli didn't react right away, he just let it hang between them, settling like something fragile, something not meant to be disturbed. The record crackled softly in the background.

Finn cleared her throat, breaking the moment before he could. "Anyway," she murmured, shaking her head as if brushing it off. "Sarah."

Eli watched her for a second longer, his expression unreadable.

Like he wasn't entirely willing to let it go.

But then, finally, he nodded.

And just like that, they let it settle.

Let the music carry the rest.

Finn finally looked up, meeting Eli's eyes head-on for the first time since the conversation shifted.

"You've known her your whole life, right?" Her voice was more certain than before. "So how do we approach this?"

For a second, he looked like he didn't know what to say—like he hadn't thought that far ahead.

Then, something flickered behind his eyes.

The poster.

The one Sarah left at The Lantern.

Not just any missing flyer—Kai's missing flyer.

She'd left it there, deliberately placed where they would see it.

That meant something.

She'd opened the door.

Now, they just had to walk through it.

Eli exhaled, rubbing the side of his jaw. "The missing poster."

Finn's brows knit together briefly. "What?"

"The one at The Lantern." Eli sat up, arms resting on his knees. "She put it there on purpose, Finn. She wanted us to see it."

Finn's expression shifted, a look of realization settling in.

Eli nodded like he could see the pieces clicking into place for her too.

"So maybe that's how we do it. We just... confront her about that." He leaned back against the wall, stretching out his legs. "Tell her we noticed—like she apparently wanted us to."

Finn nodded, already following his train of thought.

"And see if she explains herself from there."

"Exactly."

It wasn't a full plan.

But it was a way in.

Finn sat with it for a moment, considering.

Then, she lifted her gaze again. "Okay, but... how much do we tell her?"

Eli fell silent.

His jaw flexed, as if he'd already thought about this question but hadn't liked any of the answers.

Because that was the real issue, wasn't it?

Sarah had left them the bait—but that didn't mean she was ready for the whole damn truth.

And Finn knew better than anyone—knowing something and being ready to face it were two very different things.

The long weekend passed, slow and thoughtful—they let themselves sink into it, knowing that once Monday came, everything would change.

Frank's unexpected day off had been a gift, one they took for all it was worth.

They let themselves relax, let themselves breathe—but beneath it all, the reality of what was coming never fully left them.

Confronting Sarah.

By the time Monday rolled around, neither of them needed to say it. They both knew the plan.

They would get through the workday. And when it was over, they would go straight to The Hollow Stitch.

No more stalling.

No more waiting.

It was time to get answers.

The shop was steady, its familiar routine unfolding—appointments cycling in and out, the hum of the tattoo machines filling the air, the scent of antiseptic and ink grounding everything in place.

For a while, Finn let herself sink into it, moving through the motions without thinking. Wiping down stations. Prepping equipment. Greeting clients with the kind of easy familiarity she had grown into over the past few weeks.

It was normal.

Simple.

But as the afternoon stretched toward closing, she felt it—of what came next, creeping into her thoughts no matter how hard she tried to push it back.

The question of how much to say, of how much pressure to apply before Sarah either cracked open or shut down completely.

She was so lost in it, she didn't notice her mistake.

"Finn."

Eli's voice cut through the haze of her thoughts, pulling her back into the present.

She blinked, realizing he was holding out a needle cartridge—the one she had just placed on his tray.

She frowned. "What?"

"These are shaders." His brows lifted. "I needed liners."

Her stomach dipped.

She never mixed that up.

"Shit," she muttered, already reaching to fix it. "Sorry, I wasn't—"

"You're distracted."

It wasn't a question. Just a simple observation.

She gave a solitary nod.

Eli just smirked, setting the shader back down. "Just don't mix up my black ink with white, and we'll be fine."

Finn let out a soft breath, huffing a quiet laugh. "Noted."

And just like that, they fell back into step.

The last few hours slipped by without issue. Closing came and went—stations wiped down, chairs tucked away, the lingering scent of ink and disinfectant settling in the air like a finishing touch.

But this time, when the lights dimmed, the hum of the shop lulled into stillness, and the front door locked behind them—there was no forgetting what lay ahead.

No more distractions. No more waiting.

Finn pictured the brass bell over The Hollow Stitch's door and felt the rowan pendant warm against her sternum.

It was time to face Sarah.

Chapter Twenty-Two

he street outside The Hollow Stitch was still, the last few customers having already left, their cars disappearing down the road into the night.

From where they sat in the Bronco, parked just a little down the street, Finn and Eli watched as Sarah moved through the boutique before closing up.

She wasn't in a hurry.

Finn tapped her fingers against the door handle, nerves wrestling in her stomach.

They had spent the weekend thinking about this moment, waiting for it.

Now that it was happening, it didn't feel like they were as ready as they thought.

Eli exhaled sharply.

"Feels like she's stalling."

Finn glanced back at the window.

Sarah wasn't just shutting off the lights and locking up.

She was moving through the boutique, adjusting a few displays.

She took down a small "20% Off" sign, replacing it with a different one, then stepped back, tilting her head, adjusting the angle.

She smoothed out the hem of a blouse on one of the mannequins, tucking the fabric just a little differently before moving on.

She disappeared behind the counter for a moment—Finn could see the faint glow of a screen from a register or tablet—before she finally reemerged.

Only then did she begin turning off the lights.

One by one, each section of the store faded to black.

By the time she reached the front door, the boutique sat in near darkness, except for the glow of a soft streetlamp through the window.

Sarah stepped outside, pulling the door closed behind her, keys dangling in her hand as she turned the lock.

She was alone.

No coworkers, no hovering customers.

Now or never.

Eli pushed open his door, stepping out without hesitation.

Finn followed.

The sound of the Bronco doors closing in unison made Sarah pause as she slid her keys into her purse.

Then she turned.

She saw them.

And she froze.

Finn caught the briefest flicker of something across Sarah's face—not shock, not fear... something else.

Calculation.

For a moment, none of them moved.

Then Eli broke the silence.

"Sarah."

She tightened her grip on her purse strap, watching them carefully before finally speaking.

"I figured I'd be seeing you two."

Her voice was controlled.

Finn and Eli exchanged a glance.

Sarah's shoulders were stiff, her body angled like she was bracing for something.

Wary.

Finn recognized it instantly—the guarded stance of someone who wasn't sure if she was about to be cornered or questioned.

She wasn't sure what they wanted from her yet.

Finn cleared her throat, stepping forward just enough to show they weren't about to ambush her.

"You left that poster for us to see."

Sarah's fingers twitched against the strap of her purse, her weight shifting.

"And?"

Eli's jaw flexed. "You were the last person to see Kai. How he was acting... what he was wearing."

Sarah's reaction was quick—too quick.

"That's what the cops said too," she muttered. "Doesn't mean I know what happened to him."

Finn watched her carefully, reading the tension in her jaw, the way her posture stiffened further.

She kept her voice even.

"What can you tell us? About the last time you saw him?"

Sarah hesitated.

That hesitation told Finn more than any answer would.

She wasn't saying no, she was just deciding how much she was willing to give.

Sarah exhaled sharply, glancing toward the empty street like she was deciding whether this was a conversation she even wanted to have.

Finally, she muttered, "Not much." She said it too fast, thumb worrying the raw edge of her nail.

But she wasn't walking away.

Finn pressed gently. "Please."

Sarah exhaled again, shaking her head like she already regretted it.

"Fine." She angled back towards them, just a hair. "It was after school. I ran into him on my way home. He was… off."

Eli's brow furrowed. "Off how?"

"He acted like someone was watching him," she finally said. "Kept looking over his shoulder, like he expected something to jump out at him."

Finn felt her pulse kick into high gear.

Sarah shook her head. "And he wasn't making sense when he talked. Just… rambling."

Finn exchanged a glance with Eli. "Rambling about what?"

Sarah pressed her lips together, then answered. "Shadows."

A chill ran down the back of Finn's neck.

"I asked him what he meant, but he got frustrated. Kept saying he didn't know why 'they' wouldn't leave him alone."

Eli let out a slow breath.

Kai had been seeing them too.

Not just the miner in the alley.

All of them.

Sarah shook her head again, like she was still trying to make sense of it herself.

"I don't know what he was talking about," she admitted. "I figured he was just stressed. But he didn't seem okay."

Finn swallowed hard.

He wasn't okay.

And then, he was gone.

Sarah glanced between them, then let out a sharp exhale. "That's all I've got."

Finn could tell she was holding something back.

But before Finn could decide if she wanted to push, Sarah narrowed her eyes.

"I've answered your questions," she said, a seething edge to her words. "Now you tell me."

Finn barely had time to react before Sarah took a step forward.

"How the hell did you get Kai's things?"

Finn's breath caught in her throat.

"The things he was wearing the last time I—" Sarah cut off, jaw clenching. "The last time anyone saw him."

Finn knew she had to be the one to respond.

But she also knew she couldn't—at least not yet—explain how she got them.

Not to Sarah.

She took a slow breath.

"I found them."

Sarah's expression darkened.

Her voice was flat and cold.

"Bullshit."

Then, before either of them could say another word, she turned on her heel and walked away, leaving them standing there on the empty sidewalk.

The air inside Eli's room was cool and still; their conversation with Sarah sat between them like an extra presence.

Finn sat cross-legged at the foot of his bed, her fingers absently tracing the carved edges of the pendant Eli had made for her. The wood was smooth beneath her touch, the delicate curves of the sun and waning moon familiar now.

Eli was in his usual spot—the head of his bed, closest to the window—one leg bent, an arm draped over his knee, staring out at the darkened yard below.

Neither of them had spoken much since getting back.

Now, finally, Finn exhaled, breaking the silence.

"What Sarah said about Kai... the way he was acting."

Eli turned his head, listening.

Finn pressed her lips together, thinking. "It ties in with what Josiah said. About the miner spirits."

Eli raised a brow. "The ones that think Kai was supposed to help set them free?"

She nodded. "Yeah. If they really believed that... maybe they were following him. Watching him. Trying to get him to listen."

Eli huffed out a breath, rubbing a hand over his jaw. "So he was being stalked by ghosts."

Finn lifted one shoulder in a half-shrug. "Yeah. I think so. Or... something like that, anyway."

She leaned back against the bedframe, "Maybe their desperation was feeding them. Giving them just enough energy to stretch past their borders. Like how Josiah's energy let that one miner make it all the way into town."

He shook his head slowly, not in disbelief, but in some semblance of agreement.

Then, after a moment, he muttered, "She's not telling us everything."

Finn looked up.

Eli's gaze was sharper now, focused. "It felt like she knew more about Kai's behavior than she let on."

Finn didn't hesitate. "Yes. 100%."

Then Eli's amber eyes flicked to hers, unreadable.

"But she wasn't the only one holding back, was she?"

Finn sat up straighter, her fingers tightening around the pendant. "I couldn't just say that the ghost of her best friend gave me his stuff, now could I?"

Eli didn't answer right away.

He just studied her, turning that over in his mind.

Then, finally, he gave a small nod, conceding.

Finn sighed, releasing the pendant and rubbing at her temples. "For one, she doesn't know he's dead. Not for certain, the way we do. She might spiral if we tried to spring that on her."

She hesitated, then added, "And even if we did... telling her we know because I've met his ghost?" She shook her head. "I couldn't do that."

Eli hummed low in his throat, considering.

Finn could tell he agreed.

But that didn't make any of this easier.

The three of them were circling the truth, each holding something back.

And somehow, that felt just as dangerous as whatever the truth actually was.

Finn lay in bed, blankly staring at the ceiling, her mind tangled in their conversation.

There was no clear next step.

No roadmap telling her where to go from here.

The only certainty was that they were missing something.

With a slow exhale, she wrapped the blanket tighter around herself, rolling onto her side. Her body was exhausted, but her mind refused to rest.

Eventually, the pull of sleep dragged her under.

– – –

Darkness.

Then, flickering light.

A single candle flame, its glow barely holding against the deep black surrounding it.

I don't know if I'm standing or floating, but I'm here. Watching. Unseen.

The flame wavers, casting shadows against rock walls—uneven, jagged. A cave. No... a tunnel.

The air is thick, unmoving. Stale.

Two hands, fingertips barely touching in the flickering glow.

I know one of them instantly.

Kai.

The other... blurred. Indistinct.

A presence sits between them—something unseen but felt.

The candle sputters.

Then—a ripple. Like something shifting beneath the surface of water.

The air changes. The light snuffs out.

And suddenly, I'm somewhere else.

The lake.

The water is still, dark, reflecting the glow of the moon like polished glass.

Kai stands at the edge, his back to me. Watching the water.

I open my mouth to call out, but—no sound comes.

He tilts his head, like he hears something I can't. Like something else is here.

Then, slowly, he lifts his arms.

His fingers work the buttons of his jacket, one by one.

He shrugs it off, his movements careful. Intentional.

Instead of dropping it, he reaches forward and drapes it over a thick tree root jutting out near the shoreline.

But this time, I see it—the way his fingers linger.

The way he adjusts it, making sure it stays in place.

Making sure it will be found.

The realization makes my stomach drop.

He wasn't coming back for it.

He meant to leave it for someone.

Then, without hesitation, he steps forward.

Into the water.

A slow ripple expands outward, swallowing the fabric in its reflection.

The image fractures. The lake disappears.

Suddenly, I'm inside.

It's dark—colder now.

The weak glow of a small flashlight against a surface.

I can't tell where I am.

Everything feels narrow, suffocating.

Then, out of the shadows, something comes into focus.

A document.

The words blur, shifting like they don't want me to read them.

I strain my vision, trying to focus.

Then—just at the bottom of the page, the letters harden into something legible.

ASHFORD MINING COMPANY.

Ashford. Not Ash Hollow.

A shock wave sweeps through me—

And I gasp awake.

– – –

Finn woke with a sharp inhale, her pulse hammering, breath coming too fast, too shallow.

The darkness in her room felt stifling, pressing in from all sides. She shoved the covers back, barely registering the cool air against her skin as she swung her legs over the edge of the bed. The stillness of the house settled around her, the kind that only existed in the dead hours before dawn, untouched and waiting.

She didn't hesitate.

Her feet carried her into the hallway, each step soundless. The air felt heavier out here, thick with something unspoken, something unfinished.

Eli's door loomed just ahead. She reached for the handle and pushed it open with no regard.

A rustle of sheets. A groggy, half-conscious mumble. Eli stirred, shifting beneath the covers, blinking up at her in confusion as the dim gray light of early morning filtered through his window.

"Finn?" His voice was rough and sleep-thick. "What the hell—"

She didn't answer.

Didn't even look at him.

Her steps were purposeful as she crossed the room, straight to the bookshelf, her focus narrowing to the large fiction book she had noticed him adjusting the night he handed her the history texts. The one he hadn't wanted her to see past.

Eli pushed himself up onto his elbows, brows drawing together, his exhaustion quickly giving way to something sharper.

"Finn—"

Her fingers curled around the spine, yanking the book free.

'Ashford Hollow: A History.'

Ashford. There it was again.

The book he had deliberately hidden.

She turned, stepping back toward the bed, and dropped it onto his lap.

Eli barely glanced at it before looking back at her. His hands hovered over the cover, but he didn't reach for it, didn't even attempt to brush this off. Instead, something swam behind his tired amber eyes—something careful, measured, almost like regret.

Finn crossed her arms over her chest, steadying herself with a breath. Her voice was low but firm.

"Start talking."

Eli didn't rush to defend himself or push the book aside. He just sat there, taking her in, eyes searching her face like he was trying to gauge just how much she had already figured out.

Then, finally, he exhaled.

Without a word, he swung his legs over the side of the bed, shifting the book onto the mattress beside him. One hand dragged down his face before raking through his tangled curls, his fingers lingering there for a beat too long.

"Let me get dressed," he murmured, his voice low, still thick with sleep. "I'll meet you downstairs in five."

Finn didn't nod. Didn't acknowledge the words at all.

She turned on her heel and walked out, leaving his door open behind her, slipping into her own room across the hall.

Her hands were shaking.

Not with anger. Not with fear.

With something sharper. Hotter. A need for answers that burned her every synapse.

She dressed quickly, her movements stiff, yanking on a pair of jeans and a long-sleeve before stepping back out into the hallway. The house was still steeped in silence, the world outside caught between night and morning.

At the bottom of the stairs, she veered right without thinking, pushing open the screen door to the sunroom.

The crisp air wrapped around her, cool and damp with the last breaths of night. She barely registered it. Instead, her focus locked onto the large window stretching across the far wall.

The horizon was shifting now, deep purples and blues bleeding into soft golds, the first slivers of sunlight setting the sky aglow. The light spilled across the room, painting long streaks of color over the floor, catching against the brushstrokes of Nancy's painting, shifting the hues, bringing out depths Finn hadn't noticed before.

She didn't turn when she finally heard Eli step into the room behind her.

Chapter Twenty-Three

li watched the back of Finn's head for a moment, eyeing the stiff set of her shoulders.

She was waiting.

He exhaled, rubbing his sweating palms over his knees before speaking, his voice quieter than she expected—almost pleading.

"I wasn't trying to hide it from you... I mean, not really."

Finn didn't turn around.

She heard him shift, his footsteps moving away from where he'd entered.

Finally, she turned, eyes locking onto him as he sank onto the wicker couch.

His shoulders were hunched, hands clasped loosely in his lap, and head tilted downward.

Not defensive.

Just... *worn.*

She walked over briskly and planted herself in the wicker chair directly across from him.

For a moment, neither of them spoke.

Then, Eli sighed before looking up at her. "Me and my dad... we don't like to draw attention to it. To our family history with this town."

His gaze flickered down again. "It makes people look at us differently. Some treat us differently."

There was something tired in his voice. Like this was something he'd carried for a long time.

"There are still people in this town who lost family members in that mining accident." He rubbed a hand over his jaw, shaking his head. "And there have always been whispers about The Ashford Mining Company's practices. People who still believe they closed that mine, too soon, with living men still trapped inside."

She had heard the stories. Everyone had.

But sitting here now—watching Eli admit it, feeling his earnest words—it wasn't just a ghost story.

It was his story.

And maybe... Kai's story, too.

Finn's arms stayed crossed, but her tone softened, just a little. "It seems like everyone in town loves you, though."

Eli let out a scoff, shaking his head. "That's because me and my dad have spent our lives trying to distance ourselves from it. From *them.*"

His gaze flashed to the window, to the soft colors of the sunrise. But Finn could tell he wasn't really seeing it.

"My grandfather, my great-grandfather, all of them... they always swore there was no wrongdoing. Boasted about it." He clenched his jaw. "Said people were just looking for someone to blame."

Eli exhaled hard, his leg bouncing beneath his forearm. "But I don't think Frank ever really believed them."

He let the words sit there.

Then, he turned his gaze back to Finn, something darker, something final in his eyes.

"And now... now I know."

His throat bobbed as he swallowed. "Because of you. Because of everything you've seen, everything we've heard... I know for sure the evil my family has done."

His voice was rougher now, lower.

"The echo of it is still hurting people." He shook his head. "Even in death, they can't escape it."

He exhaled sharply, looking down at his hands, fingers curling into his palms before flexing open again.

"That's the curse of my family's legacy."

Finn didn't know what to say.

Because for the first time, Eli wasn't speaking in what-ifs.

There was no maybe. No possibility.

He was accepting it—all of it.

And that truth felt heavier than anything else she had learned.

Finn's lips parted, but no words came out.

Because what could she say?

Eli could tell.

So he kept going.

"Ever since the day of the mining accident, people have believed the Ashford line was cursed."

Finn's stomach tightened.

Eli stared down at his hands. "It didn't matter how much the ones that came before my dad swore they'd done nothing wrong. No matter how much they tried to make people forget."

He lifted his gaze to her, something tired, something knowing in his expression. "One by one, horrible, tragic things plagued every generation."

Finn swallowed.

Eli let out a humorless laugh, shaking his head. "And I think... somewhere deep inside him, Frank believes it too."

She frowned, watching the way Eli's fingers curled into his palms again.

"I think," he said, voice barely above a whisper, "he believes my mom's death was the curse. Exacting its revenge on him."

Finn's chest ached.

"No matter how much he tried to distance himself, to protect our family from his forefathers' past..." Eli shook his head, looking away again. "It still found us."

Finn's arms loosened from where they'd been crossed over her chest.

She wanted to say something—anything—but the words still wouldn't come.

Because deep down, she knew Eli was probably right.

This curse, this legacy, whatever it was—it wasn't done with them. Not yet.

Eli sat hunched over, his head nearly touching his knees, his entire body collapsing in on itself. He looked smaller like this, dragged down by something neither of them could see but both could feel.

Finn let out a slow breath. Then, before she could talk herself out of it, she moved around the small table between them and lowered herself to the floor in front of him.

Her arms wrapped around his shoulders, pulling him into her.

She didn't speak. Didn't try to offer meaningless reassurances. Just held him, steady and firm, anchoring him against something real. The warmth of his body pressed against hers, his breath slowing, and the tension in his muscles easing by degrees.

Eli didn't move, didn't pull away. He just let himself be held.

Finally, Finn broke the silence, her voice softer now, steady in a way she hadn't expected.

"Maybe this is your chance."

She felt the sharp inhale, the way his breath caught, but he didn't lift his head.

Her forehead brushed lightly against the side of his as she tightened her hold.

"By helping Kai, maybe we can help the miners too," she murmured. "Maybe this is your chance to put things right."

The words hung between them, thick with meaning, but Eli stayed silent, his body still tense beneath her arms.

Then, slowly, he lifted his head.

Their faces were close now, barely inches apart. Finn could feel the warmth of his breath against her skin.

He studied her, searching for something, maybe trying to decide if he wanted to believe her.

"Honestly... I've been thinking the same thing. Ever since we talked to Josiah."

Finn swallowed, her pulse drumming steady and deep beneath her skin.

Eli's fingers twitched against his knee, then he reached up, his hand closing gently around the pendant resting between them. His thumb brushed over the smooth, polished wood, the warmth of his touch seeping into the space where it met her skin.

His gaze stayed locked on hers, steady, unwavering.

"I'm with you," he said, his voice low but firm.

His thumb traced over the pendant again, slower this time, thoughtful.

"No matter if it saves me from some stupid curse—" his lips barely parted as he exhaled, his voice dipping lower, more certain—"to the end."

Finn wasn't sure what hit harder—his words, the raw honesty in his voice, or the way the air between them suddenly felt like something fragile, something that had shifted into entirely new territory.

But she believed him.

Completely.

Their foreheads pressed together, eyes closed, breathing slow and steady. Neither of them moved, neither spoke, but neither needed to. The silence between them was full. It carried weight, history, something unvoiced.

Eli's fingers remained wrapped around the pendant between them, his hand resting against Finn's chest, rising and falling with calm breaths.

Then—

The sun crested the horizon.

A golden ray of light spilled through the window, cutting across the sunroom in a soft, glowing warmth. It fell over them, drenching them both in morning gold, like the world itself had paused to acknowledge this moment.

The scent of honeysuckle drifted between them, faint but unmistakable.

Finn's breath caught as her eyes fluttered open, the whisper of familiarity echoing around her like something half-remembered, just out of reach.

Eli stilled beneath her, his body rigid with awareness. He smelled it too.

Before either of them could speak, the sunroom door creaked open.

They jerked apart so fast it was almost violent.

Frank stood in the doorway, eyes wide and brows raised.

"...Shit. My bad."

Heat rushed to Finn's face as she retreated back into her chair. Eli groaned beside her, rubbing a hand over his face like he could physically erase the last few seconds.

"Morning, Pops." His voice was strained, his attempt at seeming casual completely ruined by the awkwardness thick in the air.

Frank hovered a heartbeat too long, rubbing a hand over his jaw, his gaze darting between them like he was piecing something together. His smirk was barely concealed, the kind of smirk that made Finn want to melt straight through the floorboards.

"Uh-huh," he muttered, clearly debating whether or not to press. "Didn't know the sunroom was... occupied."

Finn dropped her face into her hands.

Eli groaned again, mumbling something unintelligible.

Frank just sighed, shaking his head as he turned toward the kitchen.

"...Coffee. I need coffee."

And then he was gone, disappearing down the hall.

For a long moment Finn and Eli stayed frozen in place, staring at the empty doorway like Frank might reappear just to make things worse.

Then, finally, Eli turned to her, wide-eyed, voice still hoarse.

"...Did we just get caught having a moment by my dad?"

Finn made a strangled noise and let her forehead drop onto the table.

"I want to die."

The morning carried on as usual—coffee was poured, breakfast was eaten, showers were taken.

But the air was different now.

Whatever had passed between them still hung around their movements. It wasn't tension, not exactly, more like an awareness. They were hyper-conscious of every shift, every glance, every accidental brush of fingers.

And Frank?

He said nothing about it.

Didn't need to.

His knowing glances and barely-contained grins spoke volumes, and if Eli had any hope of ignoring it, Frank made damn sure he felt the scrutiny.

By the time the morning routines had wrapped up and the house settled into the day, Finn thought she'd finally shaken it off.

But then—

Something else took root in her mind.

Kai.

Standing at the lake, his movements methodical, almost ritualistic. The way he'd shrugged off his jacket, tucking the pendant into the pocket like a final decision. Hanging it from the tree—not abandoned, but left behind for someone to find.

The thought wouldn't let go.

It dug deep, burrowing into her mind, demanding attention.

Without conscious thought she found herself in the garage.

Eli was there, crouched beside her bike, the faint scent of fresh paint filling the air. Not just any paint—the exact cloudy, pale blue of the bike frame.

Nancy's bike.

Now hers.

She hesitated in the doorway, watching as he carefully touched up the worn areas with delicate strokes.

Eli didn't look up right away, but when he did, his sheepish grin was already forming. "I needed an excuse to get away from the looks my dad was giving us."

Finn exhaled sharply, nodding. She understood completely.

But that wasn't why she had come.

"I need to go talk to Sarah."

Eli didn't question it. He just nodded, wiping his hands on a rag.

"You want me to drive you?"

"No," she said, "I'll just take the bike."

Eli snorted, shaking his head. "Yeah, that's not happening. The paint is still wet."

She opened her mouth to argue—

But before she could, Frank's voice cut in from the garage entrance.

"If you need a ride, I was just about to head into town." He leaned against the doorframe, keys dangling from one hand. "Meeting Danny for breakfast at The Lantern."

He studied them both for a moment before he nodded toward his truck. "I can take you."

Finn hesitated, considering, then finally nodded.

"Thanks, Frank."

Without another word, she turned back toward the house.

She needed something first.

Kai's jacket.

The crescent moon pendant.

They had been left behind on purpose.

And Finn was finally beginning to understand why.

She made it halfway out of the garage before something nagged at her—a question forming at the back of her mind.

She turned, glancing over her shoulder—

But before she could speak, Eli beat her to it.

Still bent over the bike, his focus steady on the details of his paintwork, he said, "She's usually at The Lantern this time of morning. Probably your best bet."

Finn's lips pressed together, watching him.

He didn't look up.

Didn't need to.

Like he had read her mind before she'd even had the chance to ask.

She gave a small nod in thanks, even though she knew he felt it more than he saw it.

Then she turned and headed inside.

She retrieved the jacket first, fingers tracing the edge of the pocket where the crescent moon pendant had rested.

She could feel it now—the intent behind it.

Then, from her top dresser drawer, she grabbed the rusted silver chain it had once hung from, tucking it into the pocket as well.

Finally, she slung her purse over her shoulder and headed downstairs.

Frank was already waiting, engine idling in the driveway, his old single-cab truck rumbling softly in the morning air.

Finn climbed into the passenger seat, carefully laying the jacket across her lap.

The drive into town passed in mostly comfortable silence.

Frank didn't ask who she was planning to meet, though he'd overheard them talking about it.

Still, after a few miles, he finally spoke, his voice low, contemplative.

"You know, kid..." He drummed his fingers against the steering wheel, exhaling slowly.

So that's where Eli gets that habit from, Finn thought absently.

"It's been a long time since I've seen Eli... happy."

Finn blinked, turning her head, but Frank didn't look at her. He kept his eyes on the road ahead.

"Ever since he was little, there's been this... weight on him. Like he's been carrying something that wasn't his to carry." He let out a short breath, shaking his head. "And I tried, Finn. Tried my damndest to make sure he didn't grow up with the same cloud hanging over him that I had. But I don't know if I ever really did enough."

Finn's grip tightened around the jacket in her lap.

Frank finally glanced at her, his voice softer now.

"But I do know this."

His grip on the wheel flexed briefly.

"You're good for him."

Finn turned back toward the windshield, her chest tight, pulse unsteady.

For a long moment, she didn't know what to say.

So she just nodded.

The rest of the drive passed in quiet understanding.

And when they pulled up to The Lantern, she knew—

It was time.

Chapter Twenty-Four

When Finn stepped inside The Lantern, she was met with murmurs of conversation, the occasional burst of laughter, the soft clatter of plates and silverware. The scent of coffee, mingling with the rich aroma of frying bacon and something sweet, like cinnamon or maple syrup.

At the counter, Danny sat perched on a barstool, mid-story, gesturing with a fork as Sheri chuckled and wiped down the counter in front of him.

When she spotted Frank first, then Finn, her face lit up with that familiar warmth.

"Well, good morning, stranger," she said brightly, tucking the dish towel into her apron.

Frank stepped forward, the floor creaking beneath his boots as he dropped onto the barstool beside Danny. "Just meeting this old coot for breakfast," he said, nudging Danny's elbow.

Danny snorted, shaking his head. "Didn't realize we were making it breakfast for three," he added, giving Finn a pointed look.

Finn shook her head, scanning the diner as casually as she could manage.

No sign of Sarah.

She exhaled slowly, adjusting the strap of her bag, fingers tightening around the leather draped over her arm. She had a feeling Sarah wouldn't want to be here much longer once she saw it.

"I'm just meeting someone," she said, stepping up to the counter. "I'll take a coffee to go. Cream and sugar."

Sheri nodded. "Anything else?"

Finn hesitated for only a second before adding, "And one black."

"You got it, hon."

Finn reached into her back pocket, pulling out a few bills and sliding them across the counter. Sheri made quick work of the register before setting her change down with a smooth flick of her fingers. Finn gathered it without thinking, stuffing it into her pocket as she leaned against the counter.

Frank and Danny carried on their usual banter, slipping seamlessly into some debate about fishing spots. Sheri poured fresh coffee into a waiting mug, listening with half an ear, smiling like she'd heard this argument a hundred times before.

For a brief moment, Finn let herself be distracted.

Then—

The brass bell jingled.

She felt it before she even turned.

Sarah stepped inside, shaking a few stray raindrops from her sleeves, barely across the threshold before her gaze landed on Finn.

Or, more specifically—on the jacket slung over her arm.

A glint of something passed over Sarah's face. Not shock, not fear—something colder. Sharper.

Then, before Finn could even take a step, Sarah spun on her heel and strode right back out the door.

For a second, there was nothing but silence in her wake.

Sheri blinked after her, brows knitting together. "Well," she mused, half to herself, "wonder what that was about."

Finn barely heard her.

She grabbed both Styrofoam cups from the counter, mumbled a quick, "Thanks, Sheri," and bolted for the door.

Finn stepped out into the cool morning air, the scent of damp pavement and fresh coffee mingling as she scanned the sidewalk. Sarah was already making quick work of the distance, her short brown hair bouncing with each determined step as she moved toward the main road.

"Sarah, wait—I need to talk to you!" she called, raising her voice over the steady hum of morning traffic.

Sarah didn't slow. Didn't even glance back.

"Not interested!" she shouted over her shoulder, her tone clipped and final.

Finn gritted her teeth and picked up her pace, gripping the coffee cups tightly as she pushed forward. "Just hear me out!" she yelled after her. "I think you'll want to hear what I have to say!"

That did it.

Sarah's steps faltered, her shoulders tensing as she came to an abrupt stop.

For a second, Finn thought she might just start walking again, pretending she hadn't heard. But instead, Sarah let out a sharp sigh and turned, arms crossed, expression irritable.

"You have as long as it takes to get to the boutique," she said flatly.

Finn nodded, shifting the cups in her hands before holding one out.

Sarah's milk chocolate eyes took in the offering, suspicion dancing across her face.

"It's black," Finn said simply. "Like you ordered last time."

Sarah's gaze smouldered, then burnt out before she finally reached out and took it.

She didn't say thank you.

Just turned abruptly and started walking again, bringing the lid to her lips as she moved.

Finn adjusted Kai's jacket over her arm and fell into step beside her.

For a moment, Finn wasn't sure how to start.

She walked alongside Sarah in silence as she tried to piece together the right words. How much should she say? How much would Sarah even believe?

The boutique wasn't far now, and with every step, the time to figure it out was slipping away.

Sarah must have sensed the hesitation in Finn's silence because she let out a sharp breath, glancing toward her with a pointed look.

"The shop's just up ahead. You better start talking."

They were passing a small wooden bench in front of a storefront, its slats worn smooth from years of exposure to the elements. Finn's steps faltered, then stopped entirely.

Sarah kept walking.

"Can we sit for a sec?" Finn asked, her voice almost pleading.

Sarah came to a halt a few steps ahead, turning back just enough to look at her before glancing toward the bench. Then she rolled her eyes with exaggerated reluctance and walked back, plopping down heavily. One arm crossed over her body, posture defensive but not entirely closed off.

Finn sat down beside her carefully, lowering herself onto the bench as if afraid to disrupt the delicate balance of the moment.

She inhaled deeply, centering herself before speaking, her voice soft but sure.

"You were right."

Sarah stilled, her fingers flexing around her coffee cup.

"The jacket," Finn continued, shifting her gaze to the folded leather in her lap, her hands smoothing absently over it. "The necklace. They were Kai's." She let the words sit, carefully emphasizing the past tense—not to hurt, but to acknowledge the truth.

Sarah's posture tightened just a fraction, but she stayed quiet.

"I can't explain how I got them," Finn admitted. "And I don't think you'd believe me if I tried." She exhaled, forcing herself to keep going. "But I don't think they were ever really meant for me. I think... I think Kai always intended for them to end up with you. And maybe—maybe I was just supposed to make sure that happened."

She lifted the jacket, extending it toward Sarah.

Sarah's eyes dropped to it, her expression flickering—something hesitant, something unsure, something raw.

She didn't take it immediately.

Instead, her hand hovered just above it, fingers brushing the supple leather like she was trying to reconnect with something that had slipped away long ago. When she finally let herself touch it, her fingers curled around the worn material, grip tentative at first—then firmer, like the reality of it was finally sinking in.

Slowly, carefully, she pulled the jacket from Finn's hands.

Finn watched as Sarah brought it close to her chest, hugging it to herself with an almost childlike instinct.

"The pendant's in the pocket," Finn said gently. "The chain, too."

Sarah barely nodded, her fingers tightening around the jacket's sleeves.

For a long moment, she just sat there, gripping the jacket as if letting go of it would break something fragile inside her.

Then, slowly, she lifted her gaze to Finn.

Her brown eyes were glistening—so faintly it was barely noticeable, but Finn saw it.

She saw the slight tension in Sarah's throat as she swallowed against whatever emotion had surfaced.

Seeing the way, for the first time since they had met, she wasn't looking at Finn with bitterness, jealousy, or disdain.

And then, Sarah finally spoke.

"Thank you."

Nothing more. Just those two words, simple but weighted with everything she wasn't saying.

Then, before Finn could respond, Sarah stood, her movements quick and decisive.

She turned on her heel and walked away—too fast.

Finn didn't call after her.

She just sat there, the coffee cup growing colder in her hands, watching Sarah disappear down the sidewalk.

Finn leaned against the brick façade of The Lost Boys, the rough surface cool against her back. A thin ribbon of smoke rose from the cigarette between her fingers, drifting up into the dull morning air. The rain had stopped, leaving the pavement dark and damp, reflecting muted slivers of light from the overcast sky.

She exhaled slowly, watching the tendrils of smoke unravel before her eyes, but her mind wasn't there. It was still back on that bench, still tracing every expression that had crossed Sarah's face. The hesitance. The way her fingers had ghosted over the leather before pulling the jacket into her chest. The tight, almost imperceptible waver in her voice when she had said thank you. And then the way she had taken off, like staying a second longer might break something loose inside her.

Finn turned the lighter over in her palm, flicking it open and closed absentmindedly. She hadn't thought to grab the shop keys from Bronco before they left for town, or from Frank before she fled the diner, and the idea of trekking back to The Lantern just to hover awkwardly near him didn't sit right. She wasn't ready for more conversation yet. Not with Frank. Not with anyone.

But the quiet was starting to wear on her. Her thoughts had begun circling the same track over and over, wearing deep grooves in her mind.

Then—

The low, familiar rumble of an engine.

She lifted her head just as Eli pulled up to the curb, his arrival slicing cleanly through her spiraling thoughts. He parked haphazardly, one hand draped over the wheel as he leaned back, scanning her through the windshield. Finn could see the question in his eyes, even before he stepped out—

"What happened?"

But he didn't ask. Not yet.

Instead, he pulled a fresh pack of cigarettes from his jacket pocket, tearing the cellophane with his teeth as he walked toward her. He must have stopped at the gas station on the way.

Finn arched a brow as he tapped one out, pressing it between his lips. A brief thought passed through her mind— *"Am I a bad influence?"* But then she remembered him insisting she get drunk on her birthday, and the thought made her smirk.

She flipped her lighter open, holding it out toward him. Eli leaned in, the brief flare of flame illuminating the sharp angles of his face before he straightened, exhaling a slow, steady stream of smoke.

They stood there for a while, neither of them in a hurry. The silence was like an unspoken agreement. Finn took another drag before finally breaking it.

"I found her."

Eli turned his head, tapping ash onto the wet pavement. "And?"

Finn exhaled, watching the smoke drift. "I gave her the jacket."

He turned fully toward her now. "Just like that?"

Finn shrugged. "It's what was supposed to happen, Eli. He left it for her."

Eli's jaw tightened, his gaze dropping for a moment. Then he let out a slow breath and nodded. "Alright."

But Finn could tell that "alright" didn't mean *I'm totally on board with this'*. And sure enough—

"You know your fingerprints are all over that thing now, right?" His voice was even, but there was an unmistakable edge beneath it. "The jacket and the pendant. If she turns that in, and it makes its way back into police hands—"

Finn shook her head, cutting him off. "I didn't get that feeling from her."

Eli gave her a look, one that clearly said *'you don't know that'*.

"Look, I'm not saying it's impossible. I'm just saying... if that's what happens, we'll cross that bridge when we get to it."

He exhaled sharply through his nose, but he didn't argue. He just nodded once, flicking his cigarette into the street.

"Guess we will."

Just as Finn exhaled the last drag of her cigarette, grinding the ember beneath the toe of her boot, the low rumble of Frank's truck pulled her attention toward the street. He rolled to a stop in front of the shop, engine humming for a moment before he cut it off.

The driver's side door swung open, and Frank stepped out, raising an eyebrow as he took in the sight of Finn and Eli leaning against the brick wall, the scent of tobacco still hanging in the morning air.

"Well, well," he said, locking the door behind him. "Look at this fine display of loitering."

Eli smirked, "Morning to you, too, old man."

Frank snorted, stepping up onto the sidewalk and fishing the shop keys from his pocket. "You two planning on working today? Or is this just a smoke break that never ended?"

Finn pushed off the wall and stretched. "We're here early. That should count for something."

Frank let out a low chuckle as he unlocked the shop door. "Yeah, yeah, get your asses inside."

It was a new day. A regular day. As if Finn hadn't just done something that could have very real consequences.

And yet, somehow, she felt... lighter.

The hours passed like a steady melody. Clients came and went, the buzz of machines filling the shop as usual. Finn was on point today, handling everything seamlessly—appointments, setups, clean-ups—like it was second nature.

Frank, ever the observer, finally gave her a nod of approval as he wiped down his station. "Gotta say, kid, you're catching on fast. Almost like you belong here or something."

Finn glanced up from the desk, a smile spreading across her face. "Almost."

Frank shook his head as he tossed his gloves into the trash. "Alright, I'm heading out. Try not to burn the place down."

Finn rolled her eyes and laughed playfully at the joke. "That was one time."

Frank shot Eli a knowing look. "And let's not have a repeat of her birthday night afterwards, either."

Eli groaned. "For the love of—will I ever live that down?"

Frank grinned. "Not a chance."

With that, he grabbed his keys and headed for the door, the familiar jingle of the bells marking his exit.

Finn let out a breath she hadn't realized she was holding, glancing over at Eli.

Just another normal day at The Lost Boys.

Finn and Eli wrapped up their closing routine.

Eli moved through his tasks, sanitizing the stations one last time, the scent of disinfectant mixing with the faint remnants of ink and warm skin. Finn sat behind the desk, flipping through the appointment book, double-checking deposits and marking which clients still owed.

It really was all second nature by now, this end-of-the-day regimen. Easy. Familiar.

And then—

The bells over the front door jingled.

Finn's head snapped up, her pen pausing mid-mark, her eyes instinctively flying to the pass-through window. It was late—too late for walk-ins, too late for anyone who wasn't already on the books.

The moment she saw who it was, every nerve in her body went taut.

Sarah stood just inside the door, stiff and uncomfortable, Kai's jacket still clutched tightly to her chest like a lifeline. Her wide brown eyes were slightly swollen, rimmed in the telltale pink of someone who had been crying.

Finn just stared, heart pounding, her mind scrambling to process why Sarah was here.

Behind her, Eli must have caught onto the sudden tension, because she heard his footsteps approach. A second later, he was standing behind her, his presence radiating alertness.

Sarah's gaze dashed up, landing on him briefly before shifting back to Finn. Then, finally, she took a step further inside, fingers tightening around the soft leather in her arms.

"There's more we need to talk about," she said.

And Finn knew, without a doubt—

This was about to change everything.

Chapter Twenty-Five

Eli unlocked the front door and pushed it open. The distant croak of frogs from the trees beyond the yard carried through the cracked windows. Frank wasn't home yet, but that wasn't surprising. If he left work early, he was probably still out fishing with Danny.

Without a word, the three of them stepped inside, the comfortable hush of the house washing over them. Eli led the way to the sunroom, where the warm glow of the fading day cast soft amber-hued light over the wicker furniture. Finn and Sarah followed, each holding their breath for the conversation to come.

Sarah hesitated near the doorway, clutching Kai's jacket close to her like a shield. So tightly her fingers turned pale as she took in the space around her. Finn could see the tension in her shoulders, the way she held herself rigid, as if bracing for something she wasn't sure she was ready to face.

Eli dropped onto the couch, stretching one arm along the back while his other hand absently drummed against his knee. Finn took the chair beside him, and after a long moment, Sarah finally moved. She sat stiffly on the edge of the loveseat across from them, her grip still a vise on the jacket.

The heaviness of everything they had yet to say settled over the room like a thick fog.

Then, Sarah broke the silence.

"Thank you." Her voice was raw. She lifted her gaze, meeting Finn's eyes for the first time since they left the shop and gestured to the jacket. "For this."

Finn just nodded. "It was always meant to come back to you."

Sarah let out a shaky breath, fingers smoothing over the worn leather. "I don't know how to explain it, but... I feel him. Closer than I have in a long time. Since the last time I saw him."

She exhaled slowly, like she was trying to steady herself, then looked between Finn and Eli. Her voice was steadier when she spoke again.

"Is he dead?"

It wasn't really a question. More of a statement, an inevitability she had already made peace with.

Finn's throat tightened, but before she could find the words, Eli answered for her.

"Yeah, Sarah. He's gone."

Something flickered across her face—not surprise, not even grief. Acceptance. Her lips pressed together as fresh tears shimmered in her eyes.

She gulped hard, nodding once. "How do you know?" Her gaze settled on Finn now, sharp and searching. "How did you get this?" She lifted the jacket a little, her fingers curled around the collar.

Finn and Eli exchanged a glance. Then, slowly, carefully, they told her everything.

They told her about the lake, about Kai appearing to Finn. About the mines, the spirits, the shadows that lurked beneath Ash Hollow. About Josiah and what he had told them. About the connections, the warnings.

Everything.

Sarah didn't interrupt. She just sat there, her brows drawn as she absorbed every word.

When they finally finished, Sarah exhaled slowly, then leaned forward. Her voice was low when she spoke again, almost as if she were speaking to herself.

"He told me," she murmured. "He said they were watching him. That they wouldn't leave him alone. That he had to get away from them, or *'their fire would consume him'*. I thought... I thought he was just spiraling. Losing himself in it. But now..."

She trailed off, shaking her head. Her fingers rubbed absently at the edge of the jacket's sleeve, her gaze distant. "Kai and I... we started our own coven. The crescent moon—it was our symbol, our mark. We'd been practicing witchcraft for a while, but his parents found out and freaked. They sent him to work at the church every day after school, hoping it would 'save' him, that the *proximity to the house of god'* would turn him away from what we were doing."

She let out a humorless laugh, her eyes flashing darkly. "But that backfired. Because that's where he found it."

Finn leaned forward. "Found what?"

Sarah's jaw tightened. "A document. Old. Hidden away in the church basement. It was from the Ashford Mining Company."

Her eyes landed on Eli, almost apologetic.

"Acknowledgment that they knew survivors were still alive in the mine after the explosion—but they sealed it anyway. The rescue was deemed too expensive. Too risky."

Eli swore under his breath, his knuckles going white where they rested on his knee.

"After that, he became obsessed. We started doing séances in the mine, trying to reach them. And we did. Well... Kai did. They only ever wanted to answer him. And the more they did, the more he changed. He started seeing them everywhere, hearing them. He wouldn't sleep, wouldn't eat. He said they were always there, whispering, watching."

Sarah's hands flexed into fists, her fingertips digging into the leather. "And then one day, he told me he had to go. That he had to get away, or burn with them. I tried to stop him—I did, but..." Her voice cracked, and for the first time, her composure faltered. Her eyes shone with unshed tears. "I couldn't. And then he was gone."

Silence overtook the room.

Finn's pulse roared and her breath became shallow. She felt Eli shift beside her, his presence steady, but even he seemed at a loss for words.

When Sarah finally looked back up, her expression was resolute. "I don't know what's going on. But if Kai was right—if the fire is still coming..." She paused for a shaking breath. "Then we don't have much time."

Finn met her gaze, something deep and unspoken passing between them.

No. They didn't.

Finn reached out instinctively in a gesture of consolation. But the moment her skin made contact—her fingertips grazing both Sarah's hand and the soft leather of Kai's jacket—something struck her like lightning.

A violent jolt ripped through her, seizing every nerve in her body. Her breath was sucked from her lungs like a vacuum and her spine snapped straight, her head wrenching backward as her eyes rolled into white voids.

And then—

– – –

I'm flying.

My breath is ragged, tearing through my lungs, but I can't stop.

Can't slow down.

The trees blur past me in streaks of shadow and silver, the moon barely piercing through the dense canopy.

The handlebars judder in my grip, chain grinding as I tear along the rutted path.

The pedal smashes my shin when I jump off. I let the bike skid and clatter into the ferns—front wheel ticking, ticking—then I run.

The ground is slick beneath my feet, damp with fallen leaves and rain, but I keep running.

Because they're coming.

I can feel them behind me, closing in, their presence thick in the air like smoke.

Shadows dance along the trees, flickering with fire that doesn't burn.

Eyes—dozens of them—smoldering in the darkness, watching me, waiting.

Their fire will consume me.

I know this.

It's too late to escape. But there's one thing I can still do.

The lake.

The trees break open, revealing the water ahead—black and endless, stretching into nothing.

The wind howls through the branches, but the lake remains still.

I tear off my jacket, my hands shaking as I fumble for the clasp at my neck.

The pendant.

They have to stay.

They have to find their way back.

I loop the chain over an exposed tree root, my fingers lingering on the leather of my jacket as I press it into the bark, securing it there.

A message.
A memory.
Something left behind.
I sprint toward the water.
And dive.
The cold is instant, shocking. It steals the air from my lungs, wraps around my limbs like unseen hands and I don't fight it.
I let it take me.
The water swallows me whole, dragging me down, down, down—

– – –

A sharp, shuddering gasp tore from her throat as her body lurched. The world around her snapped into focus in disorienting flashes—the sunroom, the scent of pine.

She was on the floor.

Her head was cradled in something warm—no, *someone.*

Eli's arms were around her, his body curled protectively over hers, his hands framing her face. His breath was unsteady, forehead pressed to hers, hot tears slipping from his lashes into her hair.

"Come back," he whispered, his voice wrecked and raw.

"Finn, please... come back to me."

"I'm here. I'm back."

The words scraped from Finn's throat, ragged and weak, as her awareness clawed its way back through the haze of the vision.

She felt Eli stiffen beneath her, his whole body tense where he still cradled her head in his lap. His face was close—so close.

His breath was warm against her temple, his lips moving even as he pulled back. It took her a second to register what he was saying.

Soft, urgent whispers.

"You scared the shit out of me."

She tried to push herself up, but her limbs were sluggish, her muscles weak, trembling as if they'd been wrung dry. And her skin—god, her skin—felt too tight, stretched over her bones, like she wasn't fully settled back into herself yet.

Eli reacted instantly. His hands—strong, but unmistakably shaking—slid under her arms, easing her up before she could collapse again.

Once she was upright, his grip stayed firm on her, fingers tight around her upper arms like he wasn't sure she'd stay up on her own.

He wasn't wrong.

Finn's head swam, her skin buzzing like she was still caught somewhere between the vision and reality. The frigid sensation of lake water clung to her like a phantom touch, even though she was dry.

Even though she was safe.

Sarah sat frozen, her hands clamped over her mouth, her wide brown eyes locked onto Finn like she had just witnessed something unnatural.

She had.

And then, her voice split through the silence, breaking on the edges.

"What the fuck just happened?!"

Finn inhaled slowly, deeply, trying to steady herself.

She turned toward Sarah, but before she could answer, her eyes caught Eli's instead.

And for a moment—just a moment—it was only the two of them.

He was searching her face, the normal honey of his eyes dark and stormy, gripped with concern, fear, and something deeper.

He already knew what she was going to say. She could see it in his expression. Could hear it in her mind as clearly as if he had spoken it aloud.

And he hated it.

Still—Finn didn't have a choice and spoke anyway.

"We have to go to the mines."

Eli's entire body went rigid.

His fingers twitched against her skin before—reluctantly—he pulled away.

Sarah sucked in a sharp breath beside them.

Finn held both their gazes now, unwavering.

"We have to."

She let the importance of the words sink in, let them settle in the space between them like an undeniable and inescapable truth.

"So we can help them rest. Help Kai rest."

A breath of silence.

Then—

The sound of tires crunching against gravel.

All three of them turned toward the window just as headlights swept across the room, streaking along the walls.

A second later, the deep rumble of Frank's truck engine cut out.

The moment shattered.

Eli immediately pulled further away from Finn, as if the headlights had caught them doing something they weren't supposed to.

Sarah blinked fast, wiped her eyes and straightened.

They had seconds to pull themselves together before Frank walked through the front door.

And then...

Then, they had to decide what the hell came next.

Eli moved.

He shot to his feet, crossing the room in a few quick strides, clicking on the overhead light. The sudden glow washed over them, pushing away the dim shadows that had settled in the corners.

It was too bright, almost jarring, but at least now they looked normal. Or as normal as they could manage.

Eli hurried back, sinking into the couch beside Finn. She could still feel the ghost of his warmth where he had held her moments before, holding her to reality and calling her to surface from the vision.

Sarah's breathing had finally evened out. Her grip on Kai's jacket was still white-knuckled, but she was doing her best to compose herself, her features smoothing out into something that could pass for casual—if you weren't looking too closely.

Then they just sat there, waiting, bracing.

They heard the front door swing open, and Frank's voice rumbled through the house as he entered, the *thwap* of him shaking the moist night air off his jacket.

"You would not believe how good the fish were biting tonight," he called, his voice carrying through the halls. "Haven't had a catch that good in years. Thought about heading back before dark, but Danny—man, he kept reeling 'em in, and next thing I knew—"

His footsteps were unhurried as he moved through the house. Then—he stepped through the sunroom doorway and stopped.

His eyes immediately landed on Sarah.

A glint of something observant, and mildly suspicious crossed his face. She wasn't a normal fixture in the house. And more than that—there was something about the air in the room.

Something off, that they had no hope of willing away.

His gaze swept over Eli, then Finn.

Finn forced herself to relax, sinking further into the chair, even though every muscle in her body was screaming from exhaustion. Eli was the picture of ease, one arm draped along the back of the couch, but his leg bounced.

Frank's brow furrowed.

"What's up?"

Eli didn't miss a beat.

"Oh, you know—just hanging out."

Far too casual.

Frank squinted at them, clearly not convinced. His gaze dwelled on Finn, like he was trying to read something in her face.

"No booze tonight, right?" he asked, narrowing his eyes.

Finn let out a breath, forcing herself to laugh, light and easy.

"No," she said.

Eli chuckled too, shaking his head. "Not tonight."

Frank was still watching them like he wasn't quite sure he bought it.

But after a long moment, he let out a low grunt, scratching the back of his neck.

"Alright."

He yawned, stretching his arms up with a tired groan. "I'm heading to bed. Y'all make good choices."

With that, he turned, lumbering toward the stairs.

Finn didn't breathe at all until she heard the door settle back into its frame.

They listened, waiting. No one moved, no one spoke, or barely even breathed, until the faint sound of Frank's footsteps reached the top of the stairs. The creak of his door opening, the low thud of it closing behind him.

Then, almost at the same time, they all exhaled—a collective, unsteady breath.

Eli slumped back against the couch, rubbing his hands over his face, exhaustion settling into his posture. Sarah let out a shuddering breath, arms wrapped around her torso using Kai's jacket like a security blanket, as if she were holding onto him instead.

Finn sank deeper into the cushions, muscles weak and aching, her skin pulling painfully, stretched too tight over her bones.

And then—all eyes were on her.

She felt their expectant stares, waiting for her to make sense of what had just happened.

Finn swallowed, her throat raw, lips dry to the point of splitting, but she forced the words out anyway.

"I saw him."

Finn hesitated for only a moment before continuing. "In my vision, I was him. I was running through the woods, the sky closing in around me, shadows reaching like hands. But it wasn't just the night—it was them. The miners. Their fire licking at the edges, moving in ways it shouldn't have been able to move, twisting and warping the trees."

Sarah's hand pressed back over her mouth.

Finn's chest ached at the sight of her. She hated this. Hated that she had to say it, had to force Sarah to hear what she had spent so long trying not to understand.

But the words kept coming, and she couldn't stop them now.

"He thought there was only one way to escape them," she said. "To keep them from consuming him. To stop himself from becoming one of them. He believed—really believed—that the only way out was the lake."

Sarah let out a fractured sound, fingers digging into Kai's jacket so tightly the leather creaked under her grip.

"So he ran to the water," Finn continued, her own hands curling into the fabric of her jeans, knuckles pressing hard into the muscle beneath. "He stripped off his jacket. He unclasped his necklace. He left them behind, hanging from the roots, hoping someone would find them. Hoping you would find them."

Sarah's shoulders jerked, her whole body tensing as though physically bracing for what came next.

Finn's voice softened, but the words still landed like blows. "And then he dove."

A tear slipped down Sarah's cheek, quick and silent. She wiped it away before it could fully fall, pressing her lips together in a taut line.

Eli had been quiet, letting her speak, letting her get it all out, but now he leaned forward, his forearms resting against his knees, voice low and steady.

"What does it mean?"

Finn closed her eyes for a brief second, trying to collect herself, to put into words something she knew deep in her bones but still couldn't fully explain.

"It was a mistake," she murmured, shaking her head. "A horrific, tragic misunderstanding."

Sarah's head snapped up. Eli's brows furrowed, confusion set in the lines of his face.

Finn looked at them both, voice gaining strength, the certainty settling deeper with every word.

"Kai had a connection to the dead—just like me. That's why the miners were drawn to him. They thought he could help them, that he was the one who could set them free."

Eli exhaled through his nose, rubbing a hand over his mouth.

Sarah, though—she looked lost, like the ground had suddenly shifted beneath her and she wasn't sure where to step next.

Finn turned her gaze to her now, gentler, but still unwavering.

"But he didn't understand. He didn't know how to control it. They weren't trying to hurt him, but he couldn't see that. Their persistence—it was too much. It broke him. It drove him to madness."

Sarah was shaking her head, but it wasn't in denial. It was in realization.

Finn swallowed, her own breath uneven now. "That's why he ran to the lake. That's why he thought he had to escape them."

Sarah's breathing was ragged, her hands gripping her sleeves, nails biting into the fabric.

Finn sat up straighter, the truth solidifying inside her, no longer just a theory but something she knew.

"And now he's stuck," she whispered.

Sarah's wide brown eyes lifted to meet hers, searching for something, anything.

Finn didn't look away.

"Just like them."

Eli let out a slow, measured breath, his gaze dropping to the floor, running a hand over his jaw.

"I don't think he can move on until they do," Finn added. "I think that's why I saw all of this. That's why he came to me. He's still waiting, still caught somewhere between here and whatever comes next. And we're the ones who have to help him get there."

The implications of what she had just said settled over the room like a dense fog, heavy and inescapable.

Sarah, who had been staring down at her lap, finally lifted her gaze. Her eyes, still swollen from tears, were resolute now, sharpened by something fierce and unshakable.

"I'm coming with you."

Finn blinked, taken aback by the certainty in her voice.

"I was part of what set this in motion," she said, her voice steady but thick with emotion. "I had a part to play in what happened to Kai, whether I meant to or not. I can't just sit back and do nothing. I have to help."

Eli, who had been quiet, staring down at the floor in contemplation, exhaled heavily. When he looked up, his eyes burned with conviction. "I have to, too."

Finn turned to him, heart leaping into her throat.

"This is my family's fault," he continued, his voice low, weighted. "What happened to those miners, why they became what they are—it all started with the Ashfords. If we're going to help them, if we're going to set things right, then I have to be part of it."

The three of them, bound now not just by loss but by responsibility, sat in the hush of the sunroom, the soft sounds of the night pressing in around them.

Then Eli straightened, squaring his shoulders. "That said, no one is doing anything tonight."

His voice was firm, leaving no room for argument. He turned his gaze on Finn, who still looked pale and sunken, dark shadows stark beneath her eyes. She looked drained, fragile.

"Look at you," he said gently. "You can barely sit up. Whatever we're going to have to do, it's going to take all of us. And all our strength. We need a plan first."

Finn wanted to protest, but she knew he was right. Every part of her body ached, her bones heavy, her skin on fire. Even speaking felt like an effort.

Sarah nodded. "We need to figure out how to actually release them. How to help them move on. We can't go in blind."

They all exchanged glances, silent agreement passing between them.

Eli leaned back, rubbing his hands over his thighs in an anxious motion. "Alright, then that's what we do next. We research. We find out everything we can." He exhaled, then looked at Sarah. "Come on, I'll drive you home."

She glanced at Finn. "You coming?"

Finn shook her head. "I need to rest."

Eli nodded his head once in staunch agreement, standing and grabbing his keys. He and Sarah left through the back door, their voices low as they disappeared into the night.

Finn sat still for a moment, gathering the strength to stand. Slowly, carefully, she pushed herself up and made her way to her bedroom. Taking the stairs with the waning strength of a woman many decades older.

The moment she hit the soft duvet, her body melted into the mattress, exhaustion pulling at her like gravity.

But sleep didn't come immediately.

Instead, she found herself thinking of her mother—of the way she used to hold her when she was little, arms wrapped tight, whispering soft reassurances whenever she was too afraid to sleep.

She thought of the comfort of that warmth, the safety of it, and how desperately she wished she could have that now.

A tear slipped down her temple, disappearing into the pillow. Her breath faltered. She turned onto her side, curling into herself.

Then—

A warm breeze stirred through the room, gentle and slow. Finn barely registered it at first, but then—it curled around her, soft and steady, cradling her.

Like warm arms. Like a mother's embrace.

Her lips parted, a shaky breath escaping as the tension in her body unwound, her exhaustion finally winning.

And just like that, she slipped into sleep—deep and dreamless.

Chapter Twenty-Six

A soft knock at Finn's door broke the stillness of morning.

Eli stood in the hallway, fingers still resting against the wood, waiting. When no response came, he frowned and knocked again, louder this time.

Still nothing.

That was... odd. Finn wasn't exactly a light sleeper, but she wasn't a deadweight, either.

Eli waited just a few moments longer, then finally—carefully—cracked the door open.

"Finn?" His voice was low, cautious.

She didn't stir.

The room was dim, the morning light barely creeping past the curtains. Finn lay on her side, the blankets wrapped around her like a cocoon, her breathing deep but too still. A horrible, creeping unease settled into Eli's chest.

He stepped inside, his socked feet soundless against the floor. Crouching beside the bed, he reached out, hesitating only briefly before placing a hand on her back.

"Hey," he murmured, rubbing slow, steady circles between her shoulder blades. "Time to wake up, Rowan."

Finn didn't jolt or groan in protest like usual. She just rolled slowly to her back, eyelids fluttering sluggishly before cracking open.

Eli sucked in a sharp breath at the sight of her.

She was pale. Too pale. A washed-out version of herself, her skin leeched of color, dark hollows beneath her eyes making them look sunken. The whites of her eyes glowed an angry, bloodshot red.

"Jesus, Finn," he whispered. "You look like hell."

Finn swallowed dryly, blinking blearily at him. When she finally spoke, her voice was hoarse and groggy. "Feel like hell."

That was all Eli needed to hear.

He stood so fast his knee cracked against the wooden floor, but he barely noticed as he turned and strode straight for the hallway.

Within mere minutes, he was back, with Frank in tow.

Finn could barely lift her head when they entered, but she caught the way Frank hesitated just past the doorway, clearly uncomfortable being in her space. Still, when he glanced from her to Eli, taking in the sheer worry etched into his son's face, he stepped forward without another word.

Frank crouched beside the bed, sharp eyes scanning over her. "You sure there was no boozin' last night?" he asked, tone rough but not unkind.

Eli, standing rigid behind him, crossed his arms tightly over his chest. "No," he said, firm and serious. "I swear."

Frank studied him for a long second, then finally nodded, turning his attention back to Finn.

He reached out, resting a broad, calloused palm against her forehead, then pulled away with a knowing huff.

"Looks like you caught a bug, little one."

Finn moaned weakly in response, tugging the blankets tighter around her body like they were the only thing keeping her tethered to warmth. Her skin felt clammy, her bones aching with a marrow-deep exhaustion. Her lashes fluttered before settling against the deep shadows beneath her eyes, drawn further into the haze of fever.

Frank gave her a small, almost imperceptible pat on the top of her tousled head before pushing himself upright with a low grunt—one of those noises men made when their knees weren't quite as cooperative as they used to be.

Eli and Frank moved toward the door, slipping out into the hallway without closing it fully behind them. Their voices dropped low, hushed, but Finn still caught fragments of their conversation through the fog.

"She's in rough shape," Frank muttered, voice laced with concern.

"She was fine yesterday," Eli murmured back, though there was an edge to his voice. Not defensive—just unsettled.

Frank exhaled. "Only got two clients today. I can handle 'em myself just fine."

A pause. Then Eli's voice again, cautious. "You need me to stay home too?"

"She's in no fit state to take care of herself."

Another pause. Longer this time.

Then Eli's steady voice. "I got her."

Frank's response was immediate. "Damn right."

Then Finn heard Frank's boots scuff against the wooden floor, the sound growing softer as he walked away.

She didn't open her eyes. Couldn't, really. But she felt it—felt the shift of air, the presence lingering just beyond her door.

Someone cracked it open just a little more.

No sound. No words.

Then, after a long moment, the door creaked back shut.

And Finn let herself drift, slipping back into sleep's waiting arms.

By the time Finn woke again, she felt a little more sure of herself, her strength returning in small, delicate increments. Slowly, she pushed herself up, resting her back against the wooden headboard, her muscles protesting the movement but not enough to stop her.

The sun was higher now, hanging in the sky with an intensity that suggested it was sometime well after noon. The shadows in her room had shrunk, the slats of light breaking through the blinds that at some point had been drawn, sharpening into thinner bands across the floor.

Her gaze drifted toward the short dresser beside her bed, where a plate of buttered toast sat waiting for her, next to a banana—lightly speckled with brown, just the way she preferred them. Beside them, a tall glass of water shimmered in the half-light, beads of condensation trailing down the side.

Finn reached for it first, her arms still sluggish, her fingers barely able to curl properly around the cool glass. It felt too cumbersome in her grip, but she managed to bring it to her lips, drinking greedily, the cold water soothing her dry throat.

She let out a breath as she set the glass back down, wiping the stray droplets from her lips before grabbing a wedge of toast, the scent of butter and warm bread filling her nose.

And that's when she heard it—the creak of her door, so quiet she wouldn't have noticed if she hadn't been as aware as she now was.

Her eyes lifted just in time to see the door crack open, revealing Eli's drawn face through the sliver of space. The hallway light behind him, shadowing his features, making the worry etched into his expression more stark.

His timing was impeccable.

As always.

Like he'd sensed she was finally fully conscious again.

When Eli saw that she was upright and partaking in the sustenance he'd left for her, he pushed the door open the rest of the way and stepped inside.

His movements were slow, as if he were afraid to disturb the fragile balance of her recovery. He made his way around the bed, lowering himself into the window nook across from her.

He tucked his knees in close, wrapping his arms around them, resting his chin on top as he settled into place. The afternoon light streaming in through the blinds behind him, catching the edges of his auburn curls, turning them to warm copper.

Finn took a small, tentative nibble from the corner of her toast, chewing carefully, her throat still raw and reluctant to cooperate. She swallowed, the movement rough, her body slow to accept even the simplest acts of nourishment.

Eli just watched. Waiting.

And then, finally—

"This isn't a normal flu, is it?"

There was no real question in it.

Finn shook her head gently, but even that small motion sent a dull, punishing throb through her skull. She let out a shallow breath, lowering the toast to rest limply in her lap, her fingers barely able to grip it.

"No," she rasped, her voice strained, like it was being dragged out of her against its will. She took another drink of the water before continuing, knowing she didn't have to explain but feeling the need to say it anyway. "I've gotten sick before after... experiences."

She didn't have to clarify what kind.

They both knew.

"But never anything like this."

Eli's gaze didn't waver. He just nodded, his chin rising and falling against his knees in contemplation.

"Well," he murmured, "it's a good thing we didn't try to blindly dive in and go to the mine last night."

There was the ghost of a smirk on his lips, an attempt to lighten the density in the air between them.

But it didn't reach his eyes.

Because there was too much truth in it.

Too much of a possibility that she might not have made it.

The next days blurred together.

Finn barely left her bed at first, her body too weak, her limbs heavy with exhaustion. The fever came and went, rising in waves that left her drenched in sweat, only for chills to creep in and set her teeth chattering soon after. Eli stayed close through it all.

In the mornings, he'd knock gently on her door, just loud enough to check if she was stirring. Some mornings, she wasn't. Some mornings, he had to push the door open and crouch beside her, rubbing the slow circles on her back until she blinked herself awake, bleary and pale.

And every morning, he'd ask the same thing—'*how are you feeling today?*'—his voice soft but searching, his amber eyes scanning her face for any sign of improvement.

And every morning, Finn would give the same tired answer. "Not great."

He didn't push her to eat when she couldn't stomach it, but he always left food beside her bed. Toast. Bananas. Soup. Water.

By Saturday, she managed half a piece of toast before her stomach twisted, too painful to finish. On Monday, she drank an entire glass of water without feeling like she might throw it up.

That was progress.

By the next Thursday night, Eli was finally convinced she could survive without him hovering over her. When he left for the shop Friday morning, it was the first time since she had collapsed that she was awake and alert enough to hear the front door shut behind him.

She spent the first half of the day exactly where she had been all week—wrapped in blankets, limbs aching. But by late morning, something shifted.

The fever had finally broken, and when she sat up, she didn't feel like the weight of her own body was going to drag her back down.

So she moved. Slowly and carefully. She peeled the sweat-dampened hoodie off her body, wincing at the stiffness in her joints, and pulled herself up on unsteady legs. She shuffled her way into the bathroom, eyes catching the mirror briefly as she passed.

She looked... *awful.*

Hollowed out with dark circles bruised beneath her eyes, her face paler than she'd ever seen it. Her hair a tangled mess.

She turned away quickly, not wanting to see herself like that any longer than necessary.

The tub was old but deep, and she twisted the knob until the water ran hot, nearly scalding. She let the steam fill the room as she rummaged through the cabinet beneath the sink, fingers brushing past a small, dusty bottle tucked all the way in the back.

Lavender bubble bath.

She unscrewed the cap and inhaled deeply. It smelled soothing, familiar in a way she couldn't place. Pouring a generous amount beneath the running faucet, she watched as the water frothed into thick, fragrant bubbles.

When she sank into the tub, the heat burned against her sore muscles at first, but then—relief.

For the first time all week, she felt almost normal again.

She stayed there longer than she meant to, topping the tub off with hot water every time it started to cool. Letting the lavender wrap around her, letting the warmth sink into her bones, thawing out the exhaustion still clinging to the deepest parts of her.

Eli stepped through the front door that afternoon, kicking off his boots with a tired groan. The scent of lavender still faintly wafted through the air, mixing with the comforting aroma of something warm. Soup.

He made his way through the entryway of the house, following the sounds of movement, and when he stepped into the kitchen, he froze.

Finn was sitting at the table, hunched over a bowl of soup, devouring it.

For a second, he just stood there, one hand still gripping the doorframe, like his brain needed an extra moment to process what he was seeing.

She wasn't slumped over in fevered delirium, wasn't pale as a sheet, or trembling with weakness.

She looked... awake and present.

Alive.

The dark circles beneath her eyes had faded slightly, and there was color in her cheeks again, her skin no longer the sickly, hollowed-out version of itself. Her hair was pulled up loosely, stray waves falling against the oversized sweatshirt draped over her frame. It was the most she'd looked like herself in days.

Finn glanced up mid-bite, spoon still in her mouth, brows shooting up as she noticed him standing there, staring.

Eli exhaled a small, disbelieving laugh, running a hand over his face before shaking his head.

"You're eating."

Finn swallowed her bite and smirked. "You're observant."

Eli rolled his eyes but didn't argue, finally stepping fully into the kitchen and dropping into the chair across from her.

"You scared the shit out of me, you know that?" he muttered, bracing his elbows against the table.

Her smirk softened into something smaller, and understanding. "I know."

"I swear to God, if you ever pull that again, I will force-feed you through a straw." He huffed.

Finn snorted. "You would make fun of me after I almost died."

Eli gave her a flat look. "Almost died? Dramatic much?"

She just shrugged and took another bite.

Shaking his head, Eli leaned back in his chair, but something bright flashed behind his tired expression—something lighter. For the first time in over a week, the tight knot in his chest began to loosen.

Yeah.

She was back.

And whatever came next...

She was finally getting strong enough again to face it.

Eli pushed back from the table suddenly, standing without a word. She watched as he strode back toward the front door, hearing the faint scrape of something against the wood of the entry table.

When he returned, he set a small box down in front of her.

A cell phone, still in the packaging.

"I grabbed it on the way back," he said casually, but his voice held something deeper.

"I didn't like being at work, knowing you were here like that. Not being able to check in."

Finn's fingers grazed over the box's smooth surface before pulling it closer.

Something about the gesture—the thoughtfulness behind it—made warmth bloom in her chest. It wasn't flashy, it wasn't some grand, over-the-top thing. It was practical. Because that's who Eli was. He didn't show care through words. He showed it like this.

She looked up at him, smiling softly. "Thanks, Eli."

That familiar half-smile pulled at the corner of his mouth—but as quickly as it appeared, it faded. His expression turned more serious.

"There's another reason I thought it'd be good for you to have it..."

Finn's stomach dipped at the shift in his tone.

He leaned toward her, lowering his voice.

"Sarah's been stopping by the shop," he admitted, watching her carefully. "Checking in. Asking how you've been holding up."

Finn's pulse gave a small, uneasy flutter.

"I told her you were still out of it, filled her in a little on how bad it got," Eli continued, his voice steady. "And we talked. About everything. About how we need to figure out the next steps. How to keep this—" he gestured vaguely at her, at the exhaustion still carved into her features, "—from happening again."

Finn nodded slowly.

They all knew they couldn't just charge in unprepared.

Not anymore.

Eli sighed, rubbing the back of his neck. "Look, I know you're still recovering, but we need to start figuring this shit out." His warm brown eyes met hers. "Because we both know this isn't over."

Finn nodded again, firmer this time.

No.

It wasn't.

Eli

Alright, phone is officially set up. Welcome to the modern world, Rowan.

Wow, thanks

I'm honored.

Sarah

It's about damn time. If I had to keep checking in with Eli like he was your keeper or something, I was gonna lose it.

To be fair, he's basically assigned himself that role.

Eli

Damn right, someone's gotta keep you two from burning the town down.

Sarah

Yeah well, now that Finn's back in action, we need to figure out our next steps. I've been digging through some of my books, and there's some stuff I want to show you. Protection, spirit work, that kind of thing.

Good, because I'd rather not feel like I'm dying again.

Eli

No kidding. So where are we doing this?

Sarah

Library. I found some other books there a while back that might help, and I want to check them out. Plus, fewer distractions.

Smart. When?

Sarah

Early. 8 AM. Fewer people around, fewer questions.

Eli

You two are really gonna make me wake up early on our first real Saturday off in forever, huh?

Sarah

Suck it up, Ashford.

Buy the coffee and we'll pretend to feel bad for you.

Eli

You guys are the worst.

Sarah

See you both in the morning.

Eli

Yeah, yeah. We'll see you in the morning, Sarah.

Chapter Twenty-Seven

The parking lot of the Ash Hollow Public Library was nearly empty when Finn and Eli pulled in, the only other car in sight was a maroon Saab parked near the entrance. The building itself was small, brick, with ivy creeping up one side, the faded sign near the door swaying in the wind.

It had finally stopped raining, but the sky was still darkened, dense with clouds that refused to clear. The air had taken on an unusual chill for late summer, the kind of biting wind that cut straight through clothing, down to the bone.

Eli put the Bronco in park with a sigh, scrubbing a hand down his face before rubbing at his eyes. He stifled a yawn with the back of his wrist, blinking sluggishly before glancing over at Finn.

She was balancing a tray of three to-go coffee cups in her lap, her fingers tight around the edges to keep it steady. Steam curled faintly from the lids, filling the cabin with the familiar scent of roasted beans.

"You ready for this?" Eli asked, his voice still rough with sleep.

Finn sighed, blowing warm air into her free hand before reaching for the door handle. "Not really. But here we are."

Together, they stepped into the library, the scent of musty books and polished wood greeting them. The only sound was the occasional soft clack of a keyboard from behind the front desk. The elderly librarian sat there, her silver hair pinned neatly into a bun, adjusting a pair of half-moon glasses as she eyed them briefly before returning to her computer.

There was no sign of Sarah.

Eli and Finn exchanged a glance before making their way toward the farthest corner of the library, finding a table nestled between rows of shelves lined with history books. Finn set the tray of coffee down, peeling the lid off hers and blowing on it before taking a careful sip.

"She better not be late," Eli muttered, rubbing his eyes again before slumping in his chair, blinking slowly. "She's the one who wanted to meet at the ass-crack of dawn."

Finn huffed a laugh, setting her cup down. "You wake up earlier than this most days. I think you just feel this way because you don't want to spend your Saturday at a library."

"Yeah, well, you're not wrong," he said shooting her a dry look.

Before she could say anything else, the front door creaked open.

Sarah strode in with the kind of energy that made it seem like she'd already been awake for hours. Her short brown hair was tousled from the wind, cheeks pink from the cold, a thick scarf wrapped haphazardly around her neck.

She made a beeline for their table, tossing a small stack of books onto the wooden surface with a loud *thud* before sitting down.

Eli eyed her warily. "How much coffee have you already had? And are you sure you need anymore?"

Sarah shot him a look, grabbing one of the cups marked black and taking a long, dramatic swig. "Not nearly enough to deal with you."

Finn hid a smirk behind her cup as she took another sip, watching as Sarah unwound her scarf, tossing it at a chair across from them. Eli and Finn exchanged a glance, both taking in her complete opposite energy level.

Sarah exhaled, drumming her fingers on the book stack in front of her. "Alright, listen up, because I have found some things."

Still not fully awake, Eli blinked at her. "Yeah, no kidding."

Finn set her coffee down, leaning in. "What kind of things?"

Sarah's expression turned serious as she reached for the top book. "The kind that might just keep us from getting ourselves killed."

She cracked her fingers, the small pops breaking the hush of the library as she settled in. Finn and Eli watched as she took another sip of coffee, her energy still miles ahead of theirs. The stack of books she had dropped onto the table sat between them like a waiting offering.

"Alright," she said, flipping open the first book, a leather-bound tome that looked like it belonged in some old apothecary. "I spent a good few nights going through these, and I think I've got a solid idea of what we need to do."

"Please tell me it doesn't involve any bloodletting or human sacrifice," Eli said raising an eyebrow.

She shot him a deadpan look. "I swear to the Gods, Ashford, I will hex you."

Finn smirked, but nudged her. "Ignore him. What did you find?"

Sarah turned her attention back to the open book, running a finger down the page before tapping a section. "Okay, first thing—offerings. Everything I've read says that for spirits who are bound, who haven't passed on, there must be something that anchors them here. A grievance, a tie, or in our case... an injustice."

Eli exhaled sharply, rubbing his eyes. "The miners."

She nodded. "Yeah. They were left there to die—sealed away like they were nothing. That's a grudge strong enough to hold anyone here, let alone a group of men who suffered together in the dark."

Finn felt a shiver roll over her skin. She had felt that anger, that desperation.

"So what do we do?" she asked softly.

Sarah flipped another page, eyes scanning the faded script. "There are a few ways to release bound spirits, but most of them boil down to the same thing—acknowledgment and restitution. The dead need to know they've been heard. That their suffering mattered. That we, the living, recognize what happened to them."

Finn's pulse quickened. "So... we talk to them."

Sarah met her eyes. "Yeah. A séance. But not just a *let's light some candles and hope for the best'* kind of séance. This has to be done properly. With intent."

Eli shifted, resting his forearms on the table. "And what's this about an offering?"

Sarah pulled another book from the pile, flipping to a bookmarked page. "In almost every account of restoring balance to spirits that died in suffering, there's a form of an offering. It's not always material—it can be a symbol of atonement, an act of justice. Something to show that the wrong that was done to them is finally being recognized."

Eli stilled. His gaze dropping to the worn wood.

Finn turned toward him. "Eli?"

"The pocket watch. The one my dad has... it belonged to my great-great-grandfather. The same Ashford who owned the mines." His voice was quieter now, heavier. "If anything could be a symbol of what they lost, of what my family took from them... it's that."

Sarah and Finn exchanged a glance. It made sense.

"That could work," Sarah said, more serious now. "If you're willing to part with it."

Eli gave a slow nod, jaw tight. "I am."

Sarah took another sip of coffee, then continued. "That's just part of it. The other part is protection."

Finn listened carefully as Sarah flipped to another book, this one thinner but filled with diagrams and old rituals.

"I found some stuff on energy preservation and spiritual shielding," she explained. "Because after what happened to you, Finn, we can't have you going in there completely defenseless."

Finn sat up straighter. "What kind of protection?"

Sarah skimmed through the page. "There's a few layers to it. First, we burn herbs—mugwort and rosemary seem to be the best for this kind of work. It's supposed to help create a spiritual boundary, so the spirits don't just latch onto you and siphon you dry."

Her words hung in the air, weighty and unshakable. Finn's fingers tensed around the steaming cup in her hands, absorbing the warmth as if it could chase away the sudden chill creeping over her skin.

"Latch on?" Finn echoed, a thread of uncertainty weaving through it.

Sarah nodded, taking a slow sip from her to-go cup, the lid clicking softly as she set it back down. "You said they're drawn to you. If you don't learn to put up a barrier, they'll keep coming. Not all of them mean harm, but some..." She hesitated, considering her next words carefully. "Some are suffering, yearning to be released. They don't want to stay, but they don't know how to move on. And because you can sense them so strongly, you're the most vulnerable to being overwhelmed by their pain."

Finn exhaled, her pulse quickening. She thought about the lake, about Kai's desperate stare boring into her, the way his presence had made her feel lightheaded, drained. And the way it had happened before, again and again, since she was little.

"How do I stop it?" she asked, her voice a thin whisper.

Sarah's lips curled into a knowing smile. "First, you have to want to."

"What's that supposed to mean?"

Sarah lifted her gaze, dark eyes sharp yet patient. "You're afraid of what you see, but you don't turn away. You listen. You let them in. There's a part of you that wants to help them. But if you let them take and take without protecting yourself, you'll have nothing left to give."

Finn wanted to argue, but Sarah wasn't wrong. She had always wanted to help. Even when she was a child, even when it terrified her.

Sarah leaned forward, resting her forearms on the table. "We can use what we know now to teach you how to set boundaries. How to push back when you need to. I've been reading about spiritual shields—mental walls, visualization techniques. It's all about intent and control." She tapped a finger against her temple. "Picture a barrier around yourself, like a sphere of light. The stronger you make it in your mind, the harder it is for spirits to push through."

Finn considered that. It sounded simple, but she knew it wouldn't be easy. "And that works?"

Sarah nodded. "It takes practice, but yeah, it should. There are other methods, too—grounding techniques, protective symbols. I want to check a few more books in the library to make sure we have the best chance of success for the séance."

Eli straightened. "So, we're really doing this?"

"Of course. But we need to be prepared." Sarah stood, stretching. "I saw a few books before that might help. Let's split up and search. We need all the information we can get."

With that, the three of them made their way deeper into the library, each heading in a different direction in search of the knowledge they would need for the mission ahead.

Finn ran her fingers along the spines of the books in the paranormal studies section, scanning for anything that might help them with the séance. The library had an almost sacred stillness.

Rows of towering shelves stretched high, their contents meticulously categorized, yet somehow chaotic in their vastness. A distant clock ticked softly, the only sound breaking the quiet aside from the occasional rustle of pages being turned.

She exhaled softly, trying to focus, but her mind was still reeling from everything Sarah had told them.

As she reached for a particularly worn book titled *Spiritual Gateways and Protective Circles*, a voice from behind startled her. "Looking for something specific, hon?"

Finn turned sharply, clutching the book to her chest. Standing there was Clara, her kind eyes peering at her from the other side of the shelf. Her silver-streaked hair was loosely tied back, and there was something knowing in her gaze.

"Just browsing," Finn said, her tone guarded.

Clara nodded thoughtfully, then tilted her head. "I've heard your last name around town. Rowan, isn't it?"

Finn's fingers tightened around the book. "Yeah," she said slowly.

Clara stepped around the shelf, coming to Finn's side. She studied Finn's face for a moment before asking, "Is your mother Annalise Rowan?"

"She is," she answered cautiously, heart skipping.

Clara nodded as if she had just confirmed something for herself. "I thought so. You look so much like her." She hesitated, as if choosing her next words carefully. "But there's something else... I see your father in you too."

"You knew my dad?"

Clara sighed softly, offering a gentle smile. "I did. Not as well as I knew your mother, but well enough. Annalise never talked much about what happened, and I never wanted to pry. But I do know he was a good man—just... lost in his own way."

Finn swallowed, her pulse quickening. "Do you know why he left?"

"I wish I had the full answer, Finn. All I know is that when he found out about you, he left town. I always assumed he went back home—to Louisiana." She paused, studying Finn's face for a reaction before continuing. "His name is Claude Boudreaux."

The name settled over Finn like a ghostly whisper, unfamiliar yet suddenly important. A thousand questions burned behind her lips.

"Did my mom ever try to find him?" she finally asked.

Clara's expression softened. "She never said. But I think part of her was always waiting for him to come back." She hesitated again, then offered a small smile. "I hope I'm not overstepping by telling you this."

Finn, still processing, shook her head quickly. "No, no, of course not. Thank you."

Just then, Eli and Sarah stepped into the aisle. Eli's eyes immediately went to Finn's face, his gaze sharpening as if recognizing that something significant had just happened. He didn't say anything, but Finn could feel his attention on her.

Sarah, oblivious to the tension, piped up. "Find anything good?"

Finn hesitated, then glanced back at Clara. There was something in her expression—like she wanted to ask more—but Clara must have sensed it. She gave Finn a reassuring smile.

"If you ever want to talk more, come find me," Clara said gently. Then, turning to the others, she gave a polite nod. "Nice to see you both. Take care." With that, she walked away.

Finn watched Clara's figure disappear between the shelves, her mind racing. She had spent years thinking, wondering, even daydreaming about her father—who he was, where he might be, what kind of man he had been. And now, she had a name. A place. A thread to follow.

But she couldn't stay on it now. Not when they had a séance to prepare for.

She turned back to Sarah and Eli, forcing herself to focus. "Yeah," she finally said, gripping the book tighter. "I think I did."

The three of them stepped into Sarah's attic bedroom, and Finn immediately felt like she had stepped into an episode of Charmed. The space was bathed in the glow of string lights woven through faux vines, which draped around the border of the ceiling and wrapped elegantly around the exposed wooden beams.

Richly colored tapestries hung from the walls, their intricate patterns adding a dreamlike quality to the room. The scent of incense hung in the air, mixing with the faint, earthy fragrance of dried herbs.

At the center of it all stood a grand four-poster bed, like something plucked from the pages of a fairytale. Sheer curtains cascaded from the canopy, stirring as the three of them moved through the space.

Against one wall sat a wooden altar covered in an array of crystals, candles, charms, and a tarot spread that looked as though Sarah had left it mid-reading.

A large wooden trunk rested at the foot of her bed, its lid slightly ajar, revealing an assortment of ritual supplies.

Sarah strode toward the trunk, kneeling beside it as she began pulling out unburned black candles and small bundles of dried herbs wrapped in twine. She handled each item with practiced hands, setting them in a neat pile beside her. Finally, she pulled out a small brass bell, its surface tarnished with age.

She held it up for a moment before placing it carefully with the other items.

Finn remained frozen, taking it all in with wide eyes. "I was not expecting this," she murmured, with a mixture of awe and surprise. Sarah had always had that put-together 'clean girl' aesthetic—sharp eyeliner, minimalist gold jewelry, a wardrobe full of neutrals. This room, though?

This was something entirely different.

"You promised no human sacrifices, right?" Eli quipped, clearly feeling a bit out of his depth amongst all the occult elements.

"Not on weeknights," Sarah responded impishly, not looking up from her work.

They had chosen to come here to practice Finn's guarding techniques because Sarah's parents weren't home this weekend. Even if they had been, it wouldn't have mattered—unlike Kai's strict household, Sarah's parents were openly supportive of her beliefs.

This attic, filled with its mystical warmth and personal touches, was a safe place to learn.

She picked up the bell again and gave it a small chime, ringing crisp and pure. "We'll use this to mark your chakra points," she explained. "And we'll say the incantation to help you call a white light of spiritual protection."

Sarah set to preparing, rolling up the large rug in the center of the room, exposing a wide expanse of aged wooden floor. She drew a large circle in chalk, the lines clean and unbroken.

The ritual items were placed just outside the border—each positioned with care. She reached for the particular books she had referenced earlier, as well as the one Finn had found, flipping them open to their pertinent passages and placing them just outside the circle as well.

She retrieved a lighter and a small copper bowl from the altar before turning to Finn and Eli. "Sit cross-legged inside the circle," she instructed.

They both instinctively formed a semicircle, leaving a small space open for Sarah, which she stepped into moments later. She placed the copper bowl in front of her and took a slow breath, her expression shifting into something calmer, more focused.

Sarah reached for the candles, placing them deliberately at four equidistant points along the chalk circle. She struck the lighter and, one by one, ignited their wicks, murmuring an invocation as each flame flickered to life.

"I call upon Air, the breath of life, the unseen force that carries whispers through the trees, the intellect that grants clarity and wisdom. Be present in our circle."

She set the first candle down and the small flame danced in response.

"I call upon Fire, the spark of creation, the consuming force of transformation, the courage that fuels our will. Be present in our circle."

The second candle glowed, casting a flickering golden hue against the wooden floor.

"I call upon Water, the flow of intuition, the rhythm of tides, the keeper of emotion and healing. Be present in our circle."

A soft creak echoed through the attic as if the house itself sighed.

"I call upon Earth, the steadfast guardian, the roots that ground us, the strength that shields and sustains. Be present in our circle."

The candle was placed with reverence, its flame steady and unwavering.

Finally, Sarah took the last candle and held it between her hands for a moment, as if drawing energy into it. "And I call upon Spirit, the unseen thread that binds past, present, and self. The force that connects, protects, and guides. Be present in our circle."

She lit the final candle and placed it in the center between the three of them.

Then, she grabbed the two bundles of herbs she had selected from the trunk—no doubt mugwort and rosemary, just as she had spoken about earlier. Holding them carefully, she let them catch fire, allowing the flames to rise for a moment before gently blowing them out so they smouldered and smoked.

The fragrant tendrils curled through the air as she wafted the smoke around them, tracing their forms in protective swirls before finally laying the bundles inside the copper bowl.

The air in the attic seemed to shift, thickening with something unseen, something ancient. The candles flickered, though there was no breeze, and a hush fell over them.

Sarah's voice, steady and sure, carried through the silence. "The circle is cast. We are seen."

Finn felt the shift in the atmosphere—a deep, thrumming pulse of energy undulating through the air. It pressed against them, pulling them closer together as if binding them within its unseen force. Sarah placed a steadying hand on each of their knees.

"Grasp hands," she instructed, her voice low, reverent.

The moment their fingers clasped, Finn felt it—a current, passing through them in a steady, pulsing flow. It circled through her palm into Eli's grip, through Sarah and back again, an endless loop of connection. Eli must have felt it too; his sharp gasp broke the stillness.

"Close your eyes," Sarah murmured. "Breathe. Let your breath match the rhythm of the energy."

Finn obeyed, inhaling deeply. As she exhaled, she felt her senses heightened—she could feel the dampness of rain that had not yet fallen, the radiant heat of fire long extinguished, the scent of unsettled earth. Then, without warning, a gust of wind whirled through the attic, rustling the hanging tapestries, sending a shiver down her spine.

Their eyes flew open just in time to see the candle flames leap higher, stretching upward, reaching for something unseen; the fresh breath of extra oxygen feeding their eager glow.

Sarah looked at them both with a beaming smile of success, while Eli looked thoroughly freaked out, his wide eyes darting between them as if searching for a logical explanation. But Finn's gaze floated around the room, seeking out the unseen eyes she could feel watching them. She wasn't afraid—she sensed they weren't adversaries, but allies.

Seeing nothing in the realm of sight, she settled her gaze on Sarah, who met it with steady confidence. "Okay, Finn," she said, "it's your time to shine."

Unclasping their hands, Sarah reached for the small bell, hovering it just above Finn's head.

"With the first chime, imagine a bright white light forming here," she said, "and let it spread further down your body with each subsequent chime."

Sarah rang the bell, the sound reverberating through the air. "Crown chakra, representing life's purpose." Finn imagined the pure, effervescent light blooming at the top of her head, feeling like an egg cracked over her, dripping liquid energy down her brow.

The bell chimed again, this time just between Finn's eyes. "Third eye chakra, representing intuition." The cool light spread over her closed eyes, heightening her awareness.

Sarah moved lower, stopping at Finn's throat. "Throat chakra, representing communication." Finn felt the luminous energy pooling at her collarbones, swirling there.

At her chest, Sarah rang the bell again. "Heart chakra, for love and compassion." Warmth bloomed between Finn's ribs, a steady pulse radiating outward.

Lower still, just below her belly button, Sarah called out, "Sacral chakra, ruling creativity." The light shifted, deepening into a golden warmth that settled into Finn's core.

Finally, Sarah brought the bell into Finn's lap. "Root chakra, representing safety and security." The light puddled around her feet, grounding her completely as it enveloped her in its radiance.

Just as the last chime faded into silence, Eli let out a noise unlike anything Finn had ever heard, the same moment Sarah gasped in unadulterated splendor.

Finn opened her eyes to find their stunned expressions staring back at her. An iridescent glow radiated from her body, like the angelic depictions in sacred art.

"I think you got it," Sarah said, beaming from ear to ear.

As the glow around Finn faded, Sarah blew out each candle in reverse order. One by one, she extinguished their flames, murmuring her gratitude for their guidance and power as she released them from the circle.

After the last flame dissipated, Sarah turned back to Finn, still exuberant. "You should practice calling the white light every night," she said, already prattling on about the importance of building up Finn's spiritual muscle memory. "It'll help when we do the séance in the mine."

Finn nodded, but she was only half-present in the conversation. Out of the corner of her eye, she kept watching Eli. He wasn't looking at Sarah. He was watching her. And the look in his eyes wasn't fear or disbelief—but something else entirely, something she didn't recognize.

They said their goodbyes to Sarah and made their way back home in utter, palpable silence.

Frank was in the living room, seated in his usual armchair, his posture relaxed but focused as he worked on a fishing lure. A small wooden tray rested on the coffee table in front of him, lined with bright feathers, thin copper wire, and delicate hooks. His hands moved with dexterity, threading materials together with the same practiced ease he applied to everything he built or fixed.

He barely glanced up as they entered, his attention still on the lure in his fingers. "How you feeling, kid?" he asked, his voice steady as ever.

Finn shrugged off the jacket Eli had let her borrow. "Much better." And it was true. There was something different in her now—stronger, steadier, humming just beneath her skin.

Frank nodded, twisting a thin wire around a hook. "Good." He reached for a pair of small silver scissors and snipped the excess. "So, what'd you two get up to this morning?"

She tossed her jacket over the back of the couch before answering. "Met up with Sarah for coffee at the library."

Frank glanced up at that, his lips twitching before he looked over at Eli.

"The library?"

Eli, who had just thrown himself onto the couch in an exaggerated sprawl, caught the look and scowled. "What?"

Frank let out a chuckle, tying off the lure with a final twist of wire. "What are these girls doing to you?"

Eli scoffed, but Finn could tell he was playing it up now, leaning into the moment. He turned toward her with an easy grin, eyes glinting as he leaned in. "I told you, Rowan. Now you're dead meat."

The teasing was familiar, but something in the way he said it felt different.

There was an undercurrent beneath his words, a hesitation before he spoke.

It was gone in an instant.

Eli must have realized he hadn't played it off as smoothly as he intended, because he quickly turned back to Frank, picking at a loose thread on his sleeve. "We hung out at Sarah's after," he added, sounding more casual now. "Listened to some new-age bell music." He threw Finn a quick smirk, this time landing the teasing without pause.

She rolled her eyes, nudging his arm lightly.

Frank set the completed lure aside with a chuckle. "It's nice you two are spending time with her," he said, his tone thoughtful. "I usually see her alone around town, since..." He trailed off, but they all knew how that sentence ended. Since Kai went missing.

Finn, unwilling to let the moment remain too heavy, smiled. "It's nice having a girlfriend, too," she said, stretching her legs out as she settled onto the couch beside Eli. "As much as I enjoy your company."

Eli pressed a dramatic hand to his chest. "Wow. What a brutal betrayal."

Finn laughed, nudging him again, but the feeling that had been tugging at her remained.

Something had shifted in Eli, even though he was trying to play it off.

They stayed in the living room a little longer, but the conversation with Frank had settled into a natural lull. After a moment, Eli pushed off the couch with a stretch.

"I'm gonna crash in my room for a bit," he said, his tone neutral.

She expected some kind of quip, something teasing to wrap up their usual banter—but nothing came. Eli didn't look at her before disappearing down the hall, his retreat feeling pointed in a way.

Brushing it off, Finn exhaled and made her way to her own room. She grabbed a fresh pair of comfortable clothes—an oversized tee and a pair of baggy shorts—before heading to the bathroom. They'd woken up so early that morning that only Eli had managed to get a shower before they left. After everything that had happened, the thought of standing under hot water and rinsing away the day sounded like exactly what she needed.

As the water pounded against her shoulders, she closed her eyes and focused, calling upon the white light once more.

She didn't force it—she simply let it come, imagining it the way Sarah had instructed. At first, it was just an idea, a concept. But then, like before, it responded.

It gathered inside her, subtle at first, then stronger. She could almost feel it mingling with the hot water cascading over her skin, the two sensations intertwining. The energy pulsed, radiating outward, wrapping around her like a second layer of heat.

She smiled to herself.

It was easier this time.

When she stepped out, she felt lighter, the remnants of white light still buzzing beneath her skin. Steam rolled out into the hallway as she opened the door, trailing behind her like mist.

And that was when Eli stepped out of his room.

Their eyes locked.

There was something about the way he looked at her—not a glance, not a passing acknowledgment, but a quiet pause, his gaze tracing over her face like he was trying to understand something she wasn't saying out loud.

Then, as if realizing himself, Eli adjusted his expression, schooling it into something more normal.

But not fast enough.

Finn saw it.

Felt it.

She felt caught between wanting to brush it off or acknowledging it, but before she could say anything, he cleared his throat. "Gonna go check out that knocking sound in the Bronco's engine," he muttered, already stepping past her toward the stairs.

Finn blinked, confused. "Oh—do you want to play something first? Maybe Street Fighter?"

He stopped at the top of the stairs, like he wanted to say yes. But instead, he just shook his head, already moving down the steps. "Nah. I'll be out in the garage."

And just like that, he was gone.

Finn stood in the hallway, watching after him, that odd feeling still present.

Whatever was going on with Eli was getting harder to ignore.

Chapter Twenty-Eight

The next week passed in a strange pattern of contradictions—fast in some ways, dragging in others. The motions of everyday life fell back into place—work, meals, the comfortable routine of living under Frank's roof—but the space between those moments was being pulled thinner and thinner.

Finn kept up with her practice, calling upon the light each night, strengthening her spiritual shield the way Sarah had instructed. It was becoming more instinctual, like something she was meant to do all along. It answered each time she called it forth, growing and fortifying.

But as Finn felt herself becoming more connected to this newfound power, she also felt herself drifting further away from Eli.

She tried to talk to him about it whenever they were alone, choosing her moments carefully—never at work, never when Frank might overhear. On their ride home or late at night, she'd bring it up, hoping to bring him into the conversation and pull him back toward her.

But Eli never truly engaged. His responses were short, his attention somewhere else. Before she could push too much, he'd find an excuse to leave—heading out to the garage, fixing something that didn't need fixing, or disappearing into his room with the door shut tight.

There was always something that needed his attention. But nothing that included Finn.

And yet—he was still watching her.

She caught him in moments when he thought she wouldn't notice. A glance from across the shop floor. Or in the reflection of the shop front windows. His gaze holding too long in the darkened glass of the passenger-side window as they drove home.

Something about those looks made Finn's stomach tighten and her pulse skip.

And the more it happened, the more she felt like he was watching someone he didn't quite recognize anymore.

Sarah had her own distractions—inventory at the boutique kept her locked in all week—but she never stopped checking in. Their group chat buzzed with messages, small reminders that Finn wasn't entirely alone in this.

Sarah

How's the light summoning going?

Good. Still practicing every night.

Sarah

> That's my girl. Deep breaths. Don't force it. Let it come naturally.

> I know, I know. You've drilled it into me by now lol

Sarah

> You're welcome!

By Friday evening, Finn had settled into the routine of practicing alone, strengthening herself in preparation for what was coming.

She just didn't expect the texts that came next.

Sarah

> I think you're ready.

> We shouldn't wait much longer.

> Sunday. We all have the day off. Let's do it then.

Finn just stared at the screen.

She knew this was coming. That they couldn't put it off forever.

> Okay.

Her fingers hovered over the keyboard before she added—

> A little nervous, but okay.

Sarah's response came almost immediately.

Sarah

> Of course you are! But you've got this, Finn. You're stronger than you think.

Finn took a slow breath, forcing herself to believe it.

Then Eli finally responded.

Eli

Yeah. Sunday's fine.

Unbothered. No teasing remarks, no sarcastic comment about ghost-hunting.

Just... flat.

Finn frowned, rereading the words, searching for something more beneath them. But there was nothing.

No matter how much she focused on preparing for what was coming, there was something else she couldn't prepare for.

Eli.

The way, no matter how much distance he tried to put between them, he was still watching.

Like he was waiting...

For what, Finn wasn't sure.

The sun had begun its slow descent into dusk, stretching hues of rose, amber, and coral across the sky, clouds dusted in streaks of fading gold. Light spilled through the sunrooms window in lazy ribbons across the floorboards, pooling over the threadbare rug, brushing against Finn's bare legs where she sat in the chair.

She should have found comfort in it—the way the world turned toward night. She should have been able to focus on the way the sky melted into something softer, on the hush of the house and the day's warmth still in the air.

But tonight, nothing felt steady.

Her mind wouldn't still, her thoughts looping around themselves, pulled taut beneath the impending draw of tomorrow.

The séance and the mines. The ghosts still waiting beneath the earth.

She had done everything she could to prepare, spending each night training herself, calling upon the light until it no longer felt like something separate from her that she was pulling in from the ether, but something that had always been there—waiting to be awakened.

And yet, no matter how much she practiced, or how many times Sarah reassured her she was strong enough, she couldn't shake the feeling that she was walking into something too big and unknown, too dangerous.

Not because she wasn't ready.

But because Eli wasn't really with her.

He had been there all week—beside her at the shop, sitting next to her in the Bronco, close enough that she could reach out and touch him if she wanted to. But he'd also never felt further away.

She had tried to talk to him.

To reach him in those in-between moments, when it was just the two of them, when she thought maybe he would finally open up and let her in. But every time, he found a reason to leave.

And yet, he kept looking at her.

Not just in passing.

Over and over.

It was never long enough for her to hold onto, but never gone quickly enough to be forgotten.

Finn exhaled.

She couldn't do this anymore.

She couldn't walk into that mine tomorrow with this distance still between them, with something unspoken sitting between every moment and glance.

She needed to confront him.

Her fingers tightened around her phone, her pulse hastening as she typed.

Come to the sunroom.

She hit send before she could second-guess herself.

Seconds passed.

Then minutes.

The screen stayed dark, the silence hollow.

Maybe he wouldn't come. Maybe he would see the message and let it sit, unanswered, let it disappear into the same silence he had been giving her all week. Maybe he had already made his choice, and she had been fooling herself into thinking there was still something left to hold onto.

Then—footsteps.

The sound of boots against hardwood, moving toward her.

Finn sat up a little straighter just as Eli stepped into the doorway.

For a long moment, he just stood there, framed in the fading glow of the sunset, one hand braced against the doorframe; he shifted like he was still deciding whether to step forward or turn back.

She had seen him hold himself back before.

But never like this.

"I was just—" He exhaled, scrubbing a hand over the stubble shadowing his jaw, his voice quieter than usual, as if it took effort to say even that much.

"What's up?"

Finn rose from the chair, arms uncrossing, bracing herself for whatever this was going to be.

"I think you know."

Eli's shoulders shifted in a way that looked restless, like he wanted to escape.

"Finn—"

"No." She shook her head, stepping forward, closing some of the space between them. "Not this time. Not after this whole week."

The words pushed to the surface now, rising faster than she could stop them, too much to contain.

"I don't understand what's going on with you," she admitted, her voice strained, but no less steady. "You barely talk to me anymore, but you—"

She hesitated, drew a breath, and said it anyway.

"You keep looking at me like I'm something you don't understand."

His body tensed.

For the first time, he had nothing to say.

Just silence.

She exhaled, a rawness creeping into her voice.

"Just tell me the truth."

A pause, stretching between them like a held breath.

"Please."

And then—finally—he cracked.

His breath left him in a slow, uneven exhale, looking like he was still fighting something invisible.

"The night at Sarah's," he murmured, stepping forward, slowly, like something was pulling him toward her whether he wanted it to or not.

"The light," he said, voice lower now. "The one that surrounded you."

Finn nodded, her chest tightening. "Yeah... we saw it too; it faded after."

Eli shook his head.

"No," he said, more certain.

"Not for me."

Another step, slower than the last, but just as inevitable.

Like he couldn't fight the force of some unseen gravity.

"I realized you and Sarah didn't see it anymore," he admitted, "but I did. When the ritual ended... it never really left."

His gaze was searching hers, waiting for something, waiting for her to understand before he had to say it.

"I see it every time I look at you."

Another step.

"There's always a wisp of it," he murmured, something fragile in the way he said it, like it had been sitting on the edge of his tongue all week, waiting to be spoken.

His hand lifted, his fingers hovering just over her cheek.

"It's always here," he whispered, something close to awe in his voice. "Dancing over your skin. Like I'm finally seeing something that was always there."

He touched her.

The moment his fingertips brushed her cheek, she shuddered.

And then—he kissed her.

The moment Eli's lips met hers, the world tilted, shifting at some unseen angle Finn had never experienced, like she had been waiting for this moment without ever knowing it.

The kiss started slow and tentative, like he was still unsure if he should be touching her this way. But Finn had no hesitation. The second their lips met, something cracked open inside of her, unnamed, undeniable, and she reached for him instinctively, her fingers wrapping into the fabric of his shirt, pulling him in and holding him there.

And Eli—Eli gave in.

His hands slid over her waist, like he had been holding back from this for far too long. He let out an uneven breath against her mouth, and something about that sound, the way it shook. It felt like a surrender, and sent a sharp, shivering warmth through Finn's chest.

And then—the light responded.

Finn felt it like a hum beneath her skin, a thrumming pulse before it began to move and spread, to reach for him.

And Eli felt it too.

His breath hitched, and for just a second, his fingers tightened at her waist, gripping her like he was bracing for something he couldn't see, something too big to hold onto.

But then—he stopped fighting it.

The warmth between them expanded, threading through the space where their lips met, undulating between their breaths, slipping from her into him, and then back again, looping in an endless circle. It was something more than heat, more than energy, more than anything she had ever felt before.

The glow flickered to life around them, whispering along the edges of their skin, wrapping them in something golden, weightless and eternal. It pulsed with their heartbeats, with every brush of their lips, every second that passed, unspooling through the air between them like it had been waiting for this moment—for them.

Finn barely noticed the way her hands moved, sliding up from the fabric of his shirt to the sharp line of his jaw, fingers threading through his hair. She could feel his heartbeat, the way it pounded against her own, the way it echoed through the light, weaving into it, becoming part of it.

She knew Eli felt it too.

His hands had started to tremble, but he didn't pull away. If anything, he only deepened the kiss, leaning into her, into this, into something that felt like it had always existed between them but had never been spoken aloud.

The light reached further and brighter, slipping along the edges of their fingertips, tracing over the lines of their faces, flitting across their skin like it was something sentient and watching, something weaving them together.

It slipped from Finn's lungs into Eli's, then back again, each breath shared, each inhale and exhale feeding the warmth between them, fusing them to this moment.

Time blurred.

The room around them, the house, the world itself—none of it mattered.

There was only this.

Only the feeling of being truly seen, completely known, and fully recognized.

Only the soft, shuddering gasps between them, the way his fingers traced her back, slow and unsure, like he wanted to memorize the shape of her through touch alone.

Only the glow, lingering and pulsing, fading in and out, still winding between them like an unseen tether, something unbreakable, something infinite.

Only them.

And when they finally pulled away breathless, their foreheads still pressed together, their hands still holding on, the world had completely changed.

The sun had fully set, leaving them wrapped in the endless hues of indigo, violet, and deep, burning gold.

But it didn't matter.

Because they were still glowing.

The glow that had flickered so brightly between them had begun to settle now, no longer pulsating outward but instead sinking into the spaces where their bodies touched, where their heartbeats pressed against one another, like an echo of something ancient and unbreakable.

Eli didn't pull away.

For the first time since this strange, unseen tether had begun pulling them together, for the first time since he had started resisting something he couldn't explain, he didn't run from it.

Whatever had been keeping him at a distance—fear, uncertainty, something too big to name—was gone.

Instead of retreating, he exhaled, long and slow, like the final release of something he had been holding inside of him. His hands, still warm and steady at her waist, shifted, his grip changing as he guided her down with him, sinking into the loveseat. Finn followed, moving instinctively, her legs draping over his lap, her body fitting seamlessly against his like she had always belonged there.

And maybe she had.

The moment she settled against him, every last inch of space that had stretched between them this past week vanished.

Eli let out another slow breath, his arms wrapping fully around her, one hand resting at her hip, the other trailing absentmindedly along the curve of her spine, tracing unspoken words into the fabric of her sweatshirt. He wasn't gripping her like he was afraid she might slip away. He wasn't holding on with uncertainty. He was simply holding her, touching her, existing here with her, fully and completely.

Finn pressed her cheek against his chest, listening to the deep, steady rhythm of his breathing, the thump-thump-thump of his heartbeat beneath her, unwavering, like an anchor in a restless sea. It felt like something constant and permanent, something she could trust.

There had been distance between them this last week, stretching wider with every moment he pulled away, with every unanswered question, with every long glance that said too much but never quite enough.

But now—now there was nothing left between them but certainty.

Whatever unseen thread had always been connecting them, whatever force had drawn them toward each other again and again, was no longer stretched tight.

It had wrapped around them now, woven into something unbreakable, something sacred.

They'd stopped moving in parallel and finally clicked into the same orbit.

Stronger together than they had ever been apart.

The loveseat was small, barely wide enough for both of them to fit comfortably, but Finn had never felt safer, never felt more whole than she did in that moment, cradled against Eli.

Like the waning moon in the pendant he had made for her, cupped gently in the golden arms of the sun.

Eli shifted, adjusting the way he held her, but never moving away. His fingers continued their slow, aimless tracing against the small of her back, a silent reassurance, a confirmation that he wasn't going anywhere.

Finn felt something inside of her finally, fully settled.

She hadn't realized how much she had been carrying, how much doubt had been whispering questions she hadn't wanted to ask. But now, wrapped in Eli's warmth, there was nothing left to question.

She wasn't alone in this.

She had never been alone in this.

And she never would be.

Neither of them spoke, but the silence between them wasn't empty—it was full. Filled with something more profound than words.

There had been no grand declaration, no moment of explanation or reasoning.

Because they didn't need it.

They had already said everything that needed to be said—with the way Eli had kissed her, the way Finn had reached for him without hesitation, the way the light had curled around them, binding them together in a force neither of them fully understood—but both of them fully accepted.

Whatever was coming tomorrow, whatever they would find in the mines, they would face it together.

And for the first time, Finn wasn't afraid.

She felt bolstered by this connection, strengthened by it, more ready than she ever could have imagined.

They weren't just walking toward the unknown anymore.

They were stepping into it whole.

Outside, the last colors of the sunset had faded into deep, endless indigo, the world shifting into darkness, but inside, in the glow of the sunroom, bathed in the last traces of golden light, Finn and Eli remained.

Unshaken.

Unbroken.

Exactly where they were always meant to be.

Chapter Twenty-Nine

fter a while, the glow between them had faded into something softer but no less present, neither of them moved to break the moment.

The house was quiet, the world outside shifting toward night. Finn could hear the distant croak of the frogs in the trees, the rustle of the evening wind through the leaves, but none of it felt quite real—not after what had just happened, not after what had changed.

Even now, Eli's arms remained loosely draped around her, his thumb still moving in slow, thoughtless circles against the fabric of her sweatshirt, as if even in stillness, he needed to keep touching her.

Eventually, stars began to speckle the endless blue, and Eli let out a breath, the vibration of it humming beneath Finn's cheek.

"You tired?" His voice was low, the kind of tone that rolled through her bones.

Finn blinked sleepily, reluctant to move from this moment, from him.

"A little," she admitted, tilting her head to look up at him. "But I don't want to leave yet."

Something swam in Eli's expression— something fond and entirely new. His lips twitched at the edges, not quite a smirk, not quite a smile.

"Then don't."

It was a simple answer, but it whispered to Finn like a promise.

She let him pull her gently to her feet, his hand lacing with hers as they moved through the house, stepping carefully, as if trying not to disturb whatever shift had just taken place.

When they reached his room, Eli nudged the door open, letting her step in first before following, like this was the most natural thing in the world.

And maybe it was.

Maybe it had always been leading to this.

Finn slipped onto his bed, tucking her legs beneath her, watching as Eli stepped toward his desk, absently fiddling with something that looked like a half-finished sketch, his fingers flexing like he needed to keep moving, to calm the energy still thrumming beneath his skin.

After a moment, he turned, leaning back against the desk, his arms crossed loosely over his chest.

"So," he said, like they were speaking into something fragile.

"Tomorrow."

Finn swallowed, exhaling softly.

Tomorrow.

It was strange, how close it suddenly felt.

For so long, the séance had been an idea, a plan, something to prepare for. But now, it was here.

"I don't know what to expect," she admitted, tilting her head against the wall. "I mean, I've communicated with spirits before, but nothing like this. Not... so many at once."

Eli nodded, the muscle in his jaw ticking, like he didn't love the idea of her walking into something so unknown and unpredictable. But he didn't say that.

Instead, he just said, "You're ready."

Finn's chest tightened.

"Yeah?"

Eli's gaze met hers, unwavering.

"Yes."

And somehow, that meant more than anything.

Eli stayed by the desk for a moment longer, his eyes grazing over her like he was committing this to memory, like he was watching something shift into place. Then, finally, he crossed the room, dropping onto the bed beside her, his arm looping around her waist as she curled easily into him, her body fitting against his without thought.

Finn wasn't sure when she finally drifted off, only that the last thing she remembered was the steady rise and fall of Eli's breathing, the warmth of his arms around her, the feeling of being completely, fully safe.

When she woke, the first light of morning was slipping through the curtains, and Eli was still there, holding her, his breath hot against the back of her neck.

She didn't move right away, only blinked slowly, letting herself absorb the moment, letting reality in.

Today was the day.

She inhaled, steadying herself, then shifted, turning in Eli's arms. His eyes were still closed, his breath even, but she knew he wasn't really asleep—not fully.

"...Morning," she murmured.

Eli made a low, tired sound, his grip on her waist tightening. "Five more minutes."

Finn huffed a quiet laugh, shaking her head, but she didn't move to get up.

They could have five more minutes.

Eventually, the scent of lavender-cinnamon coffee filtered through the house, and Eli finally blinked his eyes open, gaze still soft with sleep.

They stretched, moved slowly, pulling themselves into the day. By the time they made it downstairs, Frank was already up as suspected. He was rummaging through his tackle box, organizing for his fishing trip with Danny.

He glanced up when he saw them, the familiar half-smile already pulling at the corners of his mouth, but then his gaze flickered between them—taking in whatever had changed, even though they were doing their best not to draw attention to it.

Something in his expression shifted—not surprise, not even amusement. Just aware.

"What are you two up to today?" he asked, sorting through a box of lures.

Eli stretched, keeping his voice casual. "We were thinking about taking the bikes out. Probably ride around for a bit, enjoy the weather."

Frank nodded, clearly pleased, smiling around the rim of his coffee cup. "Warm blue-skied Sunday," he mused, shaking his head with something like fondness.

Finn smiled, trying to ignore the way her stomach tightened at the lie.

Because they weren't just going for a ride.

They were heading toward something unknown.

Something waiting.

But Frank didn't need to know that.

What little sun managed to slip through the tangled branches came in thin, fractured slivers, paling against the overwhelming sense of stillness. Though the day was warm, the air beneath the trees carried an unnatural chill, not from the temperature but from something deeper, something unseen.

Finn felt it pressing in from all sides—the waiting silence, the way the world seemed too enclosed, too watchful. As if the trees themselves were listening, bending toward them, waiting to see what would happen next.

Eli's fingers remained laced tightly with hers. A solid presence beside her. He didn't say anything, but she could feel his attentiveness, the way his gaze found her every so often, checking, making sure she was still okay.

And she was.

Or at least, she had been.

But with every step forward, something twisted tighter in her chest.

Because this wasn't just any place.

This was where the miners had died.

Where their souls had been left to linger, restless and yearning, their bones still encased deep in the earth like a tomb. Trapped beneath rock and time and memory, unseen but never forgotten.

And they knew she was coming.

The dirt path began to widen as they neared the clearing, the first glimpse of the mine appearing between the thinning trees.

The entrance loomed ahead, gaping like the mouth of something ancient and hungry, the rotting, splintered wood of its boarded opening jutting out at odd angles. Jagged and broken like uneven, blackened teeth. The planks, warped from time and weather, were brittle with decay, their surfaces slick with years of rain and neglect, yet somehow they still held—not just a barrier, but a warning.

She and Eli unclasped hands without speaking, but Finn felt his hesitation. The way his fingers lingered against hers for just a breath longer, reluctant.

Sarah was already there, perched on the boulder near the mine's entrance, waiting.

She must have been sitting there for some time, wrapped in Kai's jacket, the fabric hanging loose around her shoulders. His pendant rested against her chest. She looked up as they stepped into the clearing, her perceptive gaze catching the moment when their fingers slipped apart.

But whatever thought passed through her mind disappeared quickly.

Because there were more pressing things to focus on.

Sarah had been the one keeping Finn steady all week, pushing her forward. She had been the one reassuring her, making sure she felt steady enough to do this. But now, sitting here alone, her arms overloaded with supplies, her fingers tightening around the bundle of ritual tools she had brought, she looked different.

Not uncertain. Not afraid.

But heavy.

Like sitting beside the mine had allowed the reality of what they were about to do to finally sink in.

Like she had felt something already.

Finn squared her shoulders and braced herself.

Because she felt it too.

The pull, the pressure, the presence.

The air here was different—charged, brushing against her skin in a way that made the fine hairs on her arms rise. It wasn't just the temperature or the enclosed feeling of the woods. It was something else, something that waited just beyond the mine's entrance.

The feel of unseen eyes stayed, unmoving and expectant.

Finn could feel the spirits were already paying attention.

She had felt their presence before she even had to reach for them.

"You good?" Eli asked Sarah, his gaze sharp, cutting through the expectant stillness.

She shifted on the boulder before giving them a quick nod. "Yeah. Fine," she said, but something in her usual confidence wavered, just enough for Finn to notice.

Eli did too.

She quickly realized she wasn't fooling either of them. "I just—" Her fingers tightened around the bundle in her arms. "I haven't felt alone since I got here."

Finn and Eli exchanged a glance.

It wasn't exactly unexpected.

But hearing her say it aloud made it real.

"Alright, let's get this done, then." Eli's tone was matter-of-fact.

Together, he and Sarah moved toward the mine entrance, setting down the supplies as they began working loose a few of the wooden planks that sealed off the opening. The wood splintered under their hands, brittle from years of exposure, the jagged edges scraping against their palms as they pried them free.

Finn took a few steps back, her breath slowing, focusing inward.

Closing her eyes, she called upon the light, reaching for it the way she had been practicing every night since the ritual in Sarah's attic. It came easily now, like it had always been there, waiting for her to stop doubting. She felt it begin to build, pulsing outward, wrapping around her in its familiar glow.

By the time Sarah and Eli turned back to her, the last of the wooden planks discarded in the dirt, Eli had gone still.

His gaze was locked on the space around Finn, watching as the light she summoned grew, expanding with each breath she took. He had gotten used to seeing it over the past week—the wisps dancing across her skin, hovering in the air around her like something alive. But now, in the shadow of the mine, with the unshakable darkness growing just beyond, the sight of it seemed to ease something in him.

He smiled, something confident and knowing, returning to his expression.

Sarah, unaware of what was happening between them, shouldered her bundle of supplies and squared her stance. "Alright," she said, her voice resolute against the tension in the air.

"Now or never."

And with that, she turned, ducking inside the mine first.

Finn and Eli followed, stepping over loose gravel and fallen debris, as they hunched forward to fit through the narrow tunnel. The air was stagnant, dust cold and unmoving. The earthen scent of stone and decay all around them.

Sarah turned on a small flashlight, the beam cutting through the dense shadows. Their steps were cautious, the space pressing in on either side, forcing them to move in a line, heads low as they maneuvered through the passage.

Just as the tunnel began to feel impossibly claustrophobic, it opened.

They rounded a broad curve, stepping into a wider chamber—a hollowed-out cavern where the walls grew higher, giving them just enough space to stand at full height.

The darkness here was absolute.

The light from the entrance was gone, swallowed by the twist in the tunnel, leaving only the narrow glow from Sarah's flashlight. The small, bobbing circle of illumination barely enough to chase away the shadows clinging to the walls.

Finn inhaled, steadying herself. They were here.

And so were the spirits.

Sarah wasted no time. She moved to the center of the chamber and began drawing a large circle in the dirt, the fine powder shifting beneath her fingers as she carved the shape into the ground. Finn and Eli stepped forward once it was complete, sitting cross-legged within it, taking their places.

Sarah then lit the small bundle of mugwort and rosemary, wafting the fragrant smoke all around before laying the herbs aside.

Next, she began placing the candles at north, south, east, and west, arranging them precisely at the edges of the circle before sitting down to complete their inner formation.

The atmosphere in the chamber was charged now, pressing inward like an unseen force was gathering just beyond the reach of their light.

Sarah straightened her posture.

And then, just as she had before in her attic, she began calling upon the elements.

Her voice was strong, weaving through the stillness as she knelt beside the first candle. Pressing her fingers to the dirt, she closed her eyes.

"I call upon the element of Earth, the foundation beneath us, the presence that surrounds us, that has held what was lost for so long."

A deep hum pulsed through the stone walls—something ancient and unmoving was listening. The cavern itself seemed to exhale, the weight of ages settling around them.

Sarah moved to the second candle, her breath steady.

"I call upon the element of Air, to bring clarity and wisdom, to guide us through what is unseen."

A faint, unexpected breeze stirred through the chamber, sending dust curling into the dim light. The air smelled of old stone, undisturbed for lifetimes—until now.

Without hesitation, she lit the third candle, hovering her hands over the flame.

"I call upon the element of Fire, to bring strength and protection into this space."

The flame flared sharply, rising for a heartbeat before steadying, its glow casting restless shadows along the cavern walls. The warmth of it licked against Finn's skin, a stark contrast to the cold pressing in from the depths.

Sarah moved to the fourth candle, her voice unwavering.

"And I call upon the element of Water, to bring renewal, to cleanse and carry forward what has remained."

From somewhere deep within the mine, a sound echoed through the chamber.

A drip.

Soft. Steady.

Like water seeping through stone.

Finally, she reached for the last candle, placing it in the center of the circle.

"And I call upon the element of Spirit."

Her voice was quieter now, reverent. The match flared, and as she touched it to the wick, the small, trembling flame leapt to life.

"For all that has come before and all that remains unseen," Sarah whispered, watching the trembling light, "we welcome you."

The words had barely left her lips when the chamber lurched.

Not physically—but the air itself shifted, pressing in around them, warping, bending as if reality had just frayed at the edges.

Finn's breath caught.

The candle flames flickered, bending unnaturally, as if responding to something outside of the realm of sight.

And then—the light of the spirit candle pulsed, illuminating the air around them in a soft, wavering glow.

A glow that outlined something.

Someone.

The séance had begun.

Chapter Thirty

n the glow of the spirit candle, something began to take shape.

At first, it was nothing more than a shadow, a vague, wavering silhouette just beyond the border of their circle. The darkness clung to it, moving and reshaping itself, as though it was resisting definition.

Finn's breath slowed.

She wasn't afraid.

Not as the figure took on more structure, the blackness stretched until it was unmistakably human.

She realized—it wasn't alone.

The space behind the first shadow began to thicken, the void of the mine gathering, deepening, forming shapes within it.

Men.

A mass of darkened figures pressed forward from the abyss, their forms silent, their presence pushing toward the circle but never breaching its edge.

And then—one by one, their eyes began to open.

The first spirit's gaze flared to life, its light unnatural, burning against the surrounding black. A second pair blinked open, then another, then another, until the cavern was littered with glinting eyes, reflections of the candle flames that now stood as the only barrier between the living and the dead.

Finn didn't need to look at Sarah and Eli to know.

She heard it—the sudden, sharp inhalation of breath, Sarah's exhale of disbelief, the way Eli shifted beside her, his shoulders tensing and body going rigid.

They could see them now.

Dozens of golden eyes, pulsing in the dark, fixed on them from just beyond the edges of their circle.

Finn didn't flinch or shrink away.

Didn't pull back.

Because something inside her had already begun to change.

There was no conscious decision, no command of her own will. The light inside her simply responded.

It stirred first at her core, subtle, then began to push outward, expanding beyond her skin, a pulse of golden light spreading in steady waves. It wasn't something she forced—it wasn't even something she fully understood—but it was happening.

Finn felt it rise in response to the spirits, an undeniable force answering their presence, as if something within her already knew what to do.

She felt the moment Eli's gaze shifted, no longer on the eyes flickering in the dark, but on her.

She could feel his stare, the way he was watching—in steady recognition.

The light around her grew, reaching beyond the circle's boundary, stretching into the dark where the spirits hovered just out of reach.

The spirits did not recoil.

Instead, they watched.

Waiting.

Finn exhaled, and the light pulsed with her breath.

The three reached for each other's hands.

The connection was instinctual, a silent agreement that whatever came next, they would face it together.

Sarah's grip was firm but steady, her breath slowing as she adjusted to the unnatural pressure around them. Eli's was different—almost crushing, his fingers laced tightly with Finn's, an unconscious reaction to the growing force.

But Finn remained calm.

She let the warmth inside her pulse outward, sending a current of energy through their joined hands. It moved in waves, spreading through their chests until their breathing fell into sync, their grips loosening as it steadied them.

Finn, without thinking, spoke first.

"You recognize me."

The mass of shadows rippled in response, their blurred outlines bending and warping, vibrating with a silent but resounding *'yes'*.

Finn's pulse remained even, her expression unwavering.

She knew they did.

They had known from the moment she arrived.

Her gaze shifted toward Sarah, the wild candlelight flickering across her face, making her expression unreadable for a moment before she gave a small, sure nod.

Finn turned back to the spirits.

"And I know you recognize her too."

A subtle shift in the air.

A whisper of movement, a reaction that was neither hostile nor inviting, but simply acknowledging.

"She is here to help me complete what Kai—the young man you drove into the lake—wasn't able to."

The edges of the spirits shivered, their forms becoming less defined before sharpening again.

Finn's voice didn't waver.

"He wasn't able to bear your insistence. But I think you know that I can."

The darkness around them swirled, pressing inward.

The spirits didn't step forward—it wasn't movement in a traditional sense—but the blackness that composed their forms undulated and rippled, growing restless.

Finn's glow pushed outward, keeping them from overtaking the space.

And still, she remained unshaken.

"Because I have something... someone, that Kai didn't."

She turned to Eli, her gaze soft but certain.

Their eyes locked.

For a long moment, Eli didn't move.

The shadows shifted, towering over them now, pressing not just from the outer edges but from above, stretching down from the cavern ceiling, leaning over them.

A glimmer of fear passed through his eyes.

Finn saw it, felt it in the tremble in his grip, in the way his breathing grew shallower as their presence descended like a tidal wave.

But she squeezed his hand, a warm surge of light pressing into his skin, radiating from her fingertips, sending a concentrated pulse of her energy deep into his bones.

Eli's breath steadied.

His grip held firm.

Then, finally, he nodded.

His fingers unwound from Sarah's, though he didn't let go of Finn. Not for a second.

With a deliberate movement, he reached into his pocket.

Finn watched as he tore his eyes away from hers, scanning the sea of burning eyes that surrounded them.

And then, his voice cut through the silence.

"My name is Eli Ashford."

The energy reacted to the name.

A name tied to the ones who damned them.

Eli didn't falter.

"I have come in place of my forefathers," he said, voice strong despite the pressure of the moment, "who doomed you to your tortured fates."

Finn felt it, the way the air around them wobbled, the way the energy rippled in response to his words.

"I mean to make amends."

He withdrew the pocket watch, fingers curling around the metal as he pulled it free, lifting it just enough for the candlelight to catch.

The moment the watch was revealed, the cavern erupted.

The shadows exploded outward, slamming against the walls, rebounding off the stone like a living force, a current of darkness pulling back only to surge forward again.

The ground beneath them trembled, a resonant rumbling shaking through the mine like the sound of a waking beast.

Finn felt it in her spine, the roar echoing through the hollow chamber.

The spirits reacted violently, their outlines now twisting and convulsing.

Eli held his ground, the watch swaying like a pendulum in the light, its polished surface gleaming.

They had their attention now.

And whatever happened next—there was no stopping it.

The reverberation within the mine grew, swelling within the cavern walls.

And then, fire erupted from below.

It wasn't natural flame.

It didn't crackle, didn't burn like an ordinary fire. It roared like something alive, something furious—a violent burst of hellish breath surging upward from the pit of the earth, twisting through the chamber like the exhale of a dragon long buried beneath the rock.

The heat was instant, licking at the edge of their circle as it spiraled outward. Finn's light pulsed in response, shielding them as the flames closed in.

The darkness that had surrounded the spirits seemed to feed off the fire, growing larger, monstrous, the twisting shadows clawing at the edges of Finn's protective light, writhing like demons desperate to break through.

Sarah screamed.

She had hit the ground, flattened by the force of the explosion, her hair dangerously close to the wildly flickering spirit candle. The gusts of heat sent strands of it flying, the flames reaching hungrily toward the ends.

Eli had let go of Finn's hand, his fingers clasped over his ears, his teeth gritted against the deafening, all-consuming roar echoing around them.

Finn's focus remained steady, her light holding strong against the searing firestorm, keeping the darkness and flame from consuming them. But she could feel it—the heat, the battle between her energy and the fury of the trapped souls pressing against it.

They were angry.

They wanted retribution.

But they also wanted release.

Finn's voice cut through the chaos, ringing out clear and unwavering.

"Eli, love... you have to finish this!"

The instant the words left her lips, something changed.

The fire wavered.

Not extinguished—but the wild, consuming rage of it stuttered.

Sarah's head jerked up, the blaze reflecting in her wide, stunned eyes. Something about Finn's words had lit a spark inside her, a reminder of why they were here, of what had to be done. Of who they were fighting for.

Sarah dug feverishly into the dirt, clawing at the loose earth beside the spirit candle, creating a small hollow space in the ground.

The flames surged, pressing harder against Finn's shield.

She gritted her teeth, her light pulsing again, pushing back against the ever-growing heat.

But Eli was no longer bracing against the sound.

His hands had dropped from his ears.

His breath came hard and fast, but his body was still—his eyes locked onto Finn, absorbing her words.

She had called him love.

She had spoken it without doubt, even in the midst of fire and fury. And in that moment, the words pounded through his chest louder than the chaos around them.

Something new burned behind his eyes.

Resolve.

Determination.

Eli turned back to the raging mass of spirits, his voice rising above the inferno.

"This watch was made from gold pulled from this mine—the precious metal that drew you all to sign your lives away to my family."

The shadows twisted violently, their glowing eyes flashing in response.

Eli's grip on the watch tightened, the golden surface gleaming like molten fire in the candlelight, swaying like a pendulum from its chain.

"I offer it back to the earth," he declared, "to take your place and release you from its hold!"

The cavern erupted.

The fire roared higher, the shadows screaming in one deafening, over-lapping wail as the ground beneath them shook violently.

And Finn—her light flaring brighter than ever—held strong.

Eli's fingers trembled, the chain of the pocket watch biting into his palm as he held it over the small hollow Sarah had carved into the dirt. The fire raged around them, spiraling like a living force, its tendrils clawing at the edge of Finn's glowing shield. The cavern groaned under the spirits' fury, the sound of their grief and rage vibrating through the stone like the last breaths of something ancient and restless.

And then—Eli let the watch fall.

The delicate golden casing hit the dirt with a soft, metallic chime, a sound almost too quiet to be heard over the roaring inferno.

With steady hands, he reached forward, scooping the earth back over it, sealing the gleaming gold beneath the surface.

The moment the last glint of metal disappeared beneath the dirt—everything changed.

The fire lurched inward.

It didn't extinguish.

It collapsed.

The flames—wild and towering, clawing at the cavern walls just moments before—snapped back, drawn into the ground like a breath being sucked into a hollow chest. It coiled violently, spiraling downward, dragging toward the buried gold like a vortex, like something unseen had reached up from below and was pulling it in, consuming it whole.

The force of it hit like a shockwave.

Finn barely had time to brace before her protective bubble shattered.

The explosion of energy sent all three of them hurtling apart.

Finn hit the ground hard, the breath leaving her lungs in a sharp gasp as the shock tore through her body. Sarah was flung backward, rolling to a stop near the cavern wall, her arms barely shielding her head as she landed. Eli skidded against the dirt, his back colliding with the uneven stone, his breath knocked from his chest on impact.

The candles scattered.

The once-perfect ritual circle was destroyed, the small flames tossed to the edges of the cavern. Somehow, impossibly, they still flickered—weak, feeble, but burning.

And then—silence.

A cool draft moved outward, brushing their faces and combing the dust in one direction, like the exhalation of a hundred lungs.

The heat was gone.

The swirling shadows had vanished.

The violent, suffocating energy that had threatened to crush them just moments before had dissipated so completely that it left behind a void of unbelievable stillness.

The mineshaft—once trembling, once alive with sound and fury—was silent as a grave.

Finn coughed, pushing herself up on shaking arms, her ears ringing from the sheer force of the collapse. She blinked into the unnatural silence, the last tendrils of her own light glimmering faintly around her, dimming now that the fire was gone.

She turned first, scanning the cavern for Eli and Sarah.

Sarah had rolled onto her back, her chest rising and falling in quick, uneven breaths, strands of hair sticking to her face where sweat and soot had settled. The dirt streaking her skin was illuminated by the weak glow of the still-flickering spirit candle, its tiny flame somehow surviving the chaos.

For a long moment, she didn't move, staring up at the cavern ceiling as if waiting for another eruption, another impossible force to knock them back down. But slowly, she lifted herself onto her elbows, her wild, glassy eyes locking onto Finn's.

She wasn't panicked.

She wasn't afraid.

She was just stunned.

And then, Eli.

Finn's gaze snapped to him, her chest tightening as she spotted him against the cavern wall, bracing one arm against the stone as he slowly pulled himself up. His breath was heavy, his body sluggish with exhaustion, but he wasn't hurt—not in any way that mattered.

For a moment, neither of them spoke.

They didn't have to.

Because they knew.

It was over.

Finn could feel it in the air—the unbearable weight that had once filled this place was gone. The thick, suffocating pull of unfinished business, the aching, clinging energy of souls tethered to the mine—it had vanished completely.

The mine was just a mine again.

And the spirits were gone.

Sarah was the first to say it aloud.

"It worked."

Her voice was hoarse, barely more than a whisper, but the words echoed in the cavern like a final exhale, like the closing of a long-open wound.

Something inside Finn unraveled.

The tight, rigid hold she'd kept on herself throughout the séance, the force of her light stretching to shield them, the sheer, unrelenting control she'd maintained—it all gave way at once.

Her breath shuddered, the first full, complete exhale she'd taken since stepping foot inside the mine.

A sound broke from Eli's chest—not quite a laugh, not quite a sigh. He tilted his head back against the rock behind him, closing his eyes for a moment, his chest rising and falling in deep, steadying breaths. When he looked at her again, his expression was different.

There was no fear.

No hesitation.

Only certainty.

Finn had done this.

They had done this.

The fire had been claimed, the offering had been accepted, and the souls—after decades of suffering—had finally, finally been released.

Finn slowly pushed herself upright, her limbs aching, though the pressure in her chest had lightened. The adrenaline that had kept her steady through the séance was finally fading, leaving behind a kind of hollow exhaustion, but even through it, there was peace.

She turned toward the small, hollowed space where the watch had been buried.

The ground looked undisturbed, untouched—as if nothing had ever been placed there.

Sarah let out another breath, rubbing her soot-streaked forehead with shaking fingers before looking at Finn, her expression somewhere between disbelief and awe.

"You... you felt that, right?" she asked, her voice still raw from smoke and strain. "That moment when it just—lifted?"

Finn nodded, slow and sure.

Eli did too.

It hadn't been just a moment.

It had been a release.

The curse—the unbearable weight of the miners' suffering—was gone.

Sarah let out a small, breathless laugh, swiping a dirty hand down her face before shaking her head in near disbelief. "I don't know whether to cry or sleep for a year," she muttered, rubbing her sore arms.

A smile tugged at Finn's lips, exhaustion settling into her bones now that the battle was over.

"Maybe both," she murmured, voice soft.

Eli didn't hesitate.

He moved toward her, his own exhaustion evident in the heaviness of his steps, in the shock in his expression. But it didn't stop him from reaching for her.

The second his arms wrapped around her, she let herself sink into his warmth, into his solid, steady presence, into the quiet certainty of being held.

Her forehead pressed against his chest, the heat of him chasing away the last traces of the mine's cold, the scent of fire and earth clinging to him, grounding her in what was real.

She felt him exhale against her hair, a slow, steady breath that matched her own, and she knew—deep in her bones, in every piece of herself that had carried this responsibility—it was finally, truly over.

The curse had been broken.

The dead were at peace.

And they, after everything, were free.

The cavern remained still. The curse had lifted, the spirits had moved on, and yet the three of them sat in the quiet aftermath, letting reality catch up to them.

Sarah finally moved, with slow deliberate motions, she picked up one of the scattered candles, cradling the tiny flickering flame in her palm. She exhaled softly, her breath disturbing the waxy smoke as she murmured, "Thank you, fire... if that's what you were." She let out a small huff of a laugh before gently blowing out the flame.

She moved to the next candle, doing the same.

"Thank you, air."

Another breath, another extinguished light.

"Earth."

"Water."

One by one, she moved through them, her voice warm, her gratitude genuine even if she wasn't entirely sure who she was thanking.

Finally, she reached the center candle—the spirit candle, its small, determined glow barely holding on.

Sarah hesitated for just a moment before tilting her head in thought.

"...And, uh, spirit? Thanks for not letting us get absolutely wrecked."

She blew it out, the final breath of light vanishing into the cavern.

Other than the feeble flashlight glow that paled in comparison to the flickering candle flames.

Then she straightened, dusting off her hands before turning to Finn and Eli, who were still standing close, arms wrapped around each other, neither making any move to pull away.

A smirk tugged at Sarah's lips as she pointed between them.

"Well," she said, crossing her arms. "I was wondering when this would finally happen."

Finn and Eli both glanced at her, registering her meaning at the same time.

Eli let out a small, huffed laugh, finally loosening his grip enough to drag a hand through his wild, soot-streaked curls. Finn rolled her eyes, but the warmth in her chest never dimmed.

"Yeah, yeah," Eli muttered, a small grin breaking through despite his exhaustion. "You done?"

Sarah shrugged, clearly pleased with herself. "For now."

Finn shook her head, but she couldn't help the smile tugging at her lips. The tension of the past few hours—or maybe the past several weeks—had finally begun to unravel, leaving behind a strange, light-headed relief.

They gathered the candles, brushing away the dirt that clung to their wax before tucking them back into Sarah's satchel. The remnants of the ritual were packed away, leaving the cavern empty once more.

And then—they walked away.

The mine didn't fight them this time.

There was no lingering pull, no whisper of unseen hands holding them back. Just silence.

As they stepped into the warm, bright afternoon, Finn immediately noticed how different everything felt.

The forest, once dark with shadow, now seemed more open, more golden, as if the sunlight had been waiting for them to return. It cut through the trees now, filtering in beams of warmth and color where before there had been only gloom.

They walked in companionable silence, the crunch of dirt and dry pine needles beneath their boots the only sound accompanying them as they made their way back toward the dusty road where their bikes were waiting.

As they pedaled back toward Eli's, Sarah clinging to the back of Finn's bike, the sun was already beginning its descent. Finn glanced at the sky, watching the clouds turn soft shades of gold and violet, and realized with some surprise just how much time had passed.

"How long were we even in there?" she mused aloud, breaking the quiet.

Sarah exhaled a short laugh. "Time doesn't work right when the dead are involved."

Finn hummed in agreement, still trying to piece together how the entire day had slipped away. What they had experienced had been so intense, so all-consuming, that reality itself had blurred at the edges.

By the time they reached Eli's house, the sky had begun deepening into warm hues of amber and rose, the air cooling as the last remnants of daylight painted the world in soft pastels.

Just as they pulled into the driveway, Frank and Danny were arriving home.

The two men were unloading the back of Frank's truck, their voices easy and full of good-natured ribbing as they stacked a cooler packed with their haul onto the tailgate. Even from a distance, Finn could see the way Frank's weathered face was lit up with satisfaction, the way Danny gestured wildly with his hands, recounting some part of their fishing trip with the kind of enthusiasm only he could.

Frank caught sight of them first, his brows lifting as they dismounted their bikes. "Look at that," he said, shaking his head and wiping his hands on a rag. "You kids actually spent a Sunday outside instead of staring at screens all day."

Eli scoffed, kicking his bike stand down. "Yeah, well. Turns out we had an eventful day."

Frank's eyes flicked over the three of them, his usual sharp intuition missing nothing. There was dirt on their clothes, traces of soot on their faces, an exhausted but strangely content energy settling over them.

But whatever he saw in them, he didn't press.

Instead, he gave an approving nod, tossing the rag onto the truck bed. "Well, if you worked up an appetite, you're in luck. We've got fresh trout on the menu tonight."

Sarah groaned, stretching out her sore limbs. "Gods, that sounds amazing."

Finn just smiled, the past few hours fully unraveling at the familiar, easy warmth of this house, of these people.

That evening, they sat around the kitchen table, plates full of fish and roasted potatoes, warm bread and butter passed around between them. The air was light, filled with easy laughter and the occasional ridiculous fishing story. Even Danny, whose energy was usually an unrelenting force of motion, sat back in his chair, content, and at peace.

Finn felt it settle into her bones—the knowledge that they had done something incredible today.

They had set something right.

They had freed the dead.

And now, they got to return to the land of the living—at least for now.

She caught Eli's gaze across the table, and when he met her eyes, the warmth there was unmistakable.

There was no longer any tension or unspoken space between them.

Only what had always been waiting to unfold.

Chapter Thirty-One

 was walking through the graveyard.

Barefoot. Silent. Pulled forward by something unseen.

The grass beneath my feet was damp, cool from the lingering touch of night, the scent of earth and moss thick in the air. A soft mist curled along the ground, weaving between headstones and cracked marble markers, their names and dates softened by time.

I wasn't choosing to walk.

Something was guiding me.

The path ahead wound beneath the limbs of ancient oak trees, their twisting arms draped in curtains of silver moss, shifting in a slow, rhythmic *motion, as if swayed by a breeze I couldn't feel. The graveyard was silent, not ominous but expectant, waiting.*

And then—I saw her.

A woman stood several paces ahead, her back to me, her long red hair cascading in waves down her back, catching the glow of the moon. She stood perfectly still, head tilted forward, her focus on the gleaming white marble headstone before her.

Even from behind, I felt a pull toward her, something warm and familiar.

She wasn't a stranger.

She couldn't be.

I moved closer, stepping lightly, my breath steady as I approached her. The silence around me was thick, buzzing faintly beneath my skin.

Just as I was nearly at her shoulder, she spoke.

Her voice was melodic, like wind chimes in a summer breeze.

"I knew you would get here eventually."

I stopped, something inside me tightening, unfolding, knowing before I even had the words.

"...Nancy?"

She turned slowly, graceful and deliberate.

Her face was gentle, and kind in a way that had nothing to do with memory but everything to do with understanding. She had honey-brown eyes, the same shade as Eli's.

She smiled, not just with her lips but with something deeper, something that shone in her gaze, something that told me she had been waiting for me.

Without a word, she stepped aside, revealing the name etched into the marble.

Kai Gilford.

My breath hitched.

Nancy watched me carefully, her expression unreadable for a long moment, as if making sure I truly saw it, that I understood.

Then, finally, she spoke again, her voice lighter this time, carrying no urgency—only truth.

"He's ready to come home now."

A gust of wind swept through the cemetery, stirring the leaves, carrying her words into the dawn.

I blinked.

And when my eyes opened—I was awake.

– – –

Sunlight spilled through the window, painting the room in soft amber hues. The shadows of tree branches swayed gently across the floor, stretching thin in the early morning glow.

Finn inhaled steady and certain.

The dream lingered as real as any vision before it, but there was no residual fear, no confusion, no unanswered questions.

She knew.

Today she, Eli, and Sarah would make a plan.

Kai was coming home.

The dream was still pressed against her. This wasn't something she needed time to process. She knew.

Slipping from bed, she crossed the hall without a second thought, pushing open Eli's door. The room was dim, the early morning light wisping through the slats in his blinds.

Eli was still asleep, tangled in the sheets, his breath deep and unbothered.

For a moment, she just stood there, watching him, feeling the importance of everything she was about to say.

Then she moved forward, pressing a hand gently against his arm. "Eli," she whispered, giving him a small shake.

He stirred, groaning low in his throat, face half-buried in his pillow.

"Eli," she tried again, louder this time.

His eyes fluttered open, still heavy with sleep, blinking at her in disoriented confusion. He shifted onto his back, one arm flopping over his forehead as he squinted toward her.

"Finn?" His voice was rough, groggy. "What—what time is it?"

"That doesn't matter."

She didn't wait for him to wake up fully before she slipped onto the mattress beside him, curling up under the blankets. He was warm, his body still radiating the heat of sleep, and when she tucked in close, he instinctively shifted, making space for her without thinking.

She lay there listening to his breathing, feeling the rise and fall of his chest, before finally turning to face him. He mirrored her movement, their heads close, the space between them small, their words only for each other.

"I had a dream," she murmured.

Even in his half-asleep state, his gaze sharpened.

"A dream?" His voice was more alert now. "Like... a *dream* dream?"

She nodded. "I saw your mom."

Eli went completely still.

Finn felt the shift in his body, the tightening in his muscles, and the way his breathing changed.

"What do you mean?" His voice was careful, hesitant. "My mom? Like... like how you see other spirits?"

"No," she said softly. "Not like them. Not like the mine. Not like Kai."

But she could see it in his eyes—the flicker of fear. The idea that maybe his mother, too, was trapped somewhere between here and what comes next.

Before he could voice it, she reached out, threading their fingers together.

"She's not trapped, Eli," she said, her thumb brushing over his knuckles.

His throat bobbed as he swallowed. "How do you know?"

"Because I've felt her." Finn held his gaze, making sure he understood. "Not like I feel spirits who are lost, not like Kai's presence lingering at the lake. It's different. She's just... there. Warm and steady, like she's always been. She comes and goes as she pleases, staying close when she thinks you or Frank need her." Finn exhaled. "And now, she's watching over me, too."

Eli's fingers wrapped around hers, not pulling her in, not pulling away—just holding on.

Still, she could see the war in his expression, the conflict between grief and relief.

"But how?" he whispered.

Finn smiled, something soft, certain.

"Because you and Frank love her so much," she murmured. "Because you keep her memory alive—not just in stories, but in the way you live. In the small rituals, the way you haven't touched her vanity in the attic since she passed, the way you keep it just as she left it, like she might walk in and sit down at it any day." She let the words settle before continuing. "And because of Sunday mornings."

Eli's brows furrowed, but she saw the flash of recognition in his tired eyes.

"The lavender cinnamon coffee?" she prompted.

His lips parted, like he wanted to say something, but nothing came.

So she went on. "She's there for that too, you know."

Eli exhaled, shaking his head, a small, breathless chuckle escaping his lips. "Shit, Rowan." His voice was rough. "You really don't miss anything, do you?"

"Not when it comes to you."

Her smile faded and a solemness crept in.

"She says Kai is ready."

Eli nodded, not needing any further explanation.

He reached for his phone.

This couldn't wait.

The Lantern was bathed in the golden glow of late afternoon. The three of them sat in a corner booth, untouched coffee cups between them as they mapped out the final step.

Kai needed to come home.

And they finally had a plan.

Sarah would take the jacket back to the lake.

Not just to return it—but to say goodbye.

He had left it there, along with the pendant, as a message, as a hope that they would come back to her somehow. And in the end, they had.

But they couldn't just return them.

They had to make it look right.

Sarah would cover the jacket in mud and silt, making sure it looked as though it had remained untouched this whole time, hidden beneath the surface. Then, she would take both the jacket and the pendant, along with a box of handwritten notes she had never shared with investigators before—letters back and forth between her and Kai, documenting his slow descent into fear, into believing something dark was after him.

She had hidden them before, terrified they would dismiss him as a suicide.

Now, she was giving them the full truth.

Sarah exhaled sharply, rolling the coffee cup between her hands. "I still don't trust them to get it right," she admitted, her voice raw but steady. "But I have to try."

Finn nodded. "And we'll be there with you."

Eli leaned back in the booth, arms crossed over his chest. "No way in hell we're letting you do this alone."

Sarah stood on Eli's porch, the worn business card gripped tightly between her fingers. The edges were softened, the ink faded, from where she had turned it over and over for more than a year.

She had never used it.

Never thought she would.

But now—now she had to.

Finn and Eli stood on either side of her, silent, their presence grounding her. They didn't push her, didn't rush her, just let her take the time she needed.

She inhaled sharply, pressed the number into her phone, and hit call.

The line rang twice before a voice picked up.

"Gregson."

She closed her eyes, gripping the phone tighter. "Detective. It's Sarah Whitmore."

A pause. Then: "Sarah." His voice shifted—recognition and curiosity. "What's going on?"

She swallowed, keeping her voice steady.

"I went back to the lake," she said. "Kai and I used to go there when life felt hard. I just... wanted to feel close to him."

She let that sit for a beat before continuing, her voice soft but unwavering.

"I found something."

Another pause, heavier this time. "What did you find?"

She gripped the card harder in her other hand.

This had to be right.

"A jacket," she said. "Kai's jacket. Half-buried in the mud, near the water's edge. His pendant was still in the pocket."

Gregson exhaled sharply. "And you're sure it was his?"

"Yes." Her voice didn't waver. "And that's not all. I have something else—something I should've given you a long time ago."

Finn watched as Sarah reached for the small, tattered box she had placed beside her on the porch railing. The box of handwritten notes—letters exchanged between her and Kai.

Letters she had hidden before.

Letters that detailed the slow, creeping fear that had engulfed him. The paranoia, the belief that something had been following him, watching and waiting.

She had been too afraid they would dismiss him, that they would call it delusions, call it a breakdown, call it something it wasn't.

But now—now she had to trust the truth.

"I have his words," she said. "His thoughts. I think you should read them."

Gregson was silent for a long moment.

When he finally spoke, his voice was measured, careful.

"I see," he said. There was a heartbeat of hesitation, before: "Where are you?"

She glanced toward Finn and Eli before answering. "Eli Ashford's place."

Another pause.

Then: "Meet me at The Lantern in an hour."

She let out a slow breath. "Okay."

The call ended.

For a moment, no one moved.

Then Eli reached out, squeezing Sarah's shoulder.

It was time to end this.

The morning the police swept the lake, Finn and Eli stood beside Sarah.

The air was cool, dense with anticipation. The water was still, too still, as if holding its breath along with them.

Sarah pointed out the exact place where she had "found" the jacket.

Her voice was calm, her movements precise. But Finn could see the tension in her jaw, and the way her hands trembled at her sides.

The divers moved methodically, their bodies disappearing beneath the dark surface.

The minutes stretched too long, too silent.

And then—one of the divers surfaced.

He pulled off his mask, water streaming from his face, and turned toward the authorities.

Finn knew what was coming before he even spoke.

But knowing didn't make it easier.

With a small, solemn nod, he confirmed what they all already knew.

They had found Kai.

Sarah broke.

Her body folded forward, her breath hitching violently in her chest.

Finn caught her before she could hit the ground, wrapping her arms around her, holding her tight.

Sarah clung to her, her fingers gripping at Finn's shirt, her body shaking as silent sobs wracked through her.

Finn didn't say anything.

She just held on.

Eli stood close, one hand firm on Sarah's back, the other clenched at his side.

They had known this would be the result.

But that didn't make it hurt any less.

The sky was a muted gray the day they laid Kai to rest. The kind of sky that didn't press down, didn't smother—just held, like an exhale.

The air smelled like earth turned crisp with the shift in seasons, the damp scent of fallen leaves beginning to break down into the soil. The wind carried the faint bite of oncoming winter, swirling through the thinning trees, rustling the dying grass.

Summer had slipped away, and autumn had come to take its place.

Sarah stood closest to the headstone, her fingers clutching the pendant, the same one he had left for her, now hanging around her neck. The wind tugged at strands of her hair, but she didn't move to fix them, didn't move at all—just stood there, taking it in.

Kai was finally home.

Finn and Eli stood behind her, their presence unwavering, a silent pillar of support as the ceremony moved forward.

The gathering was small, but full of love. There were tears, but there were also smiles and murmured stories, the kind that felt like wrapping a wound rather than tearing it open.

And as the final words were spoken, and the last handful of dirt was laid upon the grave, a faint thread of honeysuckle and sandlewood drifted through the chill. Finn closed her eyes.

And felt it.

The air shifted—not in weight, not in temperature, but in quiet release.

A presence lifting, moving on, finding peace.

She exhaled slowly, her breath curling into the cool air, her hand finding Eli's without needing to search. He clasped hers firmly, neither of them looking away from the grave.

Sarah took in a deep, shuddering breath, then let it out just as slow.

And when she finally turned away from the headstone, walking toward them, there was something lighter in her expression.

Not healed or whole.

But finally free.

About the author

Breanna Perez writes haunting, heartfelt stories where the living and dead walk side by side, and family is found in the most unexpected places.

Living in the forest of the PNW with her little family, she pulls inspiration from her woods, her love of the paranormal, and her deep roots in fandom culture. Breanna has spent years immersed in stories of mystery, magic, and found family — training for creating *The Liminal Veil Series*.

When she isn't writing, she can usually be found tending her garden, rolling dice in tabletop campaigns, or exploring haunted places for inspiration.

Sneak Peek

From Book Two of The Liminal Veil Series- Untethered:

Finn pulled the door shut behind her, the keys in her pocket strange but satisfyingly real.

Her place.

She breathed, headed down the narrow staircase, boots tapping against the wood. Outside, the air ran cooler; a streetlamp washed the sidewalk in warm gold as she stepped out—

"Hey there."

Finn nearly launched out of her boots.

She spun, hands flying up before her brain caught up to the familiar voice.

Sarah lounged against the brick, unbothered, a giant bottle of Moscato dangling from her hand.

Finn pressed a palm to her chest. "Jesus, Sarah."

"Did I scare you?" Sarah's grin was shameless.

"Pretty sure you shaved five years off my life."

Sarah laughed and pulled her into a tight, warm hug. "Congratulations, you badass. You officially have your own place."

Finn let the tension melt, smiling into Sarah's shoulder. It felt good.

She eyed the ridiculous bottle. "Okay, but how did you even get that?"

"I have my ways."

"You totally flirted with the guy at Hollow Spirits."

A smug little sip of air. "I don't know what you're talking about."

"Uh-huh. Come on. If you're crashing my first night, you can at least grab a box."

"Crashing?" Sarah gasped. "I am blessing your first night."

Still smirking, she followed Finn to the car.

Finn took two boxes; Sarah chose one, balancing the massive bottle on top.

"If I drop this wine," Sarah muttered on the stairs, "we're going to have a problem."

"You mean you'll be heartbroken."

"Same thing."

They made it inside without tragedy.

Sarah set the box down, satisfied. "Now let's properly celebrate the fact that you're a grown-ass woman with a whole apartment."

Finn looked around the space that was hers now—the scuffed floorboards, the faint sweetness from The Drug Shoppe below, the hush of her own quiet.

A slow smile tugged at her mouth. "Yeah," she said softly. "Let's do that."

To stay updated on future publications and all things The Liminal Veil Series, follow Breanna Perez on Tiktok @ TheHauntedAuthor

FAREWELL, UNTIL WE MEET AGAIN IN THE VEIL...

www.ingramcontent.com/pod-product-compliance
Lightning Source LLC
Chambersburg PA
CBHW071736110726
47908CB00006B/1607